MIDNIGHT
CLAIM

MIDNIGHT CLAIM

WOLVES OF MIDNIGHT

BECKY MOYNIHAN

BROKEN
BOOKS

Published by Broken Books
www.beckymoynihan.com

ISBN-13: 979-8-9883737-1-1

Cover design by Becky Moynihan
Cover model by Ravven
www.depositphotos.com

To those who never felt like they fit in:
May you find your people,
the ones who accept you just as you are.

PROLOGUE

KOLTON

I wasn't known for being reckless.

Shrewd, yes. Cunning. Sometimes cold and ruthless.

But not reckless.

Being alpha required a level head. Patience was key, as was control. Without those things, I wouldn't have kept my position this long.

But today . . .

Today, I was someone else.

Today, I was a creature of reckless instinct. Nothing more.

Every nerve ending in my body—every *cell*—was raw, firing off at rapid speeds.

I let Nora go. I'd let her *go*.

What had I been thinking?

At the time, I'd only been aware of how unhappy she was, and I couldn't stand it. Couldn't stand knowing that I had been the cause. So, like a *fool*, I hadn't made her stay. I'd watched her go, ignoring the incessant voice in my head that demanded I drag her back inside the house—kicking and screaming if I had to.

You should have listened, that same voice admonished me now. *You should have stripped her naked and ravished her senseless. Should have finally taken that sweet innocence of hers. She wouldn't have wanted to leave then.*

At the mental image my wolf familiar threw my way, I bared my teeth in a silent grimace.

Enough, Shadow, I inwardly ordered, unwilling to have this conversation with him again. Unlike me, he thrived on pure instinct. Sex and violence was his answer to everything. Keeping myself in check this past month had been near impossible, at least where Nora was concerned. He couldn't understand why I still hadn't claimed what was rightfully mine.

You know I'm right, he persisted but thankfully didn't push me further. He'd won, after all. The second I'd realized Nora was in danger—the second that *witch* had threatened her life—my careful control had snapped. When it had, Shadow had howled with pride. He wanted nothing more than for me to take action. To show those witches what a terrible mistake they'd just made.

Normally, I would formulate a plan first. I'd approach the situation with caution. But not today. I'd already wasted enough time tracking down where Nora's call had come from last night. When I'd learned the location, my body had immediately burst into action, to Shadow's delight.

For once, my familiar and I both wanted the exact same thing.

To take back what was ours, no matter the cost. No matter how reckless or dangerous it could be.

The witches hadn't found Nora at her childhood home by accident. Someone had to have contacted them. Someone with a grudge against her. There was only one person who would do something so vile.

Her old alpha.

I should have killed him. I should have killed that sorry excuse for a man when I'd had the chance. When my fingers had been around his *throat.*

I wouldn't make that same mistake twice.

Alpha Hendrix was going to pay dearly for all the pain he'd caused Nora.

"Kolton, think this through," my second in command said, doggedly shadowing my footsteps as I stormed out the door and across the estate's wide front porch. "You'll need backup."

"We've been over this, Jagger. I need you to keep everything in order while I'm gone. It's your job."

"But watching your back is *also* my job," he disputed, not surprisingly. Jagger Montgomery wouldn't be my second if he submitted to my every whim. He was my sounding board, in the best and worst of times.

"Don't do this alone, Kol," Griff, my third, spoke next. He trailed closely behind Jagger, bounding down the porch steps after us.

I stubbornly shook my head, refusing to slow. "I might not come back. I need you guys here if the worst happens."

"But we *need* you to come back," Jagger snapped. He was suddenly in front of me, cutting off my path. I jerked to a halt and met his blue-gray eyes. Eyes that were slowly bleeding yellow.

Instead of demanding he stand down, I simply stared at him. At the *fear* he couldn't quite hide behind that cool mask of his. He rarely showed it, but the responsibility of being second in command to the largest pack in the country often weighed on him. He bore the weight better than most, but even he was afraid of the gaping hole I'd leave behind should something happen to me.

In a glance, I took in his closely-shaven black hair, diamond-studded earlobes, broad shoulders, and the tattoos on his light brown arms. He and Griff were my oldest friends, and I knew their features almost better than I knew my own. Barely a day had gone by in the past twenty-five years when we hadn't seen each other. When we hadn't *been* there for each other.

When I didn't argue back, the yellow in Jagger's eyes slowly faded. He knew me too. Knew that his statement had struck a chord inside me. "Let us be there for you, Kolton. For your family."

Although his words were quietly spoken, they hit me like a sledgehammer.

Family. For my *family*. Protecting them was more important than anything, and I'd failed. I hadn't been there for her. For Nora. She'd left and was now in danger, because I hadn't protected her from *myself*.

The guilt was an unbearable weight on my chest. So great that I finally gave in. Finally saw a sliver of reason.

"Fine. You and Griff can come. But nobody else."

I made sure to say the words loud enough for the person exiting the house and hurrying toward us to overhear.

"Kolton, let me go too. *Please*."

At the desperation in my sister's voice, I almost turned. Almost retraced my steps to offer her words of comfort. But I knew Vi. Knew she wouldn't appreciate them. She'd always preferred harsh truths to soft platitudes. Which was why I took off again and said, "Not happening, Vi."

"But you *know* I can be of help," she pushed, clambering down the porch steps after us. "We don't know how big the threat is."

"Exactly," I replied, reaching the white truck already waiting for me in the roundabout. In the short time since Nora had been taken, I'd packed some essentials and dismissed the staff until further notice—even Melanie's nanny, Miss Gabby. "I can't risk bringing Melanie, and I won't leave you two here alone, which is why you need to take her to our safehouse. You heard what Nora said. They want vengeance on us all."

"What about Mom?"

"They don't know about her. She's safest where she is."

"Okay, but I still think I can be of more use than a babysitter. Melanie could stay with—"

"Violet, *stop*," I barked, whirling to face her. She abruptly halted, her brunette ponytail swinging as she raised her chin to meet my stern gaze. Most wolves would look away. Would *submit* to my display of dominance. Especially females. But Vi wasn't like most females, which was why I bluntly said, "If we don't come back, you know what will happen. I'm counting on you to keep our family safe. You're the only one who can."

Her chin quivered, but only for a moment. She took a small step back, finally submitting. "Fine, but be careful." Her gaze briefly flicked in Griff's direction. "If you die, we die."

"I won't let that happen."

She didn't look convinced. When I started to turn away, her hand shot out and gripped my arm. "Promise me something."

I paused, caught off guard by her fierce tone. "Promise you what?"

"Get Nora back. No matter what."

My chest tightened. Tighter and tighter until I could barely breathe. Still, I managed to say, "I swear, Vi. I'm going to get her back."

I would get my *wife* back. Even if I had to kill every last witch who stood in my way.

CHAPTER 1

NORA

Another of Arrow's blood-curdling screams reached my ears.

The agonized sound chilled me to the bone.

I was pretty sure my sadistic captors *wanted* me to hear the screams. To scare me into giving them what they wanted.

No fuss, no muss, right?

But I couldn't do that.

"Don't tell them, don't tell them, don't tell them," I muttered under my breath, all too aware of the camera trained on me. They were probably watching me at this very moment, waiting for me to break.

The witches hadn't touched me yet, but it was only a matter of time. Thanks to my captive companion, I now knew in excruciating detail what would happen to me. What was currently happening to *him*.

When Arrow bellowed in agony once more, I curled into an even tighter ball on the floor of my cell—or rather, *cage*. One lined in silver. I hadn't tested the bars since first waking up in here two days ago, but I didn't have to. These cages were clearly designed for werewolves. Big enough to move around in as a human, but not as a wolf. The constant close contact with silver had already dulled my supernatural abilities.

I was weak. Weak and helpless.

Unable to shift once more.

How was that for irony?

The urge to laugh pressed on my throat. I'd only been in here for two days and was already on the verge of losing it, like Arrow had. But he'd been a prisoner here for almost two *months*.

Two months of enduring torture. Of being locked in a cage. Of living in darkness. Of being treated like an *animal*.

I didn't blame him one bit for his current mental state. With time, I was certain to join him. If I didn't break first.

"Don't tell them, don't tell them, don't tell them."

"Don't let them know what you are. They'll only want to torture you more," he'd warned me, right before they'd taken him from his cage. A simple spell had frozen him in place, allowing the witches to easily drag him from the dank, windowless room.

That had been roughly three hours ago.

Since then, I'd heard him scream more times than I could keep track. To distract myself, I reached for my gold wedding band and twisted it around my finger. The action served to painfully remind me of my many, many stupid mistakes.

Like leaving on my own once again. Like believing Alpha Hendrix wouldn't betray me. *Again.* Like . . . like trusting my parents without question. Was my dad even sick, or had they been a part of the plan to lure me into this trap?

I'd been stupid. *So* stupid to leave the one place that had kept me safe.

But the pain—the pain of being *near* him—had been too much.

"I won't let myself fall in love."

Won't.

Won't.

Won't.

2

Kolton Rivers, the man I'd agreed to marry, didn't love me. Wouldn't *allow* himself to.

I'd known from the beginning he didn't want love or a mate. I hadn't wanted those things either. But, over the weeks spent in his company, I'd grown attached. I'd grown *more* than attached, and that's where I'd messed up. I'd stupidly allowed my heart to fall for him. For a man that could never fully be mine.

And, according to my wolf, that very same man was my mate. My *soulmate.*

He didn't know though. Or, at least, didn't care. We might have shared several passionate moments, but that's all they were to him. Moments. Fleeting moments of desire. Nothing more.

Despite how screwed up everything was between us, I couldn't make myself regret the deal I'd made with him. Couldn't regret marrying him. I'd gained my wolf. Gained protection. Gained *acceptance.* I'd even gained a family, of sorts. One very much unlike the family I'd been born into.

But I'd left. Left to coddle my hurt feelings. Which had ended in disaster.

Now, I was who-knew-where, waiting for a bunch of crazy witches to exorcise the wolf from my body. Correction: the *spirit.* The celestial being who called herself Storm—ergo, my moody familiar.

I would ask for her help, except that she was officially giving me the silent treatment. Not surprising. She only responded when she felt like it. Still, ever since our soulmate conversation, I thought we'd had a breakthrough. Thought she was opening up to me. Guess not. I was on my own, as usual.

I'd gotten myself into this mess, and now I had to get myself out. I couldn't rely on someone to save me. Not even Kolton. Sure, I was his wife, but he had his family to consider. His sisters. His mother. His pack. He had a responsibility to protect them, and that meant making smart decisions. Attempting to rescue me would be dangerous. *Stupid* even. And he was anything but stupid.

No, I couldn't expect him to come for me. Besides, if anything happened to me, he could easily find a new wife. Loads of females would marry him in a heartbeat, even without the promise of love. He was Kolton Rivers, after all. *The* Kolton Rivers. Billionaire alpha. King of New York. Leader of the largest pack in the country. Any female would be lucky to rule by his side. To help him further secure his coveted position. To bear his children.

But the very thought of another woman taking my place in Kolton's life tore a jagged hole in my chest. I pressed a hand over my thundering heart to keep it from falling out.

The room's only door suddenly screeched open, jerking me from my self pity. All of the hair raised on my body as two witches entered the dark room, dragging a limp Arrow between them. I couldn't tell if he was conscious. A tangle of white-blond hair obscured his face, but I could see the fresh, oozing cuts on his arms and legs through his tattered clothing.

The witches unceremoniously dumped him inside his cage and secured the lock. But instead of leaving again . . .

They turned to me.

As they approached, my heart nearly gave out.

Two days. Two days without food or water. Two days of using the grate in the floor of my cage as a toilet. Two days of muscle cramps from sitting in awkward positions. Two days of no sleep. Of being watched but never approached.

Until now.

I didn't recognize either of the witches, only that they were female. When one raised a hand toward me, I cringed away. But I

4

had nowhere to run.

"*Rigescunt indutae*," she said.

Just like that, every inch of me froze. Not even my eyelids would shut. The spell seemed to be a favorite of theirs. Keisha had used it on me right before portalling us here. The spell definitely gave them the upper hand, rendering my superior strength useless. Not that I was much of a threat right now, what with the silver-lined cage having weakened me.

Still, I could understand their caution. A single drop of my toxin into their bloodstreams would immediately switch their status from witch to werewolf. According to Keisha, that was cause for instant banishment from the coven. I could still vividly remember her leaving Fang behind to face his fate after Vi had scratched him.

The memory quickly dissipated when the witches moved forward to unlock my cage. Without a word, they grabbed my feet and dragged me out. Unable to brace myself, my head fell back and thwacked against the concrete floor. They didn't seem to notice. Or care.

Through the ringing in my ears, I heard Arrow rasp, "You're wasting your time, evil crones. She's just a regular werewolf."

They ignored him, pausing only to drop my feet and grab my arms. A tangled mass of fiery red hair tumbled forward as they flipped me over and dragged me facedown from the room.

"Did you hear me, old hags?" Arrow's weak voice followed in our wake. "You can't cleanse her. She's not *possessed*."

The door slammed shut, cutting off his protests. Never having been outside the room until now, I tried to take in my new surroundings. Unfortunately, my long, curly hair effectively blocked the view. The only thing I could make out was lit candles, evenly spaced along the hallway. The witches didn't drag me far. Half a minute later, they entered a darkly-lit room and deposited me facedown on the floor.

A floor splattered with fresh blood.

Arrow's blood.

And that wasn't all. A large symbol was carved into the concrete beneath me. A five-pointed star surrounded by a circle.

A witches pentacle.

Still unable to move, I didn't react when one of the witches clamped something hard and unforgiving over my wrist. And then the pain hit.

Swift. Hot. Excruciating.

Burning. *Melting* my skin.

I tried to scream. Tried with all my might.

All that came out was a strangled whimper.

When rough hands grabbed my other wrist, there was nothing I could do. Jerking it to the side, they clamped that one in irons too. Except that this iron was coated in *silver*. Nothing else could explain the agony searing my flesh.

A familiar heat suddenly blasted through me.

Storm was finally responding. Trying to emerge at the *worst* possible moment.

No! I internally yelled, struggling to push her back down. *They can't know about you.*

You need help, Nora. Let me face them, she barked, still wrestling for control.

Not like this. We're too weak. They want to exorcise you.

She made a scoffing noise. *I'm not afraid of a few witches. They know not what power I possess.*

Neither did I, but now wasn't the time to voice my bitterness.

Before I could respond, several more pairs of feet shuffled into the room.

Ah, hell. That was *definitely* more than a few witches.

Stay down, I hissed at Storm, doubling my efforts to keep her at bay. Moments later, fresh pain lanced through me as fingers grabbed my hair and lifted my head.

I tried to squeeze my eyes shut, terrified that they were glowing blue and giving away Storm's presence. No such luck. The owner of the hand crouched to my level, bringing his face within inches of mine. At the sight of his familiar features, I froze—well, froze *more*.

"So, this is the creature responsible for my brother's fate?" he said.

"Yes, Tao. Fang fell because she refused to come with us peaceably," a voice answered him. A voice I knew all too well.

Behind him, Keisha's dark boho braids swung into view. Victory shone in her brown eyes, giving me pause. Up until now, I'd thought she was the leader of the Blackstones—the coven I'd found on the dark web. I'd also thought the coven was small. Apparently, I'd been wrong on both counts.

Not far away, I spotted the brown-haired witch, Raelyn—a Water Elemental, judging by the way she'd controlled the lake the first time we'd met. Something moved on Tao's shoulder, drawing my attention back to him. At first, I thought the black and white animal was a racoon, but it was too small, too slender. It stared at me with intelligent black eyes, twitching its pink nose.

Ferret. A ferret *familiar*.

I'd never seen one before. At least, not one that was contained purely in animal form, separate from a human body.

I refocused on Tao, just in time to see something cold darken his gaze. There and gone again in a blink. I could see now that he was older than Fang. Maybe early thirties. And instead of a top knot, his black hair was shaved on the sides and longer on top. He was handsome, but I'd thought the same thing about his brother before he'd tried to pelt me with magic fireballs.

"You will pay for taking my brother away from me," Tao said, slowly tightening his grip on my hair until tears filled my eyes. "But you will pay *less* if you cooperate."

Keisha made a sound of protest, but she didn't utter a word when Tao raised his free hand for silence.

"The Blackstone Coven isn't known for torture. Quite the opposite, actually," he continued. "Yes, we dabble in black magic when the need arises, but only to keep our community safe. As for exorcisms, it is our responsibility to protect witch lineage. Our connection to the spirit world is sacred. No other supernatural possesses this connection. Celestial beings gifted *us* their power, presence, and protection. But there have been whispers, rumors over the years, that some werewolves have the ability to perform magic."

Surprise trickled through me. Magic? Like *magic* magic?

"As you know," Tao went on, "witches and werewolves don't often cross paths. So when we were contacted not once, but *twice* about unnatural werewolf activity in a matter of months, we suspected there must be truth to these rumors. Werewolves are keeping secrets, ones that aren't theirs to keep. If some of you have the ability to wield magic, that can only mean one thing: you've been touched by the spirit world. And that is why you're here today. If Keisha's visions are correct, you possess something that doesn't belong to you. Not just a spirit's power, but the spirit itself. And the very prospect of you having it is an offense worthy of death."

As if sensing my rising panic, he gentled his hold on my hair. "Despite the trouble you've caused us, we don't wish to kill you. Yes, you must be punished for your offenses, but not out of spite. Order must be restored. We've been without the wisdom of our elders for over half a decade, and it's taken a toll on us. We're divided. Diminished.

Unsure how to proceed in an ever-shrinking world. But I do know that letting a *werewolf* possess that which makes us powerful cannot be allowed. Remember that, and we can be reasonable."

He let go of my hair then and stood. Still unable to hold up my head, my gaze fell to his shoes. They were expensive. Black and shiny. At the sight, my throat tightened miserably. Kolton wore shoes like that.

I shouldn't have left. I shouldn't have left *him*. I should have talked things out like he'd wanted. I should have stayed instead of running away like a coward.

The pain of my regret was almost worse than the silver eating away at my skin. I tried to move my numb limbs, desperate to escape. Still unresponsive.

But slowly, lethargically, I managed to blink.

The witches in the room didn't seem to notice. They were too busy setting up a ring of black candles around the pentacle. When they were finished, they each claimed a spot around the circle, evenly spaced apart. Their ages, gender, and ethnicity varied. Each wore their own style of clothing. For all intents and purposes, they looked like regular humans.

Well, until all thirteen of them joined hands and began to chant.

Seconds later, the candles lit up with a *whoosh*. Cold fingers of dread dug into my spine as the fire wildly danced on an invisible wind.

Words continued to spill from the coven member's lips, a droning chant in what sounded like Latin. Their eyes were closed, their faces pinched in concentration.

Keisha's voice suddenly rose above the rest. "Spirit of the otherworld, reveal yourself to me. Come forth from your host so that I may know thee."

The air froze in my lungs. Crap. Could they really force me to shift?

No, Storm said, clearly having picked up on my thoughts. *They aren't powerful enough.*

Well, *that* was a relief. Still . . .

Then how was Kolton able to force the change?

"Spirit of the otherworld, reveal yourself to me. Come forth from your host so that I may know thee," Keisha repeated, louder this time.

You share a strong connection with him, Storm replied, as if Keisha hadn't spoken. *The bond—although new at the time—dragged me from my slumber.*

Huh. Interesting. *You never told me why you stayed dormant for so long,* I said, hoping against hope to keep this conversation going.

"Spirit of the otherworld, reveal yourself to me. Come forth from your host so that I may know thee!" Keisha screamed.

My eyes slowly pivoted to her location, taking in her agitated state. Sweat beaded her dark brown skin while the coven chanted, the candles' flames continuing to mysteriously dance. I waited for Storm to respond. Waited and waited.

At her deafening silence, my hope petered out. Was she *ever* going to tell me about herself?

Knowing by now that our conversation was over, I stopped waiting for a response and focused on regaining control of my body. A sharp tingling in my hands had slowly begun to spread up my arms. As the chanting and screaming reached a crescendo, I tried to wiggle my fingers and toes.

Yes! I silently cheered when they finally obeyed my command. Right at that moment, I became aware of the awful silence. Ah hell, when had the chanting stopped?

I looked back up at Keisha—only to find her dark gaze on me, blazing with fury. A swallow got stuck in my throat. This wasn't good. Not wanting them to know that I'd regained partial use of my limbs, I stayed perfectly still. From behind me, footsteps approached. It took all of my effort not to react.

Don't move, don't move, don't move.

Tao stepped around me and crouched once more, allowing me a clear view of his disappointed expression. Even the ferret looked disappointed, if that were possible. When the familiar hissed at me, I tried not to flinch.

"It's unfortunate," Tao said, studying me critically. "Your suffering could have been minimal, but your resistance tells me you have no intention of cooperating."

Rising, he flicked a glance at a rather burly-looking warlock to the left of Keisha. "Fritz, begin the exorcism ritual. And if she continues to resist," he said, casting one last look at me, "break her."

I stopped breathing.

Tao swept from the room, followed by the other coven members. Leaving me alone with Fritz.

And Keisha.

"I want to watch," she said when the warlock glanced at her.

Shrugging, he turned to face me. A gleam that could only be described as excitement entered his eyes. My whole body began to tremble. I wasn't a stranger to pain, but I was pretty sure pain was this dude's middle name.

Sure enough, he wasted no time getting down to business. Stepping over me, he knelt by my side. I lost sight of him, but Keisha leaned against the wall right in front of me, crossing her ankles as if settling in for a show.

"First, I will cleanse you with holy fire. *Ignis sanctus*," Fritz said. Keisha's eyes lit up. Rough hands grabbed the back of my shirt and yanked. I swallowed a gasp as the material tore, right up the middle.

When his finger touched my bare back, I finally reacted. My body was slow, clumsy, but that didn't stop me from lunging at him. Before I could make contact, the chains snapped taut. Still, I clawed and writhed, desperate to defend myself.

"Restrain her!" Keisha ordered, without moving from her spot.

Fixing my gaze on her, I gathered my strength and prepared to pounce. Fritz slammed a knee down on my lower spine, pinning me in place. I glared at Keisha, baring my teeth in a defiant snarl.

She slowly smirked. "Proceed. Show her what happens to naughty wolves who mess with the Blackstone Coven."

Everything in me went cold.

Storm. Storm, I need—

Before I could beg Storm for help again, Fritz traced a pattern over my back and muttered, "*Internus ignis.*"

Just like that, my body burst into flames.

I screamed as liquid fire consumed me. Not my skin, but my veins. My *blood*. It was boiling. Raging hotter and hotter until I thought I would explode from the inside out.

No such luck.

The fire continued to rage. Ceaseless. Endless. Stealing my breath and sanity. I screamed myself hoarse, but my body refused to pass out. I endured the torture for *hours*. Trapped in my own personal hell. Unable to escape it.

All I could do was scream.

Scream and survive.

Even when I wished for death.

CHAPTER 2

NORA

"Nora. Nora, wake up."

For a second—a *split* second—my traitorous mind heard Kolton's voice. I jerked my heavy eyelids open and wildly looked about. Looked for *him*.

When all I found was Arrow's worried face behind the bars of his cage, my heart sank. I let my eyelids droop shut again.

Minutes passed. Then . . .

"I heard your screams."

I didn't reply. Didn't even twitch.

Another few minutes passed before Arrow asked, "What did they do?"

I tried to swallow and miserably failed. Even during my times locked in the farmhouse cellar without food or water, I'd never been this parched. My tongue was swollen, stuck to the roof of my mouth. The hours of screaming had leached my mouth of any moisture. Combined with the inferno that had baked me alive from the inside, I was nothing but a dried-out husk. I wouldn't be surprised if I floated away with the slightest breeze.

A few hours had passed since the torture had stopped. Since they'd dumped my limp body back in my cage. I'd immediately passed out from pure exhaustion, half hoping that I'd never wake up again.

But I had.

And I kind of hated Arrow right now for being the cause.

Still, he was the only one in this cursed place who actually cared about my well-being. So, I managed to croak out one word. "Fire."

Arrow quietly swore. "Those bastards. They did the same thing to me when I first arrived. Purged me with holy fire. Ironic, considering what they are. I'd love to burn them all at the stake and see how *they* like it."

His words shouldn't have comforted me, but they sort of did. Just knowing that I wasn't alone helped.

Well, I had Storm, but she wasn't exactly the type to offer comfort. Had she felt my pain earlier?

Yes.

The single word slid through my mind, confirming that she was listening to my thoughts.

I'm sorry, I told her, glad that our communication didn't require the use of my raw vocal chords. *I tried to protect you from it.*

She was silent for several beats. Then, *You tried to protect me?*

Well, yes. I didn't see a point in us both suffering. They think I'm the abomination, not you.

She fell silent again. For so long that I didn't think she would respond. *Your mate was right about you,* she suddenly said. *You have a generous heart. Too generous, in my opinion. Despite the many injustices you've endured in your short lifetime, your heart is still soft. How?*

Surprised by her question, I struggled with how best to reply. *I guess . . . I just find it better than the alternative. If I harden my heart, no one can get in. I'd be isolated and alone, and being alone in this vast world sounds like the worst kind of hell. So, I keep opening myself up to people.*

Even when it hurts?

Yes, Storm. Even when it hurts.

She didn't respond after that, but for once, I didn't mind. She'd paid me a compliment. A legit *compliment*. Another breakthrough in our strained relationship. I'd be elated if I wasn't still in so much pain. My supernatural ability to heal wasn't working like it should. The lack of sleep, no food, and close contact with silver was weakening me more and more. The shackles had been removed, but not the aftereffects. Even the slightest movement was agonizing.

Hours dragged by. I fell in and out of consciousness, all too aware that at any moment, the witches could come back to torture me some more. And if they did, I would surely break. I wasn't cut out for torture. Threaten me with some nail-and-teeth-pulling and I'd sing like a canary.

They already knew something was different about me, thanks to Keisha's creepy Oracle powers. But they didn't have physical proof. Didn't know for certain what Storm was. Demon? Angel? Something else entirely? I wasn't exactly a connoisseur of celestial beings. *I* didn't even know what Storm was—which might be a blessing in disguise. They couldn't torture the truth out of me if I didn't know.

Still, I knew enough. And that was dangerous not only for me and Storm but for Arrow as well. For months, they'd been trying to pry him open like some Pandora's Box. And it was becoming more and more clear that they had no idea what they were doing.

Guess the movies were wrong. Witches weren't exorcism experts. They kind of sucked at it, actually.

Just as I was beginning to doze off again, the door to our prison banged open. I barely flinched, still too weak to dredge up much reaction. But when heavy footsteps approached my cage, my heart started to thunder like a runaway horse.

"Dinnertime, flea bags," an annoyed male voice said, right before a metal tray clanged against the concrete near my cage. "Get it before the rats do."

Rats? My body shuddered in revulsion. I might be a carnivore by nature, but I still had standards. Rats were filthy little creatures.

Another tray clanked against the floor near Arrow's cage, then the warlock left, slamming the door shut behind him.

The second he was gone, Arrow scrambled for the tray. I watched as he reached through the bars and snatched up a small loaf of bread. Then, like a rabid animal, he savagely tore into the food. It wasn't until he'd consumed the whole loaf that he finally glanced up and caught me staring. Not the least bit embarrassed, he reached through the bars again for a cup of water.

"You should eat, Nora," he said, his mouth still full as he guzzled the water. "To keep us docile, meals are few, and the rats really will steal it. Although, if you can catch one, they're a great protein boost. It's the only meat you're going to get in here."

My stomach soured. If I had anything left in my body, I would have thrown it up.

When Arrow lowered his cup to ravenously eye my plate of food, I finally moved. Slowly reaching out, I carefully slid my hand through the bars and picked up my loaf of bread. Instead of devouring it though, I turned and stuck my hand through the bars again.

"Here," I rasped, watching as Arrow's crystal blue eyes brightened at my offering.

Without hesitation, he snatched a hand out and caught the bread—along with my fingers. Before I could pull them back, he squeezed them tightly and whispered, "Thank you."

A little disconcerted at the intense way he was looking at me, I nodded and tugged my hand free. As he settled back and demolished my loaf of bread, I focused on the one thing I desperately needed.

Water. Grasping the cup with trembling fingers, I nearly dropped it. Panic beat at my ribs, but I managed to bring the cup to my lips without spilling a drop.

When the tepid liquid touched my tongue, I almost lost it. Gripping the cup with both hands, I drank the water in greedy gulps.

"Careful," Arrow warned as I sputtered and coughed. "You won't be of much use to me if you choke to death."

At that, I almost laughed. But even the *thought* of laughing hurt. When I could speak again, I said, "How can I possibly be of use to you?"

"For one, you're pretty to look at," he replied in a perfunctory way. As if it was simply a fact. "For another, you keep me out of my head." He tapped his temple with a wink, making me wonder if he was actually referring to his wolf.

When he didn't offer further explanation, I snorted and took another sip. More carefully this time. "So, what's your story? How did the witches discover you?"

He stared at me for a long moment, then barked a laugh. "They didn't *discover* me. Someone in my pack handed me over to them, end of story."

I blinked. Blinked again. "That's what happened to me too. Well, the handing-me-over part."

"Sorry to hear. Being betrayed really sucks."

"Yeah." I licked my cracked lips, wondering what else I could say without getting us into trouble. "Where are you from?"

He tilted his head to the side. "Portland."

"Maine?"

"Yeah. You?"

"A little town in northern Vermont. Well, not anymore. I'm in New York now."

His expression froze, as if he'd been zapped with a spell. For several seconds, he simply stared at me, unblinking. Growing uncomfortable, I set my cup down and reached for my wedding band. The moment I touched it, Arrow's gaze snapped to my ring finger. I could almost see the wheels turning in his head as he stared and stared at the ring.

"So, you're a member of the Midnight Pack," he abruptly said, meeting my eyes once more.

I almost squirmed, disconcerted by his probing look. "Well, not yet. I haven't been officially initiated. But I'm sort of, um . . . married to the alpha."

Crap, were his eyes starting to glow? Maybe we should change the subject.

Before I could though, he said, "So, Alpha Rivers has finally chosen himself a bride. One who is somehow still a virgin. How is that possible?"

Every inch of me tensed. Hell, not *this* again.

Before I could say anything, he waved the question away with a laugh. "Forget I asked. You don't have to answer."

Relieved when the glow in his eyes faded and he didn't probe further, I let silence settle between us.

Arrow released a quiet chuckle before lying down. Well, as much as the cage would allow him to. "I was wrong, Nora," he said after a few minutes, a small smile on his face. "You're going to be of *great* use to me."

In the middle of the night, they came for me again.

Except that, when my blurry vision cleared, the forms creeping toward me solidified into one.

Into *Keisha*.

She was alone.

She swept into the room on eerily silent feet, avoiding my food tray with agility. Not far away, Arrow stirred awake and sat up. I remained where I was, curled into a tight ball in the middle of my cell. Only my eyes tracked her stealthy approach.

When she bent to unlock my cage, my heart started to pound. I tensed, ready to move. To spring. To take her down and make my escape.

The lock unlatched.

Adrenaline raced through me.

The gate swung open.

I gathered my strength and lunged.

A force like a battering ram threw me backward. My head hit the silver bars, and I nearly blacked out. Crumpling to the floor of my cage, I struggled to rise again. To gather my wits. Before I could clear the spots from my vision, that same force pinned me to the ground—like an elephant sitting on my chest. I tried to move my arms and legs, but they were pinned as well.

At first, I thought Keisha had used a freezing spell on me, but I could still blink. Could still move my head side to side. No, the magic she'd used on me this time was different. Testing its strength, I struggled with all my might to unlock my limbs, but to no avail.

Suddenly, she was there. *Inside* my cage.

My eyes widened as she straddled my hips and leered down at me, her boho braids creating a dark curtain around us. Still, I could see her expression, twisted in hatred. Hatred for me.

"Don't worry, little wolf," she quietly crooned. "I'm not here to kill you. This will be a short visit, I promise. I only want to confirm what I already know."

Without warning, she reached down and dragged one of her dagger-like nails up my inner forearm. So deep that the skin split like butter. I cried out as pain lanced up my arm, sharp and swift.

"Shhhh," Keisha continued to croon, covering my mouth with her other hand. "It's not that bad. Just a little cut." She viciously dug her nail into the open wound, warm blood spilling out and coating my skin.

Her hand muffled my screams.

"Let her go, witch," Arrow growled, "or I'll call for the guards."

Keisha scoffed. "Go right ahead. They won't hear you. I put them under a little sleeping spell. Not too long, of course. Just long enough to disable the camera and slip inside unnoticed. I really don't plan to overstay my welcome. I just want to confirm that my findings are correct."

"What findings?" Arrow asked, when it was clear that I couldn't.

"That there is indeed a spirit trapped inside this body," Keisha replied, gouging her nail even deeper into my flesh. I cried out again, unable to do anything else. She was powerful, no doubt about it. Powerful and sadistic.

Arrow barked a laugh. "You're delusional. You've been trying to crack me open for *weeks*, and look where that has gotten us."

She ignored him this time, focusing on me. "You made me look like a fool today, little wolf. I want justice for Fang, but I also want satisfaction. You *are* harboring a dirty little secret, and I won't rest until it's revealed to the entire coven. Even if I have to cut you open every night. Even if I have to tear you apart, piece by piece, until I find the truth."

She twisted her nail inside me until she hit bone. A sob wrenched from my lungs. "Eventually, you will break. And when you do, you will tell me everything I want to know. *Everything.*"

Excitement gleamed in her eyes as she yanked her nail from my arm and whipped out a small bowl. In no time, the brim was nearly overflowing with my blood.

"*Manifesto*," she purred, then uttered a haunting spell. The same one she'd recited the first time we'd met.

Cerulean blue magic lit up her hand as she waved it over my arm. The blood in the bowl started to bubble. Without delay, she dipped her nail into the blood and brought it to her lips. I wanted to vomit as she tasted it and moaned, just like she had last time.

"The power. It has *grown*," she gasped, her eyes wild with shock. With *awe*. "So close. So close that I can almost *touch it.*"

Her eyes suddenly glazed over. She began to tremble, so violently that her teeth clacked together.

"I know you're there, spirit," she frantically whispered, digging her nails into my cheek. "You can't hide from me forever. I will find you. I will *see* you!"

Heat abruptly whipped through me.

With a startled cry, Keisha vanished. I lifted my head, just in time to see an unseen force *shove* her from the cage. She tumbled across the concrete until her back struck Arrow's cage. He lunged for her, but before he could grab her, she scrambled away with a hiss.

The distraction was enough to undo the magic hold she had on me. Ignoring my aching body, I threw myself toward the opening. Right before I could make my escape, Keisha flicked her wrist, and the gate slammed shut in my face. I jerked back, barely avoiding the silver bars.

A second later, Keisha began to laugh. More like cackle. She threw her head back and shrieked like, well, a crazy witch. "That was unexpected. And *thrilling*," she gasped out, still cackling.

The laughter abruptly stopped as she eyed me with feral excitement. I shivered at the creepy grin she wore.

"You continue to surprise me, little wolf," she said, not looking the least bit freaked out by what had just happened. "And, as an Oracle, I'm not often surprised."

Securing the lock, she came around the side of my cage and collected the bowl of blood—which miraculously hadn't spilled. I didn't move a muscle. Only my eyes moved, tracking her as she crossed the room.

At the door, she turned and looked at me one last time. Her grin was pure insanity. "Until tomorrow night, then."

With that, she left as silently as she came.

CHAPTER 3

KOLTON

"You should sleep, Kolton."

Without turning around, I acknowledged Jagger's concern with a simple, "Can't."

"It's been three days. You need rest," he quietly persisted.

At the fresh reminder, my shoulders grew rigid. I didn't budge from my spot in front of the hotel room window. For the past hour, I'd been staring out at nothing, lost in thought.

Three days. Three days of hitting dead end after dead end.

We'd discovered the witches' scent but had no trail to follow. They must have portalled away, taking Nora along with them. We also hadn't found Alpha Hendrix. He'd vanished, as if he'd known I would come for him.

Coward.

Nora's parents hadn't been any help either. They knew nothing of their alpha's whereabouts. They'd looked guilty though. So guilty that I'd mercilessly grilled them until they'd confessed to their part in luring Nora back to the farm. After thoroughly investigating the grounds, I'd left before I could take out my anger on them.

They were spineless, but they'd only been following their alpha's orders. No matter how much I detested them for not protecting their daughter, I knew how pack hierarchy worked. They'd felt like they had no choice. Disobeying the leader held consequences, and I doubted Hendrix dealt fair punishment.

Alphas had the power, no matter how corrupt they were.

From the bathroom, I heard the shower switch off. A few minutes later, Griff emerged.

"He still hasn't moved?" he said, clearly talking about me.

"Nope," Jagger replied. "Too busy brooding."

"Watch out, Jag. He's going to steal your job."

"Hey, I don't brood."

"Then what do you call that thing you do?"

"What thing?"

"That grumpy-cat-face thing."

"That's just my face, Griff."

If my eyes weren't so heavy, I would have rolled them. "Quit it, you two. You're not helping."

"Just trying to lighten the mood," Griff said. One of the beds creaked as he threw his weight onto it. I glanced back, just long enough to see him sprawl onto the mattress butt naked, both inked arms tucked beneath his head. The only thing he'd bothered with was his hair, the blond strands spiked as usual.

I faced the window again, impatiently shoving back my own hair. The dark strands were uncharacteristically limp, falling onto my forehead once more. "Until we find a new lead, I'm not in *any* mood. The only thing I care about is getting her back."

Griff and Jagger fell silent. Probably to exchange looks behind my back, but I didn't care. After seeing what the witches had done to Nora's truck and phone, I couldn't stop thinking the worst. Were they hurting her?

Three days. Three days of pure hell as my imagination went wild.

My skin was stretched tight, barely containing my fury, but a lot of that rage was directed at myself. I hadn't bothered to question Nora about the witches. Hadn't taken precautions. Hadn't even considered

24

that they would still pursue her. I'd been arrogant. Blinded by my position. A few witches wouldn't *dare* challenge the alpha of Midnight Pack, after all.

What a fool bastard I was.

All I had now was an elusive name. Blackstone.

Despite my many resources, I couldn't track down the coven's location. They'd been careful not to leave physical *or* digital footprints, snatching Nora up like ghosts and leaving without a trace.

"Still no phone call?" Jagger had the courage to ask.

My shoulders fell. "No. Nothing."

The witch who'd taken Nora had said she would be in touch soon, but no contact had been made. Which probably meant one of two things. That they were too busy tearing her apart, or . . .

She was already dead.

When fresh panic squeezed my chest, I heard Jagger rise from the table and approach. Griff rose as well, dragging on a pair of sweats as he went. Moments later, I felt their steady presence at my back. Even when I was being short-tempered, they never wavered in their support.

I didn't take that for granted. Most alphas couldn't afford to name a second, let alone a third, especially if they were dominant males. The relationship often grew strained, as the instinct to challenge their alpha arose.

But, in all of our years together, they'd never once questioned my leadership. Even as adolescents, they'd followed me. After our first shifts, when we'd learned of our deeper connection, we'd been inseparable. To be chosen by a familiar was a rare gift. Even rarer to find werewolves who possessed the same gift. An instant bond had formed—one that had only grown once we'd discovered that Vi and Melanie had also been chosen.

We looked out for each other. *Protected* each other. Our shared secret had forged us into a family, one that transcended the earthly plane.

I wasn't simply their leader and alpha. We were friends. *Brothers*, even. Our bond was ironclad, rooted in loyalty, trust, and honesty.

Which was why, when Jagger said, "I know you're worried, Kolton. We are too," I didn't hesitate to say, "No, I'm not worried. I'm *terrified*."

Griff rested a hand on my shoulder. "She's a survivor. She'll get through this."

I shook my head, unable to slow my racing pulse. "Maybe she will. But *I* won't."

"What do you mean?" Jagger asked, clearly confused.

I finally turned to them. In a rare show of vulnerability, I didn't mask the fear, turmoil, and desperation pumping through my veins. I let them see, smell, and hear it as I said, "I've been unable to eat or sleep for weeks, long before Nora was taken. There's a gaping hole in my chest that grows larger with each passing day. The only time I feel better is when I see her—like the day before she left. And now that she's gone, I can't think. Can't *breathe*. Nothing makes sense without her."

My heart pounded harder. Harder and harder until I thought it would explode.

When all they did was stare at me with concern, I finally confessed what I hadn't dared believe. Finally admitted what my heart had known from the moment I'd first laid eyes on her.

"I think Nora is my soulmate."

CHAPTER 4

NORA

Over the next few days, a schedule formed.

In the mornings, Arrow was removed from his cage and tortured.

In the afternoons, it was my turn.

The methods of torture varied.

Silver, electricity, near-drowning, hallucinations. And—when none of that worked—more fire to "cleanse" me. I'd scream and scream and scream, but my pleas always fell on deaf ears. Tao wasn't there for the torture, but Keisha was. Every single time. She'd stand in front of me, watching me scream for hours. With each day that passed, she seemed less concerned with keeping me alive and more interested in seeing me break.

I expected to be questioned, to have information pried from my cracked lips. But, after my second dinner of stale bread and water, I found out why they hadn't.

Keisha had convinced her coven that I needed to face justice first. Even Tao had agreed. She'd delivered the news personally, then once again crept into my cage in the dead of night to flay me open like a fish.

Each night that passed, the same thing happened. She'd cut me open, drain my blood, and utter incantations. But every time she did, the same thing occurred. An unseen force blasted her back. I'd asked Storm about it, certain she was responsible somehow, but she wouldn't answer. Even Arrow was tight-lipped. He'd spent the past few days staring at me intensely, refusing to take the food I'd offer him.

Guess I couldn't blame him. Between the lack of appetite, little sleep, torture sessions, and blood loss, I wasn't doing so well. My body couldn't heal, and I was growing weaker and weaker. The only way I could keep track of the passing time was by the tally marks in Arrow's cage.

Seven days.

Seven days since I'd left the best thing that had ever happened to me. Had Kolton given up on me by now? Had he announced my death to his pack? Had he . . . begun his search for a new wife?

At the mere thought, I nearly broke. Nearly succumbed to my pain.

On the eighth day, everything changed.

No one came for Arrow in the morning, and no one came for me in the afternoon. I should have felt relief, but my trepidation grew and grew as the hours dragged by. Something was about to happen, and whatever that something was wouldn't be good. Unable to sleep, I focused on the silence, straining to hear any sound. To gain even the slightest bit of information on what our captors were up to. No such luck. The silence was absolute. Deafening.

It was nearing dinnertime when the door finally opened. Several figures approached my cage en masse, causing Arrow to stir and release a low growl.

"Leave her alone," he barked at them. "She needs to heal. Take me instead."

They ignored him, unlocking my cage to drag me out. Through my hazy vision, I spotted the usuals, including Keisha. But even more surprising was the appearance of Tao.

Instead of taking me to the "interrogation room," they dumped me a few yards from my cage. I landed in a heap, too weak to even sit up. A fact they must have known, considering they hadn't bothered to restrain me, not even with a spell.

Still, several of the witches looked ready to zap me if I dared *look* at them wrong, let alone attack. Even Keisha appeared on edge. Or more like upset. She kept pursing her lips and casting glances at Tao every few seconds.

He, on the other hand, was cool as a cucumber. When he approached to tower over me, the only emotion he showed was a brief nose wrinkle—one that his ferret mimicked. Probably at the stench of my unwashed body. I couldn't even muster up the strength to be embarrassed.

"Ready to cooperate yet?" he said, standing with his hands casually tucked into his pockets. "If you do, I'll have someone administer a healing potion. It'll be like the past week never happened. I'll even make sure they provide you with clean clothes and toiletries so you can freshen up."

He flicked a glance at the cuts and dried blood on my arms but made no comment. I let a moment of silence go by, then slowly nodded.

A smile devoid of warmth tipped his mouth. "Good. You can start by making a phone call." He withdrew a hand from his pocket, along with a phone, then held it out to me.

I stupidly gaped at the device, half-expecting it to tase me or some other form of torture. When nothing happened, I cautiously accepted it.

Clearing my throat, I rasped, "Who should I call?"

Coldness darkened his gaze. "The man who killed my brother." At my startled expression, he added, "Yes, I know all about what happened that day. How Keisha was forced to leave Fang behind.

How Mr. Rivers snapped his neck. Keisha had a vision afterward. She saw everything. Fang tried to surrender, but your cruel husband murdered him in cold blood."

My mouth fell open. "That's n-not . . ." I stammered, casting Keisha a wide-eyed look. She smirked. "That's not what happened. She's *lying*. Also, she's been secretly sneaking in here at night to torture me. That's why I have these cuts on my arms. She's—"

"*Enough*," Tao snapped, whipping his other hand out. I winced as a bright translucent light engulfed his palm. Just like that, all the air left me. *Whoosh.* Gone. Ripped from my lungs. Terrified, I grabbed my throat, desperate for air. But, no matter how hard I tried to fill my lungs, nothing happened.

I gaped at Tao's cold face, realizing what he'd done.

Stolen my air. Every last drop. Sucked it right out of me with magic. He was an *Air* Elemental.

The corners of my vision began to darken.

Dimly, I heard Arrow shout. Heard Storm join in. I felt her rise to the surface, seconds away from taking over. There was nothing I could do to stop it. Not this time. Every witch in this room would see me shift. Would have *proof* of Storm's existence.

If that happened, they would stop at nothing to torture her out of me. I would break. Break into a million pieces. There would be nothing left of me.

Just when I thought all was lost, air leaked down my windpipe. Tao dropped his hand and I sucked in a loud gasp. Life-giving air rushed into my lungs, dispelling the darkness. My body exploded with pain as I began to cough. Still, the pain sure beat transforming into a werewolf. Although, wolfing out on these evil witches sounded mighty tempting right now.

Before I could follow through with my stupid idea, Tao spoke again. "I do not tolerate false accusations, especially ones about my coven members. Keisha has been invaluable to us for years. She would not lie about this. Now, make the call."

Still greedily dragging in air like it might be my last, I shook my head. "No."

I flinched when Tao curled his hands into fists. This was it then. This was how I would die. I'd always thought a werewolf would kill me, not a warlock. Guess my prediction skills weren't very good.

Refusing to cower, I looked him in the eye, waiting for him to snatch the air from me once more. Instead, Tao said to no one in particular, "Take out the other one. Torture him in front of her."

My gaze flew to Arrow, just as Raelyn and Fritz unlocked his cage and grabbed him. When he put up a fight, they pinned him to the ground with magic. Despite his vulnerable position, he bared his teeth and cursed at them. The burly warlock stepped forward and blasted a fireball straight into his chest.

"No!" I screamed, scrambling upright. Magic pinned me back down. I helplessly watched as the smoke cleared, revealing a charred hole in Arrow's shirt . . . and flesh. Rage fueled my next words. "You sadists! You all deserve to burn in *Hell*."

"Is that where your spirit is from? *Hell?* Cooperate and this can all stop," Tao said, crouching to my level. At the scathing look I gave him, he flicked his fingers. "Continue."

Raelyn stepped forward this time and, uttering a few words, waved a hand engulfed in deep blue magic over Arrow. A second later, he began to choke. Blood spewed from his mouth. When he continued to choke and cough up blood at an alarming rate, I finally started to fracture.

To *break*.

"Stop. *Stop!*" I yelled, struggling against my invisible restraints.

"I'll do it. I'll make the call. Just . . . just stop torturing him. *Please.*"

For an unbearable moment, the torture continued anyway. Until Tao raised his hand. Just like that, it stopped.

"Make it quick," he said, flicking his fingers again. The magic holding me in place vanished. "I've already been here longer than I wish to be."

Trembling, I focused on the phone. *Don't do it, don't do it, don't do it.* But I wasn't strong enough. I couldn't let them torture Arrow. Not when I could stop it. So I dialed the number. *His* number. Shaking so hard that I nearly dropped the phone.

When it began to ring, I almost hung up. Almost. One look at Arrow, and I fractured again. He'd been through so much. *So much.* I couldn't allow him to suffer more because of me. But I also knew that the witches wanted vengeance on Kolton and his family.

All because of me.

Because of my stupid, *stupid* decisions.

I didn't deserve him. Didn't deserve his help. Didn't deserve his protection. And I *certainly* didn't deserve to be his soulmate.

I'd caused him nothing but trouble. And now—

"Kolton Rivers speaking."

At the sound of his voice, I nearly lost it. Nearly bawled my eyes out then and there. Right in front of my tormentors.

A tremor shook me, so violently that I lost the ability to speak. To *breathe.*

"Tell him who's calling," Tao ordered.

I opened my mouth, but nothing came out.

"Nora?" Kolton said, the word coated in disbelief. In *hope.*

That was all it took.

Hot tears scalded my cheeks. Tears that should have long since dried up. They fell and fell, soaking the phone and my fingers.

Everything in me wanted to cry out to him. To share my pain and distress. To plead for his help. His *protection*.

But I didn't.

I gathered the remnants of my shattered strength and, in a stuttering rush, said, "Don't come for me, Kolton. They'll only kill you too."

Before I could say more, the phone flew from my grasp and into Tao's hand.

"Nora? *Nora!* Tell me you're okay. Speak to me. *Please.*"

When I opened my mouth again, Tao raised his free hand. At the sight, I flinched and snapped my mouth shut.

Satisfied, he brought the phone to his ear. "Your concern for your wife is touching, Mr. Rivers. She's fine, but I must ask for your cooperation if you wish to see her again."

Silence. Then, I heard Kolton clearly say, "Who are you and what do you want?"

It took everything in me to hold still. To stop myself from tackling Tao and wrestling the phone from him. With so many other witches in the room, I wouldn't get that far anyway.

"My name is Tao," the coven leader calmly replied, absently stroking his ferret's head. "And what I want is justice for what you did to my brother. Normally, a blood debt would extend to your family as well, but I'm a reasonable man. Turn yourself in willingly and my coven and I will leave the rest of your family alone. Provided they leave *us* alone."

I bit my tongue. *Hard.* When what I really wanted to do was scream, *Don't do it!*

Kolton didn't even pause. Didn't even hesitate to say, "Name the location, and I'll be there. But I won't turn myself over until I'm certain Nora is safe first."

"Deal," Tao said, then proceeded to give him a location. "And, Mr. Rivers? Make sure you come alone. If we sense a trap, Nora pays the price."

When the phone call ended, I felt no relief. Only bone-deep dread.

He was coming. Kolton was coming for me. And I couldn't be more terrified.

Pocketing his phone, Tao stood and commanded that Arrow and I be put back into our cages. When we were secured inside once more, he said to Raelyn, "Make sure Nora is provided with Sano, clothing, and toiletries to clean up with." Raelyn bobbed her head and left the room to do his bidding. As the other witches and warlocks started to leave, he looked down at me and said, "See? I can be reasonable. You might even get out of this alive if you continue to cooperate."

Throwing caution to the wind, I blurted, "If I cooperate, will you show mercy to Kolton?"

Tao's expression flattened. "He didn't show mercy to my brother. Therefore, I cannot show mercy to him."

He whirled and strode from the room, his shiny shoes clicking against the concrete with finality. Flicking his fingers, he used magic to slam the door shut behind him, sealing us in darkness once more.

My panic increased tenfold.

"You okay?" Arrow quietly asked. I could barely see him as he wiped the blood from his mouth and chin. The gaping wound on his chest was still horrific to look at, but I could tell the edges were slowly starting to close.

I shook my head. "I have to escape."

Now. I had to escape *now*. It was the only way to stop Kolton from turning himself in. From *sacrificing* himself.

All because of me.

Arrow's gaze sharpened. "How?"

Swallowing the terror gripping my throat, I managed to say, "By giving them what they want."

"Are you mad?" Arrow hissed, darting a glance at the camera.

A laugh burst from me. The first one I'd been unable to contain.

"Yes, Arrow, I'm mad. I'm *furious*. I've been treated like dirt most of my life, but this experience takes the cake. I'm done being tortured. *Done.* They want to know what I am? Fine. Let's see how they handle a raging werewolf."

"But we're outnumbered," Arrow continued to hiss. "We can't possibly escape them all."

I blinked. "We?"

"Yes, *we*. I may not approve, but whatever you're planning, count me in."

I shook my head. "I could get you killed."

He shrugged. "Death is better than rotting away in this hellhole."

Couldn't argue with him there.

"Okay," I begrudgingly gave in, fully aware that I could be dooming us both. "I'll think of something."

Truthfully, there was very little chance of escape. The witches had been cautious around us from the start, taking extra measures to keep us secured. Plus, we were both so weak that, even if we *did* manage to escape our cages, shifting into our wolves could take too long. A simple freezing spell was all it would take to incapacitate us once more.

As far as I could tell, we only had one hope. One *tiny* sliver of hope. And that hope came in the form of a brown-haired witch named Raelyn. She should be back soon with the supplies Tao had asked her to give me. If I could lure her close enough to the cage, I might be able to grab her. Might be able to convince her to unlock my cage. I'd have to threaten her, of course. Have to be cold and cruel.

But I would. To keep Kolton from sacrificing himself, I would do just about anything.

Minutes passed. Then hours. Dinnertime came and went. No Raelyn.

My hope slowly flickered out.

Kolton could be here by now. He could be turning himself in right this very moment. It was hopeless. We couldn't escape. I'd doomed us *all*.

But when the door suddenly creaked open and a single witch entered, my hope roared back to life.

This could work. I would *make* this work. I had no other choice. It was do or die time, and I had no intention of dying. Not today. I was going to *escape*.

The witch turned, and my heart immediately sank. It wasn't Raelyn. It was *Keisha*. She slowly closed the door behind her, not bothering to silence the squeaky hinges.

At my wide-eyed gaze, she openly smirked. "Expecting someone else, little wolf?"

I didn't respond, too busy trying to adjust my plan. But how? This was *Keisha*. She was always prepared for an attack. She wouldn't be stupid enough to get too close, not without first incapacitating me with magic. Silently cursing, I scrambled to think of something else.

"I brought your potion and clothing," Keisha said, unbothered by my silence. "Tao should have picked someone else for the task. Raelyn has always been a pushover." She approached, her footsteps intentionally loud, like she wasn't afraid of being heard this time. Stopping just shy of my reach, she crouched and raised a glass vial. "Is this what you've been waiting for?" She uncorked the vial and tipped it over. The liquid spilled onto the concrete. "Shame."

I watched her every move, refusing to make a sound. Refusing to be *baited*. Undeterred, she dropped the vial and held up the clothing. Then proceeded to shred the material with her wicked sharp nails. Soon, there was nothing left but tattered rags.

"It's unfortunate the camera went dead an hour ago. No one will see how badly I tried to help you," she said, tossing the shredded material to the ground. "Sadly, you wouldn't accept it, still determined to make my coven question me. But who do you think they'll believe? Me?" She unzipped a small bag of toiletries and dumped the contents. "Or you?"

Rising, she strode to the wall and grabbed a coiled hose. Not the garden variety but a high-pressure one. Cranking the spigot, she turned to face me again.

"And then you went rabid. No one was around to help me, so I did my best to stop you. Unfortunately, I couldn't stop you from hurting yourself."

Whoosh.

A powerful stream of cold water blasted me. I jerked away, covering my face, but Keisha was relentless. The water pounded my back and shoulders with bruising force, agitating my open wounds, but I bit my lip and refused to cry out. When I cracked my eyes open and caught Arrow staring, I shook my head.

Don't interfere, I tried to communicate. I wanted her attention on me, only me. Not that I had to worry.

She continued to blast me with the water until I curled into a ball, choking and shivering. Finally, she stopped, dropping the hose to approach my cage. "It really is sad that no one will see my moment of glory," she practically sang, pausing to unlock the cage. I didn't move a muscle. "I will cut and cut and they'll think it was you. Only this time, I will discover the truth."

Magic flipped me onto my back and pinned my arms to the floor. I blinked to find Keisha in my cage, hovering above me. Smiling that creepy smile of hers.

"Fine," I gasped, still trying to catch my breath. "Cut me all you want, but you'll only end up on your butt again."

Her eyes flashed with anger, just like I wanted.

Storm, wake up, I silently urged. *I need you.*

"Not this time," Keisha hissed. "I must dig *deeper*. It's the only way to reach the spirit and pull her out of hiding."

My heart started to hammer. "Why do you want to figure me out so badly anyway?"

"I'm an Oracle," she said, as if that explained everything. "My calling is to seek. To *know*."

"Yeah, I'm not buying it. This is personal for you. What are you *really* trying to do? Prove to your coven how awesome you are?"

She bared her teeth at me. "*Silence*, or I'll cut more than just your flesh."

"But what if you end up killing me? I don't think Tao will be very happy. Especially if it costs him Kolton."

As I predicted, Keisha's anger only grew.

"Tao is too set in the old ways. He doesn't see how important this opportunity is. How essential to our survival. He only wants to restore order when we possess the key to unlocking a new era. Witches could be powerful again, more than we've *ever* been. If werewolves have the ability to house an entire spirit, then so could witches. We just have to figure out how. Tao might not be willing to do what it takes, but I am. I'll unlock every last one of your secrets, even if it kills you."

"Aww, I'm flattered that you're so obsessed with me," I had the audacity to say, "but you do realize how psychotic you sound, right?"

She lifted a brow. "You think this is psychotic, little wolf? You have no idea what I'm capable of."

"Funny. That makes two of us," I tossed back.

Storm. Storm, wake up!

A slow grin replaced Keisha's anger. "Oh, but I'll know soon enough. No more games. It's time you gave me what I wanted."

I braced for the pain. Waited for her nails to slice into my arms.

Instead, she reached down and yanked my shirt up. I stifled a gasp as she set her sights on my bare stomach. "Interesting," she said, eyeing my skin. When she ran the tip of a nail along one of my scars, my breathing sped up. "It's like a map, showing me just where to cut."

Horror gripped me.

"No—" I blurted. Too late.

Fiery pain ripped through me as she jabbed her nail into my flesh and savagely cut. Cut and cut and cut, right where Alpha Hendrix had clawed me open. Unable to control my reaction, I screamed in pure terror. Images flashed past. Raw, painful memories. I was a child all over again, helpless as my leader tried to disembowel me. To *kill* me.

"Help!" I screamed, just like I had the day he'd attacked me.

No one came that day. No one came now. I was on my own.

"Spirit, reveal yourself to me!" Keisha yelled over my screams. She yanked out her nail, only to stab it back into my stomach.

"HELP!"

My skin and flesh tore. Over and over. Hot blood spilled. Gushed. Keisha dug deeper and *deeper*. Burrowing into my stomach. Shouting her incantations.

"I see you. *I see you!*" she screamed, clawing at my stomach with all ten nails. "I know what you are. I *know.*"

Blinding agony barreled through me. So hot that I nearly passed out.

Keisha suddenly screamed. Not in excitement, but in *terror*. When she pulled her nails from my body, I forced my eyes open. What I saw chilled me to the bone. Keisha's eyes were glowing. No, *burning*. Flames burst from her eye sockets, so intensely that I could barely stand to look.

"No, *please*. It's too much. Too much!" She reached for her eyes, then screamed anew as the fire burned her hands. Moments later, the flames vanished. All that remained were two charred holes where Keisha's eyes used to be. "My sight. *My sight*. She took my sight!"

Keisha's gut-wrenching wails froze me in place. What did she mean? Did *Storm* do this?

"Nora, *move!*"

Arrow's bellow snapped me out of it, making me realize that Keisha's magical hold on me had also vanished. A rush of adrenaline gave me the strength to shove her off me and scramble for the exit. For *freedom*. Too busy clutching her face and wailing, she didn't stop me. Didn't even see me. Sopping wet and bleeding profusely, I clambered from the cage.

"Keys, Nora. Get the keys!"

Clenching my teeth, I forced myself to backtrack and search Keisha for the cage keys. She didn't even notice when I pulled them from her pocket. Scrambling from the cage once more, I hurried to unlock Arrow's.

The lock immediately burned me, and I jerked back with a yelp.

"Here." He yanked off his tattered shirt and thrust it through the bars. I accepted it, using the material to handle the silver lock. My fingers shook so badly that I almost dropped the keys. "Hurry, Nora. Hurry."

"I'm trying!" I yelled above Keisha's sobs, terrified that she'd snap out of it at any second. The itch to *run* raced through my body, but

I couldn't leave Arrow here. I renewed my efforts and was rewarded with a *click* moments later. Still using his shirt as a barrier, I removed the lock and thick chain. Letting them clatter to the floor, I shoved on the bar keeping the cage closed. The door popped open.

The second it did, Arrow surged from the cage in one fluid move. For the first time, I saw him straighten to his full height. He towered above me for a moment, beaten and bruised but far from broken. Streaks of dried blood marred his chest and abdomen, but there was no mistaking his powerful, albeit lean, build.

"Come on. Let's get the hell out of here," he said, offering me his hand.

I didn't hesitate to take it.

CHAPTER 5

NORA

My stomach wouldn't stop bleeding.

Blood saturated the band of my shorts with each step I took, and pressing a hand over the wounds did little to stem the flow.

Keep going, keep going, keep going, I ordered myself, refusing to pass out.

Arrow was only a few steps ahead, but I knew he was moving slower for my benefit. My legs trembled, barely able to carry me. Still, I kept moving. Desperate to escape before Kolton arrived.

As we passed the "interrogation room," I tensed. As did Arrow. The room would forever haunt my dreams. Even when my body fully healed, I would always bear the scars of my time spent there. A few feet later, Arrow paused and yanked up his hand. My heart wildly pounded. He tilted his head to the side, listening.

"They're coming," he said.

I trembled harder. "How many?"

"Four. Maybe five."

I frantically searched for another way out, but the only escape route was forward. Based on the damp chill in the air and windowless rooms, we were in a basement. Finding the stairs was our only hope of getting out of here.

Resolve filled me. We'd have to *fight* our way out.

Storm, get ready. I'm giving you control.

Familiar heat surged through me in response.

"What are you doing?" Arrow hissed.

Startled, I glanced up to find his gaze on me. When our eyes locked, his mouth fell open.

"I knew it," he whispered. "I *knew* it was you."

At the sound of approaching voices, he grabbed my bicep and hauled me into the nearest room—which just happened to be the "interrogation room." It was pitch black, but I could still make out familiar shapes. The silver chains bolted to the floor. The large pentacle carved into the concrete.

Arrow's dried blood. And mine.

When my breathing sped up, Arrow pulled me into the shadows and covered my mouth. I struggled against his hold, suddenly overcome with fear.

Pain.

Touch equaled *pain.*

So focused on breaking free, I failed to notice how careful he was being. The only places he touched were my mouth and arm.

"Shhh," he whispered in my ear, refusing to let go. "They'll hear."

His words snapped some sense into me, and I froze. Just in time too.

". . . and instead of preparing for our new arrival, she's still fixated on that female werewolf. Do you think she's been acting strange lately?" I heard Raelyn say.

"It's Keisha. She's always a little strange," Fritz replied.

"Oracles," another warlock muttered, causing a smattering of laughter among the group. Arrow pulled us farther into the shadows as they passed by the door. I stopped breathing.

"Yes, but—" Raelyn began, then abruptly stopped. "Did you hear that?"

Arrow's grip on me tightened.

"Keisha?" Fritz called.

My heart lodged in my throat.

When a keening wail reached us—*Keisha's* wail—the group burst into action. The second they did, Arrow let go of me and whispered a word. One word that sent my heartrate through the roof.

"*Run.*"

I didn't need to be told twice. Together, we rushed from the room and into the hallway. While the group raced toward Keisha, we headed in the opposite direction.

Don't look back, don't look back.

I did. Just for a second. And in that second, so did Fritz.

Our eyes collided.

Ah, *hell.* There was no stopping him.

"*Hey*," he shouted, turning to point at us. "Get them!"

Everything slowed as the group whirled in our direction. I gaped like a deer in headlights, my lungs seizing with panic. Until Arrow bellowed, "*Run*, Nora!"

Whipping back around, I charged down the hallway as if my tail was on fire. When a fireball blasted the concrete wall beside me, I yelped and protected my face from the flying debris. Several more dogged my footsteps, inches away from striking me.

Arrow reached back and hauled me forward, so fast that I nearly lost my footing. He grunted as a fireball slammed into him, but he didn't stop. He continued to drag me forward, all but carrying me when we reached the stairs. He took them three at a time, surging upward at supernatural speed.

His lengthy time here might have weakened him, but his strength still far surpassed mine. I let him help me up the stairs, all too aware of the blood trail I was leaving in our wake. I might have freed us from the cages, but he was in charge now. I could only hope that his plan of escape worked.

When we reached the top, it became clear right away where we were.

"A church?" I panted. "*Really?*"

An old, abandoned one, but still. Kind of cliche for an exorcism.

We'd arrived in the vestry, where sacred vessels and records were normally kept. But all that we found was a folding chair and table containing a computer monitor. The screen was black. Only a handful of candles lit the dusty space.

"Hurry," Arrow urged, letting go of me to forge ahead.

Ignoring my wounds and the fresh burn mark on Arrow's back, I followed his lead. Yanking a door open, he ushered me through. I stumbled into the church's nave, not surprised to find it empty as well. A handful of wooden pews had been left to rot, but other than that, only candles decorated the cavernous room. They barely lit the space, leaving the ceiling high above hidden in shadow. Most of the stained-glass windows were damaged, but the flames eerily danced in the surviving pieces.

Without a moment's hesitation, we raced down the central aisle toward the narthex. The heavy mahogany doors were wide open. An invitation. Beckoning us forward to freedom.

I didn't question it.

Solely focusing on that opening, I rushed ahead of Arrow. Almost there. *Almost.* Just a few more steps. Just—

The doors slammed shut.

Arrow yanked me back as silver chains shot through the air and coiled around the door handles. Trapping us inside.

"You thought you could escape so easily?" a familiar voice said from behind us.

Cold dread slithered down my spine. I turned to face Tao and the rest of the Blackstone Coven behind him. He sliced his arm through the air. Just like that, I went flying. Arrow shouted, only to fly back as well. I caught a brief glimpse of him crashing into a pew before I painfully hit the ground.

Stars burst behind my eyelids as I rolled and rolled, finally coming to a jarring stop against a pillar. The force of it knocked the air from my lungs. I lay gasping like a fish out of water, unable to catch my breath.

Blinking away the stars, I struggled to remain conscious. To pick myself up. Before I could, shiny black shoes filled my vision.

"I'm disappointed in you, Nora," Tao said, stopping just shy of touching me. "I thought we had an understanding. Your husband will arrive at any moment, and I can't have you disrupting my plans. Guess you need more *incentive* to cooperate."

My throat suddenly closed. I grabbed it, desperate for air. When none came, I writhed on the floor, blindly swiping for Tao's leg. He easily avoided my weak attack, refusing to let up. To free me from his magic.

Just as my vision began to darken, a powerful *boom* shook the air. The windows imploded in a shower of colorful glass. The locked doors burst open, and the chains went flying. Wood exploded, becoming deadly shrapnel. Tao whirled and jerked up a hand, barely halting a piece from impaling his eye.

And yet, his magic still held me. Still robbed me of air.

My vision darkened further.

No, no, no! Don't you dare pass out, I hissed at myself, furiously blinking.

The darkness abruptly moved. Taking on a shape. It rushed—no, *loped* toward us.

When the shape grew larger and larger, ice filled my veins. I saw fangs and claws and dense fur the color of shadows. And then it was there. Picking Tao up by the neck. Rising onto its powerful hind legs. Higher, higher, higher. Eight feet. *Nine.*

The invisible grip on my throat released.

I frantically pulled in air, not once taking my eyes off the massive form. Tao's ferret familiar jumped from his shoulder and scurried away. No one else moved a muscle. We couldn't. We were all in shock. Utter shock at witnessing the impossible.

A creature of myth stood before us. A being that shouldn't exist. Part man, part beast, but mostly beast. A monster straight out of a horror movie.

And then it spoke. *Spoke.* Each word grated on my ears. Deep. Guttural. Rumbling through my insides like crashing boulders.

"You hurt what is mine. Now, you must pay."

"Wait. *Wait,*" Tao wheezed, his legs kicking uselessly in the air. "There's been a mistake."

"There's no mistake. You threatened my family, and now you must die."

Before Tao could say another word, a sickening *crack* cleaved the air. Gasps echoed throughout the cavernous room as the monster dropped Tao's limp body, his neck bent at an odd angle. Clearly dead, his eyes and mouth were still open, frozen in terror.

Magic suddenly exploded against the monster's side. He whirled toward the remaining coven and roared. So loudly that the ground beneath me shook.

Then, he charged. Straight toward them like a bullet. I couldn't look away, struck dumb by how fast he could move. His claws dug into the floor, leaving deep gouges in the concrete. He loped toward them on all fours, which was somehow even more terrifying.

Apparently, the witches felt the same.

"Retreat!" one of them screamed.

Flashes of color briefly blinded me as, one after the other, portals sprang into existence. Right before the monster could reach them, the witches vanished in a swirl of sparkles.

The beast skidded to a halt and roared again, clearly upset to have lost his prey.

I must have made a sound, then. A small gasp or whimper. Because the creature suddenly set his sights on . . .

Me.

I wasn't prepared. Wasn't ready to stare into eyes the color of spilled blood. Glowing so hotly that they burned my retinas.

It was like staring into the face of Death.

My lungs seized with panic. With fear. With *terror.*

I gasped as familiar heat blasted through me. Storm roared, fighting like a wild thing to break free. When she started to force the change, it was too much. *All* of it was too much. The pain, the blood loss, the violence. And, above all, the terror pumping through my veins as the wolf-like monster rose onto his hind legs again and stalked toward me.

My vision darkened.

No. Please, no. Don't pass out.

He came closer and closer until he was towering over me. As he bent and reached for me, I stopped breathing.

Nora, let me out! Storm continued to roar, relentlessly pushing, pushing, pushing. Making me slip farther and farther away.

The beast scooped me up like I weighed nothing. I waited for the pain, the agony of being ripped open by his wicked black claws. The pain didn't come. He lifted me with one powerful arm, then turned and exited the building, eating up the distance in great strides. He carried me out into the night, and I tasted fresh air for the first time in days.

I tried to breathe it in, but I couldn't focus. Storm continued to rage, desperate to gain control. The harder she fought, the more my vision darkened.

"Hurts. Make it stop," I whimpered.

The monster stopped dead in his tracks. I'd meant the words for Storm, but apparently, the beast thought I'd spoken to him. A violent tremor suddenly rocked his massive body. Then, he was shifting. *Changing.* All while I lay cradled in his arms. Arms that were becoming less and less furry, and more and more . . . human.

Seconds later, everything went silent. But I couldn't see. Couldn't see what had happened. My vision had fallen completely into darkness. Still, I clung to consciousness, terrified to let go. Until I heard a voice. A familiar one that whispered into the darkness . . .

"*Sleep,* Nora."

At the sound of that voice, Storm immediately stopped fighting. So did I.

I let go, finally slipping into sweet oblivion.

CHAPTER 6

KOLTON

Nora awoke with a cry.

When she flailed in the bed sheets, as if trying to escape them, I quickly stepped forward. Only to stop dead.

Terrified. She was utterly *terrified*. I'd never seen her so afraid before.

She wildly looked about the room in search of something. Or *someone*. And I immediately knew who.

She's scared of us, a voice said, one that set my blood to boiling.

Of you. She's scared of you, I growled back, forcing myself not to outwardly react when Shadow scoffed.

I hadn't meant to let him loose. Hadn't meant to lose control. It had just . . . happened. I'd heard voices inside the church. Knew Nora was in trouble. And I'd completely lost it. I hadn't reacted that strongly since the day I'd become alpha of the Midnight Pack. Thankfully, only two people had witnessed that event, and one of them was now dead. Unlike last night's fiasco.

You shouldn't have tried to hold me back, Shadow butted into my thoughts, not the least bit sorry for his actions last night. *I would have killed every last one of them.*

I didn't respond, too angry with him to think rationally.

He'd taken advantage of me last night. Made a power play that went against everything we'd been working toward for the last twenty-five years. If I had given him complete control, he wouldn't have just killed the witches. He would have razed the entire building to the ground—even with Nora watching.

When her gaze finally snapped to me, my gut twisted. Her fear was palpable.

"Where is he?" she said, her voice shrill. "Where *is* he?"

"Nora, you're safe. It's only us," Vi gently said, perching on the mattress to take Nora's hand. Before she could touch her, Nora flinched away.

The sight broke my heart.

"Everybody out," I said, speaking to the others without taking my eyes off her. Her eyes darted to me again, then nervously skittered away.

"Kolton," Jagger started, caution edging his voice, "maybe you should give her some time. She's—"

"Leave. Now."

The quietly spoken words rang with authority. Bowing his head, Jagger followed my order, as did Vi and Griff. They soundlessly shut the door behind them, leaving me alone with Nora. Despite my calm outward appearance, my heart started to pound. I'd frightened her. I'd frightened her terribly. She might never look at me the same after this.

Pain seared my chest, but I refused to show how nervous I was. How *afraid*.

I waited a moment. A moment that felt like an eternity. Then slowly stepped toward her.

She immediately bolted off the bed. And fell.

When I surged forward to help her up, she scrambled away, her back hitting the wall. More pain lanced through me.

"Stop. Please, stop," she panted, her heart trilling dangerously fast. "It was only a *nightmare*. Had to be. Doesn't make sense. W-where am I?"

"In my New York City penthouse. We came straight here from the Boston area where the coven was keeping you. They can't track you here though. You're safe."

"We?" She darted a look around the room again.

"Vi, Melanie, Griff, Jagger, and I. No one else is here."

The words did little to soothe her. She kept looking behind me, as if she expected to find someone there. Eventually, she glanced down at herself and froze, gaping at the black t-shirt she now wore. *My* shirt. The one I'd given to her the morning after our wedding.

Her eyes flew to mine, almost in accusation.

"I brought it with me," I said by way of explanation, unwilling to apologize. She hadn't washed it and the shirt still smelled like her. Like *us*. I'd carried it with me this past week, needing to feel close to her somehow. I would have certainly gone insane otherwise. "Vi changed you while you slept, and tended to your wounds."

Looking down at herself again, she lifted the shirt to reveal her abdomen. And underwear. I swallowed, keeping my gaze safely on her bandaged waist.

"You don't need stitches this time. With a little more rest and some food, your wounds should heal quickly on their own."

I'd been alarmed at her injuries. Alarmed and furious. Despite myself, I'd almost gone back to the church and finished what Shadow had started. She'd been brutalized. Ripped open. And not only her stomach. Her arms as well. Her clothing had been saturated with blood, and faint burn marks still ringed her wrists, probably from silver shackles.

As awful as her injuries were, the overall state of her body was what alarmed me the most. Of the glimpses Vi had allowed me to see, the outline of Nora's ribs were painfully obvious. She was rail thin, her skin sallow. Even her fiery curls were dull and lifeless.

At the lost look on her face, my strength finally gave out. I crouched before her, slowing my movements when she threw me another panicked look. She was like an injured animal, skittish and terrified. The sight broke my heart even more. The urge to gather her into my arms was a living, breathing thing inside me.

I needed. *Needed* to hold her. To comfort her. To bridge this awful gap between us.

But, right as I dredged up the courage to bridge that gap, she darted a look around the room again and said, "Where's Arrow?"

CHAPTER 7

NORA

Kolton shot to his feet. So fast that I bared my teeth and scrambled to my feet as well.

Seeing my defensive stance, he raised his hands in a placating manner. "I'm sorry. I didn't mean to react like that."

But he had, and I'd immediately sprung into action, fearful for my life.

Stop it, I scolded myself, willing my erratic pulse to slow. *Blood loss made you hallucinate the beast. It wasn't him. It wasn't Kolton.*

The words didn't soothe me. They only made me feel crazy. So crazy that I had to ask. Had to *know.*

"Did the monster kill Arrow too?"

The second I uttered the words, I knew I'd said them wrong. Kolton harshly exhaled, like I'd punched him in the gut. He looked away, but not before I saw the pain in his eyes. So raw and intense that it stole my breath.

"No," he roughly said, dropping his arms to his sides. "Only the coven leader."

At his confirmation, my insides turned to ice.

"No," I whispered, shaking my head in disbelief. In denial. "I imagined the beast. He . . . he wasn't *real.*"

His hands formed fists. "You didn't imagine him, Nora."

My throat closed. "But it's impossible. Something like that can't exist."

"You mean *shouldn't* exist?" He turned to look me dead in the eye.

I shivered, barely able to hold eye contact. "No, that's not . . . I didn't mean . . . Okay, fine. What was it then?"

He searched my face for a long moment, then answered, "A demon."

Holy hell.

My knees buckled, and I braced myself against the wall. It couldn't be. That would mean . . . *Don't ask, don't ask, don't ask.* "Was it Shadow? Your familiar?"

I could already tell by his resolute expression that it was.

"His true form, yes. His . . . demonic form."

All the air left me in a rush. "Wow," I said, bending forward to place my hands on my knees. I tried to catch my breath. To come to grips with this shocking news. The terrifying beast from last night . . . had been Kolton. Or, at least, a part of him. "Oh, wow."

Kolton didn't say anything, allowing me time to collect myself. He simply stood there and waited. Waited for me to accept it.

Or not.

But I didn't know. I didn't know what to think or feel or believe.

He'd known about this the entire time. Known that he could turn into this . . . this monstrous *demon.*

But if he knew that, what else did he know?

Oh no. Oh no, oh no, oh no.

Struggling to breathe, I looked up at him again and point blank asked, "What is Storm?"

His expression shuttered.

Ah, *hell.*

"Kolton. What. Is. Storm?"

At the bite in my voice, he clenched his teeth. "Nora . . ."

"Kolton, *tell me!*"

"An *angel*," he forcefully said.

I gasped when his eyes started to glow yellow. Gasped again when his words finally sank in.

"That's all I know, Nora, I swear. When you shifted for the first time, your blue eye color made me suspect. Then the way your wolf responded to mine confirmed it. She hates him because he's a demon."

"And you didn't *tell* me?" I yelled.

"Nora, I'm—"

"What else haven't you told me?" I demanded, pushing off from the wall. When I staggered a little, Kolton reached out to steady me. "*Don't*. Don't touch me."

He winced, then retreated a step. "It's a lot to take in. I didn't want to scare you."

"Scare me? I'm *terrified*," I screamed, not caring how unhinged I sounded. "You can turn into a nightmare straight out of a *horror* film."

The agony in his eyes almost made me stop. Almost. But I couldn't. Too many emotions were bottled up inside me. Too much pain and anger and fear. They demanded to be released. To be *spoken*.

"And you never told me. You never told me what you were. What *I* was. That our wolves are, what? Mortal *enemies*? Because angels and demons are on opposite sides, last time I checked. In fact, Storm warned me about you. About Shadow. That he could end up corrupting you. And if that happened, she would have to—"

Ah crap, I hadn't meant to say that much.

"Have to what, Nora?" Kolton quietly asked, slowly unclenching his fists. "What would Storm have to do?"

I pursed my lips, refusing to say more. Refusing to let *him* get the upper hand. I was mad. Mad and *hurt*. And so confused. We were supposed to be *soulmates*. How screwed up was that?

But Kolton was relentless. He took another step. "Would she kill me? Save me from the *evil* inside me?"

"That's not—"

"You didn't have to. I can see it in your eyes. You're afraid of me."

"No, I'm—"

He took a third step, and I instinctively retreated. My back struck the wall.

"You're terrified. You think I'm a monster."

"No . . ."

Another step.

"You wish you had never agreed to marry me."

"Kolton, stop—"

I sucked in a gasp as he erased the final distance between us. As he placed his hands on the wall near my head. Leaning into my personal space, he said, "You're right. I didn't tell you everything, and I'm *sorry*. I'm sorry for it all. It wasn't fair to you. *None* of this is. The way you were treated by your old pack. By the witches. By *me*. You deserve so much better. You deserve protection and safety. You deserve support and acceptance. You deserve a caring family and unconditional love. You deserve a husband of your choosing. You deserve a—"

He stopped. Stopped and simply stared at me. Stared and stared. Like he was looking for an answer. A *truth*. A revelation that would give him the courage to forge ahead.

My breath caught.

He knew. He knew about us. About our mate bond. That had to be it. Had to be why he looked so scared, like he was about to confess his deepest, darkest secret.

My heart stuttered when he inhaled. When he opened his mouth and said, "There's something else I need to tell you."

When he paused again, I nearly passed out from holding my breath.

Say it. Just say it, I silently pleaded, barely able to hold still. To bear the suspense a moment longer.

Despite the shocking news about our wolves, I still wanted Kolton the *man* to acknowledge what lay between us. To *face* it, even if he wasn't willing to accept it.

"Nora, I . . ." he began, removing a hand from the wall to touch my cheek.

At the sudden move, I flinched. *Flinched.* Only a little, but he still caught it.

His hand froze, inches from my face. He stared at me and I at him, our expressions reflecting the same emotions. Horror. Pain. Confusion. Sadness.

I hadn't meant to react that way, but I had. There was no undoing the damage.

He slowly lowered his hand and straightened, putting distance between us. I bit my tongue, refusing to say a word, no matter how much it hurt to keep silent.

When he took a step back, I knew the moment for truths was over.

Despite everything I'd just learned, my heart twisted miserably. We were still running. Still hiding. Still denying what lay between us. Only, it was worse now. He'd been right about me. There was no denying my reaction. Deep down . . .

A part of me was afraid of him.

You could have warned me that it was more than a little bad blood between you and Shadow. Oh, and learning second-hand that you're an angel really sucks, you know. Don't think I'm not mad at you too, because I am. You left me in the dark as much as Kolton did. Maybe even more.

Oblivious to my heated, albeit one-sided conversation with Storm, Vi finished unwrapping the bandage from my waist. When it fell away, she paused to critically eye my stomach.

"Hmm. The bleeding stopped. Still healing far too slowly though."

Unwilling to look at the damage Keisha had inflicted, I focused on the task before me: getting into the monstrous jet tub Vi had just filled. As soon as Kolton had left the room to give me space, his sister had invaded it. At first, I'd thought about sending her away, too exhausted for any more company. But when I'd pushed back my hair and felt how dirty it was, an idea had formed. One I couldn't get out of my head.

Clean. I wanted to be *clean.* More than needing food or even sleep, I needed to rid myself of this past week. Smells still lingered on my skin. Triggering ones. The acrid stench of magic. The metallic bite of old blood. And the cage. The scent of my cage was *everywhere.*

So I'd allowed Vi to help me, too weak to do it all by myself. Even removing my underwear had been a monumental effort.

"Whoa, slow down there," she said, reaching for me when I teetered and nearly tipped headfirst into the tub. The second she touched my bare skin, I went poker straight.

Touch is pain, touch is pain, my mind screamed at me, demanding I push her away.

Struggling to breathe, I stayed where I was. This was *Vi.* My friend. She wouldn't hurt me.

An image suddenly popped into my head. A terrifying one of her shifting into a nine-foot-tall demon werewolf with blood-red eyes. If Kolton could, then she probably could too.

"You okay?"

At the sound of her voice so close to my ear, I nearly jumped out of my skin.

"Yeah, fine," I hurriedly said, trying to calm my racing pulse as she helped me into the tub. But the second I sank beneath the water and she let go, my tension eased. I wanted to believe the soothing warm bath was the cause, but deep down, I knew better.

My fear had spread to her. To *all* of them.

Before I could stop myself, I blurted, "Do you carry a demon inside you too?"

At the startled look on her face, I internally kicked myself. Why couldn't my mouth have a filter?

"Vi, I'm—" I started, needing to apologize. Despite the trauma I'd just been through, she didn't deserve the third degree from me. I couldn't take out my hurt on her, especially after how kind she'd always been to me, treating me like a member of the family right from the start.

"You mean a monster?" she interrupted before I could finish apologizing.

I winced. "You heard?"

She shrugged, perching on the tub's edge with a long-handled loofah and some lavender body wash. "I didn't mean to, but I wanted to make sure you were okay. Normally, I wouldn't question Kolton's orders, but he's been a bit . . . unpredictable lately."

That was one word for it.

Sighing, I tipped my head back and submerged my hair in the water. After a moment, I popped back up and said, "It's my fault."

Vi stared at me like I'd grown two heads. "None of this is your fault, Nora."

"But I'm the one who brought my problems to your doorstep. The Blackstone Coven wouldn't have even crossed paths with you if it wasn't for me. And now, because of me, they've discovered Kolton's secret. Their leader might be dead, but the whole coven is pretty determined to protect what they consider their birthright. What if they go after Kolton next and try to take Shadow from him?"

Vi's purple eyes widened. "Take?"

"Remove the spirit through exorcism. That's what they were doing to me. To Storm. *Trying* to, at least."

Vi's chin began to quiver. "Oh, Nora. I'm so sorry."

A hard lump formed in my throat. Not wanting to cry, I looked away and reached for a razor on the ledge. "It's okay. I'm okay."

Thanks to Kolton.

The lump grew painful. Needing a distraction, I began to shave off a week's worth of stubble from my legs. My thighs shook from the effort of holding them up, but I stubbornly kept shaving.

Vi silently watched me for several moments, then said, "I still stand by what I said. You're not to blame for any of this. The witches are responsible for their actions, as is Kolton. What others do isn't a reflection of you. It's a reflection of them. But, to answer your previous question, yes. I carry a demon inside me too. We all do. Well, except for you," she finished with a wink.

I stopped shaving. "Even Melanie?"

"She hasn't shifted yet, but all the signs are there. Plus, she can already communicate with her spirit."

"But she's so . . . so . . ."

"Spoiled? Impish? Manipulative?"

"I was going to say bubbly and sweet."

Vi snorted. "She's been on her best behavior since you arrived.

But give it time. The little devil in her will rear its head eventually."

Despite myself, I laughed. When Vi joined me, I felt something inside me thaw. A cold wall I hadn't realized was there. It didn't disappear completely, but some of the ice had melted.

Vi seemed to notice the change. Holding up the loofah, she gave me a questioning look. After a moment, I accepted her invitation, turning in the tub so she could scrub my back. When the brush made contact with my skin, I barely flinched. Melting further, I closed my eyes and allowed her to wash me. First my body, then my hair. Her fingers were firm yet gentle, kneading my scalp the best they could around my matted curls. By the time she was done, I trembled with fatigue.

As I rinsed the last of the conditioner from my hair and fell limply against the tub, she finally spoke again. "Do you want to talk about it?"

Right away, I knew what she was referring to.

Focusing on the suds on the water's surface, I said, "No. Not yet." Maybe not ever. Except . . . I looked up at her again. "There was another werewolf imprisoned with me. I need to know if he escaped too."

She nodded. "I could probably find out about him. What's his name?"

"Arrow. I don't know his last name, but he's from Portland, Maine."

Vi shot to her feet, so fast that I violently startled. When water sloshed over the tub's edge, she lunged for a towel and began cleaning it up.

"Vi."

She didn't respond, too busy scrubbing at the floor like her life depended on it.

"Vi, what's going on?" I persisted, struggling to rise from the tub. When my arms gave out and I sloppily fell back in, Vi popped up to check on me. Seeing her concern, I waved it away and sank back against the side. "You and Kolton both reacted the same way when I mentioned Arrow's name. Why? Do you know him?"

She looked everywhere but at me, wringing the towel until water dribbled out. Finally, she said, "Yes, we know him. But it's been a long time since we've seen him."

I frowned, trying to catch her eye. "What aren't you telling me?"

"I'd rather not say."

"*Please*, Vi. I'm tired of being the last to know about everything. I just want to—"

"I was *engaged* to him," she burst out, stunning me into silence. "Betrothed, actually. But it didn't last very long. I . . ." She suddenly jumped to her feet again. "Let me help you back to bed. You look tired."

When she reached for me, I shook my head. "It's okay, Vi. You can leave if you want. I'm just going to rest here a moment longer."

She bobbed her head several times, then quickly retreated. "Okay. Shout if you need help getting out. I'll make some calls about Arrow. Promise."

With that, she fled the bathroom.

CHAPTER 8

NORA

I hadn't meant to pass out in the tub, but when I came to, the bathwater was cold.

I jerked upright, forgetting where I was for a second. The walls of the tub were like a cage, trapping me inside. The water was a new method of torture, sure to deliver pain. Breathing heavily, I gripped the edges and fought to reorient myself.

You're free. You're safe.

I repeated the words, shutting my eyes until the panic subsided. When my heart stopped pounding, I unplugged the drain and reached for a towel. The small action quickly reminded me of how weak I was. Opening my mouth, I prepared to call for Vi, then remembered why she'd left and closed it. I'd never seen her look so unsettled before. So *haunted.* Not wanting to upset her further, I gritted my teeth and made do on my own.

Getting out of the tub without tripping was the hardest part. When I safely made it out, I sat on the ledge to catch my breath, then pushed to a stand. My legs were practically jelly, but I managed to wrap the towel around myself without looking at my reflection. I didn't feel like seeing Keisha's handiwork or how thin I'd become. With my body safely hidden from view, I shuffled to the counter to peer at my face. Namely, my hair.

It was worse than I thought.

Normally a chore to untangle on a *good* day, the curls were so matted, they were almost forming dreads. Placing my hands on the counter, I inhaled a few steadying breaths, then got to work. Minutes in, I was a panting, trembling mess. As tears stung my eyes, I tossed the comb on the counter in frustration and glanced in the mirror again. When I saw how gaunt I looked, I clenched my teeth and rummaged in the drawer for a new tool. My fingers closed around the metal object and pulled it out.

Not giving myself time to reconsider, I grabbed a handful of hair and raised the scissors.

"Please, don't," a voice said.

Startled, I almost poked myself in the eye as I whirled toward the intruder. Seeing Kolton in the open doorway, I clutched the towel wrapped around me to make sure it didn't fall. Which was kind of stupid, since he'd seen me naked more than once. Seen *all* of me, up close and personal, during my heat.

I opened my mouth to scold him for entering without permission. Instead, all I said was, "Why not?"

"Because your hair is beautiful. And I would miss it."

I felt my face heat at his candidness. Flustered, I whirled toward the counter again. But the move was too sudden, too swift. My knees buckled. I dropped the scissors and barely caught myself in time, leaning heavily against the counter. As the scissors loudly clattered across the tiles, Kolton stepped forward.

"No," I said, halting him in his tracks. Trying to hide how badly I was trembling, I slowly pulled myself upright.

"Nora," he began, "let me—"

"*No*," I repeated, more forcefully this time.

I knew I was being muleheaded. He'd rescued me. *Saved* me. I'd most certainly be dead right now if it wasn't for him. I owed a life debt to him. To . . . to both of them. But maybe my reaction to him this time had nothing to do with what he was. More like everything to do with who he *wasn't*.

A man who could love me. Who would accept our soulmate bond. Who could be mine in every possible way.

I wasn't ready to be close to him again. To allow him anywhere near my bruised and fragile heart. A part of me might be afraid of him, but a bigger part still *wanted* him. All of him. Every single piece. And if he couldn't give me that . . . I didn't want anything, including his help.

Hardening my resolve, I pushed off the counter and headed for the door. I could do this. I could prove that I didn't need him either. That I could keep him at arm's length and still function. Still *survive*. I was stronger than I looked. One man wasn't going to be my undoing, soulmate or not.

I managed to brush past him. Managed to make it all the way to the door. But the second I stepped foot inside the bedroom, my body completely gave up on me.

No! I inwardly wailed, locking my knees so I wouldn't crumple to the floor. But it was no use. My legs shook harder and harder and harder until—

"Kolton—" I weakly got out before my legs collapsed beneath me. Before I could hit the floor, he was there, oh-so-carefully scooping me up. As his arms wrapped around me, so did his scent, a tantalizing woodsy musk with hints of smoke and bourbon.

Unable to stop myself, I looped my arms behind his neck and curled up against him. When he straightened, my nose was buried in the crook of his neck, greedily inhaling him. Deep, deep, deep into my lungs. Into the vast hole inside my chest. When the gaping hole began to fill, to *heal*, a small cry left me. Kolton shuddered at the sound and held me closer, pressing his mouth to my damp hair.

When he in turn inhaled my scent, my toes curled.

No, no, no, you can't have this! I yelled at myself, struggling to break free of the spell he'd so easily cast upon me. *Pain. Being close to him is PAIN.*

But I couldn't move. Couldn't tear myself away. I wanted him too much. Wanted his warmth, his strength, his care, and attention. Wanted his mouth on my hair and his arms cradling me close. Wanted the feeling I got from being near him. It hurt, but it hurt so good.

He held me for several minutes, each one lasting a lifetime. I didn't move and neither did he. We were frozen, unwilling to let go, to end the moment. But when I went limp against him, struggling to stay conscious, the spell broke.

Slowly crossing the room, he stopped at the king-sized bed and lowered me onto the mattress. "You need sleep," he said, his voice deliciously rough. With the curtains drawn, I had no idea what time it was, but he was right. I needed to catch up on days' worth, *weeks'* worth, of lost sleep.

But as he straightened, I replied, "I can't."

He slowly blinked down at me, making me aware of how tired he looked. How *exhausted*. His clothes were rumpled, his hair mussed. And his facial hair had grown far past its usual five-o'clock shadow. I wasn't the only one who needed to recharge. "Why not?"

I grabbed a chunk of matted hair and held it up. "One more day like this and it's going to be rock solid."

He blinked at me a moment longer, then said, "Turn around."

It was my turn to blink up at him. "Huh?"

"Turn around," he repeated, then sat beside me without explanation.

When the mattress dipped, threatening to throw me against him, I scooted away and turned like he'd wanted. The second I did, I felt him touch my hair. I stiffened, and he froze. But when I didn't flinch, he slowly slid his fingers into the thick mass. Tingles erupted over my scalp—pleasurable ones. Trying not to freak out, I blurted, "What are you doing?"

"Fixing your hair."

Despite my exhaustion, my eyes flew wide. "That could take *hours.*"

"Maybe not. I'm good with my hands."

At the thinly-veiled innuendo, my face flushed scarlet. I couldn't even refute that one because he *was* good with his hands. I knew that from personal experience.

When his hands started to move, I felt myself surrender. Setting aside my conflicting emotions, I let him help me. I was too tired to fight any longer. Making sure the towel was still snug around me, I held perfectly still and allowed him to work on my hair. His movements were gentle, yet he tackled the tangles with a practiced hand.

Unable to help myself, I asked, "How do you know how to untangle hair?"

"I have two younger sisters," he replied by way of explanation. "Although Melanie hasn't been too bad. She's currently in a princess, tea parties, and stuffed animals phase and doesn't go outside much. But when we were younger, Vi was always chasing after me, Griff, and Jagger, getting into mischief while exploring the outdoors. It was my job to keep her out of trouble, and that included extracting countless burrs from her hair before our parents could scold her."

My mouth twitched into a small smile. Vi used to be a rough and tumble tomboy? I could see it. My smile suddenly slipped. I didn't know why, but the way Kolton talked about his sisters made me want to cry. Maybe because it sounded so normal. So human. So loving.

Nothing like a *demon* should sound.

I bit my quivering lip and fell silent, focusing on what he was doing. It shouldn't have felt good. He was untangling my *hair*. But this was Kolton. Whatever he did to me felt good. After a moment, my eyes drifted shut and I allowed my muscles to loosen. Just a little.

As if responding to my relaxed state, he slowly shifted his position, placing one bent knee onto the bed. When it brushed against my backside, I stiffened. He froze again. Only when I relaxed once more did he resume his work. Carefully. He was being *careful* with me, diligently responding to my unspoken cues—keenly aware that there were still so many unsaid things between us. So many hurts and fears and uncertainties.

Even still, we sat together in silence. Silence that was growing less and less awkward and more and more . . . comfortable.

At one point, he left for a few seconds, only to return with a comb. When he slid onto the mattress again, I didn't flinch. Didn't even stiffen. Several minutes ticked by, and I struggled to stay awake. His hands were just so *soothing*. Tingles continued to tease my scalp, but they only served to further lull me into a catatonic state.

"Why did you come for me?" I suddenly broke the silence, startling us both.

His hands stilled, and I bit my lip again, wondering where the courage to ask that question had come from. Maybe I was simply too tired to care about the ramifications right now.

He didn't keep me waiting long. "You're my wife. As such, you're under my protection."

I mulled over his response, feeling my brow furrow. "But, by protecting me, your family's safety was put at risk. You can always find a new wife, you know. I'm insurance. Dispensable."

His reply was immediate. "I don't want a new wife, and you're *not* dispensable."

My heart went crazy, fluttering like a hummingbird's wing. Holy hell, were we really having this conversation? Did I even *want* to? It could end terribly, and I was already in a vulnerable state. But, apparently, I didn't care. Because the next words out of my mouth were, "Then what am I?"

He tensed. We both did.

Had I pushed him too far? Was he going to retreat again? *Run?*

I waited for what felt like an eternity, equally terrified that he wouldn't respond and that he *would*. I wanted to clear the air between us, but at what cost? Either way, I was going to pass out if something didn't happen soon. The suspense was *killing* me.

Finally. *Finally*, I heard him inhale, heard him open his mouth and say, "You're mine, Nora. Mine to keep safe. Mine to care for. As long as I live and breathe, that is my vow to you. I made a terrible mistake in letting you go, but I won't make that mistake again. This past week was pure hell, and I can't lose you like that again. You're irreplaceable to me. I wouldn't be able to . . ." He paused for a moment, then quietly finished, "I just can't. I can't lose you."

I stopped breathing. *Couldn't* breathe. It wasn't exactly a declaration of love or even an acknowledgement of our soulmate bond. But it was . . .

It was enough.

For now.

"Oh," I said, the word barely a whisper. Speechless, I let silence settle between us again.

Apparently satisfied to leave the conversation at that, Kolton resumed working on my hair. I didn't speak again, too busy replaying the words he'd confessed to me. So busy that I was startled when he abruptly set down the comb and said, "Done."

I blinked. "Already? But you barely started."

"We've been sitting here for an hour, sweetness," he replied, reaching a hand up to run his fingers through my hair. Through my *untangled* hair.

Shocked, I reached up to touch it. My fingers slid through without snagging. "How?"

"Patience," his voice rumbled, closer than before. I froze as he gathered my curls in one hand and rested them over my shoulder, leaving my other one bare. "Perseverance." Goosebumps pebbled my skin as his warm breath caressed the shell of my ear. "And a steady hand."

My breath came in short spurts at his closeness. When I didn't pull away, didn't *stop* him, he lowered his head. Lowered it to where my neck and shoulder met.

Then, he brushed a soft kiss there.

Despite my exhaustion, my body trembled awake. I sucked in a quiet gasp, holding perfectly still as his lips lingered on my skin. He kissed the spot again, adding more pressure this time. Delicious pressure that sent a shiver racing through me from head to toe. As if responding to my body's reaction, he gripped my shoulder and pressed another kiss to the spot. A harder one. An *open-mouthed* one.

My eyes flew wide.

At the feel of his teeth on my skin, I loudly gasped his name.

He immediately jerked back and released me.

"I'm sorry," he said, breathing heavily. "That wasn't . . . that wasn't my intention."

When I turned to look at him, he shot off the bed. But not quickly enough. Not before I saw the panic on his face. The *fear*.

I swallowed, struck mute by the sight.

Yanking a hand through his hair, he backed up a few steps. Then

71

backed up a few more, as if we were still too close. "Get some sleep, Nora. I'll be back to check on you later. Call if you need anything."

With that, he fled the room—which was becoming a rather bothersome pattern today. Except, I knew all too well why Kolton had left this time.

He'd been about to claim me.

As he would a mate.

CHAPTER 9

NORA

In the dream, Keisha was cutting me. Cutting and cutting and cutting.

She knew. She *knew* what Storm was. And she wouldn't stop cutting me open until Storm was removed from my body. Until she could possess Storm for *herself*.

"No. Please. Stop!" I cried, struggling to break free.

"She's not yours. She's not yours!" Keisha shrieked back.

She cut deeper and deeper and *deeper*.

Nora, wake up, a familiar voice invaded my head.

"You didn't tell me. You didn't tell me what you were!" I wailed at Storm. "Why?"

Because I'm not an angel, she said. *Not anymore*.

"She's not yours," Keisha shrieked again. "Give her to me."

"No! You can't have her."

"Then I'll take her by force!"

She thrust both hands into my stomach, and I screamed. Screamed and screamed as she twisted and yanked, pulling out my organs. Piece by piece, she disemboweled me until I was nothing more than a bloodied pile of broken flesh.

Nora, WAKE UP!

The sound of a door crashing open yanked me from the nightmare. I shot upright in bed, only to yelp when I opened my eyes to a sea of white.

"*Nora!*" I heard Kolton roar, but I couldn't see him. Not with this glowing aura around my body. No, not around. It was coming *from* my body. From *inside* me.

Pounding footsteps reached my ears, followed by several more startled voices. On the verge of hyperventilating, I continued to gape at the light show. Kolton got to me first. Or, at least, he tried to. Squinting past the brightness, I saw him reach for my arm, as if to snatch me away from the light. But the second his hand came into contact with the light, he jerked it back with a hiss.

"What's happening?" I cried, legitimately freaking out now. Vi, Griff, and Jagger skidded to a halt beside the bed, their shocked expressions illuminated by the glow. When Melanie's little face appeared from behind Jagger, he blocked her from view.

"You need to calm yourself, Nora," Kolton said, standing just outside the light's reach. "Storm's true form is trying to push through. Tell her to settle."

It was then that I felt the pain. The *heat* all but roasting me alive.

Storm. Storm, please stop, I cried to her. *You're hurting me!*

The light flared brighter for a moment, as if I'd startled her, then slowly began to dim. The more it did, the less pain I felt until the heat vanished completely.

The second it did, Kolton dragged me off the bed and into his arms. Still terrified, I wrapped my legs around his waist and frantically clung to him.

"It's okay," Kolton said in my ear, cupping the back of my head. "You're safe."

I buried my face in his neck, seeking solace in his scent.

Griff huffed a weak laugh. "Guess that confirms Nora's angel status."

"Nora's an *angel?*" Melanie piped up. I turned my head to see her gawking at me. Not with fear, but with awe.

"Her familiar is," Vi corrected, allowing Melanie to stand next to Jagger, now that the danger had passed. "Remember what we talked about? We all have—"

"Spirits inside us!" Melanie sang, her brunette pigtails bouncing. "Will mine light up like that too?"

Several throats cleared. I hid a grimace, feeling sorry for the person who would have to pop the six-year-old's excited bubble. Which wouldn't be me.

Before anyone else could speak, I became acutely aware of Griff's state of dress, or lack thereof. As I beheld his manhood, my face turned about fifty shades of red.

Noticing my stare, Vi rolled her eyes and groaned, "*Really*, Griffin? Not everyone wants to see your ding-dong."

He looked between us, his face a picture of innocence. "What? You all know I like to chill in the nude. Even Mellie." A devilish grin suddenly curled his lips. "And now, so does Nora."

Vi smacked his arm and shoved him toward the door. But, as he laughed, I could have sworn she hid a smile. The familiar sight of them bickering eased some of the tension in my shoulders.

"Right. It's time for bed, Mellie," Jagger said, sharing a pointed look with Kolton. As the girl moaned her displeasure, Jagger scooped her up and threw her over his shoulder. Her moans turned to giggles.

"Okay, but you have to read to me first. *Five* stories this time."

It was Jagger's turn to groan. "Two stories."

"*Six*, or I won't go to sleep!"

Jagger cast one last look at Kolton then left with Melanie, closing the door behind him.

Wow. Vi was right. Melanie *did* have a manipulative little devil inside her.

Trying not to smile and failing, I glanced up at Kolton to catch him already watching me. Heat threatened to spill across my cheeks again. "What?"

"Nothing," he said, continuing to stare at me.

I was suddenly reminded of what happened between us hours before. Of the kiss that had almost become a bite. A *claiming* bite.

When he flicked a brief glance at *the* spot, heat burst across my face. Crap. We were thinking the same thing. The urge to squirm hit me hard, but I held perfectly still, watching him as he watched me. Waiting. Waiting for what, I didn't know.

"Hungry?" he said, so abruptly that I got tongue-tied.

"Umm, I . . . maybe later. I should . . . I should sleep more. I'm still really . . . Are *you* hungry?"

I wasn't the only one who'd lost weight. His unshaven cheeks were hollower than I remembered. Not as obviously as mine, but his cheekbones were sharper than before.

"Starving," he replied, interrupting my inspection. My breath hitched when yellow flashed in his dark amber eyes, a sign that *food* might not be the only thing he was hungry for.

"You should eat something then," I said, inwardly wincing at how breathless I sounded.

"Later. Sleep first." He bent and set me on the bed.

Having put on his black t-shirt again after my bath, I tugged the hem down over my underwear. I stared up at him, clearly able to see with the bedside lamp still on. After a week of being trapped in darkness, I couldn't bear to turn it off. My night vision was still weak, only a step above a human's. Until it returned, I wasn't going to worry about wasting a little electricity.

Expecting Kolton to leave, I gaped when he simply rounded the bed, unbuttoning his white dress shirt as he went.

"What are you doing?" I said, drawing my legs up to my chest.

"Getting into my bed."

My tired eyes rounded to saucers. "*Your* bed?"

"When I visit this penthouse, I sleep in this room, yes."

His shirt started to come off, and I panicked, scooting toward the edge of the bed. "I didn't know. I'll go find a different room then."

"They're all taken."

Ah, hell.

"I'll take the couch then," I hurriedly said, swinging my legs over the side. "You have one of those in this place, right?"

"Nora."

"Also, how many penthouses do you have anyway?"

"Nora."

I jumped to my feet, pausing as the room swayed. After a few steadying breaths, I straightened and took a step toward the door.

"Nora, stay."

I froze rock solid.

With my back to him, I couldn't see his expression, which was probably a good thing. It meant he couldn't see *mine*. But he could no doubt hear my heart, which had decided to skip several beats at his soft command.

Carefully swallowing, I murmured, "Is that a good idea?"

No. It was a bad idea. A *really* bad idea.

"We're husband and wife, Nora," he evenly responded. "We both need sleep, and this is a big bed. I don't see any harm in sharing it."

Harm?

Ok, then. Guess he was ignoring what happened between us earlier and the fact that I'd almost gone supernova.

Fine. I could ignore it too.

Turning, I slipped into the bed again and yanked the sheets up to my chin. Kolton was slower to get in, toeing off his shoes before sliding onto the mattress. I barely felt the dip of his weight, but simply knowing that he was *there*, close enough to touch, made my body buzz like a live wire.

Bad idea, bad idea.

Determined not to chicken out, I rolled away from him and squeezed my eyes shut, willing myself to sleep. And, surprisingly, I did. Or started to. Until the darkness crept back in.

I jerked my eyes open with a strangled gasp. Then gasped again as a large hand gripped my shoulder.

"It's me," Kolton's deep voice rumbled behind me. When I continued to gulp down air, he said, "What's wrong?"

Struggling to speak, I managed to say, "I-I'm afraid to fall asleep. To dream again."

Wow. Look at me, being all vulnerable and stuff.

He slowly released my shoulder, then said, "I can help."

At that, too many naughty ideas popped into my head. His idea of help usually involved my clit and his fingers. Or tongue.

I quickly squeezed my thighs together. Still, I couldn't help but ask, "How?"

He was silent for a long moment. *Too* long. My thoughts went haywire until he said, "With magic. I can make you fall into a dreamless sleep."

My jaw dropped, and I rolled to face him. "I *knew* it. When you kidnapped me, I had no idea how you'd knocked me out. You used magic on me!"

He flipped onto his back and dropped an arm over his eyes. "Not my finest moment, but yes, I used a sleep spell on you. Last night as well."

Of course. It all made sense now.

Choosing not to be mad that he'd kept yet another thing from me, I asked, "Is that why the witches can't track us here? Did you put a spell on the penthouse?"

"The building is warded against magic, yes, but I didn't perform the spell. My dad hired a witch almost two decades ago to do it, shortly after I shifted for the first time. I was different, and different in our world isn't a good thing. He wanted to ensure I had a safe place to go in case I was ever hunted for my rare abilities. Didn't think I'd ever actually need it though."

I propped myself on an elbow, absently staring at his inked arm while he spoke. The most prominent tattoo suddenly caught my eye, reminding me of another occurrence I couldn't quite explain. Until now.

Before I could think better of it, I reached out and touched the tattoo. Kolton's arm flexed beneath my touch, but he didn't pull away. Growing bolder, I traced a finger up the tattoo's length, all the way to his elbow.

"When you placed this snake on my arm, did you use magic?" I hadn't thought about it before. Hadn't thought to question how he'd performed a binding ritual with a moving *tattoo*.

With his arm still draped across his face, he replied, "Yes. Shadow taught me how. Griff and Jagger can do it as well. The spell requires dark magic, which was why Griff questioned my decision to perform it on you. Not many can bear the mark. Or see it, for that matter."

What the hell? I sat straight up, so fast that Kolton finally removed his arm to look at me.

"It could have *hurt* me, and you did it anyway?"

He took in my anger, then reached up to touch my face. When I didn't flinch away, he gently swept a loose curl off my forehead before saying, "I knew it wouldn't. I knew you were different."

"But how?" I pressed, trying to ignore the tender gesture. "How did you know I possessed a spirit familiar before I'd even shifted?"

He hesitated, then slowly said, "Because my magic was drawn to yours."

I sucked in a quiet breath. He'd *almost* acknowledged our soulmate bond. So close that I nearly blurted out the rest and put us both out of our misery. But . . . it wasn't close enough.

Needing a distraction, I said, "Show me."

His brows lifted in question.

I wiggled my fingers in the air. "Show me your hocus pocus, voodoo magic."

A slow smile curved his lips, one that threatened to snatch all the air from my lungs. "Hocus pocus?"

"Hey, I still don't quite believe that it's possible. A *werewolf* performing magic? How crazy is—"

My mouth formed a large O as he lifted a hand and magic sprang to his fingertips. Deep purple magic. So dark that it almost looked black.

"Holy hell," I whispered, staring in awe for several moments. Then reached out to touch it.

"Don't. It will hurt you."

When I didn't pull my hand back quickly enough, he snuffed out the purple flame. Without thinking, I grabbed his hand and checked it for injury. The deep olive skin was smooth. Not a single burn mark. As I started to pull away, he captured one of my hands and threaded our fingers together. Delicious warmth shivered up my arm.

I stared at our joined hands, at the gold wedding bands shining in the soft light. And said, "I'm pretty sure Storm used magic to help me escape my cage." Kolton's fingers stiffened. I didn't look at him. Couldn't. Not when all I could see was Keisha's ruined eyes. "Do you think . . . do you think I'm a monster?"

His fingers tightened around mine. "No, Nora. I don't think you're a monster."

I released a trembling breath. "I don't think you're a monster either. But I made you feel like one earlier, and I'm sorry."

"Nora . . ."

For whatever reason, his soft use of my name was the final straw. A sob ripped from me. Startled, I frantically tried to stuff the emotions back in. But now that a crack had formed, they came roaring out like a flood and there was nothing I could do to hold them back.

So, I didn't. I let them out. *All* of them.

"This past week was so awful," I choked out as tears clogged my throat. "I thought I was going to die so many times. You were right about the witches. They tried to tear me apart. The things they did. The *horrible* things. They would torture me for *hours*. Day after day. Kept me in a cage like an *animal*. And they . . . they tried to cut Storm out of me. Literally. I can still feel the pain. The *agony* of being ripped open, again and again."

Each word tore from me in great, heaving sobs. At some point, Kolton pulled me into his arms, holding me so close that I could barely breathe. I cried and cried until a river of my tears ran over his chest. When the tears dried up, I continued to gasp. To sob. To let the pain, the *agony*, of the past week leave my body.

Finally, when I lay quivering against him, utterly spent, he spoke in a rough whisper, "I'm so sorry, sweetness. I'm so sorry for what you endured. I should have been there. It should have been me instead. I would do anything. *Anything*. To take your pain away."

"Kiss me."

The words slipped out all on their own. My brain didn't fully realize what I was saying. What I was asking him to do. All I knew was that I wanted, *needed*, to be close to him. So I said the words again, uttering them like a prayer.

"Please kiss me."

Without a moment's hesitation, he rolled me onto my back and pressed his lips to mine. At the sweet rush of warmth, I released a whimper that he immediately swallowed by deepening the kiss. The way our lips seamlessly fit together filled me with absolute bliss. It was like coming home after a long, exhausting day. When I reached up and slid my fingers through the scruff on his jaw and cheeks, he trembled beneath my touch.

The kiss wasn't fast or desperate. It was deep and thorough, overflowing with comfort and compassion. I felt it in every part of my being, all the way to the tips of my toes.

I drank it up in thirsty gulps, consuming every last drop he gave me. And he gave me *everything*. Everything I needed. Everything to soothe my pain and mend my hurts.

A tear escaped, and he cupped my face to wipe it away. When I sighed my gratitude, he pulled away to kiss my cheek. Then the other. My eyes fluttered open, just as he lifted one of my arms and gently kissed my slowly-healing wounds. Lifted my other arm and repeated the tender gesture.

And then he pulled down the sheets, just enough to expose my upper half. I stopped breathing as he carefully grasped the hem of my shirt and bared my stomach.

When he looked at it. At the mutilated flesh. He drew in a ragged breath. Again and again, as if breathing was the only thing keeping him from coming apart at the seams. Then, he lowered his head and kissed each mark. Each gnarled wound and jagged scar. My body shook as I silently cried. As I watched Kolton tenderly soothe each hurt, chasing the pain away.

When he was finished, he wrapped both arms around me and

carefully rested his head on my stomach. Guarding me from more pain. From more nightmares.

Within minutes, I was fast asleep.

CHAPTER 10

NORA

I slept so hard, so deeply, that not even an earthquake could wake me.

So, when something finally stirred me from my dreamless slumber, I was surprised to discover that a slight tickle on my stomach was the culprit.

Peeling my eyes open, I groggily blinked down at my stomach and froze. Kolton's head was still there. With every breath I took, his unshaven stubble tickled my sensitive skin. Had he rested there all night? *Slept* there?

Warmth rushed through my body when I realized that his arms were still around me. One of his hands had fallen between my legs—inches away from brushing against my underwear. But his eyes were closed, his body relaxed. He looked . . . peaceful. Drinking up the sight, I didn't move a muscle. I simply watched him. Watched the steady rise and fall of his back, shamelessly exploring the muscles on his powerful shoulders and the strong length of his spine.

His face, free of stress and worry, was what caught my attention the most though. I took the time to trace each line—the generous curve of his lips, the straight slope of his nose, the dark sweep of his thick eyelashes. His nearly black hair spilled across his brow, and my fingers twitched, unable to keep still a moment longer.

Giving in, I reached up and gently swept the hair off his forehead, then glanced down and found his eyes on me. Caught red-handed, a fierce blush heated my cheeks. Before I could die of embarrassment, he lifted himself off me, only to lean down and whisper in my ear, "Morning, wife."

The sound of his voice all gruff with sleep curled my toes.

I opened my mouth to respond, only to suck in a gasp as the hand between my legs shifted upward. Sliding his fingers over my underwear, he found my center and traced lazy circles through the material. My spine arched off the bed at the unexpected rush. Taking that as a good sign, he slipped his hand inside my panties and touched my clit.

"Kolton," I gasped out, trembling from the swift jolt of pleasure.

Holy hell, he'd never touched me like this before. Not without cause. In the past, there had always been a reason. But I couldn't think of one right now, other than the fact that he simply wanted to.

I should stop this. I should *really* stop this. We still had so much to discuss, namely the unspoken elephant in the room—ergo, our mate bond. But as his fingers began to expertly move, I was lost. Lost to sensation and bliss. Lost to *him*.

My core grew wet, and he inhaled, drawing in the scent of my arousal.

A growl vibrated his chest. He dipped his fingers into the wetness and found my clit again. At the rush of ecstasy it gave me, a moan burst from my lips and I gripped the sheets for dear life.

"Your scent is so intoxicating," he rumbled, brushing his nose along my jaw. "Like a field of blooming wildflowers in spring."

Holy hell, he couldn't say things like that.

Every inch of me trembled, overcome by his touch. *Drunk* on his sensual words. I no longer cared where we stood or why this was dangerous. I simply wanted it. Wanted this mind-blowing thrill to never end. He stroked me harder, increasing the pace until I panted for release.

My pleasure built and built, filling every corner of my body. I rode the high for as long as I could, refusing to come, to end this moment of pure sunshine. I held on until my muscles shook under the strain. Until I thought I would explode from the pressure.

Kolton allowed my resistance, prolonging my pleasure until darkness edged my vision. When I struggled to breathe, he finally put an end to it. "Come, sweet flower. Let me see the bliss on your face as you come for me."

Ah, hell.

His command, both sweet and wicked, buckled my resistance. The second I lost control, my climax shot through me. So swift and powerful that my back bowed off the bed and I groaned. *Loudly.* Barely suppressing a scream. My body all but floated off the bed, basking in a sea of warm bliss. When I could breathe again, I heaved a shaky laugh, not hiding how good he'd made me feel.

He all but purred with satisfaction.

"You're absolutely breathtaking when you orgasm," he murmured, pressing a soft kiss just below my ear. "I want to see it again."

My eyes flew wide as he slid his fingers into my wetness again. Holy hell, was he serious? *Two* orgasms? Oh, but he was more than serious. I choked out a surprised gasp as he plunged his finger inside me.

"Kolton, I can't," I whimpered, even as my eyes rolled back when he curled his finger.

"Yes, you can, sweetness," he purred in my ear. "For me. Do it for me."

When he slipped a second finger inside me, I moaned, announcing my surrender. He rewarded me by curling both fingers and hitting a spot that made me see stars. I savagely bit into my lip, stifling a cry of pleasure. He quietly chuckled, then started pumping his fingers in and out, so fast that my walls viciously clenched around him. Undeterred, he pushed through, further increasing the pace.

My hips bucked, instinctively responding to the rhythm. Soon, I was frantically thrusting against his fingers, chasing the ever-increasing high.

"God, Nora," Kolton groaned. "So beautifully responsive to me."

I whimpered breathlessly in reply.

"If only my cock were inside you right now. If only you were mercilessly squeezing it like you are my fingers."

Too much. His dirty talk was *too much.*

It tipped me over the edge into oblivion, and I came all over his fingers. A scream slipped past my control, and I slapped a hand over my mouth to muffle it. He kept his fingers inside me as my walls spasmed, releasing the glorious tension in my body. By the time it was over, I was slick with sweat and buzzing with contentment. *Exhausted* contentment. And also . . .

An angry growl tore through my stomach.

Yeah. That.

I opened my eyes to see a wide grin on Kolton's face. I stopped breathing, struck mute by the beautiful sight.

"Good girl. That's what I wanted to hear," he said, sliding his fingers free. "Be right back."

Speechless, I didn't move a muscle as he pressed a swift kiss to the tip of my nose and jumped off the bed.

What the—? What was happening?

Like a man on a mission, he strode from the room, leaving me to gape after him. When he didn't come back after several minutes, I scooted off the bed to use the bathroom. Although still weak, my legs easily carried me the distance and back. With a little food, I should be almost back to my normal—

The most *wonderful* smell froze me in my tracks. Just like that, I was no longer in control. On autopilot, my feet veered away from the bed and carried me to the bedroom door. Kolton had left it cracked open just enough to allow the mouthwatering scents to leak inside.

My stomach growled again, the vibrations shaking my entire body.

Needing to find the source of those delicious smells, I opened the door and stepped outside. The second I did, sunlight blasted my sensitive eyes. Cringing, I shielded my face and blinked away the spots. When I lowered my hand again, I found five pairs of eyes staring back at me.

At the looks, the *knowing* looks on some of their faces, heat flushed up my neck. I threw Vi a panicked look. "How much?"

How much had they heard of what just happened between me and Kolton?

"All of it," Griff supplied, earning a scowl from Vi.

I flicked a horrified glance at Melanie. She was sitting on a kitchen stool, picking at a bowl of cereal. The others were gathered around the kitchen island as well. Only Kolton was on the other side, manning the stove. Still bare-chested, he held a glass of orange juice in one hand and a steaming plate piled high with food in the other. Every molecule in my body wanted to make a beeline toward him. Toward the *food*. But I didn't move a muscle, still too mortified.

"Don't worry," Griff spoke again, noticing my stare. "Mellie heard you scream, but I assured her that Kolton was taking good care of you."

My jaw dropped.

"Griffin Hayes O'Neal," Vi hissed. "You're such a dickhead."

"Here we go again with the derogatory comments," Griff said with a tsk. He leapt off his stool when Vi tried to punch him.

"What's a dickhead?" Melanie asked, shoving a handful of cereal into her mouth.

"Stop, you two," Jagger grumbled, shaking his head in disapproval. "Act like mature adults for once. Innocent ears are listening."

Griff loudly guffawed. "*Innocent?* Are we talking about Melanie or Nora?"

Ignoring them all, Kolton rounded the island and approached me. At the sight, I forgot about everything else. The only thing that existed was me, Kolton . . . and the food. I watched as he came closer and closer. As the food got bigger and bigger. My mouth started to water. I clamped my lips shut to contain the drool.

So close. He was *so close.* To giving me the food.

When he finally stopped before me, I almost whimpered— just like I had in the bedroom earlier. My body trembled, ready to combust.

Kolton leaned forward. But instead of presenting me with the food, he whispered in my ear, "You didn't have to come out."

"Breakfast in bed? Aww. That's sure to earn you a happy ending, Kol." Griff's obnoxious comment was followed by a meaty thud and, "Ow!"

"You don't have to stay out here if it's too much," Kolton continued, pulling back to search my face. Worry filled his expression, but it wasn't needed. I'd spent the past week in near deafening silence. Despite my embarrassment, the chaos a few yards away was more than welcome. Besides, I was sick of being confined to a room. The penthouse's bright open floor plan was a great sigh of relief. Beyond the kitchen, a large living room filled with couches beckoned. And the wall was purely glass windows, showcasing a clear blue sky.

It felt like we were hovering in the air, safe from the dangers of the world far below.

"Thank you," I replied to Kolton, giving him a grateful smile as I accepted the food and orange juice. "But I'm okay."

And I was okay. Not fully healed. Not by a long shot. But I was on the mend, thanks to him. I was *safe*. And eating breakfast with his family would only mend my wounds faster.

So, straightening my shoulders, I brushed past him and made for the kitchen. They all stopped and stared, but that didn't deter me. Reaching the island, I plonked my food on the counter and claimed a stool. No one said a word. Not a single word as I gingerly picked up my fork and stabbed some scrambled eggs. But when I raised it to my lips, the fork shook so hard that the eggs plopped back onto the plate.

I tried again, but experienced the same outcome. Inhaling a trembling breath, I prepared to try a third time.

"Nora, it's only us," Griff quietly said, reaching out to gently pry the fork from my fingers. "We know you're hungry."

I quickly glanced at the others, noting the sympathy lining their faces. Even Melanie stopped eating and pushed her bowl of cereal toward me. Tears filled my eyes. Furiously blinking them away, I picked up a sausage and bit into it.

One taste and it was all over.

I devoured the entire sausage in one bite, barely pausing to chew. Three more swiftly followed. Next came the eggs, shoveled into my mouth at rapid speeds. When those were finished, I gobbled up several strips of bacon and two pieces of jellied toast. Pausing only briefly to swallow and inhale, I guzzled down my glass of orange juice. With that gone, I licked my fingers clean. Every last one. Then released a long, contented sigh.

Only then did I raise my head and peek at my companions. Every single one of them was grinning at me.

I burst out laughing, refusing to be embarrassed by what I'd just done. They quickly joined me, looking relieved more than anything. Even Jagger huffed a laugh. Only Kolton was silent. I hadn't even seen his face yet. I suddenly felt him behind me, his warm chest brushing against my spine. He lightly gripped my hip and said in my ear, "Better?"

I stopped laughing to nod and murmur, "Is there more?"

"Yes, but too much too soon could make you sick."

I chewed on my lip for a moment, then hopped off the stool and strode around the island. Opening a few cupboards, I found a plate and moved to the stove. Only when the plate was filled to the brim did I turn and set it on the island counter.

"Okay. Your turn," I said, looking Kolton dead in the eye.

Everyone froze.

Yeah, yeah, yeah. I'd just ordered the big powerful alpha to eat some food. Get over it.

And that's what my face said as I held eye contact, refusing to back down.

Eat, I silently commanded him, narrowing my gaze.

He slowly raised an eyebrow. *And if I don't?*

Then I'll force-feed you.

Yellow flashed in his eyes. *I'd like to see you try.*

I will. Don't make me come over there.

I continued to hold my ground. Continued to silently impose my will on him. He stared at me a moment longer, then slowly, ever so slowly, came around the island toward me. The closer he came, the more I had to tip my head back until I was craning my neck in an attempt to maintain eye contact. Stopping right in front of me, he held my gaze for several long moments. Making me wait. Making me sweat. Then bent down and whispered a mere inch from my mouth, "Yes, ma'am."

A grin stole across my face, growing wider as he turned and dug into the food with gusto—the same way I had. The others gaped in astonishment, as if they'd never seen their alpha eat before. Or maybe they'd just never seen him eat like *this*, in deference to someone else's order.

The grin stayed plastered on my face, remaining there as I watched him eat every last bite.

CHAPTER 11

NORA

I could see the entire world.

At least, that's what it seemed like from the luxurious rooftop terrace overlooking Central Park. Only a rich person could afford a view like this. A *billionaire*, more precisely. I was over one hundred floors up, the closest I'd ever been to the clouds. To flying.

Everything below looked so small. So insignificant. The trees, the buildings, the people. It was easy to pretend that I'd left all my problems down there. That nothing bad could touch me, so long as I remained up here. Where it was safe.

But it was an illusion, a fantasy. I couldn't stay up here forever. Neither could Kolton and his family. He had responsibilities, and I had to face my problems. Maybe not today, but soon. Perhaps sooner than I was ready for.

I'd spent the morning and afternoon relaxing. *Healing*. Enjoying the company of people I trusted. With each hour that passed, my wounds grew less and less noticeable. The visible ones, at least. Finally, after a hearty dinner, I'd gone in search of a moment's solitude. It was Jagger of all people who'd suggested the rooftop. Who'd assured me that it too was warded against magic.

And now, an hour later, I stood at the glass railing, watching the sun's slow descent toward the skyline. Completely alone. Except, I knew that I wasn't. Not really. Which was the real reason why I'd wanted to find a quiet place. Not to recharge, but to face the first challenge on my ever-growing list.

I won't yell at you. Promise, I thought to Storm, tucking a curl behind my ear as the cool evening air rustled my hair. *I just want to understand you better. Is it true? Are you an angel?* I pondered a moment before adding, *Or are you something else now?*

Because I couldn't get the dream out of my head. The nightmare of Keisha cutting me open. Storm had been there, and her words still haunted me.

If she was no longer an angel, then what was she?

Kolton seemed certain she was an angel, though. Keisha had apparently discovered what she was, but hadn't been able to say before her eyes caught on fire. I shivered, recalling her tortured screams and charred eye sockets. She was evil, but I wouldn't wish pain like that on anyone. I couldn't help but feel responsible, just a little.

The only other person who could offer me some insight was Arrow, but Vi had confessed that she couldn't find him. The abandoned church was empty now. The witches had cleared it out, including Tao's body. She'd contacted Arrow's pack in Maine, but they hadn't heard from him in months.

He'd vanished, and I couldn't help but feel responsible for that too. Despite his rocky past with the Rivers family, I should have asked Kolton to get him out safely too. Then again, I hadn't *known* it was Kolton. I shivered once more, remembering how terrified I'd been of his demon form. In a way, I was still afraid, but not for my life. After the day I'd just spent with him, I knew he would do anything to keep me safe. Even turn into something that *nightmares* were made of.

Can you turn into something like that too? I asked Storm, trying my best to be patient. But it was getting harder. I had so many questions, and she was the only one who could truly answer them. Besides, what was the point of having a familiar if she never talked to me? I wanted to *know* her. To understand why she was here. She had a story, and I wished to hear it.

When several minutes dragged by and all I heard was the occasional bird call and siren wail from far below, I sighed my defeat.

"Okay, I'll stop pestering you now. I know when my presence isn't wanted," I said, this time out loud. "But I have one more thing to say, so I hope you can hear me. I . . . I want to thank you for helping me escape that awful place. Thank you for . . . protecting me. I probably wouldn't have survived without you."

Unconsciously, my hand drifted to my stomach. To the healing wounds and old scars. Storm hadn't protected me when I'd been cut open by my very own alpha, but I could forgive her now. I could heal from those scars, knowing that she cared now. If only a little.

We still had so far to go, but it was a start.

By the time I headed back inside, my heart felt a little lighter. Our conversations were still woefully lopsided, but at least I'd had the courage to say my piece. When I descended the last of the stairs and opened the door leading to the living room, everyone inside stopped what they were doing. Well, except for Melanie, who was sitting on the rug and corralling several stuffed animals into tutus.

"What's up?" I asked, disconcerted by the guilty looks on both Vi and Griff's faces. Only Jagger was expressionless, which was normal for him. "Where's Kolton?"

"He received a call," Vi quickly said, standing from one of the couches. "He didn't get much work done this past week, and there are a few things that need his attention. Nothing big. It shouldn't take him long to handle them."

Suspicion narrowed my eyes. "Griff, where's Kolton?"

Still sitting on a couch, he froze like a deer in headlights.

My heart fluttered with worry. I faced Jagger, who was near the windows with his arms crossed. "Where is he, Jagger?"

"Jag, don't—"

"Out."

At Jagger's response, Griff groaned and covered his face.

Vi threw him an annoyed look. "Thanks a lot, Jag."

He shrugged unapologetically. "This place isn't that big. She was going to find out anyway."

"Yeah, but—"

"What do you mean *out?*" I interjected, searching all three of their faces with rising panic. "Like *out* out? As in, *outside?*"

Griff groaned again and flopped against the cushions.

"It's okay, Nora," Vi calmly said, sensing my panic. "He just needs to attend a meeting in person, and then he'll be back. A lot of rumors have spread since we've been gone, and he couldn't wait any longer to address them."

I balled my hands into fists, struggling to keep it together. "What kind of rumors?" I asked, my voice lower than usual.

When Vi hesitated, Jagger answered, "That the alpha of Midnight Pack is dead." My jaw dropped, but he wasn't finished yet. "There are also rumors of your death, plus the entire Rivers' family. The pack has been in an uproar. If they don't see Kolton alive and well soon, challengers will come out of the woodwork. The possibility of claiming the alpha position without having to fight Kolton will be too great of an opportunity to pass up. It'll be chaos."

My head spun from the news, but I quickly shook off the shock and said, "Then he needs me. I should be there with him so everyone knows that we're *both* alive. Call him. Call and tell him. I'm sure he'll agree."

Vi's expression fell. "Oh, Nora."

I stopped breathing. "What? What is it?"

It was Griff who answered next, sitting up on the couch with a resigned sigh. "He explicitly ordered us to keep you here. No one is to leave. We can't go against his command."

My hands began to shake. "So that's it then? I'm back to being a prisoner?"

Vi stared at me in horror. "No, that's not it at all. He just wants to keep you safe."

"But what about *him?*" I lashed back, louder than I intended. Melanie paused in her play to look up at me. I inhaled a deep breath, trying to calm myself. Quieter this time, I said, "The witches have seen who he really is. They'll come for him. I know they will."

"Then it'll be the last thing they do," Jagger responded, flicking a pointed glance at Melanie. Not wanting to scare the girl, I nodded and dropped the subject. For now. There was nothing they could do anyway. I knew their loyalty belonged to Kolton, as it should.

But that didn't mean I had to roll over and play the submissive wife. Not by a long shot. Kolton married the wrong person if he thought I'd be okay with this.

As the evening darkened to night, my ire grew. I worked myself into a frenzy, unable to relax. The others watched me with concern, trying their best to distract me. But Kolton was all I could think about. He was out there alone when he should be here with *me.*

Deep down, I knew I was doing it again. Hiding from the world. Hiding *him.* Which was irrational, considering his position. He didn't have that luxury. He'd already spent way too much time focused on me when there were far more important things for him to do.

I knew this, but that didn't stop me from pacing. From wringing my hands. From making everyone else so nervous that I finally retired to my bedroom for the night. Correction: *Kolton's* bedroom. I got ready for bed, quickly changing into his black t-shirt. Then I thought better of it and donned a gray jersey nightgown instead.

Angrily tossing his t-shirt on the floor, I glared at it for a solid minute, then bit out a curse and scooped it back up. Crawling onto the bed, I settled against the headboard and prepared to wait, strangling his t-shirt in my tight grip.

When he finally returned, it was almost midnight. As he quietly conversed with Jagger in the hall and mentioned my name, I sat up straight. Otherwise, I didn't move. Minutes later, he soundlessly entered the bedroom and shut the door. At the sight of me sitting up in bed, still wide awake, he paused.

I took the moment to give him a thorough once over. Top to bottom, checking to make sure every inch of him was wholly intact. He was wearing a dark suit, one that fit his broad frame perfectly. Underneath was a crisp white shirt buttoned up to his neck, along with a charcoal gray tie. Every square inch of him was polished, from his shiny shoes all the way up to his immaculate hairdo. Even his scruff had been shaved, leaving only a hint of dark stubble. Not too much, not too little. The perfect amount.

He looked good. *Really* good. Hotter-than-hell kind of good.

At the sight, my relief was swift. Breath-stealing. If I'd been standing, my knees would have buckled. But, now that I knew he was safe, my anger roared to the surface like a geyser.

Shoving his t-shirt beneath my pillow, I jumped to my feet on wobbly legs. They were still weak with relief, which only incensed me further. "Where were you?" I demanded, my voice deathly quiet.

He blinked, as if surprised by my angry tone. Then said, "I thought the others informed you where I was."

"They did. *They* did. Not you."

He stared at me a moment more, then heaved a tired sigh. "It's been a stressful evening, Nora. I need a shower."

With that, he stepped away from the door and toward the bathroom, removing his tie and coat as he went.

Shocked, I mutely watched as he kicked off his shoes and closed the bathroom door behind him. After a few moments, I heard the shower switch on.

My anger exploded.

Marching toward the bathroom, I ripped the door open without knocking. Kolton froze, about to remove his shirt. I ignored his state of undress and lit into him.

"You did *not* just dismiss me. I'm nowhere near done talking to you yet, *Alpha* Rivers."

Without a word, Kolton shrugged off his shirt. Then reached for his belt. "You'll have to talk to me while I'm naked then." The buckle came undone, and he reached for the button on his pants. "And we both know how uncomfortable that makes you."

A swallow got stuck in my throat. "It doesn't make me uncomfortable."

In one swift move, he yanked off his pants and underwear. "Oh?" He straightened, standing completely nude before me. "Then why are your cheeks red?"

Without waiting for an answer, he stepped into the shower.

I gaped at his foggy silhouette through the shower glass, my face flaming even hotter, then stormed over and yanked the shower door open. "Because I'm *furious*," I yelled at him. "You left without telling me first. I'm your *wife*. You should have—"

I yelped when he reached out and dragged me into the shower with him.

"Kolton," I sputtered as warm spray hit my face, soaking me within seconds. I struggled to get away only for him to press me against the tiled wall and crush his mouth over mine. When I sucked in a startled breath, he took full advantage and thrust his tongue into my mouth. I froze, struck dumb by the powerful way he took me. By his urgency. His *neediness*.

He gripped my head and kissed me almost roughly. *Desperately.* I placed my hands on his chest to push him away, only to dig my fingernails into his skin. He groaned and thrust his tongue in deeper, making a thousand butterflies erupt in my stomach.

Every thought in my head emptied as he kissed me like a man possessed. I clung to him, barely able to stand as my legs turned to jelly. He thrust his pelvis against mine to keep me from falling, aligning his hard erection with my core. A fierce ache pulsed between my thighs, and I instinctively responded by opening my legs to better accommodate him.

He growled this time, gripping my hair tightly while he ground himself against me. My core burst into flames, and I whimpered, dragging my nails down his chest and stomach. When I reached between us—reached for *him*—he let go of my head to capture my wrist.

"Touch me like that and this is all over, Nora. Your sweet innocence will be mine," he said, his voice a guttural growl. Grabbing my other wrist, he placed both of my hands on his shoulders, then hoisted me up. I gasped as he lifted me, so high that I could almost touch the ceiling. When he planted my legs on his shoulders, I braced myself against the tiles. Before I could fully catch my balance, he hiked up my nightgown and buried his face between my thighs.

I gasped again when I felt a sharp yank and heard my underwear rip. A second later, his hot tongue found my center. At the unexpected rush of euphoria, my reality splintered into a million pieces. I threw my head back against the tiles and cried out his name, unable to breathe as his tongue began to pleasure me mercilessly. I reached down and gripped his hair, tethering myself to a splinter of reality. His growl shook my core, wringing another cry from me.

I couldn't see. Couldn't hear. I was lost to everything but Kolton's tongue as it thoroughly wrecked me. A thousand embarrassing sounds left my lips, but I couldn't hear them. I trembled and writhed and bucked, but all I could see was shooting stars. When my breathing grew frantic, his tongue swirled harder. Faster. Targeting my sensitive clit until I came apart and screamed out my release.

Ecstasy pounded through me, stealing my ability to balance. I slumped forward, and he caught my waist, slowly lowering me to the ground. Still trembling from the pleasurable aftershocks, I drunkenly leaned against him, allowing him to bear my weight. He held me close under the warm spray, patiently waiting while I pieced myself back together.

When I could finally see and hear again, I huffed, "Holy hell, what was *that?*"

Quiet laughter rumbled his chest. "I missed you."

My heart did a weird little flutter. "You were only gone for a few hours."

"Every hour was agony," he said before pressing his mouth to my hair.

Any lingering anger melted away. It had been agony for me too. Every minute apart had felt like a lifetime.

Before I could say anything, he released a sigh and said, "You can come with me next time."

Startled, I peeled my eyes open. "What?"

"Jagger told me what you said earlier. It's a good idea. But I couldn't stomach the thought of exposing you so soon after your trauma. I should have told you before I left though. I'm sorry."

A small smile curved my lips. I slid my arms around his waist to give him a grateful hug. "Thank you." After a moment, I opened my mouth again, then closed it. Opened it again. "I couldn't stomach it either."

"Stomach what, sweetness?" he whispered, rubbing his thumb over my shoulder.

"The thought of something happening to you."

CHAPTER 12

KOLTON

It was happening.

My nightmare was becoming reality.

With every encounter, I lost another piece of myself to the female I'd chosen to marry. I hadn't thought it was possible. Hadn't thought one woman could wreck me so completely. But Nora Finch was unlike any female I'd ever met.

She was currently craning her neck back, taking in every inch of the looming skyscraper we were about to enter. Her childlike wonder was extraordinary. She'd just been through hell. No outward sign of the torture she'd endured remained, but I knew the scars ran deep. And yet, there was still so much life in her eyes. Eyes so vastly blue that I often drowned in their beauty.

I'd chosen well. She was strong, stronger than I could have ever hoped for. And that strength made the alpha in me howl with pride.

She had no idea. No idea how deeply I desired her.

After our shower encounter last night, I'd barely been able to wait until she'd left the bathroom before grabbing myself. All it took was a mental image of her legs wrapped around my head. A few swift pumps later, and I was spilling my release. Even then, I'd switched the water to cold, still burning with the need to take her.

She was yards away. In my *bed*. Soft and warm and alluring. It was getting harder and harder to keep my distance. To pretend I had even an *ounce* of control where she was concerned.

I'd almost claimed her the other day. Almost lowered my canines and bit into her flesh. Almost *marked* her as mine. I hadn't been prepared. The instinct had ripped through me, making me blind to reason. I couldn't even blame Shadow this time. Yes, he wanted me to take what was mine in every way possible, but ever since rescuing her, he'd been on his best behavior.

It was *me* who kept tearing down the barriers between us. Who kept leaping over every last line I'd sworn never to cross.

If I didn't rein in my desire soon, there would be no stopping me from claiming her virginity. By some miracle, I hadn't taken it while she was in heat. The very real consequence of getting her pregnant had been in the forefront of my mind. Even then, I almost hadn't cared. I ached to be inside her, in a way I'd never felt before. My previous encounters with women had been brief, the unions purely carnal. No emotions. No feelings other than lust. I'd ended each one with my heart untouched.

But with Nora, I wanted to be consumed. Not just in body, but in heart, in *soul*. And that was the problem. If I was right and she really was my soulmate, then taking her virginity would seal our bond. One act—one single, passionate act—would bind us together forever.

Mind. Heart. Body. Soul.

There would be no undoing it. No stopping the inevitable descent into madness that had claimed my mother. Nora would become my greatest obsession. My greatest *weakness*.

I knew that being married to her was a dangerous game, one I was sorely losing at. I'd meant for the union to *strengthen* my position, not cause me endless nights of lost sleep. Nights spent thinking about her. If I lost her again, I would never fully heal. The scars would be lifelong. Soul deep. Her hold on me was already that strong.

And yet, I would live on somehow. For the sake of my family, I would bear that burden to my grave. They depended on me, and I couldn't let my ever-growing attachment to Nora consume me.

Vi's words chose that moment to come back and haunt me. She was right. If I died, my family would die. Such was the way of things in the werewolf world. It was why I'd decided to seek out a wife. Nora could keep my mother and sisters safe if something happened to me. I could rest easy, knowing they were being looked after. My death wouldn't destroy them as my father's had.

But now that every sign pointed to Nora being my soulmate, she was at risk too. Not simply from the challenges she would face as alpha should I die, but from the loss of our soulmate bond.

The only chance she stood was if we didn't complete it. If we did, my death would be soul-destroying for her.

I hadn't wanted love or a mate for this very reason. Emotions, *bonds*, were dangerous for an alpha. But I hadn't considered—not even once—that the woman I chose to marry could be my soulmate. And a bond like that was the most powerful, most deadly of them all.

My only hope was to keep that part of me from her. To not cross that final line, one that would ultimately lead to death for us *both*. As much as I burned to erase all boundaries between us, my family's safety was too important. *She* was too important.

My sense of duty had to be stronger than my desire, or I would doom us all.

You're a fool, Shadow's voice invaded my thoughts.

I clenched my teeth, but otherwise showed no sign that he'd spoken to me. *Better a fool than dead. Or worse, dead on the inside, unable to protect my family.*

You might as well be dead for denying yourself that exquisite goddess. But you can't deny yourself forever. With every touch, I can feel your control weakening. It's only a matter of time before you break.

I won't break, I shot back. *Unlike you, I'm not always consumed by lust.*

You wound me. I can think of other things besides sex.

Really? Name one thing.

Shadow paused. *Okay, fine. Sex is the only thing on my mind right now. But don't get all pious on me. I know you wanted to finish what you started last night. She was right there in your bed, fresh as an unplucked daisy. What's more, I can sense her returned desire for you. She wants you to pluck her. To open her sweet, innocent petals and—*

Enough, Shadow, I growled, struggling to control my outward reaction to his colorful words. I knew all too well his thoughts on the matter. "Deny" wasn't in his vocabulary. Once he realized how much I wanted her, he'd done everything in his power to encourage that final step. He didn't care about my reasons for holding back. Didn't even care that Nora was probably my soulmate.

A forever bond didn't scare him—even one that could shackle him to an angel.

In fact, he relished the thought. His excitement had surprised me. I'd always assumed that demons hated angels. That they saw them as self-righteous zealots.

But I'd felt his intrigue when Storm had first made an appearance. He was curious about her, and he wanted to know more.

"You really own this building?" Nora asked, effectively snapping me from my thoughts.

At the awe in her voice, a smile twitched my mouth. "Yes. It's where I conduct business for one of my family's holding companies. Most of the floors are leased to my subsidiary companies though."

She blinked up at me. "How many companies do you have?"

My smile broadened. "A few. I can give you the rundown if you'd like. Or Vi can print out a list. She usually handles the paperwork."

We had all agreed earlier this morning that only Nora and I would leave the penthouse today. There had been some arguing, but the less attention we drew to ourselves, the better. I didn't know what would be worse: running into those witches again or facing even more questions from suspicious pack members. No, it was better to pretend we weren't on edge. To act like our stay here in the city was normal, and not for safety reasons.

As we reached the main entrance, a doorman stepped forward to allow us inside. Although I didn't personally know every member of the building's staff, they all recognized who I was. One look at my face, and they snapped to attention.

Nora smoothed a hand down her white pencil skirt, a skirt that I hadn't been able to take my eyes off of since Vi had helped her dress earlier. Paired with a flowy black top, she looked sophisticated and sexy as hell. When she stepped inside the building, her high-heeled shoes clicking smartly against the marble, I let my gaze caress her backside.

I know you want to bite it, Shadow purred. *I bet she's wearing a thong beneath that tight skirt. Oh, the fun you could have with that.*

Reining in a grimace, I nodded at the doorman and hoped he didn't notice the growing bulge in my pants.

When Shadow barked a laugh, I snarled, *Behave!*

He snorted but thankfully lapsed into silence.

When the door closed behind us, Nora slowed to take in the massive lobby. "How are rich people able to have any downtime? Their jobs seem so . . . busy."

Choking back laughter at her casual "rich people" comment, I replied, "Most don't balance their work and personal lives very well. It took me a few years to create a decent schedule. I personally visit my holdings and many of my subsidiaries once or twice a month but otherwise work remotely from the family estate. On occasion, I'll take an extended business trip, but try to keep those to a minimum. That allows me to be available for my other responsibilities."

Like my family and pack. And now my wife, who was anything but a responsibility.

She paused to glance back at me. "I don't know how you do it."

I stopped beside her, forcing my hands not to reach out and touch her. "Do what?"

"Live two separate lives. Be two very different people. It sounds exhausting."

I shrugged. "It can be, but it's the only thing I know."

She tilted her head like she wanted to say something. Instead, she turned and resumed her trek toward the elevators.

I silently followed, knowing that today's meeting was certain to be exhausting. The pack rumors were worse than I thought, along with the unrest that came with them. Managing a billion-dollar business was a breeze compared to being the alpha of Midnight Pack. The hierarchy was forever being tested, and not a day went by where I wasn't forced to put a pack member in their place.

With the arrival of Nora, my job had become insurmountably more challenging. At the same time, it had become more bearable. And a lot less lonely.

When we were safely ensconced in an elevator, I finally revealed to her the one meeting topic that would give us the most trouble. Then braced myself for her reaction. "I should warn you. Since Rodney's death, rumors have spread of your . . . of our unconsummated union. There will be questions."

She noticeably stiffened but didn't look up at me. "Will it . . . cause problems?"

"Not if we play our cards right."

I waited. Waited for my words to sink in. For their meaning to become clear.

When her cheeks slowly reddened, I knew she understood.

"Oh. Okay," she quickly said, looking far too flustered for someone who'd had my face buried between her thighs last night.

Her embarrassment made me hard, in the worst of ways. I angled myself away from her, not wanting to fluster her further.

"Do you remember the story?" I asked, trying to distract her.

She nodded, still not looking at me.

"Do you want to rehearse it again?"

"Nope. All good."

I paused, searching her profile for a moment, then quietly said, "You don't have to do this, Nora. We can leave right now. I can figure this out on my own."

She finally looked up at me, determination flashing in her eyes. "I'm your wife. Your responsibilities are my responsibilities. If you need my help, I'm going to give it."

God, she was so beautiful right now. What I wouldn't give to press her up against the elevator wall and discover exactly what that skirt of hers was hiding.

Yesss, Shadow purred. *That's what I'm talking about. Yank down that little zipper and smack that delicious booty. I bet she'd like that.*

When Nora's eyes widened, I knew that she'd caught a glimpse of the bastard within. I quickly shoved him back down and schooled my expression.

Thankfully, the elevator chose that moment to slow its ascent. Nora faced forward, unable to hide her nerves as her heart started to race. With a *ding,* the elevator doors opened. With the barest touch to her lower spine, I guided her forward, offering what little comfort I could. I'd prepared her to the best of my ability. The rest was up to her.

I'd ordered all meetings on the entire floor be canceled for the day, so our walk to the meeting room was met with silence. Not even the receptionist had shown up today. I wanted utmost privacy for the conversation about to happen. I'd even chosen our soundproofed room for the occasion.

Rumors were a virus in the werewolf world, and I didn't want these ones to spread any further. Which was why this meeting was so important—and potentially dangerous. The outcome would determine if the rumors spread like wildfire or were safely contained. Problem was, I couldn't command the rumors away. I had to fight them like everyone else.

Nora's presence was both a blessing and a burden. She could help quell those rumors, but could also start up new ones just by being here. How she handled herself in front of the others was essential to today's outcome. If she was the least bit timid or showed any sign of weakness, they would eat her alive.

Refusing to show how nervous *I* was, I guided her the remaining distance to the meeting room with unwavering steps. Once there, I pulled open the glass door and ushered her inside. At the sight that awaited us, I felt her tense beneath my touch. Still, she didn't miss a beat, striding inside to face all twelve of my wealthiest, most influential pack members.

When I entered, they rose as one from their seats to face me. I'd met with them all yesterday, but this time immediately felt different. Nora was here, and their body language changed in an instant. Besides Jagger and Griff, the wolves here today were the most dominant in Midnight Pack. They all held positions of power in my territory, deferring only to me.

The only problem was that each and every one of them was a normal werewolf. With the pull of a full moon only days away, I could sense their heightened restlessness. Their animalistic natures were barely concealed beneath their human skins. I could see it in their eyes. In their predatorial movements. The good thing was that the entire lot of them currently had mates. They wouldn't be interested in claiming Nora for themselves.

But they were still hungry. Hungry for a hunt. For a *kill*. And, one by one, their sights were slowly setting on . . .

Nora.

CHAPTER 13

NORA

They all stared at me like I was a filet mignon.

I'd known the meeting would be tense, but I hadn't expected them to look at me like I was their next meal.

Swallowing the panic surging up my throat, I took another step inside the room. Besides me, there was only one other female in attendance. Hoping to find a friendly face, I gave her a small smile. In reply, her eyes narrowed shrewdly.

Okay, then. She didn't want to be besties.

Trying to slow my fluttering pulse, I focused on my breathing. *Inhale. Exhale. Don't show them how freaked out you are. Inhale. Exhale.*

Before the silence could become too uncomfortable, Kolton shut the door behind him and said, "Thank you all for meeting us here today. I know you met my wife Nora at our wedding last month, but she might have forgotten a few of your names."

A light chuckle swept through the room, allowing me to breathe easier.

Until one of the males closest to me lifted his nose into the air. When his nostrils flared, all the blood drained from my face.

"So it's true," he said, taking a step toward me. "She's still unmated."

Kolton's reaction was immediate.

In one swift move, he jerked me back against him, his hand possessively gripping my hip. "Stand down, Carter," he ordered the man, a growl vibrating his chest.

Carter obeyed, returning to his spot with a slight dip of his head, but I saw the suspicion burning in his gaze. In *all* of their gazes. They wanted answers. Needed to know why their alpha hadn't claimed the body of his own wife. Not doing so made the marriage look weak. *Fake.*

Well, they were going to get answers, straight from the virgin's mouth.

Before Kolton could defend me, I raised my chin and said to the entire room, "Yes, the rumors are true. I'm still a virgin. Kolton has been gracious enough to wait for the consummation until our honeymoon, per my family's request. I come from a very . . . traditional household. And maybe a little superstitious," I finished with a small laugh.

Wow. Where had *that* come from?

Several of the pack members looked surprised by my explanation. Kolton's fingers twitched on my hip, as if he too was surprised. We definitely hadn't practiced *this* speech beforehand.

"Why haven't you been on a honeymoon?" the female asked, still eyeing me shrewdly.

I inhaled a steadying breath, then began my practiced spiel. "My dad unexpectedly became ill. It's why my parents weren't at the wedding. I didn't want to go anywhere too far away in case he . . . in case he didn't make it. A week ago, he took a turn for the worst. It's why we weren't at the estate. Kolton and his sisters went with me for moral support, and . . ." I blinked a few times, as if the memory was painful. "Anyway, my dad is stable now. But our lack of communication this past week was my fault. I've been keeping Kolton a bit . . . preoccupied."

Going all in, I tipped my head back and gave him an adoring

look. Then graced him with a secret little smile, one that told the room *exactly* what I'd been doing to keep him preoccupied. Kolton's chest expanded against my back as he beheld my face. Something like pride simmered in his gaze, and another emotion I couldn't quite define. It was intense. So powerful that my breath caught.

When he reached up and touched my chin, the room ceased to exist for a moment. I placed my hand on his forearm and leaned into the touch. As his thumb swept up and caught my bottom lip, we shared a look. One filled with heat. With promise.

Later, was all it said. Excitement shivered up my spine.

Suddenly remembering we weren't alone, my cheeks warmed. A slight smirk tipped Kolton's mouth. There and gone again in a blink.

Dropping his hand, he lifted his gaze to the room once more. "Is my wife's explanation sufficient to dispel the rumors?" he asked them, staring at each one in turn.

Carter cleared his throat and said, "Yes, Alpha Rivers. It's sufficient. We'll need a date for the honeymoon though. The sooner, the better. And we'll have to back her story with evidence. Permission to contact her family?"

"I'll get the date to you as soon as I can. And permission granted. But her parents only. The rest of her old pack is off-limits."

Fingers crossed that Kolton's call to my parents this morning had earned their cooperation. He'd laid on the guilt trip—and *threats*—thick enough. I hadn't wanted to speak to them though. Not after Kolton had confirmed that they'd been partly to blame for my kidnapping. Sure, they might not have known what Alpha Hendrix's intentions were, but they had still lied to me. Had still chosen their alpha over their own daughter once again.

"Understood," Carter said, his suspicion no longer evident. In fact, most of them looked rather appeased now, to my utmost relief.

"Good," Kolton said, gesturing for them all to sit. "Then let's continue with business, shall we?"

When he started to pull out an empty chair for me, an idea formed. Good or bad, I had no clue. It was one thing to pull off a stunt like this at a wedding, but a *business* meeting? And instead of Kolton initiating it this time, *I* was.

Not giving myself time to second-guess the decision, I grabbed his hand and went straight for the head of the table. The chair there was clearly meant for him. Bigger than the rest, which was to my benefit. Otherwise, this reckless plan of mine might not work.

Thankfully, Kolton didn't resist, allowing me to guide him toward the chair. Only when I pulled it out for him did his face register understanding. His eyes flashed yellow, only for a split second, then he unbuttoned his suit jacket and claimed the seat in one fluid move.

I was halfway around the chair when he took matters into his own hands, swiveling to drag me onto his lap. As a gasp left me, several chuckles filtered around the room. Pressing me tightly against him, Kolton leaned forward and breathed in my ear, "Clever girl." The words were barely a whisper, disguised as an affectionate gesture as he nipped at my earlobe.

At his praise, heat rose to my cheeks. When he shifted me on his lap, revealing how *hard* he was, my face burst into flames.

I dared to peek at the others and was surprised to find only amusement. Not a single one of them looked suspicious or offended by my rather bold move. And when Kolton reached down to possessively grip my thigh, no one batted an eye.

Okay, then. Apparently, PDA was a commonplace thing in this pack and highly encouraged. Now that their alpha's virgin bride was sitting on his lap, everyone seemed much more at ease.

As the meeting began in earnest, it became more and more clear that his pack enjoyed seeing our casual touches. In their eyes, the affection confirmed the legitimacy of our marriage. So when Kolton touched me, I touched him back, first his hand, then his arm. But it didn't seem to be enough—at least for him.

"I know you've all been wondering when Nora's official initiation into the pack will be," he said, tracing circles on my thigh. "Now that her father is on the mend, I'm proposing next month during the full moon."

"Why not this month?" an older male toward the back of the room asked.

"Because the full moon is only a few days away, and Nora's unmated status could cause undue tensions to rise."

"I can do it this month," I spoke up, surprised that I'd agreed to do something without fully knowing what it entailed. Plus, dealing with the unmated thing would suck. Still, I suddenly had the urge to please his pack. *Willingly*. A feeling I'd never had before and never thought I *would* have.

Kolton froze, his finger halfway through a circle. "You sure?" he quietly asked.

When I nodded, he shifted me on his lap again, angling me in a way that allowed one of his thighs to rest beside mine. A clear invitation. I reached down and placed my hand on his thigh. The second I did, a quiet purr rumbled his chest. He shifted again, encouraging my hand higher.

Just like that, my pulse shot through the roof.

I knew the table hid some of our movements, but it was still pretty obvious what we were doing. My face was no doubt beet red, and I definitely knew they could hear my rapid heartbeats. Not daring to look at our audience this time, I focused on the table as I inched my hand upward. In response, Kolton's other hand slid around my waist and slowly carved a path toward my aching center.

Holy hell, this wasn't happening right now. Oh, but it was. My body was warming in all the wrong places, and Kolton seemed all too happy about that. *Very* happy. I could feel his thick arousal beneath me, way too close to the spot where my body desperately wanted it to be.

"That's settled then. We'll spread the news of Nora's initiation to the rest of the pack," Carter said, continuing the meeting as though we weren't performing an erotic show feet away from him.

Details of the initiation were discussed next, along with our impending honeymoon, but I could barely listen. Kolton's fingers were inches away from reaching their target, and so were mine. I felt his erection swell beneath me, so large that I grew wet in response. Silently cursing, I squeezed my thighs together. Which Kolton didn't like at all.

"My wife and I need the room for a moment," he abruptly said, to the shock of no one but me. I threw a startled look at the others but only received knowing glances in return. Without a word, all twelve of them rose and quietly left the room.

The second the door shut, Kolton reached for a remote on the table and pushed a button. An opaque glaze slipped over the windows, blocking us from view.

"Kolton, what—?"

I gasped as he lifted me off him in one swift move. When he placed me on my feet, I teetered forward and grabbed the table.

"I've been wanting to do this all morning," he said, his voice almost guttural. My eyes flew wide as I felt a yank, followed by the whine of a zipper. His hands were suddenly on my backside. My *bare* backside. Pushing my skirt down to my ankles. I gasped again as they gripped both cheeks and squeezed. "Gorgeous," Kolton breathed, clearly pleased with what he'd discovered. "You were right about the thong."

"Who was?" I asked, biting back a moan when he kneaded the flesh.

He paused, then huffed a laugh. "Shadow."

"Your familiar?" I said, having a hard time following, especially when he let go of one cheek to slip his fingers beneath my G-string.

"Yes," he replied, fisting the string until it stretched taut. The action served to stimulate my clit, and a moan slipped free. When he let go of the string and it snapped back into place, I flinched in surprise. Not at the pain, but at the way my body responded, growing even wetter.

"You and Shadow have discussed my underwear?" I squirmed as the ache between my thighs intensified.

He laughed again. "We talk about many things."

At that, an emotion pricked my chest. It should have been fear. He was conversing with a *demon*, one that had terrified me only a few short days ago. But it wasn't fear I was feeling right now.

It was envy. I was jealous of the open relationship he shared with his familiar.

"Are you talking to him right now?"

"Yes."

"What is he saying?"

Kolton paused again, then gripped my inner thigh and slid his hand upward. When it brushed against my throbbing core, he purred, "That he wants me to bend you over this table and have my way with you."

Holy hell.

Once again, I should have been afraid but wasn't. I was *excited*. Knowing that Kolton's familiar wanted him to be naughty made *me* want to be naughty. Before I could think better of it, I blurted, "Maybe you should listen to him."

Oh, wow. I'd totally just said that out loud.

Time froze as my words hung in the air. As a wave of my arousal followed the clear invitation.

Kolton inhaled a ragged breath, tightening his grip on my thigh. Then, with a feral growl, he lunged to his feet and flipped me over. The second my back hit the table, he pinned me down against it and began to rock. At the feel of his hard shaft thrusting between my legs, I threw back my head and groaned. He slammed his hands down on the table and answered my groan with one of his own.

Needing something to hold on to as he increased the pace, I reached up and gripped his jacket. A huge part of me wanted to rip our clothes off, eliminating all barriers between us, but I was already too far gone. Too high on the friction our bodies were making. On the euphoria whipping through me.

In the back of my mind, I remembered the other pack members. They were probably right outside the door, all too aware of what was happening. We weren't exactly being quiet.

But I didn't care. Didn't care about anything except *this*.

Soon, our harsh panting filled the air. Kolton gripped one of my thighs, angling my body to better accommodate his. More pleasure rushed through me, and I cried out. At the sound, his thrusts became frantic. I coiled both legs around him, desperate for more. When he dug his fingers into my flesh, my release barrelled through me.

Arching my spine clean off the table, I screamed, so loudly that the entire building probably heard. Kolton jerked against me once more, then released a shuddering groan as he came. I reached for him, and he crushed me to his chest, expelling my name in a breathless rush.

For several moments, we simply held each other. I stroked his back, and he shuddered again, burying his face in my neck.

When my high slowly faded to a contented hum, I whispered, "I'm pretty sure they heard that."

He smiled against my neck. "The room is soundproof." Before I could feel relief though, he added, "But they'll definitely smell it."

Ah, *hell.*

I knew Kolton was pleased with me. He was proud of how I'd handled myself in the meeting with his pack.

I couldn't help but soak up his approval like a sponge desperate for water. I'd never received this kind of attention before. Never been anything more than the pack's bothersome disappointment.

My face was probably glowing like the sun all the way back to the penthouse. It was a wonder people didn't shield their eyes as I passed by.

In his company, I could almost pretend that the horrors of the past week had never happened. That the Blackstone Coven no longer existed. That the only thing I had to worry about now was being accepted into his pack and preparing for our honeymoon.

Crap. Honeymoon. What had I been *thinking?*

We couldn't go on a honeymoon. Not if the purpose of it was to hand Kolton my V-card. Yes, he'd been *extremely* attentive to me lately. So attentive that I'd helplessly fallen back under his spell. But we still hadn't discussed one little detail.

Our possible soulmate bond.

Not to mention his aversion to love, the reason I'd distanced myself from him in the first place.

Yeah, we really needed to have a talk before things got any more complicated. We couldn't let communication take a back seat like we had before. Doing so would only lead to more heartache.

I knew what Brielle would say. She'd say—

I sucked in a gasp, just as the elevator to the penthouse opened. "Brielle!"

"Who?" Griff immediately questioned, standing just outside the elevator like he'd been waiting for our return. Then, "*Whoa*, you two smell . . ." One look at Kolton, and he lamely finished, "Lovely."

Trying not to blush at his comment, I replied, "Brielle Lacroix. My roommate from college. She was expecting me a week ago and hasn't heard from me since. I bet she's frantic with worry. Does anyone have a phone I can use? I need to—"

"You're not thinking of leaving us again, are you?"

Catching Griff's expression, the words died on my lips. He looked like a kicked puppy.

"Griff," I said, stepping from the elevator. Uncertain how to reply, I wordlessly reached for him. When he stepped forward to take my hand, Kolton pulled me back against him.

As his arms banded around me, Griff threw him a devilish smirk. "Afraid I'm going to make a pass at your wife?"

"If you did, there's a one thousand foot drop just outside calling your name," Kolton rumbled behind me.

A swallow got stuck in my throat.

Griff stared at him for a long moment, then burst out laughing. Just like that, Kolton's hold on me loosened. I breathed out a sigh of relief, not sure if I should join in the laughter or not. Griff might not be worried, but I was pretty sure Kolton was serious about his threat.

Suddenly nervous all over again about my upcoming initiation, my palms began to sweat. Had I made the wrong decision? Would Kolton threaten *every* male who got too close to me? Would he hurt them?

"What's wrong, Nora?" Kolton quietly said, sensing my unease.

I bit my lip, then decided to go for honesty. "I don't want to be the cause of contention in your pack."

"Aww, that's cute," Griff crooned. "Little Miss Innocence doesn't want to be in the spotlight. I don't think you understand how this works, gorgeous. As the alpha's wife, you're going to get a lot of attention. Most of it from thirsty males. Fights *will* happen. Might as well accept the inevitable."

Ah, hell. Not what I wanted to hear.

"Griff, stop scaring Nora," Vi said from behind him. Nudging him aside with a hip check, she held out her phone to me. "And if she wants to leave, that's up to her."

Kolton went rigid. "Vi . . ."

"Don't *Vi* me, Kolton. If she wants to go see her friend, then we should let her."

Kolton bristled even more. "It's too dangerous. She could get attacked again."

Vi managed to toss her sleek ponytail without disturbing her perfectly straight bangs. "An attack in *your* territory? Sounds like an alpha problem to me. Figure it out."

Oh, snap. Time to make myself scarce.

Letting my intentions be known, I squirmed in Kolton's arms. He tightened his hold for a moment, refusing to let me go, then abruptly dropped his arms with a sigh. Stepping away, I threw Vi a grateful look and accepted her phone. No one stopped me from making my escape to the rooftop. Once there, I quickly dialed Brielle's number.

She answered on the first ring.

"This better not be a spam call. I'll talk your ear off until you're begging me to hang up. Don't say I didn't warn you."

A grin split my face. "Hey, Brielle."

"Nora? *Nora Bora?*"

I held the phone away from my ear as she shrieked my name a few more times, then dove headfirst into demanding where I was.

"I've been trying to reach you all week. I even contacted your parents—and you know I don't do that—but even *they* didn't know where you were. Are you okay? Is it—" She suddenly gasped. "It is your wolf? Did you . . . did you finally *shift?*"

I winced, realizing how out of touch we'd been since graduating college and going our separate ways. She'd moved into an apartment and started her first "real" job. I, on the other hand, had been forced back home to work on the family farm. They'd only allowed me to get a degree so I wouldn't run away. So I wouldn't be tempted to strike out on my own and become an even bigger pack problem.

Brielle knew all of this. I'd told her everything, including the forbidden supernatural stuff. Even though she was human, she'd been the first person in my life who'd actually listened. Who'd *wanted* to listen. Breaking the silent rule for her had been one of the best decisions I'd ever made.

But since leaving home two months ago, I hadn't seen her, let alone told her about all the changes in my life. She was going to flip big time.

Bracing myself for the conversation ahead, I answered, "Yes, I finally shifted into my wolf."

Another shriek, this time of excitement. I couldn't help but smile at the sound.

"Oh, Nora, I'm so happy for you. I know how badly you've wanted this."

My smile slipped a little. I *had* wanted it. More than anything in the world, I'd wanted to be a normal werewolf. To prove to my pack that I wasn't a disappointment. But . . . that wasn't exactly what had happened.

Before I could tell her the details, she asked, "Did you take off into the woods or something? Wait, don't you need the full moon to shift? Where are you calling from anyway?"

I chewed on my lip, debating how much information to share. After I hadn't shown up last week, she deserved answers, but I still didn't want to drag her into my problems. Once she knew what I'd been through, she'd want to see me, and being around me could be dangerous—especially for her. There was no way she could survive a witch attack, or a werewolf one for that matter.

The practically-human girl she'd known in college no longer existed. My life had been simple then. Uncomplicated. Now, it was a crazy ball of chaos.

Sighing, I said, "No, I'm not in the woods right now. I'm . . . I'm not sure I can tell you where I am. A lot has happened lately, and . . . it's not safe for you to get involved."

I winced again as silence greeted me. It wouldn't last. She was going to have a conniption in three, two . . .

"*Safe?* Well, now you've *got* to tell me. If you're in danger, I'll come get you right away. Tell me where you're staying, and I'll drop everything to get you. I mean it, Nora. Don't start that crap your parents taught you. I don't care *what* trouble you're in. You're not a disappointment or a waste of time. You're my best friend, and I love you."

My bottom lip quivered. "I love you too," I whispered, blinking back tears. "I've missed you so much, Brie."

"Nora Bora," she whispered back, followed by a loud sniffle. "Please let me see you. Whatever problems you're facing, I can help."

If she only knew.

"Invite her to the family estate," a voice said from behind me. I nearly jumped out of my skin, so focused on the phone call that I hadn't heard his approach.

"Who is that, Nora?" Brielle said, clearly paying more attention than I was.

Quickly putting her on hold, I whirled to face Kolton. He stood in the rooftop's open doorway, casually leaning against the frame with his arms crossed. He'd removed his jacket and tie, and the top button of his white shirt was undone. The sleeves were rolled up to his elbows, revealing his dark tattoos, a look I was beginning to appreciate way too much.

I forced my gaze to his and said, "I can't do that. She's human."

He studied me, intently enough that I struggled to hold eye contact. Finally, he said, "Does she know what you are?"

"Yes," I admitted, suddenly nervous of his reaction. I'd chastised him for hiring human staff, and here I was, best friends with one. I'd known the risks but had pursued the friendship anyway.

"Then she's under my protection," he replied, not a hint of judgment in his eyes. "Tell her she can stay at the estate for as long as she wants. We leave in the morning. That is, if you want to go."

That's when I saw it. The flicker of fear.

He was afraid that I'd leave again. That I'd pack my bags and go without a backward glance.

I'd thought about it. We still had so much to sort out between us. Still needed to *heal*. But I'd rather face things—face *him*—head on this time. Not run, no matter how painful it might be to stay.

So, crossing the terrace, I stopped in front of him and said, "Okay."

He searched my face, not daring to believe. "Okay, what?"

"Okay, I want to go home. With you."

It was like I'd offered him the moon. Joy lit up his face. Then an emotion I couldn't quite define. The same one I'd seen during the meeting this morning.

The emotion was soft. Tender. As tender as the caress he gave my cheek and the words he whispered in reply, "Okay, sweetness. Let's go home."

CHAPTER 14

NORA

I didn't think I would be this nervous.

What if they didn't like Brielle? What if she didn't like *them?*

The nervous energy had followed me all the way back to the estate. At least it prevented me from focusing on *other* things, like the fact that we were no longer protected by magical wards. Or the fact that the witches knew about this location. Or the fact that my pack initiation was only *two days* away.

I now knew that the initiation involved shifting into my wolf and running with the pack. It was a test to see if our wolves were compatible—and an indication of how *alpha* my wolf was. If the pack didn't recognize her dominance, they would challenge her status. She could fall within the ranks and be seen as a lesser member, unworthy of a leader position. If that happened, they might not accept my role as their alpha's wife. Might even rise up to have me removed.

Kolton didn't seem concerned though. About *any* of it. In fact, he'd looked rather serene the whole ride back to the estate. *Content,* even. When I'd started to nervously twist my wedding band, he'd reached over the middle console and laced our fingers together. Just like that. As if it was the most natural thing in the world.

From the backseat, Vi and Melanie had silently looked on. But when I'd sneaked a peek at Vi, she had a little smile on her face.

At least Griff and Jagger had been riding in the Jeep. Griff would have certainly made a teasing comment, then regaled me with more stories about past initiations gone wrong. Apparently, the pack rejected a newcomer on occasion. And if the new wolf didn't accept the outcome, fights would ensue, often resulting in injury. Sometimes even death.

"But you don't need to worry about that," he'd quickly said when both Vi and Kolton had scowled at him. *"Kolton will skin anyone alive who dares to pick a fight with you."*

Yeah, that didn't make me feel any better.

But I could fret about all of that later. Right now, I needed to focus on *another* initiation. One involving the introduction of my best friend to my . . . well, my new family. I knew what she thought of the *old* one, and it was nothing good. I could only hope that she saw how accepting my new family was of me. How caring and protective. But protective in a *good* way, not controlling like Alpha Hendrix.

By the time I heard her car pull into the roundabout, I'd worked myself into a cold sweat. Quickly wiping my damp palms on my shorts, I headed for the front door. The others didn't follow me, as planned. Despite their protests, they'd agreed to stay in the front sitting room while I greeted my friend alone. I didn't want her overwhelmed by a literal pack of predators. Besides me, she'd never actually met another werewolf.

On account of the full moon's approach, the human staff hadn't returned to the estate yet. The only one who'd arrived back was Miss Gabby, Melanie's nanny. She doubled as the girl's teacher, since homeschooling was a common practice for families with natural-born offspring. The children normally experienced their first shift by the age of six, so enrolling them in local school programs before then was too dangerous.

They were currently both sequestered in Melanie's "school room," which meant that the foyer was empty as I hurried to open the door.

At the same time, I struggled to slow my racing pulse.

Everything's going to be fine. They'll love her, and she'll love them. No need to worry.

The pep talk did little to soothe my nerves. My human best friend was about to meet my billionaire werewolf *husband*, after all. Introducing them could be disastrous on so many levels. For one, Brielle wasn't shy about expressing her opinions. For another, she couldn't possibly understand how complicated my relationship with him was. She tended to see things in black and white, and my marriage to him was anything but.

What could possibly go wrong, right?

Everything. Absolutely everything.

Kolton was an alpha, and I doubted he would tolerate criticism from a regular human girl.

But the second I opened the door, I shoved aside my worries and plastered a smile on my face. No need to freak Brielle out before she'd even met the guy. Even so, she knew all my tells and would certainly pick up on my anxiety. I braced myself for the explosion of questions heading my way.

Before I could finish crossing the porch, Brielle whipped open her car door and stepped out. Wearing a pair of her colorful high-heeled shoes, she straightened effortlessly and gaped up at the mansion. Her red lips were rounded in an O as she slowly lowered her designer sunglasses, revealing wide green eyes.

"*Ooh, la la,*" she exclaimed. "You *live* here now?"

"Um, yeah," I replied with an awkward shrug, reaching for my ring finger. "Surprise?"

Like a bee drawn to honey, her gaze snapped downward, expertly landing on my fingers. Or rather, my *wedding* ring. Ah, crap.

Here we go in three, two, one . . .

"No way. Finch, you little *minx*. Is that what I think it is?" A pair of deep dimples appeared on her olive cheeks. "It *is*. I can tell by your red face! You totally went and got yourself *hitched*. To a sugar daddy, by the looks of it."

When my smile became a scowl, she beelined for the stairs with a laugh. Her wavy honey-brown hair bounced as she hurried forward to greet me with open arms. Chunky gold bangles flashed in the early afternoon light, along with several thin gold necklaces. If anything, my friend loved to accessorize. She even had a few new ear piercings.

Unable to hold the scowl, I grinned at her zealous approach, striding forward to meet her. We clashed in a tangle of limbs, so forcefully that she teetered just the slightest bit.

"Whoa," she exclaimed in surprise, pulling back to hold me at arm's length. "You're *strong*. I can feel the difference." Her dimples suddenly winked out as she caught sight of the rest of me. "But you've lost weight. A *lot*. You okay?"

Ah, hell. I knew that look. She was already thinking about the worst case scenario, picturing my new husband as the villain.

I opened my mouth to explain, not wanting her to blame my weight loss on Kolton. Before I could, a deep voice spoke. A shockingly familiar one. One I'd half-expected never to hear again.

"I think she looks great. Already starting to fill out some."

My eyes flew wide, and I glanced around Brielle to find a man with white-blond hair standing on the porch steps. The once tangled hair was now smooth, neatly tucked behind his ears. He wore a ripped pair of blue jeans and a tight t-shirt that showed off his lean, muscular build. The look was topped off by a black leather biker's jacket. When I met his crystal blue eyes, he flashed me a lopsided grin.

"Hey, Nora."

I blinked several times to make sure I wasn't hallucinating. Then whispered, "Arrow?"

"Oh, yeah, forgot to mention," Brielle spoke up. "He was hanging out by the gate when I arrived, so I gave him a ride up here. Said he's been waiting for you to get back."

Still facing me, she wiggled her eyebrows and mouthed, *Hottie.*

"I didn't get a chance to thank you," Arrow said, ascending the steps to stand on the porch. "I just wanted to—"

The front door suddenly burst open with a loud *bang.*

Before I could turn, arms banded around my middle and yanked me clean off my feet. A second later, I was set down again near the open doorway, so fast that I stumbled and caught myself on the frame. I barely had time to register Kolton's presence before he was across the porch and in Arrow's face.

"*You,*" he said, so deathly quiet that a chill skated up my spine. "You have *no* right to be here."

Sensing the others close by, I glanced over to find Vi beside me. Her face was blanched white as she stared at Arrow. Directly behind her, Griff's face was the exact opposite, nearly purple with rage. Standing where I'd left her, Brielle gawked at the standoff, unaware that Jagger was now hovering behind her like a silent sentinel. Only Melanie and her nanny were still inside.

"Leave my territory," Kolton continued, standing so close to Arrow that their noses nearly touched. "Unless you're here to challenge me. In which case, I'll gladly rip you limb from limb."

Tension lined Arrow's face. Still, he held his ground, not budging an inch. He wasn't broad like Kolton, but he was equally as tall. When he broke the staredown to flick me a glance, Kolton's growl practically shook the porch.

"Eyes on me, Pemberton. She's none of your concern."

A smirk twisted Arrow's mouth. "Oh, but that's where you're

wrong, Rivers. She concerns me a great deal."

Kolton went preternaturally still.

Ah, hell. This wasn't good. Arrow was going to get himself killed if he didn't stand down.

Before I could intervene, he winked at me and said, "Isn't that right, *angel?*"

My breath caught.

He was suddenly shifting. Changing. Morphing into a huge silver wolf. I watched in horror as Kolton released a bellowing roar and started to shift as well. Deadly claws shot from his fingertips and dark fur sprouted over his arms and face. When his bones began to crack, giving way to his wolf, I finally burst into motion.

"Stop!" I shouted, racing toward them. Jagger tried to snag my arm in passing but missed. Brielle continued to stand in the middle of the porch, too shell-shocked to move. I skirted around them both, only to stop dead as Arrow's eyes locked on mine. They were glowing the brightest of blues, wholly animal now. The sight of them made Storm stir awake. She rose up without warning, stealing my breath with the force of her presence. Before I could stop her, she began the shifting process.

Stop, Storm, stop! I yelled at her, but she was deaf to my cries.

When I dropped to all fours on the porch and whimpered from the pain, Kolton whirled. He stopped his own shift mid-transformation and strode toward me. Storm forced me to snarl a warning, and he froze. At the flash of hurt in his glowing yellow eyes, remorse filled me. I tried to apologize, but my vocal chords were gone, taken over by Storm's relentless change.

Seconds later, I was fully wolf, struggling to hold onto consciousness as Storm attempted to shake me off. She took one look at Kolton's half-shifted state and laid her ears back. When a growl rumbled in her chest, his clawed hands curled into tight fists. I couldn't tell if she was growling at Kolton or Shadow—or maybe both. All I knew was that she didn't want him near.

Really, Storm? I snapped at her, angry at her irrational behavior. *You decide to shift now, in front of my human best friend? What's gotten into you?*

She ignored me, so completely that I might as well have been a flea on her back. Sidestepping Kolton, she set her sights on Arrow. Or rather, Arrow's *familiar*. The moment their gazes locked, a tremor shook her body.

Zuriel, she breathed, stepping toward him.

Which Kolton didn't like *at all.*

"*Storm*," he barked, with so much authority that she paused. She didn't look at him though. She was too busy staring at *Zuriel*, if that was indeed the familiar's name.

Do you know him or something? I couldn't help but ask, not that I was expecting an answer.

I was shocked witless when she said, *Zuriel was the leader of my legion.*

Legion?

A unit of angels. He's an archangel. So was I.

Was. Past tense. So it hadn't been a dream. She didn't consider herself an angel anymore.

Before I could question her further, Zuriel began to shift back. In no time, Arrow stood where the silver wolf had been. He was stark naked, his clothing in tatters at his feet. Storm didn't look away, and neither could I. Resigning myself to seeing yet another penis, I blew out a frustrated sigh. Storm didn't even twitch an ear.

"As you all saw," Arrow said, not the least bit uncomfortable in his birthday suit, "Nora and I possess angelic spirits. Not only that, her spirit and mine share a celestial bond, one spanning thousands of years. Essentially, that makes her mine."

What. The. Hell?

Everything went silent. Not even the wind dared stir the air.

Then, it was chaos.

"She's not yours, you pompous douchebag," Vi roared, followed by a sound of protest as Griff stopped her from storming across the porch.

"You're a dickhead for showing up here like this," Griff said, in a voice I barely recognized. The guy was *livid.*

"Want me to send him packing, boss?" Jagger this time. "I can think of a few creative ways."

"Can someone pinch me? This can't be real," Brielle said, her voice surprisingly calm.

Through it all, Storm didn't move a muscle. Didn't show any sign that she'd heard a single word anyone said. Until Kolton spoke, so low that the fur raised on her back.

"I don't care what you are or what she is. Nora doesn't belong to you in any shape or form. She's my wife. She is and always will be *mine.*"

Arrow was quiet for a moment, then burst out laughing. The kind that hinged on the crazy side. Still chuckling, he said in a rather theatrical voice, "I don't know what twisted game you're playing, but she's *unmated.* You have no claim on her, Rivers. Regardless, she belongs with her own kind. I can protect her in a way you never can."

Oh. Oh no.

He might as well have stuck his claws into Kolton's chest. Sure enough, Kolton went ramrod straight. "What is that supposed to mean?"

"Simple. It means that angels belong with angels and demons

belong with demons. Our essence isn't the same, neither is our magic. You can't help her come into her powers the way I can. If she's to survive this world in the form she's in, then she needs me. The witches aren't done with her yet."

"Correct me if I'm wrong," Kolton quietly seethed, taking a step toward him, "but *you* were imprisoned too. You didn't get Nora out of there. *I* did. Seems like I'm the one who can protect her better than you can."

Oh boy. This was turning into a pissing contest real fast. I struggled to regain control, but Storm wouldn't budge.

Come on, Storm, work with me here. They need to be stopped.

Agreed. But standing naked between them isn't going to help matters.

Okay, fair point.

"Why are you *really* here, Arrow?" Vi butted in, saving the day. I'd throw her a grateful look, but Storm insisted on remaining a statue.

Arrow's attention drifted to Vi. I tried to read his expression but couldn't. "I'm here for Nora," he simply said, his voice devoid of emotion.

"Bull," she shot back. "You want something else out of this visit."

He stared at her for a long moment, then huffed a laugh. "Fine, you got me. I do want something. Currently, I lack the resources to track down the Blackstone Coven. I need help finding them. Surely you want them silenced as much as I do."

"Why can't your pack help you?"

"Someone in Northwood Pack betrayed me to the witches. Until I find out who, I can't trust them to help me."

Griff scoffed. "And why should *we* help you?"

"Because I know your big secret."

"Really? That's all you've got?" Vi again. "Lame, Arrow. Even for you. We know your big secret too."

"Not *that* secret," he said, switching his attention back to Kolton. "I'm talking about the other secret. The one you've been hiding since the day you brutally killed my dad. Yeah, that's right. I was there, and you didn't even know. I saw everything. Your mom didn't die in childbirth. She went *insane*. And I know she's still alive."

CHAPTER 15

NORA

The tension in the air was palpable.

While the others quickly recovered from their shock, I still reeled over the news that Kolton had killed Arrow's dad. My brain struggled to piece everything together. Had Arrow's father been the one to challenge and kill Kolton's dad, only to turn around and challenge Kolton's mom while she was in labor with Melanie?

"What do you want, Arrow?" Kolton said through gritted teeth, his fists noticeably shaking.

"I want your help finding the coven."

"What else?"

"I want to remain here until the traitor in my pack is brought to justice."

"No way are you staying in my territory."

"Let me stay, and I won't tell everyone that your marriage to Nora is a lie."

Oh *crap*. That was too far. How did he even *know* that?

Kolton looked two seconds away from ripping Arrow's throat out. "It's not a lie," he said, taking another step.

Storm, give me back control.

"Oh, really?" Arrow challenged, refusing to back down. "Well, I happened to bump into a few members of your pack who believe otherwise. It wouldn't be hard to spread some damaging rumors, especially with witnesses in my corner."

Storm. NOW.

"I could kill you right now and save us all the trouble," Kolton replied, nearly nose-to-nose with Arrow again.

Arrow smirked. "You could try. But if I best you, that'll leave Nora squarely in my hands."

Fur erupted over Kolton's arms once more. I shoved at my wolfy prison, desperate to stop them before a fight broke out. When Storm visibly shuddered under my assault, I struggled harder. Over and over, I pushed at my prison until she finally started to relent. The change was slow and painful, but I continued to claw my way out, refusing to back down.

When it was finished, I lay trembling and gasping on the porch. Within seconds, a blanket was draped over my naked form. I gratefully wrapped it around me and tried to stand. When a hand materialized before me, I didn't hesitate to take it. Kolton pulled me to my feet and immediately tucked me against his side. His hand slid to my hip and gripped it tightly, a sure sign that he was feeling possessive.

I didn't pull away, instinctively knowing the closeness could prevent them from fighting. Instead, I burrowed even more into his side, which he seemed to like. A *lot*. He heaved a sigh, one that I felt all the way to my toes. The hard planes of his body noticeably relaxed, molding around mine to fit me perfectly against him.

Before I could get too comfortable, I set my jaw and locked eyes with Arrow. "I think we should help him." Kolton immediately stiffened against me, but I forged ahead anyway. "He helped me, and I'd like to repay the favor. Besides, we need to find those witches before they hurt anyone else. Also, he should be allowed to stay here. In return for our hospitality, he agrees to keep our secrets and leave when he no longer needs our help. Deal?"

I waited for the arguing to begin. None came.

Unwilling to take my eyes off Arrow, I watched as he cocked his head to the side and studied me thoughtfully. Kolton's hold on my hip tightened further. After a lengthy moment, Arrow said, "And what about you?"

"What *about* me?"

"You belong with your own kind. With me."

"Says who? *Zuriel?*"

He blinked at me in surprise.

Not waiting for his response, I stuck out my hand and said, "So, do we have a deal or not?"

I thought for sure Kolton would stop the deal from happening, but he kept quiet, allowing me to take the lead. Something warmed my chest, a feeling that made me melt even more against him.

Finally, Arrow raised his own hand and firmly clasped mine. "Fine. We have a deal. But I hope you'll still consider my offer. You're meant to be with me. Not him."

When I felt Kolton's muscles bunch, I quickly dropped Arrow's hand. "I'll decide who I want to be with, not you. Oh, and Arrow? I'm glad you're okay. Really, I am. But mention my husband's mother to anyone, and I'll kill you myself."

With that, I pulled free of Kolton's grip. The edge of my blanket trailed behind me like a cape as I strode into the house without a backward glance.

Hours. I spent *hours* answering Brielle's probing questions. She wanted to know everything, every last detail. The entire time, her mouth was open in a large O. I was pretty sure it was stuck that way now. Couldn't blame her though. I still struggled to believe most of it myself.

After I'd made the deal with Arrow, we'd all gone our separate ways to cool off. Arrow had been given a place to stay in the guest apartment above the garage. I didn't know how long he'd been in the area waiting for us to arrive, but he hadn't come unprepared. I'd heard the loud rev of a motorcycle engine before he'd parked his bike. Not inside the garage but in front of it. They didn't even trust him near their vehicles.

He hadn't emerged from the apartment since then. Still, I'd seen both Jagger and Griff walking the grounds, clearly intent on keeping a close eye on him. I hadn't seen Kolton or Vi all afternoon though. The itch to find them was hard to ignore. Even as my mind stayed busy recounting the past couple months to Brielle, my heart ached to apologize to Vi. Only after I'd made the deal with Arrow did I consider how hard it might be for her to have him nearby. And I could only imagine what Kolton was thinking and feeling right now.

Was he mad at me for making the deal? For stepping in and taking charge? For shifting into my wolf and *growling* at him?

The need to see him, to speak with him and clear the air, was almost more than I could bear.

"I still can't believe you're married," Brielle said, dragging my attention back to her. I glanced over to find her staring at my ring finger. At the thin gold band I was unconsciously twisting round and round.

Sighing, I dropped my hands to the mattress on either side of me. "Neither can I. And to an *alpha.*"

"An extremely hot one with lots and lots of money."

A laugh burst from me.

"I bet the sex is mind-blowing."

I nearly swallowed my tongue. When I choked on a cough, she

sat up in my bed to gape down at me.

"You've had sex, right?"

Trying and failing not to blush, I hurriedly said, "Well, not exactly."

"What do you mean *not exactly?*"

"I mean that we've done stuff, but haven't . . . you know."

Her green eyes rounded further. "How is that possible? He looks at you like you're the sun, moon, and stars. And don't get me started on how possessive he is." When she dramatically fanned herself, I snorted and rolled my eyes. "Seriously, Nora, you'd have to be blind not to see how much he's into you."

I chewed on my lip hard enough to draw blood. Sighing again, I said, "It's not that simple, Brie."

"Hey, I've had my fair share of relationships, Nora Bora. I know how complicated they can get. But you like Kolton, right?"

My chest tightened to the point of pain. Barely able to speak, I whispered, "Yes."

She was silent for a beat, then quietly said, "Are you in love with him?"

Just like that, all the air left the room. Shooting upright, I clutched my chest and struggled to breathe.

"It's okay," Brielle said, placing a hand on my back to rub comforting circles. "You're okay, Nora Bora. It's only a panic attack. Just breathe. In and out. That's it."

I focused on her soothing voice, forcing myself to obey her soft commands. Within a minute, the tightness in my chest eased. Groaning, I slumped forward and stuck my head between my knees. "Oh, Brie, I'm so screwed."

She continued to rub my back, using her other hand to tuck curls behind my ear. "I don't know what's happened between you two, but talk it out. If not with me, then with him. I think there's something special between you. Something worth fighting for."

She was right. This thing between us *was* worth fighting for. Even if it broke me into a million pieces, which was a high likelihood. But what if I was alone in this? What if I fought for us . . . and he didn't? Still, my feelings for Kolton were very much real and only growing stronger. If I didn't express them soon, I was going to explode.

Despite my mini meltdown, we went on to discuss lighter topics. Like her new accountant job and how amazing the kitchen here was. Thankfully, when we headed down for an impromptu dinner for two, we found the fridge stocked with fresh food.

If only Kolton were here to make you both a mouth-watering meal, my mind decided to goad me. Shoving the tantalizing thought aside, I heaped my plate high with fruit and cold cuts, to Brielle's delight. I'd told her about the witches and what I'd endured this past week. Dried mascara still streaked her face.

The only thing I hadn't told her about was my possible soulmate bond to Kolton. Sharing that highly personal detail hadn't felt right. I needed to tell *him* first. Once I dredged up the courage.

When the day came to an end, my bestie cup was full and I was almost content enough to fall asleep. Almost. Listening to Brielle's steady breathing beside me, the itch to find Kolton rose in intensity. Several minutes dragged by until I couldn't stand it any longer.

I'd just whipped the covers aside when the bedroom door cracked open. I froze, suddenly doused with fear. *Terror.* The witches had found me. Unable to move, I watched as the door soundlessly creeped open to reveal a shadowy figure. Shoving my fear aside, I prepared to attack. To defend my friend if they tried to hurt her.

When the figure stepped into the room, my heart leapt into my throat. I was just about to spring from the bed when my night vision kicked in.

Pure relief rushed through me.

I left the bed and hurried to him. Without a word, he lifted me up. When I wrapped my legs around him, he slid his fingers into my hair and held me tight. Burrowing my face in his neck, I inhaled his scent in greedy gulps. He turned, silently closing the door behind him.

All the way back to his room, he held me tightly, as if the contact was breathing life back into him as well. If anyone else was still awake, I didn't see. All I saw and heard and felt was him. Kolton. The man I couldn't stop falling for. Didn't *want* to stop falling for.

With every step he took, my questions and worries fell away. Everything else could wait. He was here. With me. The only thing that truly mattered right now.

The second we were locked inside his room, he tilted my head back and kissed me. Fully. Deeply. Filling me up to overflowing. With a breathless whimper, I arched against him and parted my lips.

More, I silently pleaded.

Gripping my hair, he deepened the kiss. At the feel of his tongue in my mouth, I whimpered again.

More. Please. I need more.

He broke the kiss and reached between us. With one swift move, he removed his shirt. Another swift move and mine disappeared as well. He crushed our heated skin together and took my mouth again, deeply stroking my tongue with his. After several moments of passionate kissing, I started to beg again.

More. MORE.

He immediately responded to my silent signals, setting me down to tug off his pants. My pajama bottoms quickly followed. When our bodies were at last free of all barriers, I sighed in relief. He kissed me again, swallowing the sound, then lifted me up. I straddled his waist, relishing the warmth of his skin. When the kissing grew passionate once more, he slowly walked to his bed and lowered me onto the mattress.

Yes.

As he covered me with his body, pressing me firmly into the mattress with his weight, every inch of me exploded awake.

Yes. YES.

I quivered beneath him, spreading my thighs to accommodate his thick arousal. He groaned, so loud and gutturally that heat shot to my core. He reached between us and slid his fingers through my wetness.

"God, Nora," he roughly said. "So ready for me."

When he slipped a finger inside me, a moan rolled up my throat. I placed my hands on his back and dug my fingernails in.

Suddenly remembering the last time we'd been in this room together, panic fluttered in my chest. He'd left. For *three* weeks.

"Don't run," I pleaded, shaking uncontrollably when his finger curled inside me. "Don't leave me."

"I can't," he breathed, adding a second finger. "Not this time. I need . . . Need to . . ."

"Need to . . ." I moaned again as his fingers began to pump. "Need to . . . what?"

"Need to *claim*."

The words tore from his throat as if an unseen force had ripped them from him.

"I need to bite. Need to mark. Need to make you mine."

The confession sent euphoria cascading through my body.

"Then do it. Claim me. Mark me as yours."

He blew out a harsh curse. "You should stop me. I'm only

responding to another male's threat. I'm not in my right mind."

His words pinged off me like harmless grains of sand. All that mattered was *this*. The heat between us. The passion. It was electric. Lightning in my veins.

"What does Shadow want you to do?" I said, struggling to speak as he thrust his fingers in deep, hitting the spot that made me see stars.

Kolton blew out another curse. "He wants me to claim you."

More pleasure shivered through me.

"You said I'm yours, so make me yours. I want you to—*Aah!*" I cried out as he lunged for my neck and bit down *hard*. Pain mixed with pleasure, his fingers continuing to move inside me. When I felt his canines puncture my skin, every inch of me stiffened. Gripping the nape of my neck, he held me in place, slowly digging his teeth in deeper.

As I violently shuddered, he growled in warning. I stilled again, only to whine when his fingers slowed. He pressed his thumb to my clit, rubbing circles over the sensitive nub until I panted for release. With a few more thrusts of his fingers, he wrung my climax from me. Viciously digging my nails into his back, I choked back a scream. In reply, he growled again and bit me harder.

My world was exquisite pain and breath-stealing pleasure, a heady mix I'd never experienced before. I didn't know how long the ordeal lasted, only that I was slick with sweat by the time it ended. When he finally pulled his canines from my neck, I was on a high I never wanted to come down from.

He raised his head, just enough to look down at me. I met his stare, my expression open and vulnerable. Whatever he saw made his breath catch. He stared a moment more, then lowered his head and tenderly kissed the spot he'd bitten.

His mark.
His claim.

CHAPTER 16

KOLTON

It was beautiful.

The mark on her neck. *My* mark.

It was the most beautiful thing I'd ever seen.

Until I pulled back and saw her face. The way she looked at me. With trust. With raw vulnerability. With adoration.

There was no one to convince this time. No one here but me and her.

This was real. The way she looked at me. The way she felt about me. It was *real*.

My heart swelled to the point that I thought it would burst. Overwhelmed, I ducked my head and kissed the claim mark. The mark that was already starting to fade. But my scent would remain, buried deep beneath her skin. Any male who came near her would know she was taken. The realization eased some of the raging possessiveness that had risen up the moment Arrow Pemberton had arrived. Nora might still be unmated, but there was no denying now that she was mine.

Another possessive growl pushed at my throat, but I forced it back down. He couldn't touch her. She was mine now. *Mine.*

But not entirely, Shadow whispered in my mind, fanning my territorial instincts to an inferno once more. *Her innocence remains untouched. Males will still want to claim it before you can. Including Arrow. Claim her now. She's soft and warm beneath you, wholly ripe for the plucking. Take what's yours before someone else does.*

At that, a violent shudder ripped through me. Fresh need pounded through every inch of my body, stealing the last of my control. I crushed Nora to me, pressing my throbbing cock to her wet core. When she made a small sound of surprise, my cock painfully swelled in response.

Yes, she wants it, Shadow purred, driving my instincts wild. *She's ready for you. Take her now. Slam into her until she screams your name.*

I trembled in agony. The need to take her was all-consuming, riding me to the brink of insanity.

Take her, take her, take her.

"NO!" I bellowed and tore myself off her. I was halfway across the room in a second flat, heaving in breath after breath as if I'd just sprinted a hundred miles.

Nora stirred on the bed, but I didn't dare turn around. Didn't dare move a muscle lest I lose control again. I simply stood there, shaking and panting, desperately trying to regain some sense.

"Kolton?"

I squeezed my eyes shut. Even the sound of her *voice* made me hard. The pain was almost unbearable now.

"What happened? Did I do something wrong?"

Another shudder racked my frame. "No," I managed to get out. "You did nothing."

And everything. Absolutely everything.

"Then what is it?"

Unable to stop myself, I said, "I crossed another line. I'm sorry. I shouldn't have claimed you."

The second the words left my lips, I hated myself for saying them.

She was silent, for so long that I almost turned and begged for her forgiveness. She didn't deserve this. Everything about this situation was unfair.

But before I could apologize, she said, "Well, *I'm* not sorry."

The words wrapped around my heart and squeezed, cutting off my air supply. "Nora . . ."

"No, I'm not done." Every inch of me stiffened when I heard her scoot off the bed and stand. "What are we doing, Kolton?"

I dragged a hand through my hair and shook my head. "I don't . . . I don't know."

"Well, I do. We're *torturing* ourselves, and it has to stop. You either want me or you don't. Which is it?"

"It's not that simple, Nora—"

"Well, I'm *making* it that simple. I know you desire me, but what I'm asking is, do you *want* me?"

"Of course I do, but that's not the problem here."

"Then what is? Your fear of getting too attached? Of falling in *love?* I'm sorry for what happened to your parents, but that doesn't mean we'll suffer the same fate."

"No," I said, the pain in my chest doubling. "Our fate will be so much worse."

Nora didn't speak for a long moment. Then, she quietly said, "Why? Because we're soulmates?"

My heart stopped. *Time* stopped. The only thing that remained was the question Nora had just thrown into the void. There was no denying it now. No hiding from it. The only thing left for me to do was face the truth.

So I did, turning toward her. Seeing the tears in her eyes, I trembled again, this time with the need to comfort her. I stayed where I was, my throat working as I tried to form words. The only thing that came out was, "When?"

Gripping the bed sheet she'd wrapped around herself, she

whispered, "The day I went into heat."

I closed my eyes again, remorse hitting me hard as I recalled that day. She'd left the day after. Left . . . because she'd *known*, and I'd all but rejected her.

"Nora," I began, needing to make this right somehow. She was hurt. My *soulmate* was hurt. And I was to blame.

"It's okay, Kolton," she said before I could say anything. "I know you never wanted a mate. You don't have to accept the bond. In fact, I don't want you to. Not if your heart doesn't want it. Not if you only want the parts that allow you to keep me at arm's length. Either way, I can no longer give you pieces of myself. I need you to choose. All of me or none of me. Anything else is too painful."

It was agony to breathe. To listen to the words falling from her lips. Forcing my eyes open, I met her gaze and said, "What are you saying?"

A tear slipped down her cheek. I stayed where I was, resisting the urge to brush it away. A tremor shook her voice, but she lifted her chin as she replied, "I'm saying that I care about you too much to drag this on any longer. Before we do anything else we can't take back, you need to accept or reject me. And not just pieces. *All* of me."

Every last drop of air fled my lungs.

"I won't make you decide right now," she continued, her voice gaining momentum. *Strength.* "But until you've made your choice, I think it's best we sleep in separate beds."

With that, she gathered her discarded clothing and slipped from the room, leaving me to face this impossible decision alone.

CHAPTER 17

NORA

I'd finally done it. Finally *ripped* the bandaid off.

It had stung like hell, but the pain was also a relief. It meant that I'd finally made a stand instead of allowing silence to dictate my life. Kolton knew how I felt now. Knew that I was no longer okay with maybes and uncertainties. If he wanted me, then he had to take it all. Even the parts he was too afraid to touch.

And if he didn't . . . then I at least had an answer. At least I'd know where we stood.

Even if my heart never recovered from the rejection.

I didn't expect an answer from him so soon, but the problem was, everyone at the breakfast table knew something was up. Hell, most of them had probably *overheard* the conversation.

At least they seemed to have accepted my best friend's presence here. Even Jagger. Although I hadn't seen him speak to her yet, he hadn't expressed any misgivings over her learning the family secrets. I should have known better than to worry. Brielle had a knack for weaseling inside even the most guarded heart. She'd managed to burrow into mine pretty deeply.

So, I wasn't at all surprised when Griff set down his fork and blurted for everyone to hear, "Soooo, last night was interesting. Cat's finally out of the bag."

From beside me, Vi kicked him under the table.

"Ow. What? Their bond is no longer a secret. That's a good thing.

It's been killing me to keep quiet."

"It's still none of your business, Griffin."

"Well, as the pack healer, I say it is. Especially when it's affecting the health of the alpha and his mate."

Brielle choked on a sip of her coffee. From my other side, she threw me a startled look, which I pretended not to see. "Mate?"

"What cat?" Melanie piped up next to Vi, oblivious to the rising tension. "I want to see."

"Soulmate," Griff replied to Brielle, earning himself another kick. "I've known for a week now. Longest week of my life."

Surprised, I glanced across the table at Kolton, who hadn't said a word all morning. When I caught him already staring at me, my mouth dried. He looked . . . exhausted. Like he hadn't slept a wink all night. That made two of us. Unable to bear his haunted gaze, I looked down at my untouched plate of food.

"At least he finally claimed her," Griff went on, completely ignoring Vi's death glare. "That should keep *Arrowhead* away. Hopefully."

"Claim?" Brielle said, still gaping at me.

"Griff, stop talking," Jagger finally spoke up with so much authority that I lifted my eyes again. Expecting his attention to be on Griff, I was surprised to find him staring at Brielle. She didn't seem to notice, too busy gawking at the side of my face.

Suddenly desperate for air, I grabbed my plate and stood. "I don't think Arrow has any food in the guest apartment. I'll take him some breakfast."

Before I could move, Kolton was on his feet. "I'll do it."

Not giving me time to protest, he took the plate from me and left without a word.

The moment he was gone, Griff released a low whistle. "You might want to go with him, Jag. Just in case he tries to ram that plate down our *guest's* throat."

"On it."

When Jagger left, Vi slumped against her seat with a groan. "Well, this is a crapfest."

Slowly sinking back into my chair, I worried my lip for a moment before blurting, "I'm sorry."

Vi shot me a quizzical frown. "For what?"

"For telling Arrow he could stay. I didn't stop to think if you'd be okay with it."

She snorted. "I'm not, but you made the right call. We all think so, even Kolton. Arrow has dangerous leverage on us. Keep your enemies close, right? This way, we can stop him from doing anything stupid."

Glancing at Melanie, who was still chomping away at her bowl of cereal, I carefully said, "What happened between Kolton and Arrow's father?"

I watched as the blood slowly drained from Vi's face. Griff leaned forward, as if to lend her comfort. Blinking a few times, she cleared her throat and replied, "Marcus Pemberton was the reason Kolton became alpha."

Oh, wow. I'd been right then. No wonder they all hated Arrow. Seeing him after all these years must have ripped their scars wide open.

"I'm so sorry," I said again, feeling awful that I'd dredged up the painful memory.

"Oh, Nora, you couldn't have known," Vi replied, taking my hand. "But Arrow can't be trusted. If he kept our secret all these years and only now decided to show up, he wants more than our help. And I'm not buying his benevolent angel crap. He doesn't care about your welfare. The only person he cares about is himself."

I turned over her words, comparing her version of Arrow to the man I'd been imprisoned with. Maybe I was too trusting, but I could have sworn he cared about what happened to me. Vi knew him better than I did though. She'd been *engaged* to him, after all. Which meant . . .

"Were you seriously only sixteen when you got engaged?"

Griff scoffed, not sounding the least bit amused.

"Betrothed, actually," Vi said. "Our parents set it up, hoping to unite both packs. Kind of an old tradition among alphas. Guess you could say I know a little about arranged marriages too," she finished with a wink.

Griff scoffed again.

"But you decided not to marry him?" I tentatively asked, hoping I wasn't overstepping.

She looked down, but not before I saw the flicker of hurt in her eyes.

"More like he rejected her," Griff answered, watching her closely. "Because he's a pompous dickhead with an angelic stick up his butt."

"Griff," Vi said, but without the usual bite.

"You know it's true, Vi. He didn't want his pure bloodline tainted by demon spawn. As soon as he found out what you were, he threw you to the curb and poisoned his father against the entire Rivers family. That challenge wouldn't have taken place otherwise. Everything that happened was *his* fault."

Normally prepared with a sharp comeback, Vi didn't respond.

"Vi." When she still didn't respond, Griff's tone softened. "Vi, look at me."

She finally did, looking uncharacteristically vulnerable.

"You aren't to blame, Violet Jane Rivers. Say it."

She stared at him for a moment, and then quietly said, "I'm not to blame."

"Good girl." He rose to his feet and rounded the table. Pausing behind Vi, he bent to whisper in her ear, "And maybe someday, you'll actually believe it."

Then he straightened, but not before brushing a featherlight kiss to her cheek. Her fingers spasmed around mine before she released my hand. When he left the dining room, she watched him go through lowered lashes.

For all their bluster, they truly did care about each other. There was more to their relationship, much more than lifelong friendship and the occasional hookup. But maybe it was complicated. Something I understood all too well.

"Right," Vi said, scooting her chair out and hopping to her feet. No trace of her earlier vulnerability could be found. "Now that the boys are gone, how about we have some fun before Nora's initiation tonight?"

Just like that, a thousand nervous butterflies erupted in my stomach.

Melanie looked up from her cereal to say, "Tea party, tea party! I've got extra dresses!"

Despite my nervousness, I shared a look with Vi and Brielle, then burst out laughing.

Thunder rumbled in the distance.

A bad omen? Maybe. It sure felt ominous as more and more members of Midnight Pack arrived. They filled the grassy clearing, each taking my measure as they passed by. I hadn't expected the *entire* pack to be at my initiation, but apparently, no one wanted to miss out on the occasion.

Only a few were missing. Jagger had gone to stay with Kolton's mom while her caretaker Darlene wolfed out. So far, the friendly middle-aged woman was one of only a few who'd actually looked at me with kindness. The Rivers' old and current nannies were also here, nodding their support. The rest of the pack either looked skeptical, suspicious, or downright hostile.

Jasmine Deveron, the blonde-haired Barbie doll who used to "hook up" with Kolton while she was in heat, was one of the latter. It was weird seeing her without Rodney, the guy that had recently challenged Kolton and lost. I supposed her reaction toward me was kind of justified, given that Rodney had been her boyfriend. Although, given the chance, she'd gladly crawl back into Kolton's bed. When she passed by me, I ignored her look, pretending she wasn't even there.

Melanie and Brielle had stayed back at the house, the former too young for a pack run. It was only a matter of time though before she experienced her first shift. Arrow had also stayed behind, for obvious reasons. This was a pack-only event. The only non-member allowed was, well, *me.*

But hopefully, by the end of tonight, that wouldn't be the case. Hopefully. The pack wasn't going to make this easy, that much I knew. Dozens of males had already strayed too close, intent on getting a whiff of me. They could no doubt smell Kolton's claim on me, but they could also scent that I was still unmated. No one questioned it though. At least, not aloud. Which hopefully meant that our meeting with the influential members of Kolton's pack had been successful.

Another rumble of thunder shook the clearing, this time closer.

We'd driven hours to get here, a privately-owned stretch of land barely accessible by vehicle. There was nothing for hundreds of miles except mountains and trees and lakes. The perfect spot for a pack of two hundred werewolves to run without being seen—and to hide any howls or screams should things go south.

You'll be fine. You're strong. Tenacious. They'll soon see that too.

But it wasn't *me* they would see. The success of this initiation was riding on Storm, and she hadn't said a peep all day. What if she didn't feel like cooperating? What if they all wolfed out . . . and I didn't? Old fears of being ripped to shreds came back to haunt me. Without Storm's help, I was a sitting duck out here. I doubted even Kolton could stop the pack from attacking me if I didn't shed my human form.

It's almost time, Storm, I tried again, desperately hoping for a response this time. *If we don't act like the rest of them, they'll know something's off. They're purely wolves when they shift, controlled by instinct. They won't think twice about killing me.*

When she didn't respond, I barely held back a frustrated scream.

"What's wrong, Nora?" Kolton's voice rumbled in my ear.

I suppressed a shiver, forcing myself to lean away instead of toward him. For the last hour, he'd been at my back, close enough that I could feel his steady warmth. Every time a male invaded my personal space, he was there, gripping my hip possessively. I tried to allow it. Tried not to react. But every time, I stiffened. Every time, his touch sent a yearning ache through me.

It had been almost twenty-four hours since he'd claimed me. Since I'd laid everything on the table and given him my all-or-nothing ultimatum. Since then, he'd barely said two words to me. The tension between us hurt. Every glance was a painful reminder that he hadn't given me an answer yet. If not for Vi and Griff's company, the drive up here would have been unbearable.

And now, we were minutes away from shifting into wolves. From confirming if I was *alpha* enough to stand by his side. Not knowing what the outcome would be was quickly fraying the last of my nerves.

Realizing I'd paused for too long, I quickly answered, "Nothing. I'll be fine."

He was silent for a beat, then he said, "You don't have to do this today. We can still call it off if you're not ready."

Yeah, right. Something told me that chickening out would *not* gain me any favors with his pack. I couldn't let Kolton protect me from this any longer. It was time to face the music.

"I've got this," I insisted, standing tall as another pack member passed by me. More thunder vibrated the air, and I looked up at the full moon just as a raindrop hit my nose.

Great. Two hundred werewolves chasing each other around in a thunderstorm. What could go wrong?

Lightning sliced the sky like a sharp knife, opening up the clouds. Rain poured out, soaking my hair and shirt within seconds. As if responding to some unspoken cue, everyone began removing their clothes. Shirt, pants, shoes. Everything. Not a stitch of clothing remained on their bodies. When I stood there like an idiot, frozen in shock at the sight of so much naked flesh, Kolton's voice rumbled in my ear again.

"Look at me, Nora."

Trying not to hyperventilate, I did, turning to face him. Even through the rain and darkness, I could clearly make out his expression. It was serious. More serious than I'd ever seen him before. I tried to swallow and failed.

"Just follow my lead," he said over the pounding rain, loud enough for only me to hear.

When he reached up and tugged off his shirt, I raised shaking fingers and did the same. All the while, I kept my eyes on him. On his face. Slowly gaining confidence from his unwavering gaze. His movements were sure. Practiced. Like he'd done this a hundred times before. He probably had. When we were both naked, he stared at me a moment more. Long and deep. Checking for signs of distress. Of *fear*.

Apparently satisfied with what he found, he nodded and raised his eyes to the clearing. Then, in a loud voice, said, "You all know why we're here tonight. For the initiation of Nora Elizabeth Finch, my wife. I expect you to treat her as you would any other pack candidate. With respect and fair judgment. During the moon's pull, you will all get the chance to interact with her wolf. But keep in mind who she is. I will not hesitate to punish anyone who behaves inappropriately toward her."

No one said a word. It was eerie. I shivered, disconcerted by the strange sight.

Expecting Kolton to say more to the pack, I was surprised when he looked down at me and said, "They're waiting for me to shift first. The moment I do, things will progress quickly. They'll follow my lead, but I can't stop them from approaching you. Whatever you do, don't run away. They'll see that as weakness. Ready?"

Shivering even harder, I nodded, suddenly terrified.

"No fear, Nora," he said, so quietly that I almost didn't catch the words. "Show them how strong you are."

I nodded again, softly gasping when his irises flared yellow.

"Don't give Storm control yet. Shadow wants to meet you first." When my eyes widened, he added, "He won't hurt you. I promise. Don't be afraid."

"I won't," I said, even as my teeth chattered.

He searched my face for a long moment, then nodded and took a step back.

Storm, I really hope you're paying attention. Because your least favorite person is about to make an appearance. Storm? Are you listening? You—

Dark fur erupted over Kolton's skin, so swiftly that I almost took a step back. At the last second, I stopped myself, refusing to look weak in any way. I hadn't seen Shadow since he'd charged inside the abandoned church in all his demonic glory.

Knowing that he wouldn't take that form tonight did nothing to soothe my nerves. The only thing keeping me from freaking out was Kolton's steady gaze. Even when his bones began to crack and shift into new positions, he watched me, as if his need to reassure me was stronger than any pain he felt.

Quicker than I thought possible, his form took on the appearance of a wolf. One that towered over me by several inches. As he shook out his wet fur, he continued to watch me. Only now, his gaze was sharper. Keener. Pure predator.

It wasn't Kolton looking at me anymore.

It was Shadow.

CHAPTER 18

She really was an exquisite creature.

Supple. Luscious. And, above all, *innocent.*

That innocence was reflected in her stunning aqua eyes. They were wide, watching my every move with rapt attention. I expected to find fear. *Terror.* Similar to the last time I'd appeared before her.

I couldn't find any. Couldn't sense anything but a wary caution.

Pride warmed my chest, which caught me by surprise. I usually basked in the fear of others, taking perverse pleasure in the sight of them cowering before me.

But she wasn't just anyone. What's more, I wanted her to *like* me. So, I lowered my head to her level, making my appearance less threatening. Less monstrous. The move brought us closer together. She stiffened but didn't pull away.

That's it, I silently crooned to her, wishing she could hear me. *I won't hurt you, little one.*

The very thought of hurting her soured my stomach, another reaction that surprised me. I didn't often care what happened to the corporeal beings who walked this earth. Most of them were embarrassingly weak, both physically and mentally. They acted like sheep, and that only brought out the predator in me.

But *this* female wasn't weak. Scarred, yes. A little bit broken. But not weak, not even when she couldn't shift, when she'd been *afraid* of me. Buried deep down inside her, she possessed a powerful strength.

It had drawn me to her. Had made me seek her out in that nightclub. Even before she'd bumped into us, I had sensed her presence.

Kolton still didn't know. I'd allowed him to believe that he had discovered her. That standing in that hallway right as she'd turned the corner had been pure coincidence. If he'd known that I'd orchestrated the whole thing, he wouldn't have chosen her. He would have picked a *lesser* female, one not worthy to stand beside us.

So I'd kept quiet, only whispering in his ear suggestions, ones meant to slowly break down his many defenses. It was only a matter of time. He was hurting. Barely functioning after what happened last night. Just looking at her sent shards of agony through him.

Good.

It meant that my plan was working.

Her ultimatum had come at the perfect time. It was wickedly clever, delivered with a determination that had caught even me off guard. She was done being played with. It was all or nothing for her now. The moment she'd made a stand, I'd howled with pleasure, even as I'd felt Kolton's chest rip wide open. He didn't realize what a gift this was. Not yet. But he would. Sooner than he knew.

Lowering my head another inch, I took a step toward her. Only a small one. She didn't retreat or even flinch. But her eyes. They flared bright. Revealing the celestial spirit hidden within.

Sensing Storm's presence, I flashed her a wolfish grin. Her eyes flared brighter. A clear warning. Knowing that she couldn't hear me, I still purred, *You gonna come out and play? I know you want to. You've been cooped up for far too long. Why don't you stretch your legs a little?*

When I took another small step, I could practically hear her warning growl. Could imagine her barking, *That's close enough, demon.*

I inwardly chuckled, secretly enjoying it when she got riled up. She was a spitfire, no doubt about it. A credit to her host in every way. But her unpredictable nature was what intrigued me most. She'd chosen her earthly name well. Storm had violence in her heart, along with a great deal of pain. She might hate me, but that didn't stop me from wanting to know her.

Excitement was already shivering through me, eagerness for the moments to come. Despite her animosity and coldness, I knew she would shift tonight. Knew she would face me. And when she did, I had every intention of wearing her down. The time had finally arrived for me to make my move.

With one final step, I stopped before Nora, close enough for her to touch me. I doubted she would though. Through the rain pelting us both, I could see her trembling. She might not be showing fear, but she was definitely—

She suddenly lifted a hand toward me. Every inch of my earthly form stilled. I tracked the hand, watching as it came closer and closer. Her fingers made contact with my damp fur. Hesitantly at first, then gently stroked the side of my neck. Shocked, I simply stared at her, searching her face as she continued to . . . to *pet* me. I'd never been touched like this before. Had never allowed it.

But being petted by her felt . . . nice. *More* than nice.

I wanted to lean into her hand and further encourage the touch, but I didn't dare. Her movements were still cautious, like she expected me to attack at any second. I didn't move a muscle, allowing her to explore my fur. Slowly, her fingers reached higher, until she was scratching the side of my ear.

A tremor shook my body. That felt *good.* Unable to stop myself, I pushed into her hand, a growl of contentment vibrating my chest.

The moment I moved, the spell broke. Nora cried out and

stumbled back. A shock of white fur rippled up her arms, followed by the tell-tale cracks of her bones breaking. Unable to help her, I remained close by, acting as a guard while she shifted.

None of the others in the clearing moved a muscle, but they were all watching Nora's transformation. I had a sudden urge to snarl at them. To demand they go away. I wanted this moment alone with her. To finally run and hunt with her. To *chase*.

But I didn't, knowing how important this moment was for Kolton. For them both. The only hope she had of proving her strength to the pack was if I gave her space. Sharing wasn't in my nature though. Good thing I had Kolton to rein me in. Although he was often far too uptight for his own good, he was my voice of reason. Even now, I could feel him keeping me in check, making sure I behaved like an alpha was supposed to.

In less than a minute, a snowy white wolf with a single patch of fire on her front paw stood where Nora had been. She didn't even bother to shake out her wet fur. The moment she was fully shifted, she looked me square in the eye and growled in my face.

I grinned again.

Hello, angel.

CHAPTER 19

The insufferable demon was *grinning* at me. I could tell by the way his eyes crinkled at the corners.

I glared back, showing him how angry I was that he'd *dared* get close to Nora again. Whatever game he was playing, I was onto him. One false move, and I'd remind him of what I was. *Painfully.* The only reason why I didn't attack him now was because I owed Nora. I'd allowed her to suffer at the hands of those witches for far too long. I'd only stopped them when their probing had threatened to expose my identity. I'd looked out for *myself* once again, letting her fend for herself when it was within my power to help.

When Shadow had arrived like a hound out of Hell to rescue her, I'd actually felt . . . guilty. For better or for worse, Nora was under my protection. And a *demon* had been the one to save her. Ever since then, I'd been quiet. Contemplative. Uncertain. My misery wasn't the only thing I could feel anymore. Now, I could sense Nora's emotions as well. Her fears and desires. Her loneliness and determination. The more I felt from her, the more I observed and listened, trying to understand.

I hadn't asked for this existence, but neither had she. And yet, she was still trying to make the most of it. So why couldn't I?

Still glaring at Shadow, I waited for Nora to start chattering at me. The girl was always on the move. Always *doing* before considering the consequences. Her spontaneity had gotten her into trouble countless times. It was a miracle she was still alive—no thanks to me.

I secretly admired her plucky courage though. Maybe if I had been more like her during my time as an angel, I wouldn't be in this mess. Maybe if I'd been stronger—if I'd obeyed Zuriel's final order—I would be back at my post by now.

Guilt plagued me again. Blaming Zuriel, even a little, was blasphemy. He hadn't caused my banishment. My disloyalty had. If I'd been brave enough to obey his command, my punishment could already be over. I wouldn't still be here, *stuck* in this purgatory.

My only thought should be on how to get out of it. On how to *redeem* myself. But it wasn't that simple. Not anymore. Not since I'd started to care about the fiery-haired girl I was bound to.

Thanks for shifting, Storm, she suddenly broke into my thoughts. *I was really starting to get worried.*

I almost didn't respond. It was ingrained in me to keep quiet. To observe from afar without being seen or heard. To only act when my presence was required. Centuries of training had taught me the importance of dutiful silence, especially after what had happened with Zuriel.

But I sensed her unease. Her uncertainty as, one by one, the werewolves in the clearing began to shift.

I'll keep you safe, I finally answered her.

Safe. After all these years of hiding, the word felt strange on my tongue. Strange, yet . . . right.

Shaking off the feeling, I focused on the pops and cracks rending the air. The sound of breaking bones was everywhere, followed by agonized groans and whimpers as human flesh gave way to the savage predator within. Not far away, a brown wolf rose up, sleek and agile. Patches of blond littered its tawny coat. As I caught its scent, my ears immediately flattened against my skull.

Demon, I snarled, baring my teeth.

That's Griff, Nora said. *He's like us. Oh, and Vi is the one next to him. The dark gray wolf with the white marking on her chest.*

They're not like us.

Well, not like you and your pal Zuriel, but they're still different like we are.

I bristled at her casual description of my commanding officer but didn't comment. She couldn't possibly understand his importance or what he meant to me. His host had spoken true. Zuriel and I shared a bond, one that couldn't easily be broken. No matter the current strain between us, I still owed him my loyalty.

Quick, they're heading this way, Nora said with nervous anticipation. *Act like a wolf.*

If I could, I would have rolled my eyes. *I am a wolf.*

Well, not technically. I still don't know what you actually are, since you said you're not an angel anymore.

At the fresh reminder, pain tightened my chest. I didn't respond, still unable to face the truth of who I now was.

Thankfully, the two demon wolves arrived, providing a distraction from Nora's inquisitiveness. They each approached cautiously, and for good reason. My hackles had risen, and my lips were pulled back in a silent snarl. The reaction was pure instinct, borne from centuries of conditioning and growing only stronger the closer they came.

I was outnumbered three-to-one. If they decided to attack, I needed to be prepared. I was alone here. The only one I could rely on was myself.

It's okay, Storm, Nora said, clearly noticing my defensive state. *They're friends.*

I snorted. *These aren't your friends, Nora. They are demons disguised as wolves. Their hosts might be benevolent, but the same can't be said for them.*

Can you at least give them a chance? Shadow hasn't hurt either of us.

Yet, I thought, but didn't voice. She didn't understand the spirit world like I did. Celestial beings were immortal. Time was irrelevant to them. They could go decades pretending to be your friend, only to turn on you in an instant. Zuriel's angelic visage flashed in my mind, but I quickly shoved it aside.

For the sake of your initiation, I will endure their presence. But only for tonight.

I heard Nora sigh with relief. *Thanks, Storm. I appreciate it.*

Warmth stirred in my chest. Unsettled by the feeling, I refocused on the brown and charcoal gray wolves. They were watching me carefully with their glowing yellow eyes, staying well out of biting range. Nora's soulmate had probably warned them ahead of time.

Despite my loathing of his demon counterpart, I actually liked Kolton. He treated Nora kindly and with respect. But his continued fear of an unknown future was causing them both undue pain. Not that I could blame him. I myself feared the unknown before me. Still, I didn't enjoy feeling Nora suffer. Maybe it was time for me to have another talk with her.

The brown wolf chose that moment to get a little too close. Before I could warn him away, Shadow growled and stepped between us. Surprise filtered through me. Was he protecting Nora right now . . . or me? Disconcerted either way, I stepped away from him.

Only to bump into another wolf.

I immediately leapt to the side, baring my teeth. The gray wolf was unfamiliar, smaller than the demon wolves. One sniff and I knew it was a regular werewolf. At my reaction, it flattened to the ground submissively. When the creature softly whined, I hid my teeth from view.

Soon, another approached. Then another and another. I held my ground, greeting each one with a similar reaction. They all lowered themselves before me. During each encounter, Shadow remained nearby. Not too close, but not too far away. He keenly watched every exchange, allowing me to handle the interactions.

When the brown demon wolf approached for a second time, Shadow tensed, but he didn't interfere like before. I bristled as the wolf invaded my personal space, not submitting like the rest had. He rubbed his body along the length of mine, earning a low growl from Shadow. Undeterred, he came back around and brazenly nudged my muzzle with his nose, then had the audacity to *lick* me.

An explosion of dark fur was suddenly in my face. I leapt back as Shadow barreled into the brown wolf, almost taking him to the ground. With agile grace, the brown wolf slipped away and danced out of reach. When Shadow snapped his teeth at him, I was fairly certain the wolf tossed him a playful grin. Huffing, Shadow turned and trotted back to me.

Expecting him to take up guard nearby again, I froze when he walked right up to me and rubbed his muzzle over my neck. Over the spot where Nora's mate had claimed her last night. A growl rumbled his chest as he pressed his nose to the spot, keeping it there as if to say, *Stay away. She's mine.*

Overwhelmed, I quickly backed away. Then stopped, realizing my mistake. The other wolves looked on, clearly confused by my retreat. As the alpha's wife, I should have welcomed his touch. Not run from it. Suddenly uncertain, I looked to Shadow. When he lifted his head and met my gaze, I silently questioned him.

What should I do?

He cocked his head to the side. *Show them you're not afraid of me.*

I laid my ears back. *I'm not afraid.*

Lightning lit up the night, intensifying his stare. *Then prove it.*

As a boom of thunder shook the ground, I took a step. Then another and another until I stood before him. My nemesis. My mortal enemy. I stared into his glowing eyes, scrambling to think of another way out. There wasn't one. I had no choice but to prove my devotion as a female wolf would to her alpha mate.

Before I could think too hard on what I was about to do, I stepped forward and nuzzled him with my nose. When I started to pull away, a soft growl vibrated his throat.

Stay, the sound ordered, making me internally howl with displeasure.

I continued to nuzzle, then nipped at his snout for good measure. He immediately nipped me back, causing me to jolt in surprise. When I stood stock still like a startled deer, he nipped me again, this time on my ear. I sharply nipped him in return, this time harder. Which he seemed to *like.* He softly bit my neck, inches from my throat.

As I stiffened, he brushed past me, only to turn and nip at my hindquarters. I jumped and whirled to face him, ready with a snarl. Before I could bare my teeth, he bumped into my side and nipped me again. Over and over until his actions sank in.

Run. He wanted me to *run* with him.

Excitement shivered through me.

Without a moment's hesitation, I took off, racing for the trees. When he tore after me, I put on a fresh burst of speed. With an excited bark, he gave chase, dogging my every step. Soon, I heard the others follow. All two hundred of them. Yips and howls rose into the air, only slightly muffled by the rain and thunder.

A thrill shot through me and I ran faster, leading the wolf pack on a merry chase through the woods. On occasion, Shadow would run beside me, brushing my body with his. I didn't pull away, even when he'd turn and playfully nip at my neck.

The chase lasted for hours, pausing only when someone caught fresh prey. I reveled in the simple comradery, basking in the oneness. I could pretend that I was nothing more than a cog in a well-oiled machine. A soldier in a legion. My identity was restored. My *purpose*.

The pain of the past few decades melted away as I allowed myself this moment.

This single moment of feeling whole again.

CHAPTER 20

NORA

I should have known this had been too easy. Should have known it wouldn't last.

It all fell apart with one little nip. A playful nip that turned into a possessive *bite*. Not from Kolton, but from another male. The entire pack had stopped at a stream to slake their thirst, and the overeager male had caught us completely unaware.

The pain of the bite startled a yelp out of Storm. In a split second, that one little sound flipped the carefree mood on its head. Several more males reacted to the distress call, raising their heads to sniff the air. To sniff the *blood* now trickling from Storm's neck. Storm jerked away from the wolf, but the damage had already been done.

She was injured and surrounded by predators whose instincts were to flush out all weakness.

Farther down the stream, Shadow's head shot up. He took in the scene and immediately bared his teeth. Not at Storm, but at the males who were eyeing her hungrily. He growled, but the warning came too late.

Several wolves surged toward us en masse.

Storm! I cried in warning, but she was already moving. Already meeting the first wolf head on. Teeth and claws flashed. Fur flew through the air as they grappled for dominance. Snarls rang up and down the riverbed as more and more wolves joined the fight.

Storm was a whirlwind, dodging snapping teeth left and right.

Every time a wolf got too close, she lashed out in fury, her claws and teeth finding purchase. More blood saturated the air, but not hers. Rather, from the countless males getting their *butts* kicked.

Hell, yeah! I whooped, despite the danger. My familiar was a vicious fighting *machine*. The fight only lasted minutes, but when it ended, her muzzle was covered in blood.

Sensing another wolf behind us, Storm whirled, ready for the next fight. At the sight of Shadow, she stopped short, just shy of biting his muzzle. His *bloodied* muzzle. Fat red drops fell from his mouth, as if he'd recently ripped into flesh. Storm flicked a sideways glance at the stream and found the wolf who'd first bitten her. A huge chunk of fur and flesh was now missing from his hide. Blood ran into the stream, darkening the water.

When he struggled to rise, several wolves pinned him back down with warning snarls. He cowered, thoroughly put in his place.

Storm looked back at Shadow, just as he stepped forward and licked her muzzle. She stiffened all over but didn't move a muscle. He continued to lick, carefully cleaning the blood from her face. Then gently nosed the bite on her neck and licked that too. A tremor shook her body, but she held perfectly still. So did the other wolves. I didn't say a word, too shocked by what was happening.

Shadow was taking care of Storm . . . and Storm was *letting* him.

Only when Shadow had finished cleaning her wound did anyone dare move. But not before he gave them all a look. Every single one of them. As if responding to some unspoken message, they slowly left the stream and headed for the path we'd just come from. I watched them go, confused as they each lowered their heads a notch when passing by me.

What's happening? I asked Storm, who still hadn't moved.

She was quiet for a long moment, then said, *They're acknowledging our position. They've accepted us into their pack.*

Relief flooded me, followed by an overwhelming sense of joy.

They'd accepted me. *Accepted.* I was a member of the Midnight Pack now.

I wanted to cry, but I knew Storm didn't feel the same. She simply watched them go until every last one had disappeared from view. Then moved to follow them. A second later, a warm body brushed against hers.

Shadow.

She stiffened again, but I could have sworn she leaned into him. Just a little. Before breaking into a run and loping up the trail.

With the dawn came pain.

Whimpers and groans filled the clearing as the full moon lost its pull. I joined them, allowing the shift to overtake me. Minutes later, an exhausted group of werewolves in their human skins littered the damp ground. The rain had stopped, leaving the long grass thoroughly saturated. The cool wetness helped to soothe my overheated skin and sore muscles.

I'd never been shifted for that long before. Every inch of me ached, but I welcomed the pain. It was a reminder of all I had just gained. Acceptance. Respect. A *pack*. One that didn't see me as a burden and disappointment.

A tired grin stole across my face.

The moment was suddenly interrupted by a gasp and breathy moan. Frowning, I sat up in the grass and scanned the clearing. At the sight that greeted me, my jaw dropped. Not too far away, Vi and Griff were making out. *Heavily.* Too shell-shocked to move, I watched like a creeper as their kiss became frantic. Hands started to roam. *Everywhere.* Making my face flush scarlet. When Griff lowered Vi to the grass and covered her naked body with his, I forced my eyes away.

Holy hell, I definitely hadn't been expecting *that.*

Checking to see if anyone else had witnessed the heated moment, I nearly swallowed my tongue as I caught sight of several more entwined pairs. There were even a few *threesomes.*

What the hell was happening? Was this a pack *orgie?*

As soft moans and panting rolled across the clearing, I jumped to my feet and hurried toward the trees. Only when I was hidden behind a large pine did I stop to catch my breath. Were they all in heat or something? Yeah, right. At the same time?

I suddenly felt a presence at my back. When his scent drifted my way, my body immediately responded by warming in all the wrong places. Ah hell, even *I* was feeling horny. He stopped directly behind me, so close that his heat warmed my back. Panicking, I said a bit forcefully, "You didn't warn me about this."

"It doesn't usually happen," Kolton said, the deep rumble of his voice only turning me on more. "I think they're just extra excited about having a new alpha female in the pack. As am I."

At his quietly spoken confession, heat rushed to my core. Oh, this wasn't good. This wasn't good at *all.* I'd given him an ultimatum. One I intended to stand by. But I suddenly wanted nothing more than to jump his bones.

Responding to my clearly aroused state, he eased into my personal space. I tensed all over but didn't pull away. I couldn't. I was surrounded by his heat and scent. *Drowning* in it. When he slowly slid a hand around my waist, I helplessly melted. Encouraged, he let his hand roam upward, gliding over my ribs to cup my right breast. A sigh shuddered from me, and I arched into his hand. When his other hand gripped my hip and pulled me back against him, my eyes blissfully rolled shut.

I couldn't help it. I wanted him so bad. Every time he touched me, I forgot everything else. Where I was. *Who* I was. All I could focus on was him and the way he made me feel.

Leaning against his chest, I allowed him to knead my breast and play with my hardened nipple. When his other hand began tracing lazy circles on my lower stomach, a whimper burst from me. My body was a riot of sensation, firing off on all synapses. He grew bolder and bolder, his movements becoming rough. Frantic. I trembled in his arms, gripping them as need coursed through me.

I had to end this. I *needed* to. I couldn't fall back into the painful pattern we'd woven for ourselves. Our passion would only lead to more and more *heartache*.

"Kolton," I whispered, digging my nails into his arms as he pressed his hard arousal against my backside.

"Nora," he answered, and then shocked me senseless by saying, "I can feel how my touch affects you. I can feel your *emotions*. They're beautiful. So breathtakingly beautiful."

I jerked my eyes open. "What do you mean?"

"Our mate bond. It's grown stronger."

My heart practically pounded out of my ribcage. Up until now, a small part of me had still questioned our bond. Had still doubted that we were soulmates. But that doubt quickly melted away. This was undeniable *proof* that we were.

Kolton Rivers was well and truly my soulmate.

Fresh awe trembled through me, despite my conflicted emotions. It was still surreal. Still unbelievable that he of all people would be my soulmate. Maybe running into him at that nightclub hadn't been a coincidence after all. Maybe this had all been predestined somehow.

His need for a wife. My need for help. Our paths had brought us together, whether we believed in fate or not.

The connection between soulmates was powerful. Feeling drawn to each other was the first sign, followed by an incessant need to complete the bond. If that wasn't distracting enough, the ability to feel each other's emotions should do the trick. I didn't know everything about the soulmate bond, but I knew that it couldn't strengthen without the couple's permission.

But that would mean . . . that would mean we'd *fed* the bond. That would mean we'd inadvertently, yet willingly, done something to encourage it. How? And then it came to me.

"Y-your bite. Your claim."

"Yes," he affirmed, slowly thrusting against me.

Ah *hell*, that felt good. So good that my shock over his words faded. So good that I never wanted this moment to end. But moments like this further strengthened our bond. Moments like this only led to more confusion. More *pain*.

I had to end this. *Now.*

Gritting my teeth, I shoved his arms away. He immediately let go, allowing me to put much-needed space between us. Stopping several yards away, I turned my back to him and forced myself to say, "I can't. I need more than *feelings*, Kolton. I need you to be mine."

"I *am* yours."

My breath caught. Whirling to face him, I burst out, "Not just parts of you, Kolton. I want your heart. Your *soul*. I'm honored to have you as my alpha and husband, but I want *all* of you. If that makes me selfish, then so be it. I want your full acceptance and love. If that's too much to ask of you, then just tell me. Put me out of my misery, because being with you but not fully having you *hurts*. I can't do it anymore. I can't . . . I can't bear it."

Unable to control my tears, I turned again, not wanting him to see. I was already naked before him, wholly vulnerable. He didn't get to witness me completely break down. When I heard the shuffle of feet, a sliver of hope pricked my heart. But then I heard a voice.

Her voice.

The very last person I wanted to face right now.

"Lovers' quarrel?" Jasmine said, in a tone dripping with false sympathy.

"Not right now, Jasmine," Kolton said, the warning clear.

A warning she ignored.

"It pains me to see you so unhappy, Kolton. I've heard the rumors. Seen for myself that you don't really want your wife. If you did, she wouldn't still be unmated. I know you. I know your desires. Your appetites."

At that, I turned. At the sight of her perfect naked body so close to Kolton's, a violent tremor shook me from head to toe.

"I know how hungry you get after a run," she continued, gliding even closer. "I feel the same way. I have all these *urges* and no one to help me with them. What happened to Rodney was unfortunate, but I understand why you had to kill him. You still want me for yourself. I'm sure Nora wouldn't mind sharing a little. After all, she doesn't know how to please you like I do. She can watch. I can show her *exactly* how you like it."

Sidling up to him, she had the gall to place her hand on his chest. But when she slid it downward and reached for his swollen cock— like she *owned* it—I saw red.

"MINE!" I roared.

Before she could touch him, Kolton grabbed her wrist and stopped her. But I was already moving. Already charging toward the seductress and yanking her around. When she saw the fury on my face, her eyes widened comically. I cocked back my arm and punched her square in the nose.

She went down *hard*. Blood spurted from her perfect nose. Well, not so perfect anymore. It was clearly broken.

"My *nose!*" she wailed, clutching her face.

Still boiling with fury, I grabbed her hair and yanked her head back. When her fear-filled eyes met mine, I snarled, "If you *ever* touch him again, I'll break more than just your nose."

Before I could make good on my promise right that very moment, I released her and stormed off into the woods.

"Nora!"

Kolton's voice only made me walk faster, until I was all out running. I ran without direction, fleeing the violent *rage* burning me up inside. I still saw red. Still craved to rip Jasmine to pieces. Her words—her blatant *touch*—were branded in my mind. They were a promise should Kolton choose not to accept our bond. Should he choose to *reject* me. There would be nothing left to stop him from going back to her.

"Nora, *wait.*"

Startled that he'd followed me, I almost stumbled. Catching myself, I said over my shoulder, "I'm sorry. I shouldn't have called you mine."

"Yes, you should have."

Nearly stumbling again, I forced myself to slow. "You don't really mean that."

"Yes, I do."

"You can't be mine if you don't even know what you want."

"I know what I want."

"Well, if it's Jasmine, I won't . . . I won't stop you from being with her."

Hell, if that didn't hurt to say. Like swallowing a mouthful of nails.

"I don't want Jasmine. I want you. You're the only one I'll ever want."

"Why are you doing this, Kolton?" I cried, unable to keep the anger, the *hurt* from my voice any longer. "Why are you torturing me?"

"Because I'm in *love* with you."

I stopped dead.

So did he.

Silence stretched between us. All I could hear was the frantic fluttering of my disbelieving heart. I must have heard wrong. Must have imagined the words into existence.

But I spoke anyway. Managed to say in the barest of whispers, "I thought you didn't want love."

"I didn't, but I couldn't help myself. Once I started to fall for you, it was over. Nothing I did could stop it from happening. The more I resisted, the more I wanted. Until I wanted *all* of you. Every last piece. I can't live without you, Nora. Can't *breathe*. I'm sorry it took me this long to admit how I feel, but I'm done running. Done denying what's between us. Done keeping parts of myself from you."

My chin quivered uncontrollably. This couldn't be real. I had to be hallucinating. He was saying everything. *Everything* I'd longed to hear.

"I'm yours, Nora," he continued, slowly stepping toward me. "Every last broken piece of me. You were right. My parents' fate doesn't have to be ours. I'm still terrified that it will, so terrified that I was willing to sacrifice my love for you. But I can't anymore. The pain of not having you is more than I can bear. So I've chosen to accept the risks. To accept *us*. No other outcome makes sense. Fate gave you to me. Who am I to reject such a precious gift?"

Tears blurred my vision.

He stopped again, this time directly behind me. Reaching up, he gently swept aside my hair, revealing the spot where he'd claimed me. When I felt his breath warm the spot, a shiver skated across my skin. "Nora Elizabeth Finch, you are so much more than a business deal to me. You are the air I breathe. My darkest craving and deepest desire. I want to be more than your alpha and husband. I want to be your mate. Your *soulmate*," he said, his voice thick with emotion. "Will you accept me?"

A strangled sob fled my lungs. Whirling, I threw myself at him, so forcefully that he staggered back. I openly cried, clinging to him with all of my might. "*Yes*. Yes, I accept you. I accept all of you, Kolton Anthony Rivers."

Relief rushed through me. So intensely. So powerfully that I knew, just *knew* the emotion wasn't mine. It was his. Kolton's. I could . . . I could *feel* him. Through every part of me. Not just my body, but in my heart. In the depths of my very soul.

CHAPTER 21

NORA

He kept looking at me. Every few seconds, he'd tear his eyes off the road to softly caress my face. There was so much love in every glance that my heart threatened to burst.

Not only that, I could *feel* his love. The emotion ran deep, deeper than I could have ever hoped for. It stole my breath and wrapped me in infinite warmth.

When Kolton placed his hand palm up on the middle console, I laced my fingers through his. Then grinned like an idiot at the way our hands looked twined together. Perfect. Like they'd been made for each other.

"So, I heard someone broke Jasmine's nose after the initiation," Griff said from the truck's backseat. "You two know anything about that?"

A faint smirk twitched Kolton's mouth. "Nora did it."

Biting my lip, I glanced back and saw Vi's face light up with shock.

"Our innocent little Nora?" Griff loudly guffawed, making Kolton's smirk widen. "Well, that's good news. And I'm guessing you two made up, based on all the googly eyes."

"Kind of like you and Vi?" I shot back, openly admitting that I'd seen them.

Griff choked. Vi's eyes widened even more. Wait, was she *blushing?* At least they were wearing clothes now, which made speaking about it a lot less creepy.

"Yeah, not quite like that," Griff said. "I can tell you're still very much a virgin."

Fair point.

"Speaking of," he went on, "may I suggest you two take that honeymoon pronto? I hear the mating frenzy is intense, and I have no desire to hear you two banging twenty-four-seven. Ow!"

"Still not your business, Griffin."

"I still say it is, Violet. Sex therapy falls under my job description."

"Frenzy?" I said. Too late, I realized my mistake.

"You don't know about the *sex* frenzy that all soulmates experience once the bond is complete?" Griff incredulously replied, gripping the back of my seat.

"Griff," Kolton lightly growled in warning. Which he completely ignored.

"Oh, you're in for the ride of your life, gorgeous. Literally. The ride being Kolton's—"

"*Gross!* Don't you dare finish that sentence, Griffin O'Neal," Vi yelled. "We are not discussing my brother's penis!"

"You said it, not me."

"*Ugh.* I don't know why I put up with you."

"Probably because you're obsessed with my—" He let out a loud *ooph*, then choked on laughter.

Despite my embarrassment—and growing alarm—I heard myself laugh. Earlier this week, I'd been terrified at the thought of going on a honeymoon with Kolton. Now, I wanted nothing more.

When Kolton lifted our joined hands to kiss my knuckles, I practically melted into a puddle in my seat. Griff was right. We needed to take that honeymoon as soon as possible. Every square inch of my being wanted to be Kolton's, in the worst of ways. Despite my innocence, I possessed a healthy imagination. The things I wanted him to do to me—the things I wanted to do to *him*—dominated my every thought. And I knew one thing for certain . . .

I did *not* want an audience.

Griff suddenly groaned, jarring me from my wicked thoughts. "That honeymoon can't come soon enough. You two *reek* of pheromones."

"GRIFF!"

I laughed again.

The minute we arrived back at the family estate, I knew something had happened while we were gone.

For one, Melanie came bursting out the front door. Not with a big, welcoming smile, but with a face covered in tears. "Kol," she sobbed, running to her big brother. He scooped her up with a concerned expression, asking her what was wrong.

My immediate thought was of the Blackstone Coven. I went on high alert, searching the grounds for any sign of them.

Brielle came outside next, looking more frazzled than I'd ever seen her before. She was pale, tightly hugging her arms to her chest.

"Where are they?" I said, hurrying up to her. When she stared at me blankly, my alarm grew. Pushing past her, I darted into the house.

"Nora!" Kolton shouted after me, but I didn't pause. I had to see them for myself. I had to stop them from hurting my *family*.

The second I crossed the door's threshold, I smacked into a hard body. My fight or flight instincts roared to the surface, and I blindly lashed out. Fist connected with flesh as I punched the intruder's face. They staggered back but didn't go down, giving me a clear view of their features.

"Arrow," I gasped, stopping just short of hitting him again.

Huffing a laugh, he straightened and rubbed at the sizable bruise already forming on his jaw. "Hey to you, too."

"Where are they?" I repeated, panicking when I spotted the wreckage behind him. The house was in shambles. Tables were overturned. Vases lay in pieces, shattered across the floor. Deep gouges decorated the walls, cutting straight through the plaster. Gouges that looked a lot like . . .

Claw marks.

My brain screeched to a halt. Then quickly reversed track.

"Where is he?" I hissed. Heat surged to the surface. Heat that had nothing to do with Storm's presence. This was *all* me. I was livid. *Furious.* How *dare* he come here. "Show yourself, Alpha Hendrix, you *coward!*"

Holy hell, I'd never spoken to him like that before. Not in a million years would I have ever dared. But now that I had . . . it felt *good*. Like the words allowed me to finally liberate myself from the abusive man who'd called himself my alpha.

"He's not here," Arrow said. "No one is."

Not comprehending, I blinked at him. "Then what happened? Who destroyed the house?"

"The little rugrat did. She went full-on demon last night. If I hadn't heard the commotion from the apartment, your human friend would have been toast."

Fresh panic pounded through me. "No," I whispered. Whirling, I burst outside again and beelined for Brielle.

Before I could reach her, Jagger was there. Jumping from an idling gray Porsche, he surged up the porch steps to grab one of her arms. I skidded to a halt and nervously watched as he ran his hands over her skin. First one arm, then the other.

"Any bites? Scratches?" he said, brushing her honey-brown hair aside to check her neck. "Even the smallest cut can be enough."

"No," she quietly replied, allowing him to thoroughly inspect her.

Then, "Arrow already checked me over."

At that, he froze. Then slowly straightened and stepped back. Only to cast a withering look at the open doorway. Not at me, but at the person right behind me.

"I thought you were warned not to step foot inside this house," he quietly growled at Arrow.

"I thought you were supposed to be watching a certain someone who shall-not-be-named," Arrow tossed back.

"Her caretaker returned this morning. I came back to check if you were *behaving*. Good thing too, since you obviously can't follow simple orders."

"Good thing I didn't, or the person you *really* came back to check on would be in pieces."

"Step away from my wife, Pemberton," Kolton interjected, his voice a low warning. Still holding Melanie, he took a threatening step forward.

Arrow loudly scoffed. "Really? You're worried about *me* right now? What about the little she-devil you're holding who tried to *eat* a helpless human last night?"

Melanie burst into fresh tears and pressed her face to Kolton's shoulder. He cupped the back of her head as she wailed, "I didn't mean to. I'm a bad, bad girl."

"We know you didn't mean to, Mellie," he told her softly, even as he pinned Arrow with a death glare. "You're not a bad girl. It was your first time shifting, and you simply lost control."

"It hurt," she whimpered, tightly clinging to his neck. "I don't remember making the mess. I'm sorry."

Remorse lined Kolton's face. "No, *I'm* sorry. I should have been more prepared for this to happen. I should have been here for you."

She sniffled. "It's okay. I knew that Nora needed you."

With a sigh, he hugged her to him and squeezed his eyes shut. At the sight, my heart turned over for them both. A part of me felt responsible. If not for me, she wouldn't have been left here to experience her first shift alone. But before I could bury myself in guilt for taking Kolton away from his family, he opened his eyes and gave me a look. One that said he knew *exactly* where my thoughts had just gone.

Stop. You aren't to blame, the look said. Then, *Come here.*

I hesitated, certain I'd misunderstood the look. But when he lifted his hand to crook a finger at me, I forced my feet across the porch and down to where he stood. When I stopped beside them, Melanie lifted her face to peek at me.

Sniffling again, she said, "I don't think I have a white light, Nora. I think I'm dark. And scary."

At the sad expression on her adorable little face, I wrapped my arms around her from behind. My face was inches from hers, resting on Kolton's chest. As we stared into each other's eyes, I whispered, "It doesn't matter what you are, Melanie. It matters *who* you are. And I think you're kind, sweet, and full of sunshine."

A grin stole across her rosy cheeks. She reached out and grabbed one of my curls. Then surprised me with a softly spoken, "I love you."

Emotion tightened my throat. "I love you too," I whispered back, pushing up to rub our noses together. I smiled when she giggled and clutched my curl like one of her stuffed animals.

Kolton adjusted his hold to slide an arm around me. When he pressed a kiss to my hair, I melted into the embrace. So this was what it felt like to be surrounded by family.

A family who *loved* me.

My heart filled to overflowing.

We spent the afternoon cleaning up Melanie's mess. It wasn't uncommon for inexperienced werewolves to shift inside their homes, but I hadn't expected this much destruction from someone so small. Everywhere I looked, something was damaged. She'd torn through all three floors like a wrecking ball.

Or rather, her demon familiar had.

"If you want to leave, I'll understand," I quietly said to Brielle, tossing another destroyed pillow into the garbage bag she held out to me. "This place isn't exactly safe for humans."

Not recently anyway.

The thought of her leaving saddened me, but I didn't want to traumatize her more than she already had been.

She snorted, sounding more amused than traumatized. "Even after all of our late-night dorm chats, a part of me still didn't believe the supernatural world existed. But after the terrifying night I just had, there's no denying how out of place I am here. Still . . ."

She scrunched her nose in thought, then blurted, "I want to stay. I've really missed you, and we've barely had a chance to catch up. Besides, my job lets me work remotely. They won't miss me for a few weeks. Plus, I kind of like all the excitement. Well, not the almost dying part, but the guys here are ridiculously hot. I wouldn't mind getting a little werewolf side action, if you know what I mean."

I hid a smirk, knowing that said guys could no doubt overhear her. Before she could blurt out more, I stepped forward and drew her into a tight hug. "I'm so glad you're here, Brie. I've missed our chats so much."

"Me too, bestie," she replied, squeezing me back. "Speaking of, do I sense something different between you and your hubby? A *good* something?"

A grin split my face. Not even caring who overheard, I said, "He told me he loved me."

Brielle squealed. Legit *squealed.* "Oh, Nora, that's the *best* news. I'm so happy for you!"

Before I could reply, footsteps came rushing into the room. Startled, I looked up, just as Vi barrelled into us. We all hit the living room rug in a tangle of limbs. As a flurry of loose pillow feathers poofed in my face, I burst out laughing. They both joined me, taking turns showering me with awkward hugs.

"It's about time that doofus told you how he felt," Vi said, plopping onto her back beside me. A fresh poof of feathers tickled my face. "I couldn't stand much more of the tension between you two. Your will-they-won't-they energy was sapping the life out of me."

Snorting, I flicked her a pointed glance. "Speaking of . . ."

"Nope. What Griff and I have is not remotely the same. You heard him at the bar the day before you left. He's too embarrassed to even admit that we hook up."

Brielle's head popped up from my other side. "You and Golden Retriever Eyes are a thing? Noted. I'll make sure not to hit on him then."

"No, go right ahead. I have no claim on him."

"Vi . . ." I softly began, sensing far more than her flippant words would suggest. But before I could say anything else, she forged ahead.

"No, I mean it. We've always been there for each other, but Griff and I aren't . . . we aren't *mate* material. I'm not, anyway. But you and Kolton are, and I couldn't be happier. How you handled the pack last night was nothing short of amazing. Storm was *fierce.* No one will question your right to be the alpha's mate after this."

I knew what she was doing. Knew that she was once again

slamming the door shut on the topic of her and Griff. I allowed it—for now—knowing that pushing her into talking wouldn't end well. Instead, I focused on the thrill her last words gave me.

Alpha's mate. I liked the sound of that. *Really* liked it.

As we got back to work cleaning the house, I daydreamed about the honeymoon Kolton and I still needed to plan. Now that he'd verbally accepted our mate bond, the desire to complete it was never far from my mind.

By the time evening rolled around, I'd worked myself into a frenzy. The only thing that kept me from seeking him out was the house full of people. Arrow had sequestered himself in the guest apartment, and Jagger had left right before dinner to resume watching Kolton's mom, but there were still far too many witnesses.

Plus, Kolton was too busy watching Melanie like a hawk. The full moon's pull would last for another night or two, and although she wasn't a normal werewolf, he'd decided that caution was best.

Which meant that we'd once again be sleeping in separate bedrooms. If we slept at all.

Knowing that Brielle didn't want to sleep alone tonight, I settled in for another night with my best friend. I thought for sure I wouldn't be able to sleep, but exhaustion from the pack run finally caught up to me. My head hit the pillow, and I was out like a light. But, as nothingness consumed me, a voice drifted into my subconscious. A dreadfully familiar one. One filled with malice and *hate*.

I see you, little wolf. Did you think I would forget about you?

CHAPTER 22

NORA

I awoke drenched in sweat, gasping for air.

Keisha, Keisha, Keisha.

My heart thundered to the sound of her name thrashing inside my head.

Barely able to breathe, I whipped back the covers and stood. Brielle muttered in her sleep and rolled over, oblivious to my inner turmoil. Not wanting to wake her, I silently padded across the room and slipped into the hallway, tiptoeing on autopilot toward Kolton's room. Only, he wasn't there. Of course he wasn't. He was still with Melanie, keeping an eye on her while she slept.

Unable to bear the thought of falling back to sleep, I kept going. Not back up to the third floor, but to the ground floor. My feet were silent, carrying me to the back patio doors and out into the night. A blast of chilly air struck my face, and I greedily gulped it down. Still struggling to breathe, I crept across the patio and down the steps. The pool glittered invitingly under the full moon's light, but I skirted past it.

If I couldn't be with Kolton, there was only one other thing that could soothe my frayed nerves. Every step closer to it helped ease the panic in my chest. The damp grass whispered beneath my bare soles as I hurried toward my place of solace. The moment I reached my destination, I noticed a few shrubs that needed tending to.

"Miss me?" I whispered to them, reaching out to pluck off a few dead leaves. The simple action further loosened the tension in my chest. With a relieved sigh, I threw myself into my task, grateful for the distraction. In no time, I was on my hands and knees, searching the soil for even the tiniest weed. The groundskeeper was way too good at his job. I could barely find a single one.

I was so immersed in my task that I barely heard the approach of footsteps before a voice was saying, "Not surprised to find you here."

Startled, I stood and whirled, ready to defend myself. When I caught sight of Arrow's white-blond hair shining brightly in the dark like an angelic halo, I lowered my arms.

"Why's that?" I asked, watching as he silently approached to stand a couple yards away. He still wore jeans and a t-shirt, but his feet were bare.

"Your celestial is an elemental. She's always had an affinity for living things, especially nature," he replied, studying me thoughtfully. "Did she never tell you?"

I glanced down at my dirt-encrusted fingers, suddenly feeling vulnerable. "I . . . Storm and I don't talk much." Clearing my dry throat, I glanced back up at him. "Why are you out here, Arrow?"

He shrugged. "Couldn't sleep. Not used to being in a bed. The wide open air helps me stay in the present."

I found myself nodding. "I get that. I just had a nightmare about Keisha. That's why I came out here. To get my mind off things."

He studied me a moment more, then quietly said, "I can help with that."

I frowned, suddenly uncertain. It was in the middle of the night, and I was alone with Arrow. Kolton would go ballistic if he knew I was out here with him. Still, curiosity got the best of me. "How?"

"I can teach you how to use your powers."

I stared at him as if he'd just told me I could fly. Wait. Could I?

"Your celestial is quite gifted, you know," he went on, smiling a little at my dumbfounded look. "She was second in command to the largest legion of archangels."

Holy. Hell. Mind blown.

Why didn't you tell me, Storm? I internally said, my voice filled with accusation. *That would have been useful to know.*

When she didn't respond, I wasn't surprised.

Still, I was frustrated and more than a little hurt. Especially when others knew more about her than *I* did.

Suddenly desperate to learn more, I said, "Okay, then. Teach me everything you know."

He slowly raised an eyebrow. "You sure? What will your *husband* think?"

Nothing good, I knew that much. He didn't even want me to *speak* with Arrow, let alone be trained by him.

"Let me worry about Kolton," I replied, hoping I wasn't making a huge mistake. "I just want to learn who I am."

"You mean *what* you are? I heard what you said to that little demon girl earlier. Do you really believe that?"

It was my turn to shrug. "Yes. I know you're big into the 'angels are good, demons are bad' thing, but I don't think it's that black and white."

A muscle thrummed in his jaw. Besides that, he didn't react. "And what does *Storm* think?"

I opened my mouth, only to snap it shut. Crap. He had me there. But as I recalled her behavior during my pack initiation last night, I firmly replied, "I think she's learning that there's more to people than meets the eye."

He huffed a laugh devoid of humor. "Well, for her sake, I hope life on Earth hasn't clouded her judgment. I'd hate to see her spirit permanently tainted."

I frowned again. "What does *that* mean?"

He clicked his tongue sympathetically. "She really *hasn't* told you anything. Celestial spirits are tied to either Heaven or Hell. Even when they come to the earthly plane in corporeal form, their spirits will return someday to the otherworld. Angels to Heaven. Demons to Hell. But an angelic spirit that strays from their righteous path is destined for ruin. If they didn't initially *fall* to earth, they most certainly will if their time here corrupts them."

My heart skipped several beats. "Fall? As in *fallen* angel?"

"Exactly. Although, we just call them Fallen."

Holy hell. Was *that* what Storm believed herself to be? A Fallen?

"How can you tell if an angelic spirit has fallen?"

"Violent mood swings. Selfish deeds. Unstable power. They're in a state of purgatory at first, riding the line of good and evil. Through toil and tribulation, they can redeem themselves. Or not. The direction they lean decides their fate."

"So, an angel can be cast into Hell?"

"Yes. If they fall beyond redemption. Lucifer himself was once Heaven's most powerful angel."

Wow. So, by spending time with werewolves who possessed demonic spirits, was I damning Storm's spirit? I shivered, unsettled by the thought.

As if sensing my turmoil, Arrow took a step forward. Lowering his voice an octave, he urgently said, "You don't have to stay here, Nora. I have leverage on Midnight Pack. Kolton will release you if I threaten to expose his secrets. I can take you somewhere safe, a place the Blackstone Coven will never find you."

I gaped at him, shocked by his bold words. "Arrow . . ."

"We can go right now while they're asleep. Then, when we're in a neutral location, we can schedule a meeting to absolve your marriage and obligations to the pack. They have the upper hand right now, so let's even the playing field."

"*Arrow.*"

"Kolton has no claim on you. He may have placed his mark upon your flesh, but his scent will fade. What matters is that you are still unmated. That means your marriage can be annulled and you'll be free to walk away. Come with me. I can keep you and Storm safe. It wasn't a coincidence that we were imprisoned together. We are fated, in this life and the next. We—"

"Kolton is my *soulmate*," I blurted.

I didn't know who looked more shocked by my outburst. Him or me.

"That's impossible." Even as he shook his head, there was no mistaking his horror. "You must be mistaken."

"She isn't," a new voice said, startling us both. Arrow went ramrod straight as Kolton materialized out of the darkness like a phantom shadow. "Nora is my mate, and I demand you step away from her before I rip out your treacherous tongue."

"I would listen to him, Arrowhead," another voice said. Griff slid into view, equally as silent. "Better yet, don't. I would enjoy seeing you choke on your own blood."

At their menacing approach, Arrow curled his upper lip in a silent snarl. For a dreadful moment, I thought he wouldn't budge. But when Kolton kept coming, he stepped back. Reaching me, Kolton firmly gripped my arm and tucked me behind him. As he squared off with Arrow, Griff stood guard by my side.

"She can't be your soulmate," Arrow said before Kolton could speak.

Kolton's hands tightened into fists. "Says who?"

"Says the Universe. Your earthly souls might share a bond, but the spirits you house could never. One is divine while the other is foul. Their fates will never intertwine."

"Says the man who rejected my sister simply because he thought himself superior to her. In my estimation, that makes you lower than scum."

Arrow scoffed. "If not for my superior *honor*, I would smite you where you stand."

"Honor? *Smite?* You are incapable of either. As was your father."

I peeked around Kolton, just in time to see Arrow's eyes flash a terrifying blue. Panicking at the sight, I slipped forward and planted myself between them.

"Stop. *Both* of you," I snapped, throwing my arms out to ward them off. Not that I could even remotely stop them if they chose to fight. Still, I held my ground. "Let's end this before things get any more heated. I'm going back inside now. I shouldn't have even come out here."

Kolton shifted on his feet but didn't make a move toward Arrow. "Why *did* you come out here?"

"Because she had a nightmare of her time spent with the witches," Arrow responded before I could. "Probably because she doesn't feel *safe* here."

"*Enough*, Arrow," I barked, even as a voice inside my head said, *It wasn't a dream.*

At Storm's softly spoken words, my insides turned to ice.

Kolton must have felt the swift emotional change because he was suddenly in front of me. "What's wrong, Nora?"

I opened my mouth, but nothing came out. A dull ringing began in my ears, growing louder by the second.

"What do you mean it wasn't a dream?" I whispered aloud to

Storm, hoping against hope that I'd heard wrong.

It's called astral projection. Only Oracles who have opened their third eye can perform this level of magic. Using her connection to the spirit plane, Keisha slipped into our subconscious while we slept. Our guards were lowered, and she used the opportunity to access our whereabouts.

What the hell? Witches could *do* that?

When I pressed trembling fingers to my mouth, Kolton captured my face between his hands. His expression was calm, the exact opposite of mine, as he said, "What does Storm know?"

This is my fault. With the amount of blood she consumed while we were imprisoned, I should have known Keisha could do something like this. I stole her physical eyesight, but her mental powers haven't dimmed. She must have forced a connection. A bond.

A bond?

A blood bond. Making it possible for her to commune with you on a deeper level.

At Storm's words, I trembled even harder. "I should have killed her when I had the chance."

You were merciful. There is no shame in that.

"Nora, speak to me."

Feeling Kolton's worry, I finally focused on him. "Keisha contacted me while I was asleep. She can track where I am through astral projection."

"Keisha?"

"The Oracle who tried to tear Nora apart with her bare hands," Arrow replied. "This is exactly why the coven needs to be silenced. They won't leave us alone until they get what they want."

Kolton's eyes flashed yellow. When my breath caught, he squeezed them shut with a muttered curse. Letting go of my face, he slowly reopened his eyes, the yellow fading to a dark amber.

"Now that Nora's initiation is complete, we can shift our focus to finding the coven," he said. "Until they're located, no one wanders off alone. Keep a sharp eye and ear out, and inform the others immediately if you sense anything amiss. The coven might know where we are, but they're leaderless. Without a head, the body is weakened."

"One vengeful witch can still do a lot of damage," Arrow pressed. "We're still in danger, especially Nora."

Kolton narrowed his gaze on him. "If you're so worried about Nora's safety, then I suggest you keep watch tonight. Shout if you see anything."

With that, he swept me into his arms and turned for the house. Surprised, I glanced back to find Arrow staring daggers at Kolton's retreating form. A quiet chuckle drew my attention to Griff, who was trailing us with a wicked smirk on his face. When he caught my look, he unapologetically winked.

Rolling my eyes, I focused on Kolton. Despite his sure strides, I could feel his continued worry. Not knowing what to do or say, I bit my lip and kept quiet. Only when we'd entered the house did I finally say, "Where are you taking me?"

"To my room," he firmly said. "From now on, you're not to leave my sight."

I blinked at the possessive growl in his tone.

When Griff chuckled again, Kolton shot him a look. "I need you to keep an eye on Pemberton tonight. Make sure he doesn't do anything reckless."

Griff sobered and nodded his assent. Turning, he slipped back outside.

"What about the others?" I said, trying not to panic. This had become real all too quickly.

"Vi is with Melanie. Brielle will be right above us. I'll hear if anything disturbs them."

I nodded, willing my thundering pulse to slow. When we entered his room, I asked, "Do you think Keisha would actually come here?"

He paused, then silently shut the door and carried me to his bed. Instead of setting me down, he sat on the mattress with me in his lap and leaned against the headboard. Only when I was comfortably situated did he say, "If she does, she'll wish for death before I'm done with her."

I shivered, oddly reassured by his words. He slid his fingers into my hair, and I snuggled against him, closing my eyes.

As my body started to relax, I whispered, "Do you think I belong here?"

His fingers stilled. "Yes."

"Even though our wolves come from such different worlds? Even though they aren't . . . compatible?"

"That never mattered to me. I think you belong where you want to belong. The rest will work itself out."

His words warmed my heart. Yawning, I sleepily murmured, "You called me your mate."

"I did."

At his easy response, a small smile curved my lips. "I liked hearing it."

"Me too."

My smile widened.

"Sleep, Nora," he whispered, gently winding a curl around his finger. "I won't let anyone get to you. Even in your dreams."

I believed him. I truly believed that our bond was strong enough to ward off Keisha. That his presence alone would keep her away.

With a relieved sigh, I allowed sleep to claim me, knowing there was no safer place to be.

CHAPTER 23

KOLTON

With the rising of a new day came the overwhelming weight of my responsibilities.

They pressed down on me more than ever. Down, down, down, demanding I bear their burden. Forcing my attention away from the woman currently sleeping in my arms, when all I wanted to do was make her fully mine.

I'd overheard what Arrow had whispered to Nora last night. Knew that he still wanted to claim her for himself. To what end, I wasn't sure. All I knew was that his presence here further amplified my need to complete the bond. To slam my cock inside Nora until she was thoroughly mated.

Until that happened, I was a ticking time bomb.

Every interaction with the male who wanted to poison Nora against me was rife with tension. If he'd been any other male, I would have challenged him by now. Would have gladly swept the floor with his entrails for having dared threaten my family's safety.

But Arrow Pemberton was a wild card. His power was unknown. If I tested his strength and it surpassed mine, my family would pay the price.

I knew he wouldn't hesitate to kill my sisters and mother if I fell—unless Nora stopped him. But, deep down, a part of me worried that she wouldn't. That she'd submit to him, on account of the bond their familiars shared.

Just the thought of her submitting to him, of allowing him to *claim* her, sent heat raging through me. Not wanting to wake her, I carefully slid out from beneath her and stood. The first thing I felt was my painfully swollen cock straining against my pants. Ignoring it as best I could, I shut myself inside the bathroom and started the shower.

Sharing a bed with my virgin soulmate would be the death of me. I couldn't leave her alone though, not after last night. Not after the fresh reminder of who still hunted her. Hunted *us*. Arrow wasn't the only threat I needed to worry about.

Despite my exhaustion, I mentally prepared myself for a day spent in Arrow's company. The deal Nora had struck with him sat heavy on my mind. Although I'd felt great pride at her willingness to take charge, I would have much rather bartered a deal in our favor. He was too close. Too *present*. I couldn't relax while he was near. Couldn't properly pursue my mate now that I'd accepted our bond.

Your dick in her pussy is all the pursuing your mate needs, Shadow unhelpfully supplied. *Now that you've finally come to your senses, why waste another precious second? She's in your bed, waiting for you at this very moment.*

Stifling a groan, I quickly shucked off my clothes and stepped into the shower. The water did little to soothe my overheated skin.

The self-righteous prick can wait. So can the witches. Focus on what you really want. Your sweet and delectable mate.

I endured Shadow's prodding, growing more and more accepting with each word. He wasn't wrong. The most pressing matters had been taken care of. Nora was now a respected member of the pack. Melanie's familiar was currently contained. Another full moon was waning. The threat that Arrow and the Blackstone Coven posed could wait for another day.

Now we're talking, Shadow purred. *Order the others away so we can slake our thirst.*

"Watch it," I quietly growled, not liking how possessive he sounded. "She's *my* mate, not yours."

He chuckled. *Of course she's yours. But I still enjoy it when you touch her. When you taste her.*

Unable to stifle a groan this time, I grabbed my hardened shaft and squeezed.

The second I did, I felt a presence. *Her* presence.

I turned my head and there she was, standing just outside the shower door. *Naked.* The sight stole my breath. When my cock swelled even more, I gripped it harder.

Her gaze dropped, then flicked back up to mine. "I obviously interrupted something important, so I can come back later if you want. Or—" Her lips curved into an impish grin, one that made my stiff cock twitch. "—I could help you finish what you started."

Shadow roared with laughter. *Oh, she's a clever one. You said the very same thing to her when your situations were reversed.*

I had. When she'd been in heat. My knees weakened as I recalled the memory of her pleasuring herself in that mountain-fed pool.

Roughly swallowing, I refocused on the present. On the *challenge* sparkling in Nora's eyes.

She wants to play, Shadow sang, his excitement matching mine. *She wants to play with her* mate.

Unable to deny her—not *wanting* to—I met her challenge breath for breath.

"Yes," I simply answered, already knowing how this would play out.

Sure enough, she lifted an eyebrow and said, "Yes, what? Use your words, Kolton."

I couldn't hold back a smirk. "Yes, I want you to help me finish."

Her grin faltered, as if she hadn't expected me to play this far. I could feel her uncertainty, but that didn't stop me.

Go on, I silently challenged her, my smirk widening.

Blinking rapidly, she said in a less confident voice, "Say please."

"Please," I immediately purred, then slowly pumped my shaft.

She gaped at the sight, watching as the tip engorged with blood. I did it again, then openly moaned when pleasure rolled through me.

At the sound, she jerked her gaze to mine and demanded, "Stop touching yourself."

My smirk grew wicked. "Say please."

When she remained frozen in place, I pumped faster. A clear challenge. One she rose to meet.

Ripping the shower door open, she stepped inside and grabbed my wrist. The second she said, "*Please*," I let go.

Now that she had my full attention, a flustered look crossed her face. She seemed lost. Wholly unprepared. Even so, she boldly met my gaze and said, "I know we're not truly alone, but I want to touch you. To *taste* you before life tears us apart once more. Will you let me?"

At her words, desire roared through me. It took every ounce of willpower not to crush her against the shower wall and claim her in every way possible. There was a reason I hadn't allowed her to touch me in the past. One simple touch was all it would take. One touch, and I would be branded. *Claimed.* No other female had that kind of power over me. Only Nora. If she touched me, there was no going back. I would be hers forever.

Except . . . I already was.

So, I held perfectly still and said, "I am yours, Nora. To touch. To taste. Whatever you desire, I will gladly give."

She stared at me for a long moment. I openly allowed her to see my sincerity. To *feel* it. I was hers for the taking. I wouldn't hold back this time. Wouldn't retreat or push her away. Releasing a trembling breath, she finally nodded. Then dropped to her knees. I sharply inhaled, rocked to my core. Humbled by the sight of this sweet angel kneeling before me.

Of her *submitting*.

Nothing could have prepared me for this. She was beautiful, so beautiful as she looked up at me with innocence in her soulful eyes. I held her gaze, wanting her to see how much I desired this.

Yours. Take what is yours, I silently encouraged her, gratified when she shyly bit her lip, then lowered her gaze.

At the sight of my cock inches from her face, she audibly swallowed and whispered, "Holy hell."

My smirk returned.

I was just about to make a teasing remark when she abruptly leaned forward and took me into her mouth. I jerked, sucking in a startled breath, then groaned as I felt her warm tongue slide over my swollen tip. Emboldened by the sound, she swallowed more of me. Her cheeks hollowed out as she sucked on the hard flesh, making me see stars.

My legs weakened, and I caught myself on the tiles above her head.

She abruptly pulled back, her mouth releasing my flesh with a wet *pop*. "I don't know what I'm doing."

At her vulnerable confession, warmth flooded my chest. "You're doing just fine, sweetness," I said, reaching down to cup the back of her head. To help guide her movements.

She followed my lead, opening her mouth once more to take me inside. I kept pushing, encouraging her to take more of me. To fill her mouth with my length. She obediently opened wider, allowing me to thrust my cock in deep. When her lips closed around my flesh, I marveled at the sight, taking time to savor the moment.

"That's my good girl," I purred, digging my fingers into her hair as she began to suck. To fill my body with utmost bliss. "You're doing so well." I slowly guided her head back and forth, making sure not to thrust too deep. I didn't want to choke her—not on her maiden voyage, anyway.

With each thrust, her confidence grew, until she was the one setting the pace. Loosening my grip on her hair, I allowed it. Allowed her to thoroughly pleasure me until I was overcome. Wholly undone. Humbled and awed by what she was doing. My control was hers. She was no longer submitting to me but I to her. I was ruined and remade as she freely gave another piece of herself. As she boldly claimed me as hers.

When my balls tightened, she reached up and gripped the base of my shaft. *Hard.* A wild thrill shot through me. I squeezed my eyes shut, blowing out a harsh breath. She increased her pace, her mouth and hand working together. Every inch of me trembled, on the verge of falling apart. Of unraveling completely.

"Nora," I panted, straining to hold back my orgasm. "Nora, I'm going to come." But when I tugged her head back, she leaned forward and took even more of me into her mouth. So deep that I hit the back of her throat.

Euphoria slammed into me. Jerking, I spilled my release with a guttural groan. It filled her mouth, and she didn't even flinch, taking every last drop.

As my climax ran its course, I forced my eyes open to watch her. Her own eyes were closed, as if she were wholly lost in the moment. She waited until the end, then slowly released me. I couldn't stop staring in awe.

This was my mate. My *mate.*

There was no denying that now. No going back. I had to see this through. Had to claim every last piece of her. Maybe not today, but soon. Soon, she would be mine in every way possible. Soon, we would be one flesh. One mind. One soul.

That moment couldn't come soon enough.

Feeling my eyes on her, she finally lifted her gaze to mine. Whatever she saw made her face flush red. My satiated dick twitched at the sight. God, I loved it when she blushed.

Clearing her throat, she whispered, "How did I do?"

A soft smile tilted my lips. "You were perfect, sweetness. Absolutely perfect."

CHAPTER 24

"We should meet with Nora's old pack. They knew about the coven before she was taken."

"Out of the question," Kolton immediately responded to Arrow's suggestion. "The alpha is the only one who knows anything, and the coward has gone into hiding."

"Then we should find him," Arrow countered. "Use some of that money of yours to track him down."

"Or," Jagger interjected when tension lined Kolton's body, "we could contact *your* pack and see who knows anything."

Now it was Arrow's turn to stiffen. "If you do that, the one who betrayed me could figure out that I'm staying here."

"So? You're still their alpha, right? Or did you lose your position when the witches took you?" Griff said from his spot at the kitchen island. He and Vi had claimed the two stools, while the rest of us sat in the main room of the guest apartment where Arrow was staying.

Well, except for Jagger, who was leaning against the wall with his tattooed arms crossed. Arrow was on one side of the large L-shaped couch, while Kolton and I sat at the other. Even Brielle had been allowed to attend the late-morning meeting. She knew practically everything anyway. She was in the couch's center, studiously watching us all like a referee at a game.

Arrow bristled at Griff's question. "My right as alpha hasn't been taken from me, but I've been gone for two months now. Who knows what the traitor has been up to since then. They might have turned the pack against me."

"Sounds like your problem, not ours," Vi said with a hair toss.

"Now, now, let's not forget our deal." Arrow slid a look her way, one devoid of warmth. When she went poker straight, I shifted on the couch, ready to intervene if the tension reached a boiling point. "You're stuck with me until the traitor is brought to justice. If you want me gone, then I suggest you make it your problem too."

Vi curled her lip at him but didn't say a word.

In the silence that followed, I heard myself speaking. Heard myself saying words I'd never expected to utter again. "I'll contact my parents and say I'm coming to visit. Alpha Hendrix is sure to come running back then."

Kolton's fingers immediately tightened around mine. Ever since the intimate moment we'd shared earlier this morning, he'd kept me close. So close that I'd practically been glued to his side. And his hands. His hands were never far away, touching me at every opportunity.

I still couldn't believe I'd done it. Still couldn't believe I'd had the courage to pursue him so openly. To submit myself before him and ask for what was mine. He'd tasted and felt so amazing. I never thought I'd enjoy such a thing, but I already wanted to do it again. To feel him tremble. To hear him groan. Knowing that I had been the cause.

He'd given himself to me so completely. Without hesitation. Without doubt. Without reservation. His willingness had quickly healed any lingering doubt. And the emotions pouring from him had filled my heart with joy. This was *real*. He really was well and truly mine. The only thing left was to take that final step. To unite our bodies as one and seal our mate bond.

I could hardly wait. The only thing stopping me from initiating it now was the people surrounding us. That and the pressing matter at hand. In the meantime, I'd have to make do with stolen moments, ones that drew us closer and closer together.

Like a cat curled up in a beam of sunlight, I basked in our current connection. The only reason why I wasn't on his lap right now was because we both needed to focus on the meeting. That and I didn't want to rub our closeness in Arrow's face. A sentiment that Kolton didn't share. The moment we'd sat down, he'd tucked me against him, making sure our legs were firmly touching. Then had possessively gripped my thigh a little higher than was publicly appropriate.

Arrow had glared at the sight, but hadn't commented.

"You don't have to do that, Nora," Kolton replied to my offer, knowing how strained things currently were between me and my old pack. "We'll find another way."

I shook my head. "It's the best lead we have right now. For all we know, Alpha Hendrix is still in contact with the coven. Besides, it's time I face him for what he did to me. I need closure."

"If he *is* still in contact with the coven, he could inform them of your visit. You could be walking into a trap all over again."

I chewed on my lip in thought. "I don't think he will. At least, not right away. I know him. He has too much pride to pass up a prime opportunity like this. His plans were ruined, and he was forced to hide from you. He'll want to take out his humiliation on me personally."

A low growl rumbled in Kolton's chest. "If he dares lay a *finger* on you—"

"I won't let him. I'm not the same person anymore. He can't hurt me, Kolton," I quietly said, trying to calm him.

His hold on my hand only tightened more, just shy of hurting. "I won't let you go alone."

"Then come with me."

"I can't. The second I see him again, I won't hesitate to kill him. Doing that would cost us our best lead."

"I'll go with her."

At Arrow's words, Kolton went preternaturally still. A blast of possessiveness surged through me.

Wow. That reaction was *definitely* not mine.

Before I could intervene, Jagger did. "Griff and I will go with her."

"And me," Vi spoke up, giving Kolton a pleading look.

"Me too," Brielle said, with such finality that I cracked a small smile.

Kolton looked around the room, staring at each of them in turn. He saved the longest look for Jagger. An unspoken message passed between them, one that had Jagger tilting his head in deference. In *obedience*.

Finally, Kolton's grip on my hand eased. Sighing, he replied, "I'll allow it. If only because killing Hendrix would require me to take over Nora's old pack, and I don't want their poor opinion of her polluting Midnight Pack. But we're *all* going, including Melanie. If Hendrix does contact the coven, I don't want anyone left unprotected. I'll keep my distance though, so long as I don't think any of you are in danger."

Relieved that he was going along with my plan, I leaned into him a little bit more. "That's settled then. I'll contact my parents, and we can leave first thing. Only, I could really use a new phone."

It was Kolton's turn to crack a smile. "I think that can be arranged."

The entire ride to my hometown, I was oddly calm. Maybe because there were so many emotions whirling inside me. Too many to sort out and name. I was almost numb. Detached.

Which, fortunately, allowed for better focus on the task before me.

As planned, Kolton, Arrow, and Melanie all hung back in one vehicle, while I drove ahead with Jagger, Griff, Vi, and Brielle. Despite my calmness, I knew that Kolton was still on edge. Enough that I'd worried he would change his mind at the last second. It was one thing to take risks on his own land, but we were venturing into enemy territory. Any number of things could go wrong.

Still, I was grateful when he didn't stop us. He'd pulled over on the stretch of road leading to my childhood home, allowing us to go on without him. We wouldn't be far, but far enough that Kolton might not be able to reach us in time if things went south.

Before we'd left the estate, he'd pulled Jagger and Griff aside for a private conversation. Although I hadn't been able to eavesdrop, I knew he wasn't taking any unnecessary risks with our safety. There was a good chance he'd told them to protect us by any means necessary if they caught even the slightest whiff of danger.

It was odd, thinking of my hometown as enemy territory. I'd always known my old pack was dangerous, but had never considered them my enemy. They were both now. A threat to the family that had found and accepted me. When we pulled into the driveway leading to my parents' farmhouse, I hardened my resolve. Today, even my parents were my enemies. If they forced me to choose between them and my new family . . .

They would be sorely disappointed.

Jagger stopped the truck at the end of the drive, not far from the mailbox. Even from here, I could see Alpha Hendrix's giant black Hummer parked by the house. But that wasn't what sucked all the air from my lungs.

It was my truck. My poor rustbucket pickup, now little more than a burnt-out metal shell. The windows had all been blown to pieces by the witches' magic attack. Fire had demolished the cab and melted the tires. The vehicle had been tossed aside next to my dad's broken heap of old farm equipment. It just sat there, painfully reminding me that I too had been tossed aside.

"I'm so sorry, baby," I whispered, loud enough that everyone turned my way.

"We can bring her back with us. Try to fix her up again," Griff said from the front passenger seat, realizing what had caught my eye.

Blinking back tears, I shook my head. "Thanks, but not this time."

The broken part of me was gone, as was my truck. I needed to let that part of me go. Let *her* go. She represented my past, and I didn't want to hold on to it anymore.

"Come on," I said, unbuckling my seat belt. "Alpha Hendrix is here. Let's get this over with."

Jagger threw the truck into park but didn't kill the engine. "Remember the plan, everyone. Unless I say otherwise, only Nora, Griff, and I leave this vehicle. Vi, keep a lookout for the witches. Warn us if you see or hear anything."

"I will too," Brielle said, not one to be left out.

I could have sworn Jagger smiled, just a little.

"Make sure you all come back in one piece," Vi ordered, giving all three of us stern looks. She stared the longest at Griff, who met her gaze with uncharacteristic solemnness. "Get the information we need, then get out. Don't pick any fights."

"Not unless he forces our hand."

"Griff," Vi warned, sounding more worried than annoyed.

His expression softened. "We'll be fine, Vi. It's Hendrix who needs to be worried."

"There he is," Jagger said. I jerked my gaze to the house, just as my old alpha emerged. At the sight of him, the blood in my veins started to boil. Crap, maybe Kolton wasn't the only one who wanted to kill him. Trying to calm myself, I reached for the door handle. Jagger and Griff beat me to it.

"Guys, *wait*," I hissed when they swung their doors wide and jumped out. I scrambled to follow them, but the damage had already been done. Alpha Hendrix took one look at Kolton's formidable second and third . . .

And bolted.

Cursing, I leapt from the truck and took off after him.

"Nora!" Jagger barked, making a grab for me and missing.

"We can't let him escape!" I shouted, picking up speed as I tore down the driveaway. Despite his age, Alpha Hendrix was already halfway to the treeline behind the house. He knew those woods like the back of his hand. He could easily throw us off his scent and evade capture, especially with evening fast approaching. The trees were thick, plunging the forest into premature darkness. He could hide in the shadows, even call for backup before we could find him. Before I could *face* him.

Storm, I need you! I inwardly yelled, completely ignoring my parents when they stepped outside the front door and gaped at the sight of me charging past. *Can you boost my speed without fully shifting?*

I can, she immediately responded, filling me with relief. Maybe she secretly wanted me to catch the bastard too.

A second later, pain shot down both legs. Startled, I nearly stumbled and fell. White fur sprouted over my legs as the bones began to shift, to *lengthen*. Lending me a powerful burst of speed. Of *strength*.

Thank you! I sang to Storm, pushing past the pain to focus on my new appendages.

Whoa, this was trippy. In a matter of seconds, my feet had transformed into paws and I'd grown several inches. Each stride I took was triple what I normally could run, making me eat up the distance between me and my target at an alarming rate. My upper half was human, my lower half werewolf, which probably looked really weird. At least I hadn't sprouted a tail through my shorts.

Barely able to suppress a grin, I raced forward, gaining on Alpha Hendrix. He didn't glance back once, too busy running with a metaphorical tail between his legs. He reached the treeline and vanished inside. I bounded after him, easily dodging trees and leaping over thorny bushes until only a few yards stood between me and my prey. With one last hurdling leap, I flew through the air and tackled him to the ground.

Dirt and pine needles exploded everywhere as we fell in a tangle of limbs. When he tumbled into a steep ravine with a startled cry, I dug my claws into the packed earth and skidded to a halt. As he hit the bottom with a jarring thud, Griff and Jagger caught up with me.

They had shifted too, their legs now like mine. Griff had managed to retain his shorts, but jet black fur had sprouted from several torn spots on Jagger's jeans. Right before my eyes, their legs began to shift back. Not wanting to lose my edge, I didn't bother to do the same.

As I prepared to slide down into the ravine after Alpha Hendrix, they each grabbed one of my arms. "He's *mine*," I growled at them, trying to yank free. "Let go!"

"We will, but only when you've calmed down," Jagger said, grunting when I managed to jab my elbow into his ribs.

"He can't escape us, gorgeous. Settle your wolf before he sees," Griff added, barely avoiding his own rib jab.

Still juiced up, it took me a moment to fully process their words.

When I did, I blew out a frustrated sigh and asked Storm to shift back. Then grumbled, "There. Can you let me go now?"

"Look at me."

I bristled at Jagger's command, unwilling to tear my eyes off of Alpha Hendrix, who was struggling to stand.

"Look at me or you're not going anywhere, Nora."

Gritting my teeth, I forced myself to drag in a calming breath and meet his gaze. His blue-gray eyes bored into mine. Searching. Assessing. With a sharp nod, he murmured, "Better. I'm letting go now."

The second he did, I stepped away, only for Griff to reel me in.

"Griff," I warned, glaring up at him when he pulled me close.

The sound of Alpha Hendrix lumbering to his feet reached my ears.

Still, Griff didn't relax his hold. "If you're going to be the alpha female of this pack, Nora, you have to keep a cool head. Kolton is entrusting you with the safety of his family. Can we count on you?"

Well, *that* instantly sobered me up.

"Yes. You can count on me," I quietly replied, even as my prey took off once more.

A slow smile curved Griff's lips. "Good. Then let's go hunting."

Excitement shivered through me, and I was suddenly smiling too.

Without a word, all three of us took off after Alpha Hendrix. As a unit this time. As a *pack*. While I went straight down the middle, they branched off to the sides. Flanking our prey. Corralling him.

I didn't bother asking for Storm's help this time. Alpha Hendrix didn't stand a chance. In no time, I was gaining on him. He glanced back. Just once. At the sight of me, his eyes rounded comically. He'd probably been expecting Kolton. Not *me*, of all people.

When I threw him a feral grin, he stumbled over a root and fell. Before he could get to his feet again, Jagger was on him. Alpha Hendrix growled and lashed out at him, but Jagger easily dodged the attack. When Griff arrived, I slowed, enjoying the sight of my old alpha trapped and helpless. Realizing he was surrounded, he surged to his feet and whipped out his phone.

"I have allies!" he bellowed, waving the phone in the air like a madman with a gun. "Ones that would love nothing more than to see the alpha of Midnight Pack fall. He can't withstand a dozen challenges at once. And when he falls, I'll make sure the rest of you do too."

I slowed even more, calmly replying, "And what allies would that be? I've never seen you so much as bat an eye at another pack, let alone form an alliance. I know you have *enemies*. Friends, not so much. You have no one to blame but yourself. Maybe if you'd bothered to protect your own *pack*, things would be different."

He sputtered, his face reddening. "You've forgotten your place, young lady. I will *not* tolerate you speaking to me this way."

"Haven't you heard?" Griff said, his arms loose at his sides as he carefully watched the agitated man. "Nora has officially been initiated into Midnight Pack. As our *alpha* female. She has every right to speak to you however she wants."

At the dumbfounded look on Alpha Hendrix's face, I wanted to howl with glee.

Finally stopping, I let the silence between us stretch before saying, "You underestimated me. Thanks to you, I underestimated *myself* for far too long. I allowed you to mistreat me. To talk *down* to me. But no longer. I know my worth now. I've been accepted for who I am. I've *grown*. You can't take that away from me, and I won't be controlled by you anymore."

His beard twitched with barely-restrained fury. "If you're so *self-assured* now, then why are you even here? Why return to a place where you're *unwanted?*"

Despite my resolve, it still stung. Still hurt to hear that my old pack didn't want me. But I hardened my jaw and replied, "I think you know why. You put me at risk by contacting those witches. You put my *pack* at risk. Be grateful my husband isn't here, or you'd be dead right now."

"I already told you. The coven contacted *me*. I only gave them what they wanted."

"Well, now you're going to give me what *I* want," I shot back. "How did they first contact you? Phone call?"

His face was almost purple now. I was shocked when he actually responded, spitting out, "Text."

"Jagger," was all I had to say. Alpha Hendrix sputtered out a weak protest as Jagger plucked the phone from his hand. "Thanks. I'll also need your password."

"Fine. Take it. Are we done now?"

I shrugged. "That depends on you. What else do you know about the Blackstone Coven? And don't bother lying. I'll know if you do."

His salt-and-pepper whiskers started twitching again. "Nothing. After you were taken, they stopped contacting me. I didn't even realize they no longer had you until today."

Well, *that* was surprising to hear. My parents hadn't ratted us out then. I'd thought for sure they would have after Kolton had called them, despite the guilt and threats. They normally told Alpha Hendrix *everything*.

Swallowing the sudden lump in my throat, I pressed, "I need names and locations. Anything they might have mentioned in your presence. No information is too small."

He flicked a glance at Jagger, then Griff. When they both stared at him expectantly, he said, "I wasn't given any more information. I didn't ask."

Anger heated my blood once again. "So you just let them take me, not even knowing what they were going to *do* to me? Not even—"

I cut off my words, struggling to remain calm. I couldn't let him get to me. Of course he hadn't cared what would happen to me. He was just relieved to finally be rid of the pack's bothersome disappointment. To have his *pride* reinstated.

"Go," I forced myself to say, the word like sandpaper on my tongue. "Leave before I change my mind and have Kolton tear you to pieces. But know this, Hendrix," I said, deliberately removing his title. "If you *ever* come after me and my family again, I will hunt you down. I'll humble you in front of the entire Underhill Pack so they can see just how weak and pathetic their alpha really is. And then I'll end you."

Holy hell, that felt good to say.

Even better was the look on Hendrix's face. There were no words to describe the shock, the disbelief, the *fear* I saw there.

Having said my piece, I crossed my arms and waited. Waited for him to skulk away like the coward he was. When he did, I could barely contain my relief. It trembled through me, filling me with adrenaline. Did that really just happen? Did I really just threaten to *end* the man who'd brutally scarred me, inside and out?

"That was wicked hot," Griff said the second we could no longer hear Hendrix.

"Griff," Jagger said with an eye roll, pocketing Hendrix's phone.

"What? You know it's true. Our little Nora has *fire*."

Jagger snorted, but I didn't miss the newfound respect in his eyes as he replied, "She does."

My chest warmed at their praise. I practically floated as we trekked back the way we'd come. We hadn't gained a ton of information, but it was a start. Plus, I'd received the closure I was after. Hendrix could no longer control me. I'd finally broken his hold.

You did good.

Startled by the words, words I'd never expected her to utter, I stayed silent for several moments. Eventually, a smile tugged at my mouth. Growing wider and wider with each passing second.

Thanks, Storm.

CHAPTER 25

NORA

I almost ignored them. Almost walked on by without a word, only pausing to slip on my discarded shoes.

Hendrix's Hummer was no longer in the driveway. In its place were two familiar figures, a man with graying red hair and a petite woman with aqua blue eyes. At my approach, they both nervously shifted on their feet. When I was nearly even with them, my mom blurted, "Nora, wait. Please. We . . . we need to tell you something."

I stopped. So did Griff and Jagger. They flanked me like two loyal guards. Two *overprotective* guards. Refusing to leave me alone, even with my parents.

Grateful for their support, I let them stay while I faced my parents.

Tears stained my mom's cheeks, and my dad looked uncharacteristically rueful.

"We should have protected you," my mom began, wringing her hands. "Both as a child and as an adult. You're our baby, and we . . . we failed you. We're sorry. So very sorry."

Just like that, my eyes started to burn. Not knowing what to say, I didn't say anything.

"Take us with you, Nora."

I blinked, struck dumb by my dad's words. "You know I can't do that. Your home is here. Your *pack* is here."

"Alpha Hendrix has become unreliable and weak. We don't feel safe under his leadership anymore. We want to join Midnight Pack.

We'll submit to your alpha. And you."

At the near desperation in his voice, I paused to inhale a calming breath. Then said, "I appreciate your words. Both of you. But I need time to think about it. You should too. Don't make any rash decisions."

Wow. Look at me, being the voice of reason.

They both nodded, respecting what I had to say. *Submitting*, even. Seeing them so agreeable was like stepping into an alternate universe.

When I moved to leave, my mom hurried forward and drew me into a tearful hug. The embrace was awkward but also . . . nice. Despite everything, I'd missed my parents. I would always care about them, even when they failed me. I returned the hug, blinking back tears before gently pulling away.

I left then, but not before giving them each a tentative smile. I needed time to think. To heal. Yet, my heart felt lighter as I walked away.

The moment I lifted my eyes, I saw him. My husband. My *mate*. He was standing beside the idling truck at the end of the long drive. At the sight, I broke into a run. He immediately strode forward to meet me. I threw myself at him, and he crushed me to his chest, burying his face in my neck. His relief hit me hard, mixing with my own. Wrapping my arms and legs around him, I held on as if I hadn't seen him in months.

"Hendrix left," he needlessly said, pressing soft kisses to the spot where he'd claimed me. In reply, I squeezed him tighter.

"You should have seen it, Kol," Griff said, coming up behind me. "Nora was *fierce*, a force to be reckoned with. Hendrix was putty in her hands."

"You would have been proud," Jagger added, stopping beside us to hold up Hendrix's phone like a trophy.

"I *am* proud," Kolton murmured against my neck, making me

shiver with pleasure. Then, more quietly, he said, "I knew you could do it."

My chin wobbled. "Thanks to you. You gave me the courage to stand up to him."

"No, sweetness," he whispered and kissed me again. "You found the courage all on your own."

The power of Midnight Pack never ceased to amaze me. Besides being the largest pack in the country, many of its members were wealthy or worked in high places. Sometimes both.

My latest amazement was learning that one of the pack members worked for the NYPD. After discovering that the coven had sent Hendrix *anonymous* texts, we decided to ask for his help. Vi had some hacking skills, but even she couldn't trace them.

"Darin's the best. If anyone can crack it, he can," Kolton said when Vi blew out another frustrated sigh. "There's nothing we can do at this late hour though. Let's call it a night and start fresh in the morning."

Besides Arrow, we had all piled into Kolton's study the second we arrived back at the estate. Then we'd watched with bated breath while Vi attempted to find a location behind the coven's texts. No such luck.

The texts themselves hadn't been fruitful either. All messages from the coven had been erased, due to the privacy app they'd used. Arrow had wanted to text the coven and pretend to be Hendrix, but Kolton had argued against it. The minute they knew it wasn't him, they'd cover their tracks again. A cautious, well-thought-out approach was the only way to catch them by surprise.

Arrow had all but stormed off, clearly not happy that his idea had been shot down. Up until recently, I would have agreed with him. But now, I saw the wisdom of Kolton's methodical approach to things. It left less room for error.

"I guess," Vi responded to Kolton's suggestion, reluctantly setting Hendrix's phone on his desk. "I could use a drink though. Anyone want to join me in the den for a nightcap and movie?"

"Me," four voices chorused at once.

Brielle, Jagger, and Griff all turned to Melanie with amusement.

Kolton crossed the room and scooped her up. "*You* are going to sleep. It's way past your bedtime."

"But I'm not tired," she protested, then shrieked with laughter when he tossed her over his shoulder fireman style and strode from the study.

I smiled, staying where I was as the rest filed from the room.

"You coming?" Vi asked, pausing when I didn't follow.

I shook my head. "I could use a moment to myself. It's been a long day."

She nodded her understanding, casting one more look at Hendrix's phone before joining the others.

When silence settled over the room, I released a pent-up sigh. I hadn't been alone all day, and a moment to myself was just what I needed. Unlike them, I'd practically grown up alone. Spending so much time with this many people was overwhelming, even people I thoroughly enjoyed being with.

Hoping no one would notice, I slipped into the foyer and out the front door. I wouldn't go far this time. Kolton was still acting uber protective and didn't want any of us to wander off alone. But I needed some fresh air. Some *space*. I couldn't think otherwise. Couldn't process everything that had happened today.

Deciding that the porch was as far as I should go, I sat on the top step and looked out into the clear night. I could easily pick out a patchwork of brilliant stars and the waning moon. With the start of September, the leaves were already turning. Normally, I would need to wear a sweater on cool evenings like this. But those days were gone. As with all werewolves, my blood ran hot. The chill air didn't bother me in the slightest.

As I sat and pondered over the day's events, my mind kept drifting back to Storm. To the way she'd helped and spoken to me. Not just today, but during my initiation as well. She'd looked out for me. She'd acted . . . like she *cared* about me.

Daring to hope, I disrupted the silence to say, "Thanks again for helping me with Hendrix today, Storm."

As usual, she didn't respond right away. But, just as my little kernel of hope started to crumble, she replied, *You're welcome.*

Hope rose once more. I bit my lip, scrambling to think of what to say next. When it came to me, I grabbed my wedding band and nervously twisted it. *Don't do it. She'll go into hiding again,* I told myself. *You'll ruin all the progress you've made with her.*

But I had to. I had to *know*. I'd wanted to know for so long.

"That day," I began, trying to keep the tremor from my voice. "The day Hendrix almost killed me as a child. Why didn't you help me?"

She didn't speak for several moments. But eventually, she said, *Back then, I was too wrapped up in my own self pity. I didn't see you.*

I blinked, wholly caught off guard by her confession. It stung. At the same time, it made a lot of sense. Forging ahead, I replied, "And now?"

I see you. More and more each day.

Tears welled in my eyes, and I hurriedly blinked them away. "I never asked before, but why are you here, Storm? Why did you come to Earth?"

Silence stretched. For so long that I didn't think she would answer. And then, *It wasn't by choice. I . . . fell.*

Oh, wow. And there it was. She hadn't *decided* to become my familiar. She'd been cast from Heaven and thrown into my body. Her melancholy behavior suddenly made all the sense in the world.

She was in purgatory. *I* was her purgatory.

Pain gripped my chest. Struggling to breathe, my voice shook as I asked, "What happened? I mean, you don't have to tell me. I just know that it helps me to talk things out with someone I trust. Not that you trust me, but I hope you do. I—"

For several millennia, I served under the command of Zuriel, she began. I quickly snapped my mouth shut. *I was but one of thousands who served under his leadership. Every archangel's duty is to safeguard the wellbeing of mankind, and each archangel has a different task. Zuriel's was to protect humans against evil spirits. Mine was to nurture and heal. For many millennia, he barely noticed me. I performed my duties in obedient silence, only coming forth when needed.*

And then one day about a century ago, he recognized my strength. I was suddenly promoted as his second in command. Everywhere he went, I went. He taught me skills beyond my natural abilities. Taught me to fight and defend. Soon, my power grew, until our entire legion recognized Zuriel and me as a bonded pair. Our strength was different, yet seen as equal, and I owed it all to him. So, I pledged my eternal loyalty to him.

I stopped breathing, clinging to every word she uttered. The way she spoke, it almost sounded like Zuriel was her *soulmate.*

But about three decades ago, things started to change, she went on. *Zuriel was no longer pleased with my performance. Everything I did upset him. I didn't understand why at first, but as time passed, it became clear that I was to blame. My power was surpassing his. When our legion started looking to me for orders more than him, he finally put his foot down. He sentenced me to Earth. I was to serve out my punishment until he saw fit, sacrificing a piece of my spirit by taking on a corporeal form. In doing so, balance would be restored. But . . .*

I disobeyed. For the first time in my long existence, I ignored a direct order. I didn't want to go. I didn't want to be separated from my legion. From him. His fury at my disobedience was absolute. Like a coward, I hid from him. When I finally reemerged, he was gone. Once again, I was to blame. My disloyalty drove him away. Drove him to do the very thing I was supposed to do. A few years later, Heaven cast me out for my treachery. So here I am, cut off for my faithlessness. Destined for an eternity as a Fallen. Or worse, should I fail to redeem myself.

When she was done, I gaped, speechless. Her story was utterly surreal. And heartbreaking. How could Zuriel do that to her? How could *Heaven* do that to her? It was so unfair. All she had wanted was to be loved and accepted, kind of like . . .

Like me.

"Oh, Storm," I whispered, not bothering to hold back my tears this time. "I am so sorry. You didn't deserve this fate."

Thank you, Nora, but disobedience in my world isn't tolerated. I knew this and now must face the consequences. I didn't expect to see Zuriel again though. At least, not like this. His presence here . . . complicates things.

I sat up straighter, brushing the tears from my cheeks. "How so?"

Despite everything, I am still loyal to him. When his host asked you to leave with him last night, my first instinct was to obey.

Every muscle in my body tensed. "But what about me and Kolton? What about our place here in Midnight Pack?" Pain suddenly tightened my chest. "Or is staying here . . . being this close to demon spirits . . . harming you?"

A pause. Then, *I once thought so, but I'm not so sure anymore. You were right earlier. I'm beginning to see that not everything is black and white. So do not fret, child. I won't take you from your soulmate. At least, not willingly. But I can't say the same for Zuriel and his host. You will do well to be cautious.*

My eyes widened in alarm. "Do you think Vi is right? Do you think Arrow came here for reasons other than what he's telling us?"

I wouldn't doubt it. Zuriel is extremely ambitious. If his host is anything like him, then he might have ulterior motives.

Crap. I should warn the others. I should—

Please don't tell anyone that I have fallen, especially Zuriel. I am . . . I'm ashamed of who I've become.

At the vulnerable tone in Storm's voice, something I'd never expected to hear, my heart turned over for her. "I won't. I promise. Your secret is safe with me. But, for what it's worth, I think you're pretty awesome."

"Who's awesome?"

At the unexpected voice, I jumped to my feet. Heat blasted through me as Storm surged to the surface. I was just about to let her take over when a familiar figure slid into view. Arrow sauntered toward us, hands in his pockets as he took in our defensive stance. Meeting my eyes, he hiked his brows in surprise.

"Well, well. It's good to see you again, *Storm.*"

Struggling to hide my sudden wariness, I said, "Why do you always say her name like that?"

He shrugged, halting at the base of the steps. "Because it's not her name. Not her *real* name anyway."

Curiosity got the best of me. "Then what is?"

"Seraphina."

I could have sworn I felt a swift stab of pain. Pain that wasn't mine.

Resisting the urge to rub at the phantom wound, I said, "That's a beautiful name."

"It means fiery. Burning one. Seraphina is The Purifying Angel and Goddess of Wild Nature. Her healing power is legendary among our kind."

Intrigued, I allowed my guard to slip. Just a little. Now that I knew some of her story, I was starving for more. "You said she's an elemental. Which one?"

Arrow's lips twitched into a faint grin. "All of them."

My jaw dropped. "All? As in, *all* all? Earth, Air, Water, and Fire?"

"She can command all four elements, yes. But her affinity is Earth."

Before I could stop myself, I blurted, "Show me."

He huffed a laugh and crooked a finger at me. Descending the steps, I eagerly stood before him like a kid about to receive candy. I could feel Storm stirring restlessly just beneath my skin, but she didn't comment. Didn't stop him from grasping my hand and flipping it palm up.

"Magic is most easily wielded with our hands. No matter which element you choose to work with, you will direct its power to your fingertips. Witches teach their young how to use magic this way. But, unlike them, we contain a greater store of power."

"Because of the unique connection we share with our familiars?"

"Yes. Although their spirits are no longer whole, they are fully contained within one body. That allows for a fuller range of power."

Excitement shivered through me. "What do I do?"

"Intention is key. *Will* the magic to your fingertips. It's a part of you, simmering in your veins like blood. Envision the magic leaving your body. Focus on the area you want it to exit, which would be your hand. Close your eyes and form the magic into existence."

I did as instructed, squeezing my eyes shut to better concentrate on my task.

"Call out to your celestial for help. She has wielded this power for thousands of years. Your body is but a vessel for the magic to live inside."

I focused harder, asking Storm for guidance. I'd only seen evidence of her power a few times, but I knew she was capable of so much more. The magic inside of us both was a dormant volcano about to erupt. Energy suddenly zapped through my body, traveling down my arm and out through my fingertips.

Arrow whooped, startling my eyes open. I glanced at my hand and gasped. It was glowing white. Pure white. Losing my concentration, the light abruptly winked out, leaving behind a metallic scent.

Magic. I'd just performed *magic*.

"Did you see that?" I breathlessly asked, touching my palm. It was barely warm. No sign of the magic remained.

"You bet I did," Arrow said with an excited laugh, then grabbed my face and kissed me. *Kiss* kissed me. Full on the mouth. His lips moved against mine, urging them to respond to his. To *accept* the kiss.

I pushed him away, so fast and hard that he stumbled backward.

"What the hell was *that?*" I burst out, stopping myself from shoving him again. From *hitting* him.

He raked his fingers through his hair. "I thought we were having a moment."

"A moment? I was letting you *train* me. Never once did I express an interest in anything more."

Agitation crossed his face. "Nora, I'm sorry. I didn't mean to upset you."

"Well, you did. You *really* did. This training session is over. *Goodnight*, Arrow."

CHAPTER 26

NORA

I stormed through the front door, my anger mixing with desperation.

I needed to see him. I needed to see my *mate*.

As I hurried up the stairs, I heard my name called. I didn't even pause, focused on only one thing.

Kolton, Kolton, Kolton.

His name was a chant inside my head, spurring me onward until I was taking the stairs three at a time. When I reached the third floor, I set my sights on the far end. On Melanie's room. The door was closed. As I reached for the handle, I forced myself to slow. To open the door gently. Quietly. Once it was open, I burst inside. Only to halt in my tracks.

Inside the frilly pink room, fast asleep on the canopy bed, was Melanie and Kolton. She was snuggled up against him, her favorite stuffed unicorn tucked beneath her chin. He'd obviously been reading to her and had dozed off halfway through. Couldn't blame him. He hadn't exactly been getting much sleep lately. His face was relaxed, free of stress and worry as he held his baby sister.

Never in my life had I seen a more precious sight.

Suddenly overcome with emotion, I inhaled a trembling breath. Loud enough that Kolton stirred in his sleep. Not wanting to wake him, I eased back a step. But before I could shut the door, his eyes opened, immediately finding mine. I froze, watching as he carefully slid out from beneath Melanie and rose from the bed.

"One more story," Melanie murmured in her sleep, squeezing the stuffed unicorn.

Kolton smiled and bent to kiss her forehead. Setting the children's book on the nightstand, he straightened and crossed the room. The closer he came, the more my body trembled. Yet, I made myself take another step back so he could exit the room and shut the door.

The moment he did though, I lost all composure. Reaching up, I grabbed his face and kissed him. *Hard.* With all of the turbulent emotion brewing inside me. The second our mouths met, the emotions erupted. They spilled out in a mess of desperate gasps and frantic clashing of lips. I kissed him like I never had before, needing to feel his warmth. Needing to taste him. To breathe in his scent. To bathe myself in his essence.

He eagerly met my kisses, banding his arms around me to lift me up. To draw me closer. So close that our bodies might as well have been one.

But they weren't. They *weren't.* And that was the problem.

"I can't wait anymore," I said against his mouth, trembling almost violently now. "I need to be yours in every way."

When he stilled, I almost cried out. Almost *begged* him to take me.

"What's wrong, Nora?" he said, pulling back to search my face. I internally wailed, close to tears.

"N-nothing," I replied, my teeth chattering. "I just . . . I *n-need* you. I need you to—"

When I cut myself off, worry filled me. *His* worry. I froze as he leaned forward and deeply inhaled, then jerked back with a low growl.

"Why do I smell magic on you? And why do I smell *Arrow?*"

Ah hell. I should have known he'd be able to scent him on me.

When I hesitated, Kolton growled again. An influx of emotions blasted me, all of them his. I flinched, and the emotions amplified further.

"What happened?" he demanded, the words barely containing his rage.

I tried to look away, and he grabbed my chin, forcing my eyes back to his. "Kolton . . ."

"Tell me, Nora. Tell me before I rip off his—"

"He kissed me."

Shock pierced my chest. Then pain. Then wild fury.

Kolton's eyes burst into yellow flames. "I'm going to kill him. I'm going to—"

"*Don't,*" I cried, a little too forcefully. "Please don't. I asked him to teach me magic, and he got the wrong idea. He knows now that I'm not interested. I'm sorry. I should have been more careful around him."

"It's not your fault, Nora. This is on him. He deliberately tried to take what's mine, right under my very nose. I can't allow this grave violation. I must challenge him."

My eyes widened in horror. "No. Kolton, *please.*"

Resolve hardened his jaw, and he released me. I tried to pull him back, but he was already storming for the stairs. Terror gripped me.

"Kolton, you *can't.*" I raced after him, only to slam to a halt as he drew up short.

"Step aside, Jagger."

"No."

Shocked by his second's direct disobedience, I peered around Kolton to see not only Jagger blocking the stairs, but also Griff, Vi, and even Brielle.

Every inch of Kolton stiffened. "Want to repeat that?"

At the deathly soft warning in his voice, I broke into a cold sweat.

"I said *no*," Jagger repeated, his resolve just as firm. "You can't challenge Arrow. Not like this. You're too emotional. Too *distracted*. Don't make me remind you of how dangerous that combination is in a fight."

A fresh wave of Kolton's pain struck me, knocking all the air from my lungs.

"Jag is right, Kolton," Griff added, his expression dead serious. "As much as I'd love to see you eviscerate Arrow, you'd be risking us all by fighting him like this. Save that fury for another day, brother."

More pain. So much that I couldn't hold still a moment longer. I slipped forward and tucked myself against him. At the press of my body against his, he blew out a trembling breath and folded me into his arms. I melted into his embrace, resting my cheek against his thundering heart.

The hallway fell into silence.

Then, Vi quietly said, "It's time."

Kolton released another ragged breath before replying, "Time for what?"

"It's time for you to seal your mate bond."

Kolton stopped breathing. So did I.

"*Tonight*," she added with finality.

"Vi . . ."

"Don't *Vi* me, big brother. We all know the only reason why you haven't yet is because of us. But enough is enough. If you want to take care of this family, then you must take care of yourself first."

"But I have a duty to—"

"Your *mate*. Your pack and family can do without you for a day. We can protect each other while you're gone. Your responsibilities will be right where you left them when you return."

"Return?"

"Yes, return. You both are leaving. I don't care where. Just *go*."

A tiny flare of amusement trickled through our bond. Still, he hesitated, clearly warring with his sense of duty and need to protect.

So, I looked up at him and said, "The cabin. I want a wedding night do-over." When he glanced down at me in surprise, I gave him a small smile. "It's only an hour away. We don't have to be gone long."

Griff snorted. "Long enough to get the mating frenzy out of your systems, please. We don't need to be exposed to all of that."

Vi whacked him in the stomach.

The hard planes of Kolton's body slowly started to relax. "One day. That's all we can afford right now."

I bit my lip. "One day will work."

When his eyes suddenly lit up again, this time with unbridled desire, a swallow got stuck in my throat. Holy hell, was this really happening? Was I *finally* going to lose my virginity? To none other than Kolton Rivers, the hottest alpha, husband, and mate in existence?

I hoped so. I *really* hoped so.

My own desire raced through me, and Kolton's eyes flared brighter.

Soon, they clearly promised. *Soon, you will be mine in every way.*

I'd expected Arrow to storm from his apartment the second he found out we were leaving, but he didn't emerge. Probably realizing how thin the ice he stood on was after the dick move he'd pulled. Good thing too. Kolton's emotions were everywhere. Or maybe they were mine.

I couldn't tell them apart anymore. They were too intense. Too *identical.* I could barely focus on anything else.

As we left the estate behind, our combined energy swam through my senses, making me hyper-aware of the man beside me. The energy practically leapt from my skin, filling the cab with electric pulses.

Several minutes into our trip, Kolton finally broke the silence. "I'm sorry."

I blinked in confusion. "For what?"

"For putting you in this position again."

"Again?"

"This isn't the first time we've made this trip, Nora. I didn't want it to be like this. Not this time. I wanted it to be special."

Understanding now, a huge grin split my face.

He glanced over and saw, clearly the confused one now. "What?"

Still smiling, I said, "The first time we made this trip, I was scared out of my mind. You were a complete stranger, and I half expected you to murder me and dump my body in the woods." At the frown he gave me, I laughed. "Since then, I've grown to know you. To respect and trust you. You gave me a second chance at life. A new beginning. You gave me protection, strength, compassion, and purpose. You gave me *love*, and I've never been so happy in my entire life."

He blinked several times, as if he couldn't quite believe the words I'd said. "You're happy?"

"So very happy. Which is why this trip is special. I want to be one with you. I *crave* it. Where or how that happens isn't important to me. I just want to be with my soulmate."

His throat worked, like he was having a hard time swallowing. I waited while he processed my words and his emotions, but I didn't have to wait long. Reaching over the middle console, he grasped my hand and lifted it to his lips. With a featherlight kiss to my knuckles, he murmured, "Then be with me you will, sweetness. It would give me no greater pleasure."

The soft press of his lips was electricity beneath my skin. His *words*, however, ignited a fire within, one that threatened to burn out of control. I squeezed my legs together, desperate to reach our destination before combusting.

I felt Kolton's lips on my skin twist into a devilish grin. "Do my words arouse you, wife?"

I squirmed in my seat, silently cursing him for goading me on. He knew. He *very well* knew what his words and touch did to me. "Maybe."

Goosebumps erupted over my flesh as he quietly chuckled. "I can keep going if you'd like. We have an hour to kill before I put those words into action."

Holy hell, I was so screwed. I was going to orgasm in this truck if he didn't stop.

Struggling to compose myself, I didn't respond. Which he took as a green light.

"As an alpha, I like to dominate," he purred, sensually brushing his mouth over my knuckles. "This pertains to the bedroom as well."

Yup. I was screwed. I could already feel myself growing wet.

"But first," he continued, "I like to pursue my prey. To hunt. To *chase*." He grinned against my skin again. "To capture."

Trying not to give away how turned on I was, I tartly replied, "Is that all I am to you? Your prey? Your *plaything*? To be hunted down and consumed by you?"

His grin widened. "For tonight, yes. And every night that follows. You are mine to hunt, Nora. Mine to *consume*. I relish the thought of pursuing you for the rest of our lives together."

Oh. Oh my.

I was now a puddle in my seat. Any more of this exquisite

torture and I'd be nothing but vapors. Somehow, I managed to hold it together though. Somehow, I survived the next hour without turning into a drooling mess.

I had it *bad* for him. So bad that, as we pulled up to the cabin an hour later, every part of me ached to be dominated by him.

But the alpha part of me wanted to challenge him first. To make him *work* for my submission. I wasn't going to hand it to him on a golden platter.

He had to *earn* it.

So, the second he killed the engine, I was out of the truck in a flash. Like a deer, like *prey*, I shot into the woods at breakneck speed. A moment later, an excited howl lit up the night. And then . . .

He took off after me.

Resisting the powerful urge to laugh, I focused my energy on the ground before me. On making sure I gave my mate the chase of a lifetime. Although the woods were nearly pitch black, my night vision allowed me to pick out every rock, bush, and tree. A frightened rabbit skittered out of my way, but I didn't pursue it. Neither did Kolton.

This hunt was different. It wasn't about food. It was about primal need. Lust. *Desire.* The carnal instinct to consume flesh of a different nature.

I'd been chased before, but not like this. This chase filled me with excitement, not fear. I *wanted* to be caught, knowing that pleasure instead of pain awaited me. But that didn't make me slow. I wasn't going to make this easy for Kolton. If he wanted to catch me, then he needed to prove himself worthy of doing so.

So I continued to dash through the forest, using every last ounce of supernatural speed I possessed. I could have called on Storm for help, but this moment was solely for me and my soulmate. Only he and I existed right now. A sentiment that he too seemed to share. Not once did I hear him lengthen his stride beyond that of his human form. He pursued me as Kolton, dogging my every step with clear determination.

It was only a matter of time before he caught me, though. I was much faster and nimbler than I used to be, but his raw male strength still far surpassed mine. Sure enough, after several minutes of nonstop running, my stamina started to fade. Behind me, Kolton's pursuit became more and more clear as he gained on me. At the realization, he released another throaty howl.

I laughed this time, panting heavily as I scrambled up a steep hill. When I reached the top, I made the mistake of looking back. One glance was all it took. Directly at the bottom of the hill stood Kolton. At the sight, I froze. He did too. We stared at each other for a long moment, our breaths loud in the silence. And then . . .

He whipped off his shirt.

Holy hell. He looked scrumptious enough to eat. His skin glistened with sweat. Every muscle was engorged from the run, rippling over his arms, chest, and stomach. I ogled him for a moment more, then tugged off my own shirt. I let it fall to the ground, standing in just my bra and shorts. Even from here, I could hear his heart skip several beats.

A slow grin spread across my face.

When I tensed, ready to take off again, he crooned, "Come here, mate. The chase is over."

I barked a laugh. "Says who? The *loser* at the bottom of the hill?"

I shivered at the feral smirk he gave me. "Careful, sweetness. I might have to punish you now."

Oh, I liked the sound of that *way* too much.

"Only if you can catch me," I threw back.

"Oh, I will," he said, a wicked gleam entering his dark amber eyes.

"And when I do, I'm going to make you scream my name."

All the air stuttered from my lungs.

He suddenly lunged up the hill, so fast that I shrieked and nearly fell backward. Scrambling to right myself, I took off again. When I heard Kolton reach the top seconds later, my heart leapt into my throat. He was serious about capturing me now. *Really* serious. The playful hunt had just become a wild obsession.

He tore after me at a breath-stealing pace, not giving me an ounce of mercy. Each second that passed, I lost more and more ground. Until I could practically feel him breathing down my neck. I started to zigzag around trees, desperate to evade his clutches. But he tracked my every move, a predator about to strike.

One false move was all it took. I went left when I should have gone right. Just like that, he tackled me. I yelped and braced for the fall. The ground rose up, but he twisted at the last second, softening the blow by rolling us. Before I could wrench myself away and escape, he firmly pinned me beneath him. When I struggled, he grabbed my wrists and pressed them into the carpet of pine needles above my head.

Thoroughly captured, I finally stilled. Finally looked up at him and said, "You got me."

Grinning like a fiend, he panted, "I did."

"So, now what?" I said, trying to catch my own breath.

"So . . ." he said, releasing one of my wrists to tenderly touch my cheek. "Now you're mine. Mine to claim. Mine to pleasure. Mine to love in every way possible."

My lips trembled. "So I am. Take what is yours then."

He searched my face for a long moment. Then quietly said, "Are you sure? You can still change your mind. You can still walk away."

I huffed a laugh and shook my head. "That's where you're wrong,

Kolton. It's far too late for that. I don't want to be with anyone else but you. I can't. Because . . ."

"Because?"

I bit my lip, then whispered, "Because I love you."

CHAPTER 27

NORA

I thought my profession of love would shock him. I couldn't have been more wrong.

Smiling softly, he stroked my cheek and murmured, "I know. It's why I had the courage to tell you how I felt. It's why I had the strength to accept you and our bond. Your love is powerful, Nora. You give it with your whole heart, and I couldn't help but do the same."

My lips trembled again, and he lowered his head to kiss them. Gently. Tenderly. With so much love that my heart swelled inside my chest. He slowly deepened the kiss with infinite care, kissing me as if for the very first time. As if I was a rare flower he could coax into blooming.

So I did.

I bloomed for him, opening my mouth to accept him inside. His tongue reverently touched mine, sweeping over every inch until heat filled my body. He pulled away, only to trail soft kisses down my neck. To the spot where he'd first left his claim on me. When he nuzzled the spot, I reached up and slid my fingers into his hair. Encouraging his closeness. Encouraging more.

He gave, kissing a path to the swell of my breasts. Giving them his undivided attention until I ached for more. Arching my back, I wiggled a hand beneath me and undid my bra clasp. Kolton met my gaze. Watched my face as he slowly slid a strap off my shoulder, then the other. When the bra fell away, his eyes lowered and devoured every inch of bare flesh. My nipples hardened, and he emitted a soft groan.

"You are breathtaking," he breathed, before dipping his head and taking a nipple into his mouth. At the swift rush of pleasure, my eyes rolled back. I dug my fingers into his hair, quivering as he worshiped each breast. Only when they were thoroughly pleasured did he move on, pressing soft kisses to my ribs and stomach. Then lower. And lower. Until my entire body trembled with anticipation.

When his fingers found the button of my shorts, I sucked in a gasp. He paused, making sure I was okay, then slowly undid the button. Barely able to breathe, I watched as he slid my shorts down. Inch-by-painstakingly-slow inch. Exposing more and more skin. Until I was wholly naked before him.

He'd seen me naked before, more than once, but this time felt different. This time, I allowed myself to become entirely vulnerable. As he gazed upon me, nothing was hidden. Inside and out, I was raw. Exposed. Open to him in every way.

And when he gripped my thigh and kissed the sensitive inner skin, I didn't hold back. Every kiss was met with a reaction. A quiver. A gasp. A breathy moan. He kissed a deliberate path up my thigh, each press of his lips causing more and more heat to build in my core. Until he finally reached *the* spot. The spot I'd been yearning for him to kiss for the past several minutes.

His mouth covered the sensitive flesh, then gently nipped at it. At the powerful jolt of pleasure that swept through me, I released a breathless cry.

"I'll never get enough," he whispered, kissing me again. *Nipping* me again. I cried out once more, and he visibly trembled. "Your scent. Your taste. Every sound that you make. I'll never get enough of you, sweetness."

Unable to respond, I focused on breathing. On holding still as he kissed me again and again, each kiss more urgent than the last. When I arched off the ground and gasped his name, he drew back and undid his pants. By the time he was naked before me, I was ready. *So* ready for him. So was he, judging by how hard he was.

My reaction to his engorged shaft was pure instinct as I opened my thighs to him. At the sight of my readiness, his chest heaved.

"Nora . . ."

"I'm ready," I said, my voice trembling. "I'm so ready to be yours."

His shaft swelled even more. Raising his eyes to mine, he slowly lowered onto his hands and knees, positioning himself between my legs. Despite how ready I was, my breathing sped up.

"Look at me," he softly commanded, never once taking his eyes off mine. Trying not to hyperventilate, I obeyed him, keeping my gaze locked on his. He lowered himself inch by inch, aligning his body with mine. Making every nerve ending fire awake. My heart frantically thundered, drowning out my uneven breaths as I felt his cock brush against my inner thigh.

I could do this. I could *do* this.

I squeezed my eyes shut.

"Look at me, sweetness," Kolton repeated, coaxing my eyes back open. When my gaze locked onto his once more, he whispered, "I've got you. I would never hurt you."

I nodded. "I know."

"Good. Then hold onto me and relax. I'll take this as slowly as you need."

Nodding again, I grabbed onto his shoulders as he dropped to his elbows. The move brought our chests together. My hardened nipples rubbed against his pecs, the sensation distracting me for a moment. Just long enough for him to ease on top of me. At the feel of his swollen tip pressing against my entrance, my eyes flew wide.

"I don't think you're going to fit. You're *way* too big."

At my outburst, a small smile twitched his mouth. "Trust me, Nora, I'll fit. Your body is made for mine. Just relax. Deep breaths. Unclench your thighs. I won't do anything until you're ready."

At his reassuring words, I felt my body start to relax. To accept this new and somewhat terrifying position. The moment I relaxed, he pushed inside of me. I felt myself stretch to accommodate his thickness.

"Aah!" I cried out in surprise, digging my nails into his shoulders.

"You okay?" he said, pausing to search my face.

"Yeah." I swallowed and struggled to remain calm.

"The discomfort will be over soon," he said, reaching up to touch my cheek. "Only a little bit more."

I nodded again. "Okay. I trust you."

Emotion warmed my chest. Soft and tender. It was him. His *love* for me. I focused on the feeling as he started to push again. To slowly fill me with utmost care. He watched my reaction, making sure to pause when I stiffened. Until, little by little, he sank down on top of me. Fully. Completely. Our bodies flush together. Which meant . . .

"You did it," I breathed, staring up at him in wonder. "You fit."

He graced me with the most beautiful smile. "Yes, sweetness, I fit. You are perfect for me in every way."

I returned his smile, suddenly overwhelmed with emotion. He was inside me. My *mate* was inside me. We were one. One body. As he lowered his head and gently kissed me, I marveled at the feeling of our bodies joined together. It felt strange at first. But, as he slowly began to thrust inside me, it felt more and more natural. *Right.* Our bodies were made for this. We were meant to be one.

He took his time, allowing me to adjust to the new sensations.

They were overwhelming, but in a good way. The more he hardened inside me, the more pleasure I felt. My hips instinctively rose to meet him, wanting to experience the sensations more frequently. When he continued to thrust slowly. Carefully. My patience snapped.

"Faster," I panted, raking my nails down his back. "*Harder.*"

In response, his cock swelled even more. My walls eagerly stretched to accommodate him.

"Nora, I don't think you're ready for—"

"*Please*, Kolton," I begged, desperately rocking my hips again. "Don't hold back anymore. I want all of you."

At that, a violent shudder ripped through his body. Without a word, he grabbed one of my hips and slammed into me. *Hard.*

I cried out as pleasure splintered my vision. Splintered *me*. It felt like he'd sliced me in half. "Don't stop," I pleaded, desperate to feel it again.

"My sweet, sweet flower," he groaned, digging his fingers into my hip. "You are perfect. *So* perfect for me."

And then he slammed into me again.

He did it over and over, spurred on by my cries of encouragement. I could barely breathe under the assault, but I'd never felt more alive. More free. More *whole*. Neither of us held back. We made love deeply. Passionately. Recklessly.

Our bodies were slick with sweat. Our moans echoing through the trees. Wild need drove us together again and again with a fierce possessiveness that branded me. *Claimed* me. Body, heart, and soul.

I came first. My walls tightened, mercilessly squeezing his cock. As euphoria exploded inside me, I threw back my head and screamed his name to the heavens.

He slammed into me once more, burying himself impossibly deep. Then bellowed his release. The roar was so powerful that the very ground beneath us shook.

The orgasm seemed to last forever, filling me with wondrous bliss. I lost myself in it. Floating higher and higher until I reached the stars. But I wasn't alone. He was there too. My husband. My soulmate. Floating with me. *Reaching* for me. I reached back, sighing when he wrapped me up tight.

It was like being embraced by his soul. It *was* his soul. Twining with mine. Making them one.

Joy filled my heart to overflowing.

Our bond was sealed. We were one now.

In every way possible.

When I'd said I wanted a wedding night do-over, I hadn't meant an exact play-by-play.

But, apparently, Kolton had taken my words *literally*.

After our time spent in the woods, he'd scooped me up and carried me all the way back to the cabin. Naked. Only this time, I didn't mind in the least. I was content to rest in his arms and listen to the steady rhythm of his heart. The press of his warm skin to mine was calming. Reassuring.

This wasn't a dream.

I was *really* here, fully mated to the man I loved.

Like a groom carrying his bride over the threshold, Kolton swept me through the cabin's entrance and up the stairs to the second floor. Unlike last time, I wasn't even a little bit afraid. Whatever he had in store, I was fully ready for. When he entered the bathroom, I couldn't help but smile. My face wasn't covered in blood this time, but other parts of me were. I could smell the coppery tang. Not a lot of it, but enough to surprise me.

As he set me on the counter, I peeked between my legs.

Yup. I definitely wasn't a virgin anymore.

At the sound of water running, I looked over to see Kolton soaking a washcloth. I watched him, fascinated with every little thing he did. Even the way he squeezed the excess water out and folded the washcloth was intriguing. Catching me watching him, he came over, his expression oddly serious.

"I'm sorry," he said, gently grasping one of my thighs. He eased it open and glanced down at the blood with a slight wince. "I shouldn't have taken you so hard."

Remorse filled me. *His* remorse.

Oh. He thought he'd *hurt* me.

When he placed the washcloth between my legs and began to clean me up, I flinched. Not from pain, but from how unexpectedly warm the cloth was.

Kolton's face twisted in misery. "I'm so sorry," he repeated, gentling his touch even more. Achingly so. With so much tender care that a lump formed in my throat.

"Kolton, stop." At my words, he immediately started to pull back. I grabbed his hand to halt his retreat. "No, stop *this*." I ran my fingers over his face, trying to smooth away the guilt lines. "You have nothing to be sorry for."

He lifted tortured eyes to mine. "I hurt you."

"No, you didn't. Bleeding is normal for the first time. The only thing you made me feel was good." A small laugh escaped me. "Like *really* good. I had no idea sex could be like that."

He stared at me, his face still lined with worry. As if he expected me to break down in tears at any moment.

Wanting to reassure him, I leaned forward and breathed into his ear, "In fact, I like it when you're rough. The rougher, the better. I like knowing that you're as desperate for me as I am for you."

He trembled beneath my fingertips.

Encouraged, I placed his hand between my legs again and said, "I'm excited to learn all there is to know about you. The sweet and gentle side. The wild and feral side. I don't want pieces, Kolton. I want all that you are, including the part that wants to split me in half."

He blew out a harsh breath and groaned my name. As he began to sweep the cloth over my sensitive center, it was my turn to expel his name. Scooting my butt to the counter's edge, I wrapped my legs around his waist and drew him close. A thrill shot through me when I discovered him hard once more.

"Nora," he said, groaning again as I took the cloth from him and guided his hand to my backside. Finding his other hand, I placed that one behind me too. "Nora, you need time to heal."

"Werewolf, remember? I'm not fragile like I used to be." I boldly reached between us and grabbed his thick shaft. He sucked in a sharp hiss, digging his fingers into my flesh. "In fact, I'm already healed and desperate to have my mate inside me again."

That was all he needed to hear. Roughly exhaling, he aligned the head of his cock with my entrance, then thrust inside. As his entire shaft slid in deep, I gasped and threw my arms around his neck to steady myself. He stilled.

"I'm fine," I panted, struggling to breathe past the shock. "Don't you dare pull out."

A rumble vibrated his chest. Was he . . . was he *laughing?*

"So eager for me," he purred, tightly gripping my butt to angle himself in deeper. His tip hit a spot deep inside, one that sent a blast of energy charging through me. When my walls viciously clenched around him, he chuckled once more. "Do you like that, sweetness?

Do you like it when I go deep?"

I released a breathy moan in reply, too focused on how good he was making me feel.

He slowly drew out, then thrust inside me again, hitting that same spot. My entire body shook from the pleasure. I tightened my arms and legs around him to keep from falling apart. Angling me back a few inches, he withdrew, then drove inside me again. Harder. *Deeper.* So deep that I cried out, overwhelmed by the heat exploding in my core.

This time, he didn't pause or even slow. He drove inside me again and again, hitting that blissful spot each time. I clung to him, holding on for dear life as he thrust in and out like a man possessed. And I loved it. The closeness. The oneness. The wild frenzy of it all.

I'd been wrong. *So* wrong.

One day of this wasn't enough. A *lifetime* wouldn't be enough.

I wanted to spend all of eternity having moments like this with him. Making love. Strengthening our bond. Reassuring myself over and over that this was real. That he was *mine.*

It was all that mattered right now. Everything else ceased to exist. My only thought was of him. My every action and reaction. Against all odds, we'd found each other. Accepted each other. *Claimed* each other. And I didn't want to stop. Didn't want this crazy ride to ever end.

Our fates were the same now. There was no undoing it. No returning to the person I used to be.

I knew I was forever changed as he thoroughly mated me once more. As his ragged breaths matched mine. As our sweat and pleasure mingled. As we stiffened together and came as one.

I was his. Only his. And he was mine. Only mine.

All the pain and suffering of the past had led us to this moment.

This inevitable destiny. And it was worth it. The pain. The suffering. The heartache. I would endure each hurtful thing all over again, if it meant finding my soulmate at the end of it all.

CHAPTER 28

I awoke to insatiable hunger.

Not for food. For *him.*

It felt like I was in heat again, so great was my need.

I reached for him on the bed beside me, but my hand caught nothing but air. Panic raced up my spine. Had I imagined it all? Had the most incredible night of my life only been a dream?

Before I could succumb to a full-blown panic attack, I heard whistling. Followed by the tantalizing aroma of breakfast. And not just any breakfast. *Kolton's* breakfast.

A grin stretched across my face a mile wide. Scrambling out of bed, I beelined for the door. Halfway there, I caught sight of myself and stopped dead. I was still naked. That wouldn't do. That wouldn't do at all. If Kolton was going to recreate our wedding night scene for scene, then the least I could do was play along.

Grinning even wider now, I changed course and grabbed my overnight bag. We hadn't brought much with us. Only a change of clothing and some toiletries, along with a small cooler of food. But I'd made sure to pack one particular item. Something that Kolton hadn't been allowed to fully appreciate the first time around.

Hurrying to the bathroom, I quickly donned my outfit and fixed my hair as best I could. Several leaves and pine needles were lodged in the mass, and I grinned at the sight. I never thought I'd be happy to see my hair so messy, but it reminded me of our first time last night.

I almost left the evidence where it was. Almost. Then scoffed at my silliness and picked my hair clean.

When I was done, I took a moment to stare at my reflection. Holy hell, I was practically *glowing*. Every inch of me spoke of vibrance. Of *life*.

Guess I could thank Kolton's dick for that.

Stifling a laugh, I turned and followed Kolton's whistling out the door. I descended the stairs at a more sedate pace this time, sneaking glances at my mate down below in the kitchen. His back was to me as he whipped up a batch of scrambled eggs over the stove. He was wearing an apron again, along with a pair of gray sweatpants. Nothing else.

I started to drool, and not because of the delicious scents wafting toward me.

He could no doubt hear my approach, but he continued to merrily whistle as he cooked. I could barely stand it. He was just so cute. And *hot*. How was this man mine? How did I get so lucky?

When I hit the bottom floor and rounded the railing, he finally turned to face me. Seeing the robe and nightgown I was wearing— *the* robe and nightgown—his whistling petered out. He stared and stared, his jaw slowly dropping.

Unable to hide my smirk, I glided forward. With each step, the satin robe fluttered open, revealing a peek of the tiny white nightgown beneath. The lace top was practically translucent, leaving little to the imagination. He watched me the entire way to the kitchen, his throat bobbing as I swept around the island and stopped before him.

"Morning, husband," I sang, rising up on tiptoe to chastely kiss his lips. "Breakfast smells amazing. Is it almost ready? I'm *starving*."

When I seductively purred the last word, he swayed toward me for another kiss. I danced away with a teasing laugh, rounding the island again to perch on a stool. When I looked up at him, he was still staring at me. Still gawking like he'd never seen a woman before.

"Wow, is it hot in here?" I continued to tease him, even as my face flushed scarlet. Not allowing myself a moment's shyness, I slipped the robe off my shoulders and let it pool around my waist. "Much better."

The spatula in Kolton's hand clattered to the floor. I bit my lip, holding in my mirth as his eyes greedily roved over my nightgown. Unlike last time, he wasn't even *trying* to look away.

Emboldened, I thrust my chest out just the tiniest bit, giving him an even better view. Then batted my lashes at him. "Like what you see?"

At my question, he finally tore his eyes off my chest to look at me. "Very much. I'm glad you brought it."

My body immediately responded to the roughness of his voice, filling me with heat. Squeezing my legs together, I replied, "Me too. You didn't get to properly appreciate it last time."

His swallow was audible as his gaze dipped again. "No, I didn't. I wanted to, but I wouldn't have been able to control my instinct to take you if I had."

I huffed a surprised laugh. "Why, husband, are you saying you wanted to ravish me even then?"

Heat built in his gaze, making me squirm in my seat. "Oh, you have no idea, sweetness. Seeing you in that nightgown and enjoying my food made me want to do *wicked* things to you."

I immediately grew wet. Struggling to compose myself, I leaned over the island and crooned, "Well, I'm in the nightgown now. All you need to do is feed me."

As my hardened nipples strained against the delicate material, his gaze turned feral. I basked in the heat, loving every torturous second of our naughty banter. I'd never thought *words* could turn me on so much, but I thoroughly enjoyed it when he talked dirty. What's more, he seemed thrilled when I did it back.

So I waited. Waited for him to make the next move. He didn't disappoint.

Turning, he removed a plate from a cabinet and loaded it up with food. My stomach loudly growled in response, earning me a quiet chuckle. When he turned to face me again, I didn't move a muscle, curious to see if he would do it. If he would really feed me. Setting the plate on the counter, he joined me in leaning over the island. With one hand planted on the granite surface, he picked up a plump sausage and dangled it in front of me, just out of reach. "Open wide."

At the wicked gleam in his eyes, all the air stuttered from my lungs. Holy hell, he was so much better at this than me. It was like playing in the big leagues for the first time. Still, I wasn't going to reveal how intimidated I was by his natural sensual energy.

Leaning even more over the counter, I opened my mouth for him. He rewarded me by placing a third of the sausage onto my tongue. At the instant taste bud explosion, I tried to bite down on more than he was offering. He jerked the sausage away with a soft tsk. "Naughty girl. You'll take it how I want you to. Now open up, nice and slowly."

Resisting the urge to stick my tongue out at him, I obeyed. But not before shooting him a warning look. He tossed me a roguish grin in response, one that made my lady bits all tingly.

"That's my good girl," he crooned, sticking the sausage in my mouth again. I bit into it just where he wanted me to, then closed my eyes and moaned loudly. When I reopened my eyes, he was gaping at me again, like a man starved for air. It was my turn to grin.

Swallowing, I opened my mouth for more. He obliged, giving me another third. *Torturing* me with slow, tiny bites when all I wanted to do was devour the food. Well, two could play that game. When

I opened my mouth for the final bite, I waited until the last second. As he placed the small morsel on my tongue, I struck. In went the sausage . . . and his finger.

Before he could pull away, I clamped my teeth down on the digit. Not too hard, but not gentle either. A warning growl rumbled in his chest, and I fixed my gaze on him in challenge. He growled again, and I bit down harder. When the growl faded, I rewarded him by wrapping my tongue around the tip, soothing the bite. Heat flared in his eyes.

"Do that again," he said, his voice deeper than usual. There was no mistaking his desire. He liked what I was doing. He *really* liked it.

I did as he commanded, gratified when he inhaled a sharp breath. Quickly swallowing the sausage, I claimed his finger again. Not just one, but *two* this time. I took them deep into my mouth and began to suck. *Hard.*

Kolton hissed through his teeth.

I grabbed his hand and pumped his fingers in and out, watching as his eyes hooded.

"Is this how you would take my cock?" he said, his breathing uneven. "Hard and deep?"

In reply, I sucked harder. He blew out a soft curse, watching hungrily as I devoured his fingers. When I made a sound of pleasure deep in my throat, he broke.

I yelped as he suddenly dragged me onto the counter facedown. I squirmed to get away, but Kolton firmly positioned me lengthwise on the island, spreading my body out like a buffet.

"What are you doing?" I said with mock irritation, still struggling to break free. When he effortlessly kept me pinned down, I huffed and reached for the plate of food still balanced on the edge.

He jerked it out of my reach and set it on the counter behind him.

I stuck my lip out in a pout. "What was that for?"

"I'm starving," he replied, running a hand up the back of my thigh. "It's my turn to feast."

Oh. *Oh.* Meaning, *I* was to be his feast.

Why was this so *hot?*

As his hand reached the top of my thigh, I stilled. Any moment now. Any moment and he would discover . . .

He swept his hand higher to grip one of my cheeks, then froze. I stifled a laugh. A blast of cool air suddenly struck my backside as he flipped up the hem of my nightgown. At the sight of my bare butt, he released a guttural groan.

"My wicked, wicked girl. I knew you were an angel with a naughty little devil on her shoulder."

My laugh slipped free. "Are you going to punish me?"

A strangled sound left him. I snickered, then squealed in surprise when something sharp pricked my left cheek.

"You bit me!"

It was his turn to snicker. "So I did."

Then, he did it again. I squirmed against the counter, but his attack was relentless. Soon, my entire backside was covered in bite marks. The mix of pain and pleasure did crazy things to my insides. When he began to nip at my inner thighs, a moan burst from me. So close. He was *so close* to reaching my—

He pried my thighs apart and buried his face between them.

"Kolton!" I gasped out, nearly coming on the spot when his tongue found my entrance. It darted inside, hungrily licking at the sensitive walls. I gripped the counter edge to keep from writhing against the slick surface. This was new. *Everything* he did was new. New and exciting.

Would it always be like this? So intense and breath-stealing that

I nearly passed out from the pleasure?

I hoped so. I *really* hoped so.

If he kept surprising me with experiences like this, I was pretty sure it would.

After several blissful moments of feeling his tongue thrust inside me, he pulled back to groan, "You taste like sweet nectar. I could feast on you all day."

Heat shot straight to my clit. Despite my best efforts, I started to writhe, desperate to relieve the ache. As if sensing my need, Kolton pushed me up onto my knees and delved deeper between my legs. When his greedy tongue found my throbbing clit, I well and truly blacked out. When I came to, he was still mercilessly pleasuring my center, making me feel things in a whole new way. Making me a panting, trembling *mess.*

"I'm going to—" I started but couldn't finish. My orgasm whipped through me, stealing the breath from my lungs. I stiffened and screamed out my release, almost losing consciousness again. He kept pleasuring me until I whimpered and went limp, completely spent.

With one final lick, he pulled away and released my thighs. Only to come around the island with a plateful of food, once again whistling a merry tune.

Still struggling to catch my breath, I panted, "What are you doing now?"

"Feeding you breakfast in bed," he replied, handing me the plate before scooping me into his arms. "You'll need your strength before the next round."

As he carried me toward the stairs, I couldn't help but gape at the satisfied look on his face. I'd made that happen. *I* had. It was humbling, knowing that I could make him so happy. Because he was. I could *feel* his happiness.

Barely able to contain my joy, I let my eyes caress his beautiful face a moment more before saying, "Next round?"

His expression suddenly softened. "If we only have one day of this, then I'm not wasting a single moment. Each one will be spent making you mine. I intend to take you as many times as I possibly can, sealing our bond so tight that not even the smallest crack remains. So eat up, sweetness," he said, nodding at the plate of food still in my hand. "Once you're fed, we're going to put the beds upstairs to proper use."

Heat rushed into my cheeks. He said beds. *Plural.* I shouldn't be this turned on so soon after an orgasm, but I was. He seemed determined to have sex on every surface of this cabin before the day was over, and I was more than okay with that.

In fact, an insatiable beast seemed to have awakened inside of me. I wanted nothing more than to be taken by my mate over and over and over again. And he did. He took me on each bed, proving just how useful beds could be. He took me so hard on one of them that the frame snapped in two.

As the day slowly wore itself out, so did we. Until we finally collapsed against the mattress in a tangle of sweaty limbs. He wrapped me up in his arms, and I melted against him, content to listen to his thundering heart. But, instead of falling asleep, we talked. About anything and nothing. Learning about each other. Teasing each other. Strengthening our bond in every way possible.

It was heaven, being here with him like this. I couldn't imagine a day being better than this one. Couldn't imagine a *peace* greater than this.

Squeezing him to me, I whispered in my mind, *I'll love you forever, Kolton Anthony Rivers.*

He abruptly inhaled, so sharply that I lifted my head to look at him. Startled to find his eyes wide open, I said, "You okay?"

Instead of answering, he said, *Do that again.*

"Do what?" I asked, then gasped and scrambled upright. "You just . . . you just spoke in my head. In my *mind.*"

"So did you," he responded, his eyes still wide. "I heard what you said. 'I'll love you forever, Kolton Anthony Rivers.' Clear as day."

I placed my hand over my mouth, murmuring, "It's real then. The telepathic connection between soulmates is real. I thought for sure it was a hoax. The concept is too . . . too unbelievable. Too . . ."

"Scary?"

I nodded, not bothering to hide how freaked out I was. Having Storm inside my head was one thing, but *Kolton?* I thought such naughty things about him all the time. He was sure to look at me differently if he knew how dirty my mind could be.

He slowly rose into a sitting position, then reached out to tuck a stray curl behind my ear. "I knew it would happen," he quietly said, searching my face. "I scoured every resource I could find the moment I realized we could be soulmates. I wanted to be prepared."

"Wish I had thought of that," I said, huffing a weak laugh. "But you're the planner and I'm the pantser." I nervously chewed on my lip, then blurted, "Are you okay with it? Do you . . . do you regret this? Regret falling in love with me?"

He studied me carefully, no doubt feeling my nervousness. Then replied, "I could never regret this, Nora. It's scary, yes. Terrifying, even. I keep thinking of how easily it could be taken away. How easily I could *lose* you. I thought I knew what love was before you came into my life. Thought I was prepared for the inevitable pain that came with it.

"But *this.* This right here is beyond anything I could have prepared for. This love is transcendent. It consumes every part of me. I would do anything, *anything* to protect it. And that terrifies me the most. But I could never regret falling in love with you. I was broken into pieces before I met you. And now . . . it's like I've been remade. Still weak in some areas, but growing stronger in others. Determined to build myself into the man you deserve. Come what may, I am better for loving you. I am whole. I am *complete*. And I will forever carry that love with me, in this life and the next."

A tear slipped down my cheek before I could catch it. He watched the tear for a moment, then gently wiped it away. Overwhelmed with love for him, I crawled onto his lap. Our bodies instantly fit together like two halves of a whole. The sight—the *feel* of it—filled me with wonder.

"I will never take our love for granted," I replied, despite the tremor in my voice. "You've given me something I never expected to have, something priceless and irreplaceable. I will treasure it always. Even when life gets hard, I will tightly hold on to what we have. And heaven help anyone who tries to tear us apart, because I will fight tooth and nail to stop that from happening."

For the first time ever, I could have sworn I saw tears in Kolton's eyes.

"Those words should have been our wedding vows to each other," he said, his voice gruff with emotion.

"They can be our personal vows to each other. Ones that no one else knows about but us," I suggested.

He smiled, then pressed a kiss to my forehead. "I love that. Vows only meant for us. Now, whisper them to me in your mind. I want to hear your sweet voice in my head again."

Grinning, I gladly did just that.

CHAPTER 29

KOLTON

She kept stroking my arm, tracing my snake tattoo over and over.

I could barely focus on anything else, including the road before us. It didn't matter that I'd taken her seven times in the past twenty-four hours. I was starving for more.

Realizing how quiet I'd become ever since we'd hit the road half an hour ago, Nora said, "You okay?"

I thought about quickly reassuring her, then decided against it. Everything was different now. Forever changed. If I thought too hard, too deep, she'd hear every word. If I felt too much, she'd pick up on my emotions. I was surprised she hadn't already figured out exactly what was bothering me.

Glancing at her, I openly replied, "I'm not ready to share you. Not with anyone, including my family. One day to seal our bond wasn't nearly enough."

She bit her lip, a habit that always made me want to kiss her senseless. I forced my eyes back to the road, but not before the bulge in my pants hardened even more.

"We could ask for more time," she suggested, still tracing patterns over my skin. "One more day couldn't hurt, right? I'm sure the others would understand."

Way too excited by her willingness to spend more time with me, I gripped the steering wheel harder than necessary. "The others would understand, but not Arrow." I grimaced, his name tasting like poison on my tongue. "Vi and Jagger texted me earlier. He's been causing tension for the past several hours, demanding they tell him where we went. He's also been making demands about Hendrix's phone, insisting that our window of opportunity to contact the witches is swiftly closing. If not for my mom, I would have ordered him off pack lands days ago, but I don't trust him to keep silent about her."

Nora sighed. "Neither do I. He wants more than our help finding the witches. I thought he wanted *me*, but something else is at play here. Storm told me about Zuriel, his familiar. I think they might be soulmates."

Before I fully realized what I was doing, I swerved the truck onto the shoulder and slammed the brakes. Throwing the gear into park, I faced Nora to demand, "Explain."

She looked startled by my strong reaction, but I couldn't seem to calm myself. It felt like a knife had just pierced my chest.

"*Please*, Nora," I pressed, trying to soften my brusque tone. "Tell me everything you learned about him. I need to know."

After searching my face—and probably sifting through my turbulent emotions—she did. Every single word was a fresh stab to the chest. By the way she described Storm and Zuriel's past connection, there was no disputing the bond they shared, one that did indeed sound like a soulmate bond. I couldn't be sure though. Compared to *our* bond, theirs seemed . . . small. Weak. Fragile.

When Nora started to explain how powerful Storm became, her strength surpassing Zuriel's, she abruptly stopped. Nervous energy pulsed through me, clearly hers. Confused, I tried to read her thoughts, but nothing came through. Like she was intentionally hiding from me. *Blocking* me from her thoughts.

Seeing my frown, she hurriedly said, "Storm and Zuriel had a falling out after that. Storm didn't say so, but I think Zuriel was jealous of her power. Maybe he still is. Maybe that's why he decided to come here, to get as far away from her as he could."

My frown deepened. "If they're soulmates, that doesn't make much sense. Unless he decided to reject the bond. Distance is the best way to do that."

An ache filled me, an emotion that was decidedly Nora's.

"That's awful," she said, clearly upset at the thought. Then, "Do you think he would try to harm her?"

"If he does, he'll face not only my wrath, but Shadow's."

She wrinkled her nose. "Shadow?"

I cracked a smile. "He may or may not have a little crush on your familiar."

He chose that moment to rear up, clearly not wanting to be left out of the conversation, especially one that involved him.

Oh, it's more than a little crush. I'm quite smitten with the sassy angel, especially after our romp through the woods a few days ago.

Shadow, settle, I ordered him, stifling an eye roll. *You promised not to make a peep until the day was over.*

But it is over. The important part anyway, which was introducing your mate to pound town. You did good, by the way. I especially enjoyed that kitchen island scene. Very creative. Also, I've been dying to mention how surprised I am by your mate. I thought she was this innocent little thing, but she's actually a feral beast in the sheets.

Nora made a choking noise, distracting me from my inner dialogue. I focused on her and froze, caught off guard by the supernatural glow in her blue eyes.

Aww, my angel baby is emerging.

Ignoring Shadow's comment, I said to Nora, "What's wrong?"

She opened her mouth, but only a squeak emerged. Trying again, she flapped her hands in the air and sputtered, "You . . . I can *hear* you. I can hear you and *Shadow*."

I stared at her, still frozen solid. Impossible. My research hadn't mentioned this. Hadn't *prepared* me for this.

But my denial didn't last long. Not when a deeper female voice— an *irritated* one—suddenly spoke inside my head: *Tell him I am not his angel baby.*

An incredulous laugh burst from me.

Nora's eyes rounded like saucers. "Did you just hear Storm?"

"Yes."

So did I, Shadow loudly crowed. *Her voice is as angelic as her earthly form. The very sound of it turns me on.*

Take that back, you scoundrel, Storm's angry voice once again filled my head.

Never, my lady. That would be dishonest, and I am nothing but completely truthful at all times.

"Okay, stop!" Nora yelled, clutching at her head. "There are *way* too many voices inside here. Look, this is exciting and all, but it's also really overwhelming. Can we set some ground rules or something so my brain doesn't explode?"

Sorry, Shadow immediately replied, truly sounding contrite. *I'll shut up now.*

"Thank you, Shadow," Nora said, rubbing her temples. "I appreciate that."

You're welcome.

I will leave as well, Storm spoke up, also sounding sincere. *This day is for you and your mate. I will not interfere.*

"Thank you, Storm," I replied, sharing a look with Nora.

When the voices in our heads fell silent, we both started laughing.

"Holy *crap*," Nora blurted, throwing her head back against the seat. "I had *no* idea this would happen."

Still chuckling, I said, "Neither did I. It will definitely make things more interesting. Shadow doesn't exactly have a filter."

"Yeah. I figured that out in all of two seconds. *Feral beast* in the sheets?"

I shook my head, unable to hide my smirk. "Sorry about that. His verbiage is extra colorful when he's passionate about something."

"He's passionate about our sex life?"

"*Very* passionate."

Even in the darkness, I could see the tell-tale sign of a blush staining her cheeks. My smirk only grew. Throwing the truck into drive, I pulled onto the road once again. The mood was decidedly lighter now. At least the shock of this new discovery had somewhat cooled my libido. I was still stiff, but not painfully so.

After a moment of silence, Nora said, "Tell me about him."

"About Shadow?"

"Yeah. Besides being obviously *horny*, what's he like? Why did he come to Earth? Was it his decision?"

I silently mulled over her questions, then answered, "He's impulsive, violent, and addicted to pleasure, but he's also protective and unfailingly loyal. I wouldn't be who I am without him. His nature sharpens mine, which has allowed me to become a formidable alpha. In the otherworld, he was highly regarded among his kind. A prince, in their world's standards. He only left because he has an obsession with humans and their way of life. He wanted to know what it felt like to be one. Well, as close to one as he could. Contrary to popular belief, not all demons are evil, mindless monsters. They feel pain and love. They know how to empathize and form connections. In my opinion, they're not all that different from humans."

She blinked in surprise, clearly not expecting that response.

"Wow. I had no idea demons could be . . ."

"Decent?"

She shrugged sheepishly. "Yeah."

"He's flawed, just like every other created being, but he has his good points too. If not for him, this day might not have happened."

"What do you mean?"

"Right from the beginning, he knew that you and I belonged together. Ever since the day I met you, he's been the incessant voice in my head urging me to claim you. It's been absolute torture, but he was right all along."

Nora huffed a laugh. "Maybe he thinks I'm *his*."

When Shadow quietly snickered, I scowled. "He knows very well that you are mine," I said, more to him than Nora. "But I can tell he likes you, which is a first."

"A first?"

I winced, suddenly realizing my mistake. We'd been so candid with each other all day that I'd completely lowered my guard. But this was one topic I did *not* want to discuss with her. When she continued to stare at me expectantly, I blew out a resigned sigh and decided to be honest.

"He hasn't liked any of the other females I've been with."

Nora was quiet for a long moment. Then said, "Oh."

When a slew of tangled-up emotions suddenly bombarded my senses, I tightened my grip on the steering wheel. Don't ask, I wanted to plead with her, but forced myself to remain silent.

Sure enough, she did. But I couldn't blame her. If she was half as obsessed with me as I was with her, I would want to know every last detail, no matter how painful.

Still, I winced again when she murmured, "How many were there?"

"Nora . . ."

"Please tell me, Kolton. I won't get mad."

She said that *now*.

Heaving another sigh, I finally answered her. "Eight."

"*EIGHT?*"

I groaned. "I *knew* you would get mad."

"No, I'm not mad. I'm . . . I'm . . ."

"You're mad."

"Fine. Maybe a little. But it's irrational anger. I didn't even know you back then. Still . . . *eight?* I kinda get where the womanizer rumor came from now."

I frowned. "That rumor was false. I never have and never will be a womanizer."

"Hey, *I* didn't call you a womanizer."

"Well, you kind of did, once or twice."

"No, I was only repeating what I *heard*. And how was I supposed to know? I mean, you're *insanely* gorgeous. Women trip all over themselves when they see you. I know it was lust-at-first-sight for me."

I barked a laugh. "I love it when you're jealous, just so you know."

She snorted. "Lucky me."

Still smiling, I openly admitted, "It was lust-at-first-sight for me too. One look and I was done for, even if I spent way too long denying it."

Leaning over, she rested her cheek on my shoulder and whispered, "Well, you're here now."

Warmth filled my chest. I couldn't get over how good it felt to be close to her. To allow her deeper and deeper into my heart. It was comforting. Satisfying. Thrilling. I'd never experienced anything like it. Had never wanted to. But that was before her. Now, I couldn't imagine a world where this didn't exist. Where she and *I* didn't exist.

She was right earlier. Heaven help anyone who tried to tear us apart. It wouldn't end well for them. I would make absolutely certain of it.

Kissing the top of her head, I whispered back, "Yes, I'm here now, sweetness. And I always will be."

CHAPTER 30

The second we arrived back at the estate, I knew our happy little honeymoon was over.

One step. One step out of the truck and Arrow materialized out of nowhere.

Kolton loosed a warning growl, but it was too late. Arrow lifted his nose to scent the air and stopped dead.

I watched as shock, then fury contorted his face.

Setting his sights on Kolton, he roared, "You *mated* her?"

The front door burst open and Vi, Griff, Jagger, and Brielle filed outside.

Never once taking his eyes off Arrow, Kolton quietly said, "Stand down, Pemberton. This is none of your business."

Shaking with barely-restrained rage, Arrow spat, "You've stolen her innocence. You've *polluted* her."

Holy hell, I'd never seen him so angry before. So *unhinged*. Even during our time locked inside cages.

When I saw Kolton stiffen all over, I quickly intervened. "He didn't steal my innocence, Arrow. I gave it to him freely."

Arrow scoffed. "That's what all demons would have you believe, Nora. That you *chose* to be tainted. They are manipulators. *Deceivers.* Why do you think angels are sent to banish them from Earth? Because they desire nothing more than to *corrupt* humans. There's no saving you from this. You've allowed your soul to be forever tarnished.

What's more, you've placed your celestial spirit in grave peril."

His condemning words struck me like stones, each one causing me to flinch.

"*Enough!*" Kolton barked, taking a threatening step toward Arrow. When both Jagger and Griff lunged forward as if to stop him, he yanked up a hand. They immediately halted in their tracks. "If your self-righteous disposition is this repulsed by the *bond* I share with Nora, then you can leave. No one is stopping you."

Arrow's upper lip curled in a silent snarl, but he remained where he was. "I'm not going anywhere. Not until I get what I came here for."

"And what is that, exactly?" Kolton pressed, taking another step. "*Nora?* She's been thoroughly mated. *Seven times*, to be exact. There's not a single piece I haven't claimed. Nothing left for you to take. She is mine in every possible way. If that doesn't convince you, I will gladly describe the many ways I took her."

My mouth fell open, as did Vi's and Brielle's. Griff, on the other hand, looked two seconds away from laughing. Even Jagger was struggling to keep a straight face.

Great. Just great. They *all* knew how many times we'd had sex now. That wasn't mortifying or anything.

The only one upset by the news was Arrow. There was only one word to describe his expression. *Livid.* Unsettled by the sight, I shivered.

Come here, a voice abruptly filled my head. Kolton's. *I need to hold you.*

Immediately responding, I hurried over to his side of the truck. The second I was within reach, he pulled me into his arms. Melting against him, I inhaled his scent, equally needing comfort. The contact instantly calmed us both, draining the tension from our bodies.

"I've already told you," Arrow quietly seethed, watching our close interaction with thinly-veiled contempt. "I want justice for what the witches did and for the traitor who gave me to them. What Nora does with her body is up to her. I only hoped she would see reason, considering the bond our celestial's share."

"The bond that Zuriel *broke*, you mean?"

At Kolton's words, Arrow shot me a look. "*Storm* has finally been talking, I see."

I lifted my chin. "Yes, she has. She told me not to trust you, right before you *kissed* me."

Kolton bristled at the reminder. I snuggled deeper into his embrace, trying to calm him once more.

It's okay, I whispered into his mind. *He can't touch me again. I'm yours. Even Arrow can't argue that now.*

I still want to rip out his throat for touching you, Kolton quietly growled back, tightening his hold on me.

I looked up at him. *I understand, but please don't. Let's just give him what he wants so he can return to his pack.*

"Wait, wait, wait," Griff suddenly said, drawing our gazes to the porch. "Are you guys doing the *thing?* The telepathic soulmate thing?"

"Telepathic?" Brielle said, her mouth still open. Poor girl. She'd had a major crash course in all things supernatural this past week.

"Oh, a telepathic connection is only one of the things soulmates share," Griff answered her. "They can also feel each other's emotions, which I assume makes sex that much more intense. Speaking of, seven times isn't very much. I bet they haven't even started the mating frenzy."

"*Griff*," Vi stopped him with an eye roll. Stepping forward, she pulled a phone from her pocket and said, "If justice is all you really seek, Arrow, then I've got bad news. I just got off the phone with Darin at NYPD, and the Hendrix lead is a bust. The texts are untraceable. The witches covered their tracks too thoroughly."

Arrow shook his head in disbelief. "There has to be a way. There *has* to be."

Vi shrugged. "If Darin said there isn't, then there isn't."

"Then give me the phone. I'll pretend to be Hendrix." When he stepped toward Vi, several growls brought him up short. Vi rolled her eyes again as Griff tried to block her from Arrow's view.

"Vi, secure the phone so Pemberton can't do anything *stupid* with it," Kolton ordered. With a nod, Vi slipped back inside the house. To Arrow, he said, "Contacting the coven is a *last* resort. If they fall for a trap, we have to make it ironclad. They can too easily retaliate. We have brute strength, but they have greater numbers and magic."

"We have magic too," Arrow challenged, staring Kolton up and down. "Unless your *demon* hasn't taught you how to wield it."

Without a word, Kolton raised a hand and snapped his fingers. Deep purple flames sprang to his fingertips, lighting up the night.

Brielle gasped.

"You're a Darken," Arrow said with a lip curl, glaring at the flames. "Not surprised. Only the *darkest* spirits possess such magic. Still, your conjuring is a simple parlor trick. No witch will be intimidated by a single flame."

The flames winked out. "Do you need a bigger demonstration?" Kolton replied, releasing me to step forward. My eyes widened when he slashed his arm through the air like a whip. Just like that, I heard a *crack*. Arrow leapt back with a hiss as the ground beneath his feet split open. Kolton brought his arm down again and again, driving Arrow back, back, back. "Is this demonstration enough for you? Do I need to demonstrate on your *face?*"

"Okay!" Arrow snapped, raising his hands in surrender. Kolton lowered his arm. Arrow glared at him for a long moment before saying, "If you're so powerful, then why didn't you strike down the entire coven when you had the chance? Why let them *escape?*"

Kolton didn't respond, for so long that I didn't think he would. And then . . . "Because I have a family. Every decision—every single move I make—I think about them first. I want those witches dead as much as you do, but I won't jeopardize my family's safety to appease my bloodlust."

Arrow shook his head, looking almost disappointed in Kolton. "If this was my family, I would hunt down and destroy every last thing that could cause them harm."

"And if you die in the process?" Kolton quietly replied. "Who will protect them from harm then?"

Arrow's lips thinned. He didn't answer.

I could feel how frustrated Kolton was over Arrow and our one solid lead ending in failure. The coven obviously didn't want to be found. We probably could have lived with never finding them . . . if it wasn't for the cryptic message Keisha had left in my mind.

That, and the little problem of Arrow's continued presence here. Neither threat could be ignored.

We joined the others in the den for a meeting, going over the day's events and how best to proceed now that the coven's location still eluded us. Kolton was adamant that directly contacting the witches could bring them right to our doorstep, so that option was off the table. For now.

"What about Arrow's pack?" I suggested, watching with concern as Kolton tossed back another glass of whiskey. It was his third one in the past half hour. "Hendrix didn't initially contact the coven, but someone in Arrow's pack did. They must know more about the witches than Hendrix does."

"True," Jagger responded, "but contact with Northwood Pack could cause suspicion. Midnight Pack broke ties with them a long time ago, and Vi already reached out to them once. If we do it again, the traitor could inform Blackstone Coven that we've been sniffing around."

"Or they could help us," I said with a shrug. "If they betrayed Arrow, maybe they don't hate Midnight Pack. As long as they don't realize we're working with Arrow, maybe we can incentivize them to throw us a bone."

Griff snorted. "You mean pay them off with loads of money."

I shrugged again. "A lot of people would sell their own grandmother for enough money. It could work."

"It could. Good idea, Nora," Vi said, tossing back her own drink. She too was watching Kolton. When he stood to refill his glass, she shot me a look.

Do something, the look seemed to plead. When I gave her a helpless look in return, her expression shifted to a clear, *You've got to be kidding me.*

My eyes widened in understanding. *Now?*

Yes, silly. NOW.

Okay, this was officially the strangest "conversation" I'd ever had. Especially since my husband's sister was practically *begging* me to bang her brother.

Clearing my throat, I abruptly stood. The move made Kolton pause in his task. Deciding to really sell it, I threw my arms above my head in a full-body stretch. "Well, I'm done for tonight. Today really took a lot out of me." Ignoring Griff's loud guffaw, I added, "I'll just be going to bed now. Goodnight."

"Do you need me to move my stuff?" Brielle asked, starting to stand.

I quickly waved her back down. "No need. I've switched rooms. Permanently." Sliding Kolton a suggestive look, I left the den and headed upstairs. Not to the third floor, but to the second. To Kolton's room.

To *our* room.

He didn't keep me waiting long. I'd barely started to unpack my bag when he arrived, slipping inside and shutting the door with a firm click. Without turning from my task, I said, "Are all these drawers taken? I only need one. I can stick the rest of my stuff in the closet."

Silence greeted me.

I chewed on my lip to hide a smirk, already knowing that Kolton wasn't upset at the sight of me invading his personal space. I could feel how turned on he was. How *pleased*. I began rifling through his drawers, pausing when I found a plain white t-shirt.

"Perfect," I murmured, then removed my clothes. *All* of them, including my bra and panties. I knew Kolton was watching. Knew he was getting more and more turned on with each passing second. I could barely keep from laughing.

The second I tugged on his white shirt, he said, *Take it off.*

Not out loud. Mind to mind.

The way he rumbled the words inside my head sent a thrill up my spine. Still not turning around, I obeyed his command. Then waited. Waited for the next order. He didn't disappoint.

Get on the bed.

Oh my. We were doing this whole thing telepathically then. I liked it. I liked it a *lot*.

Walking backward, I found the bed and crawled on top. I sat with my back to him, already anticipating his next command.

He kept me waiting this time, but for good reason. I heard the tell-tale rustle of clothing as he removed his shirt, pants, and shoes. Naked. He was completely naked now.

When silence stretched between us and he didn't move toward the bed, I started to squirm.

What next? I asked, finally losing my patience.

Now, be a good girl and grab onto the headboard for me.

My eyes flew wide.

When I started to turn around, he said in a commanding tone, *Don't turn around. Obey me, wife. Grab the headboard.*

Nervous, but also more than a little excited for what he had planned, I whispered, "Yes, Alpha."

Inside voice only.

Yes, Alpha.

Pure male satisfaction poured through our bond.

Grinning, I crawled over to the headboard and gripped the top. *Like this?*

Alpha.

My grin broadened. *Like this, Alpha?*

He moved then, crossing the room to join me on the bed. I felt the heat from his body as he purred, *Perfect. Now spread your thighs, just a little wider. That's it. Such a good girl.*

Holy hell, I was thoroughly enjoying this. Who knew that calling him "alpha" could be so sexy. Same with following his orders like a good little omega. I didn't feel like an omega though. I felt like a strong female submitting to her dominant mate. *Willingly.* With relish. My submission excited him, which in turn excited me.

When I was in the exact position he wanted, Kolton finally made contact. His large hand slid up the length of my spine, stirring all my nerve endings awake. I shut my eyes, basking in the warmth. In the feel of his touch. It had only been a few hours since we'd last been together like this, but those few hours had been a lifetime.

His hand went all the way up my spine, rounding my neck to lightly grip my throat. I sucked in a quiet gasp, surprised by the move. He'd never held me this way before.

Do you trust me? he whispered into my mind, his body hovering just behind me without touching.

Swallowing roughly, I nodded.

Use your words, Nora.

Yes, Alpha. I trust you.

More satisfaction pulsed through our bond.

Then get ready for the ride of your life, sweetness. You haven't experienced deep *until now.*

With that, he thrust into my entrance from behind. So hard and fast that I arched my back, releasing a strangled cry.

He paused to let me adjust. *You okay?*

Yes. More than okay. And I was. I was already wet for him, and he'd easily slid inside. The new angle was breath-stealing in the best of ways. I felt fuller. His cock was everywhere, hitting every spot that gave me pleasure.

Pleased by my response, he placed his other hand on my stomach and pressed our bodies together. The action drove his length even deeper, wringing a moan from me.

He was practically mounting me now, his lips near my ear as he whispered mind-to-mind, *Did you think to distract me with sex, wife?*

"Yes," I replied out loud.

When he nipped at my ear in admonishment, I repeated the word in my head, along with an "alpha."

Is it okay that I did? I asked.

You can distract me with sex any time you want, he replied, then licked the shell of my ear.

Goosebumps erupted over my flesh. *Even during important meetings?*

Especially during important meetings.

A laugh burst from me, one that quickly turned into a moan as he began to thrust. Gently squeezing my throat, he drove his cock in and out. My walls quivered and tightened as the new angle filled me with pleasure. The blissful sensations were swift and *deep.* My body weakened under the assault, and I gripped the headboard to keep from collapsing against the mattress.

Do you like this, sweetness? Kolton purred

I nodded, unable to speak, even in my mind.

I could tell he liked this too. Liked the way my walls were squeezing him in a tight vice. His length hardened even more, pushing through to drive deeper and deeper, stealing my sanity.

Do you know why I chose this position tonight? he asked, inching his hand lower on my stomach.

Trembling uncontrollably, I shook my head.

Because I wanted to pound and finger you at the same time.

Holy hell. If he did that, I wouldn't survive much longer.

When all I did was whimper, he slid his hand down and touched my clit. I immediately bucked against his hand, sucking in a sharp hiss. The pleasure was almost too much. My body didn't know what to do with it all. I began to pant and writhe, unable to control my reaction. Kolton kept me firmly in place, one hand still circling my throat while the other mercilessly pleasured my center.

When sweat beaded our bodies, our breathing frantic, he released me to grab my hands on the headboard. Lacing his fingers through mine, he went wild. There was no pace anymore. Only a primal need.

He pounded into me again and again, making me gasp each time.

He was right. I hadn't experienced deep until this moment.

My hips were wide open, allowing a penetration so intense that I was lost to sensation. The animalistic part of my nature growled in satisfaction, loving how feral our union was. It was pure instinct, urging us to *act*, not think. We were simply two bodies seeking pleasure from each other. Driving each other to the brink of ecstasy.

When I finally reached orgasm, it took all of my willpower not to scream my lungs out. Wave after wave of bliss pounded through me, making me clench around Kolton's cock. Making me milk out his own orgasm. Gripping my fingers, he slammed deep inside me and groaned out his release. We rode the high together, shuddering from the pleasurable aftershocks. Basking in the oneness.

When I started to collapse from exhaustion, Kolton lowered me to the mattress, then slowly pulled out.

Or *tried* to.

I suddenly realized how full I felt. Full of *him*. Fuller than I'd ever felt before. His shaft was impossibly thick. Swelling so huge that my walls were forced to stretch even more to accommodate him. I felt a tug as Kolton tried to pull out again, but nothing changed.

When he quietly swore, my eyes popped open.

"What's wrong?" I said out loud, trying to help him. When his swollen cock held me in place, I sucked in a gasp and started to squirm. "Kolton, what's happening?"

"Hold still, Nora," he said, laying on top of me to keep me from squirming. "It'll release you soon."

I stilled. "*What* will?" At his silence, I started to panic. I wiggled and squirmed, but to no avail. We were *stuck*.

Settling more firmly on top of me, Kolton finally said, "It's no use trying to get free. When a knot has formed, the couple is locked together until the instinct fades."

I nearly swallowed my tongue. "You *knotted* me?" I whisper-yelled, truly panicking now.

"I'm sorry, Nora. It just happened. I didn't mean to."

"But I'm not in heat. I thought knotting only happened when a female was in heat."

"An alpha can't control his instinct to knot when a female's in heat, but he can intentionally knot at any time. The mating frenzy must have kicked in, causing me to lose control."

Just the mention of the words heat and knot made his shaft engorge even more. It pushed against my walls, filling me with pleasure instead of pain. Despite my panic, I closed my eyes and focused on the sensation. He almost felt ribbed now, as if his cock had changed shape in order to keep us tightly locked together. The ribbed texture was oddly stimulating, making me flush with heat.

"Don't do that," he rumbled in my ear, sliding his arms beneath me to hold me close.

"Don't do what?" I whispered, sighing when his lips found my neck.

"Don't take pleasure from this. If you orgasm again, I'll have no choice but to spill more seed inside you."

That shouldn't have turned me on, but it did. I could feel myself growing wet again, making the ribbed texture even more pleasurable.

"Not helping, Nora," he growled against my neck, lightly nipping it. "Think about something else."

"Like what?" I panted, digging my nails into the sheets.

"Anything. Anything but my cock and your wet pussy."

"But it feels so good. I can't . . . I can't think."

With a groan, he buried his face in the crook of my neck and held me impossibly close. Yup. This was definitely my new favorite position. I loved being taken by him from behind. Loved being pressed face-first into the mattress. Loved being *stuck* with him.

"God, Nora, you're killing me," he groaned again, loosening his hold so that his hands could roam. When they found my breasts, I released a breathless whimper. His cock pulsed at the sound, and my core immediately tightened in response. He stiffened, blowing out a harsh breath. Then delved a hand between my legs.

At the swift rush of pleasure his touch gave me, I trembled and arched against him. He continued to stroke the sensitive flesh at an almost feverish pace, his only goal to make me come. Already aroused, it didn't take long before I was writhing against his fingers, desperate for release. When I started to softly whine, on the verge of coming, he pinched my clit. *Hard.*

The sharp bite of pleasure-pain shoved me over the edge. My orgasm slammed into me, and I pressed my face into a pillow to muffle my scream. A second later, Kolton jerked against me and moaned into my neck, spilling his hot release once more.

Spent and completely satiated, I sagged against the mattress and listened to our labored breathing. Neither of us moved a muscle, allowing the knot to slowly soften. Several minutes later, Kolton was finally able to pull out. At the loss of his cock, I actually *whimpered.*

Quietly chuckling, he kissed my shoulder, then gently rolled me over. I stared up at him, marveling at the contented look on his face. I knew mine looked the same.

Biting my lip, I whispered, "How worried should I be?"

He studied me for a moment, then said, "About getting pregnant?"

"Yeah."

"You're not in heat, so the chances are low. Almost nonexistent, even with a knot. If you're worried, I could start using protection. Although, condoms won't be able to contain me if I accidentally knot you again."

I gave him a sleepy smile. "No, that's okay. I was just wondering." When he continued to stare at me, I lifted up and pressed my lips to his. Then whispered, "That was the best one yet."

I felt his mouth curl into a smile. "Are we keeping score, wife?"

"You bet I am. Expect a detailed *daily* report on your performance, husband," I impishly said, pulling back to grin at him.

He slowly raised an eyebrow. "Oh? It's going to be like that then?"

"Yes, it's going to be like that."

When I lifted a finger to *boop* his nose, he simply stared at me, all expression wiped clean. Whoops. Maybe *booping* a big, bad alpha's nose was going a little too far. Still, I wasn't going to take it back.

We stared at each other, locked in a stalemate. Alpha versus alpha. I didn't look away, determined not to break. He could deal with the boop. It wasn't like I had—

He suddenly pounced on me and began to tickle my sides. I shrieked with laughter and tried to get away, but he was merciless. *Determined.* Eventually, I surrendered. I *had* to. Any more of this torture and I was going to pee myself.

"Okay, I *submit*," I cried out, tears streaming down my face. "Just stop. Please *stop*."

He immediately did, pulling back to grin at me victoriously. "Who's your alpha?"

I stuck out my tongue at him. "You are."

"That's right, sweetness," he said, leaning down to press a toe-curling kiss to my lips. "Don't ever forget it."

Oh, I wouldn't. I didn't *want* to. He had me completely. Every part of my being was his. Submitting to him was easy because I was so desperately in love. I would submit to him for the rest of my life, knowing that it was safe to do so. That he would shower me with nothing but love in return.

CHAPTER 31

"What's with all the blankets, Nora Bora? Planning to redecorate the house?"

Confused, I glanced at Brielle, then down at my overflowing shopping cart. "No, I just need more blankets. I like cuddling with them."

She snorted, her dimples flashing. "The only thing you like cuddling with these days is your hunky husband. Even *I* heard you two last night. More than once."

Vi groaned, stopping behind us with her own cart. "Please don't remind me. I had on headphones but still heard far too much. My ears are forever scarred."

Three days had passed since we'd returned from the cabin. Since then, Kolton and I had spent a lot of time "cuddling" in bed. We couldn't help it. The mating frenzy was driving our instincts haywire. All we wanted to do was have sex, sex, sex.

Each time we did, Kolton ended up knotting me. He couldn't seem to help that either. Our bodies were running on autopilot, driving us into the bedroom at all hours of the day. The only reason why we weren't having sex right now was because Vi insisted that we all needed some fresh air.

According to Griff, the entire house smelled of sex. He'd asked the household staff to open up every single window while we were gone for the afternoon. I hadn't even blushed at his blunt comments.

I was too busy being horny.

"Don't forget that I *saw* you and Griff right after my pack initiation," I teased Vi, dropping another blanket into my cart. "That image will forever be stamped into my brain."

Expecting her to snort or laugh, I was surprised when she did neither. As if embarrassed, she focused on the shelves of blankets, running her fingers over the varying textures.

"You okay?" I softly asked, worried that I'd overstepped.

She shrugged, still staring at the blankets. "I only let it happen because of Arrow. Seeing him again made me feel vulnerable, so I sought Griff out like a security blanket."

"Oh, Vi. You know he means more to you than that."

"Yeah," she said, a slight tremor in her voice. "Which is why I need to let him go."

Shocked, I sputtered, "But . . . but why?"

She dropped her hand and released a frustrated sigh. "Because I'm no different than *Jasmine*, that's why. I've been holding onto Griff for purely selfish reasons, not allowing him to move on. He deserves better than that."

Better than *me*, she practically shouted, but didn't say.

My heart ached for her. Vi was always so strong that it was easy to forget she had insecurities like everyone else.

"You're not anything like Jasmine," I told her, reaching out to give her a tight squeeze. "I can tell that you care about Griff and he cares about you. If anything, you'll always have your friendship. Whatever you decide, we'll be here to support you."

Brielle joined the hug, and Vi blew out a shaky laugh. "Thanks, guys. I appreciate it." When we pulled away, she sniffed back tears and put on that brave face of hers. "Anyway, I didn't mean to make this moment about me. This afternoon is about *retail* therapy. Boy drama can wait, as can everything else."

"How long until they come looking for us?" I asked, allowing the subject change.

"Half an hour, maybe. Melanie roped the boys into getting ice cream across the street."

My mouth started watering. "Ice cream sounds really good, actually. Maybe I should—"

"*Later,*" Vi said, firmly nudging me toward my cart. "Shopping first. And please don't tell me you're only getting blankets."

"Right?" Brielle replied. "The blankets are a little weird."

"Hey, they're not weird. Tell her they're not weird, Vi."

"They are. Just a little." Vi laughed when I threw her a mock glare. "At *least* stop by the intimates section. I know you're sorely lacking in that department."

"You *seriously* want her stocking up on sexy lingerie?" Brielle incredulously asked. "After what we heard last night?"

"You're right. Scratch that idea. We're going to find you some granny panties and lots of heavy flannel."

I rolled my eyes good-naturedly, secretly enjoying their teasing. It was nice being able to act "normal" for once. To spend the afternoon hanging out with friends instead of being stuck in another meeting. Or doing my best to avoid a hovering Arrow. I knew he wanted to talk with me alone, but I wouldn't give him the chance. His accusations and judgment had hurt, and I was done letting him plant doubt in my heart.

If he wanted to talk to me, then he needed a change of attitude first. Every time he saw me with Kolton, he did nothing but silently glare. If not for our deal, I would have sent him packing myself. I was so done with his behavior.

At least we'd made progress with his pack. A meeting was

scheduled first thing Monday morning. We'd agreed to meet on neutral land, hoping to keep the peace. Only the pack's highest ranking members were to attend. Kolton was certain we'd find the wolf who betrayed Arrow among them. Probably a discontent beta wanting to change the hierarchy in Arrow's absence.

Having spent time with his pack in the past, Vi knew who his closest confidants were. Arrow had confirmed that they still were. He had wholeheartedly approved of our plan to flush out the traitor, agreeing to stay behind for the meeting. All he asked was that we keep him in the loop.

Besides the upcoming meeting, we hadn't made any other plans. Kolton was still worried about the message Keisha had sent me. Enough that he was constantly vigilant, cautioning us to do the same. No venturing off alone without first checking in, *especially* me.

To ease his worries, I hadn't stepped foot outside the house until this afternoon, not even to tend the gardens. Less chance of running into Arrow that way. I couldn't stop thinking about his cruel words and that stupid *kiss*. Even if Storm and Zuriel *were* soulmates, he didn't have the right to treat me that way. My blood boiled every time I replayed his condescending words in my head. Good thing he hadn't come into town with us. Not that we'd invited him.

We were almost finished checking out when the guys strode inside the store with Melanie. At the sight of Kolton, butterflies erupted in my stomach. I still couldn't believe this incredible man was mine. He was kind and gentle and protective, not to mention sexy as hell in the bedroom. I started to grin as he turned my way, then frowned as I felt his worry surge through me.

What's wrong? I said through our bond, grabbing my bags and hurrying toward him.

Spotting me, he quickly checked me over, then did the same with

Vi and Brielle. Still not relaxing, he replied, "There's been a break-in at the house."

My eyes flew wide. "Are the staff okay?"

"They're fine. No one was injured. Still, I dismissed them until further notice," Kolton replied, nodding when Vi and Brielle joined us. Instead of explaining further, he ushered us toward the exit.

"Do you think it's the coven?" Vi quietly said, glancing about as if she expected them to appear at any moment.

"No. Miss Gabby said that only the downstairs safe was broken into."

Vi shot him a panicked look. "Hendrix's phone."

"Was stolen, yes."

Anger flashed in her purple eyes. "*Arrow.*"

"Exactly. He made a play while we were gone. I should have known he would."

"Is he still there?" I asked, relinquishing my bags so he could toss them in the truck.

"I checked the security cameras. His motorcycle is missing."

"That *bastard*," Vi spat, yanking the door of her Jeep open a little too hard. "I'm going to skin him alive for double-crossing us."

"Our focus needs to be on *protecting* each other, not revenge, Violet."

At Kolton's stern tone, Vi's anger fizzled out. "Yes, Alpha."

"Good. You and Griff are taking Brielle back to the house. Jagger and I have Nora and Mellie. Keep an eye out for trouble. Who knows what Pemberton will do next."

Nodding, she slid inside the Jeep, her focus sharp. I tried to give Brielle a reassuring look before she hopped into the back, but couldn't quite manage it. I was too miserable. Too *guilty*. Once again, this all felt like my fault. Without meaning to, I'd put the people I loved in more danger. If I hadn't made that deal with Arrow. If I hadn't suggested we question Hendrix. If I hadn't taken that stupid *phone*.

This wouldn't be happening.

Don't beat yourself up, little one, Shadow spoke in my mind, surprising me. *You did what you thought was right. That's all any of us can ask for. You're not responsible for that weasel's actions.*

I glanced at Kolton to find him already watching me, empathy clear in his expression. *You heard me too?* I asked him, wincing when he slowly nodded.

We all did, another voice spoke, this time Storm's. *Shadow is . . . Shadow is right. You want to see the best in people, and that's nothing to be ashamed of. You tried to make the most of a bad situation, and we don't fault you for the outcome. If anyone's to blame, it's me. Zuriel is obviously not happy with how things have turned out.*

You're not to blame either, angel, Shadow said. *Zuriel is clearly a prick and doesn't deserve you.*

Despite the dire situation, a laugh burst from me. *Okay, I have to agree with you there, Shadow. Zuriel is totally a prick.*

Agreed. Such a prick, Kolton's voice rumbled through my mind, making me laugh again.

He smiled at the sound, then nodded at the truck. Right. Clear and present danger. Time to go. But, as I scrambled into the back with Melanie, my heart felt lighter. I had my very own little support group, one I could rely on when doubt crept in. I didn't fail to see how fortunate I was. How *blessed*.

These were my *people*. No matter the threat, I would do everything in my power to keep them safe.

When we arrived back at the estate, Arrow was well and truly gone.

Seeing the physical evidence of his treachery filled me with so much hurt and disappointment that I knew the feelings weren't solely mine.

They were Storm's.

I'd felt her pain before but hadn't fully realized it at the time. The bond that she and I shared was growing. She was feeling less and less like a stranger to me and more and more like a friend. One filled with so much sadness that all I wanted to do was protect her from it.

In her eyes, Arrow's disappearance was like Zuriel leaving her all over again. I knew how awful it felt to be abandoned. To be *rejected*. Her hurt was mine, which oddly made me feel that much closer to her. We had something in common. I could relate to her on some level. I could lend a listening ear and offer comfort. I could *understand*.

She'd simply wanted to be a respected member of the "pack." Instead, the person who was supposed to protect her at all costs had mistreated and betrayed her. She'd been cast aside, all because she hadn't properly *fit*. I understood that pain all too well.

You'll always have a place here with us, I whispered to her, knowing she would understand my meaning. *No matter what you are, we accept you.*

I felt a flare of gratitude, right before she whispered back, *Thank you.*

As evening crept up on us, tensions arose. We had gathered in the sitting room for another meeting, and the only one not in attendance was Melanie. We'd waited until her nanny had taken her upstairs for a bath, then started debating what we should do next. Problem was, everyone had a different opinion. Vi wanted to contact Arrow's pack again to see if they'd heard from him. Jagger wanted us to return to the NYC penthouse. Griff wanted to track Arrow down using Hendrix's phone location. Brielle simply wanted to be a part of it all, despite the continued danger.

Only Kolton hadn't expressed his opinion. Instead, he calmly listened to everyone's input, then looked at me and said, "What about you, Nora? What do you think we should do?"

I blinked, caught off guard that he was asking *me*. Sure, I was his wife and now the alpha female of Midnight Pack, but my last suggestion hadn't exactly panned out well. Arrow was now in possession of something that could cause us serious harm.

When I hesitated, Kolton's voice filtered through my mind. *You aren't to blame for what happened with Arrow, remember? We all supported the deal you made with him. He didn't give us much choice anyway. Unless I'd killed him, I always knew there was a chance he would betray us.*

Swallowing the lump in my throat, I replied, *But what if I continue to make bad decisions because I'm a poor judge of character? I thought the witches were going to help me at first, and I truly thought Arrow wanted our help. What if all I do is misjudge people and cause more harm than good?*

Even the people we are closest to can hide who they truly are, Kolton said. *Putting our trust in others is a scary thing. Trust can be abused and broken, which can cause us to doubt ourselves, but that doesn't mean we are broken. We're all flawed beings living in a flawed world. No one is exempt. We decide who to trust and not to trust every day, and learn from the choices we make. Mistakes will be made, but we aren't defined by them. We live, we learn, and we do better. That's all any of us can do, Nora. And at the end of the day, all we can hope to find is someone worthy of our trust.*

Like *him.*

I knew I could trust Kolton without a shadow of a doubt. I hadn't at first though. I'd doubted and straight up thought he was the bad guy. I nearly laughed at how foolish I'd been. How ignorant and blind.

But I'd learned, just like he said. I'd made plenty of mistakes along the way, but I'd learned to trust him. To look beyond the surface and see him for who he truly was.

If I could do that, then maybe I wasn't completely hopeless after all. Maybe I could be relied upon to make sound decisions. To be a *leader*. Maybe my pack could look to me for advice . . . and trust that my intentions were pure. That I was flawed but trying my best to keep them safe.

Sensing my shift in mood, my growing *confidence*, Kolton slowly smiled.

I smiled back. *Remind me to properly thank you after this*, I suggestively told him, smiling wider when heat filled his gaze. Finally noticing how quiet the room had become, I glanced at the others.

Busted, Kolton said with a quiet chuckle.

Yeah. We were. I could tell by the looks we were receiving that everyone was aware of our private conversation. We'd been having them a *lot* lately. Hey, speaking mind-to-mind was super handy, especially if the conversation got a little naughty. There were a lot of people in this house with supernatural hearing, after all.

"Care to clue us in?" Jagger said, raising an eyebrow. He was standing by the fireplace with an arm propped on the mantle.

Trying to adopt his serious expression, I replied, "Kolton was just telling me that it's hard to know who to trust sometimes. I haven't always trusted the right people, but I know with absolute certainty that I can trust every single person in this room. And that's why I think we should stay right where we are. We don't know what Arrow plans to do with that phone, but hiding doesn't guarantee protection, and looking for trouble doesn't guarantee answers. All I know is that we can count on each other. This is our home, and I think we should defend it against any possible threat."

Kolton's pride filtered through our bond. "I agree with Nora. We should stay put and prepare for any possible outcome. We've never allowed threats to drive us from our home in the past. Why should we start now?"

One by one, the others nodded their agreement. I bit my lip, overwhelmed by their support.

Come here, wife, Kolton crooned inside my mind. *You look way too adorable to be sitting over there, so far away from my lonely lap.*

Grinning like an idiot, I jumped up from the couch and hurried over to his chair. Not thinking twice about our audience, I curled up on his lap. Kolton released a pleased rumble, fitting me more securely against him.

"Well, I'm out," Vi said from the couch I'd just vacated, shooting to her feet.

"Me too," Brielle replied, hopping up.

"Me three."

"Me four."

Both Griff and Jagger were already halfway across the room when Kolton murmured against my neck, "Where are you all going in such a hurry?"

"Anywhere but here, boss," Jagger said, so seriously that I burst out laughing.

Are we really that bad? Kolton said in my mind, kissing the spot where he'd claimed me.

We're really that bad, I breathlessly replied as my body flushed with heat. *I think they know now when we need some alone time.*

His lips curled into a smile against my neck. *Good. Then let's go be bad some more.*

I squealed as he picked me up and charged across the room like a linebacker. He made it all the way up to our bedroom in seven seconds flat.

You thought to trick me, naughty wolf.
Thought to trap me, shame shame shame.
You thought to best me, little wolf.
Now you must pay, pay, pay.

Keisha! I silently screamed, shooting up in bed. I tore open my eyes to discover the room blindingly bright.

I tried to stop her, Storm roared, and the light flared brighter. *She evaded my attack and slipped past long enough to leave a message. I'm sorry, Nora.*

Before I could respond, Kolton charged in from the bathroom. At the sight of my glow worm appearance, a wave of his panic struck my chest.

"What happened?" he said, wrapping a towel around his waist as he strode toward the bed. "Did the witch contact you again?"

I nodded, gulping in air as I tried to calm myself. The moment Storm's true form dimmed, he pulled me into his arms.

"I'm sorry, sweetness," he said, holding me impossibly tight. "I shouldn't have left you alone."

I clung to him, seeking comfort from his warmth and scent. His skin was still wet from the shower and dampened my thin nightgown. "It's not your fault. I chose to sleep in instead of joining you in the shower. Neither of us could have known that Keisha was waiting for that very opportunity. Storm tried to stop her, but she still managed to leave a creepy little message. A *rhyming* one, of all things."

A knock had us both glancing at the door.

"Come in," Kolton called. When Vi, Griff, and Jagger entered, he explained, "The witch contacted Nora again."

"We heard," Jagger replied. "What did she have to say this time?"

I quickly recited the message, then said, "Arrow must have texted the coven through Hendrix's phone."

"He's such an *idiot*," Vi seethed. "We *told* him this would happen."

Griff gave her shoulder a comforting squeeze, and she unconsciously leaned into his touch.

"What should we do, boss?" Jagger said, already dressed for the day in his usual black garb.

Kolton blew out a resigned sigh. "I think we need to prepare for an attack."

Jagger hiked up both brows. "Here?"

"Here."

CHAPTER 32

The attack came three hours later, but not in the form we'd expected.

I was in the kitchen with Brielle, begging her to return home to Albany where it was safe. The witches didn't know about her yet. Getting far away from here was the best thing for her, considering she was human. She'd barely escaped an attack from a six-year-old *girl*. No way would she survive an entire witch coven.

"But you need my *help*, Nora," she adamantly replied, refusing to listen to reason. "You said the coven has at least a dozen members. Even without their leader, they have you outnumbered two to one. I can at least help even the odds."

"A strong werewolf can easily handle two witches at once in a fight," I argued back, losing my patience. "But one bolt of magic could kill you in a second. I won't have your death on my conscience, Brie. You're leaving."

Anger sparked in her green eyes, an emotion I'd never seen her direct my way before. I braced myself, knowing that she was about to unleash a torrent of words. Sure enough, she opened her mouth. I tensed, ready for the deluge.

Before she could blast me with her fury, Vi stepped into the room. At the expression on her face, the argument came to an abrupt halt.

"What is it, Vi?" I asked with concern. She looked pale, like she'd seen a ghost.

"A package just arrived," she said, her voice a quiet rasp. "It's addressed to you."

I frowned. "To me? I didn't order anything."

"It's . . . it's from the witches."

At her words, my senses went on high alert. "Show me."

She blinked, then quickly said, "Kolton thinks I should just tell you. He doesn't want you to see."

I was moving a second later, ignoring Vi's protests as I shouldered past. It wasn't long before the *smell* hit me. I was suddenly running, following my nose toward the source. There was no mistaking that scent.

Blood.

Lots of it. Disturbingly fresh and . . . familiar.

At the sound of my approach, Kolton met me in the foyer.

"Nora . . ." he started, his voice filled with caution.

"Let me see," I demanded, slowing as I tried to get around him. To see what he was hiding in his office.

"It's horrific," he said, grabbing my arms when I attempted to slip past him. "You don't want this image to be your last memory of him."

My eyes snapped up to his. At the haunted look I found there, all the air whooshed from my lungs. "Him who?" I whispered, starting to shake. When he didn't respond, my jaw hardened. "I want to see."

He stared at me for a long moment, no doubt feeling my firm resolve. He wouldn't find an ounce of weakness. I was nothing but determined now. I *had* to know.

After a moment more, he sighed and slowly released me.

In a flash, I pulled away and entered his study. Jagger and Griff straightened at the sight of me, throwing worried glances at Kolton over my shoulder.

"Let her see," he quietly said. They looked two seconds away from arguing but didn't say a word when I made my way to Kolton's desk.

To the square box perched on top.

The smell was definitely coming from inside the box. This close, it was overwhelming. So powerful that I almost gagged. Instinctively, I knew that the blood didn't belong to an animal of prey. That fact alone was what drew me closer and closer, despite the warning bells ringing in my head.

When I stopped beside the desk, Griff reached into the box and pulled off what looked like a cooler lid. The smell hit me tenfold. Holding my breath, I steeled my spine and peered into the box. At first, I didn't know what I was looking at. Inside the box was indeed a cooler. And inside the cooler was a roundish shape. At the base of the shape was a pool of dark blood. I looked up at the shape again and suddenly realized what it was.

A head.

I was staring at a decapitated *head*.

One with missing eyes.

The gory black holes seemed to glare back at me. *This is your fault, young lady*, they accused. *If you'd only obeyed me, this never would have happened.*

Alpha Hendrix. They'd *killed* Alpha Hendrix.

You put me in an early grave, Nora. You've brought me nothing but trouble and disappointment. You—

Slapping a hand over my mouth, I stumbled back. Strong arms were immediately there, offering their support. Kolton turned me to face him, cupping the back of my head so I couldn't look back. It didn't matter. The image of Hendrix's mutilated head was already etched into my memory. Strangled gasps left me as bile rushed up my throat.

"I'm sorry," Kolton whispered, pulling me tight against him. "I'm so sorry."

Struggling to breathe, I managed to get out, "Is that it? Is th-that all they sent?"

Silence greeted me.

"Kolton, *tell me!*" I practically screamed, nearly in hysterics. When I pulled away, he let me go. Staring him dead in the eye, I slowly demanded, "Was. There. Anything. Else?"

Sorrow lined his face. He nodded at Jagger, who handed him a slip of paper. When he held it out to me, I snatched it from him and quickly began to read.

You stole my eyes, so I stole his. I'll steal more eyes 'til you turn yourself in. —Keisha, Blackstone Coven Leader

My legs nearly gave out.

Keisha was their *leader* now?

I shot Kolton a panicked look. "My parents."

"Already on it. The minute we opened the box, I called them. They're shaken up over the news of Hendrix's death, but they're currently unharmed. I sent one of my most trusted pack members to secure them. Buck knows how to get in and out without being seen. He'll relocate your parents to a safehouse on pack land for the time being."

I nodded, blinking back tears. "Thank you. Sorry I snapped at you."

His expression softened. "You have nothing to be sorry for, Nora. I just wish we could have stopped this from happening." When my gaze dropped to the note again, he deftly plucked it from my fingers. "*That* won't be happening."

My gaze went back up to his. "But she wants *me*. I could stop anyone else from getting hurt."

"By sacrificing yourself? I'll say it one more time, sweetness. Not happening."

I pressed my lips together, refusing to argue. I wouldn't win anyway. The strong emotions flooding our bond told me that much. Still, I wasn't going to sit idly by, waiting for the witches to attack again. To kill someone I actually *loved* next time. I needed to be prepared. I needed to *protect* them.

"Train me," I blurted, crossing my arms over my chest.

Kolton's brow furrowed. "Train you?"

"Yes. You know how to fight. You know how to *protect*. So teach me. Teach me everything you know."

It's what I should have done from the beginning. Asked Kolton to help me instead of Arrow.

"Nora," Kolton began, searching my face. "You're in shock. You should take a moment to grieve. To process your emotions."

"I'm not in shock, and I don't need to process anything. I'm sad that Hendrix died in such a brutal way, but he never once showed me an ounce of love. He *hated* me, and I don't . . . I don't want to grieve for him. I want to *act*. To train. To keep myself busy so I don't do something stupid like turn myself in."

On second thought, I probably shouldn't have admitted that last part. Kolton looked two seconds away from locking me in our room and throwing away the key.

Please, Kolton, I said mind-to-mind, hoping to keep him from doing just that. *I don't want to think about what just happened. I need to do something. I need to feel strong and in control, or I'm going to break.*

It was the perfect thing to say. I immediately sensed his understanding. Saw it in his eyes. Gently tucking a curl behind my ear, he nodded and said, "Okay. Then let's go train."

302

It helped. Staying active. Not allowing myself to overthink. I'd taken karate classes as a teen, but had learned the *human* way. The werewolf way of fighting was a lot more brutal, to say the least. The more blood spilled, the better.

We spent the afternoon outdoors, using the lawn space that had once held our wedding to spar. Even Melanie joined us, quietly playing with her stuffed unicorn in the grass. I'd watched with barely-concealed horror as Kolton and Jagger had demonstrated, each drawing their fair share of blood. Thankfully, no bones were broken and they remained in their human forms. Despite my horror, I'd greedily soaked up every maneuver, asking again and again when it was my turn to practice.

"Don't you get enough practice in the bedroom?" Griff had said, earning several groans. I'd then watched with glee as Vi had challenged him to a match. The girl could *fight*, which shouldn't have surprised me. Griff was physically stronger, but she was by far the fastest. He was flat on his back in no time, wheezing his surrender as she dug a knee into his sternum.

"I expected more out of you, Griffin," she teased him, lifting her knee to offer him a hand up.

"I'm a little rusty," he admitted with a good-natured smirk, accepting her help. But when he was on his feet, he pulled her close and murmured, "Maybe you can give me some private lessons later."

She shoved him away with a snort, but I could have sworn I saw longing in her eyes. Longing that quickly turned into an eye roll.

By the end of the day, I'd received enough training that my tired body was more than ready for sleep. Only, once I stopped moving, the looming threat the witches posed dominated my thoughts again. Namely, Keisha's latest message.

I could fall asleep right now. Allow Keisha to invade my mind.

Turn myself in. It was *that* simple.

In the past, I might have seriously considered it. Might have recklessly put myself in danger without a second thought, believing it was the only way.

But I knew better now. Knew that risking my life would only hurt the people I loved, not help them. No matter how badly I wanted to keep them safe, handing myself over to Keisha wasn't the solution. She would only torture me to death then set her sights on the rest of my family.

She was obsessed. And obsessed people didn't stop until they got what they wanted.

No, I had to think things through. Had to be *patient*. Two of my least favorite activities.

"Welcome to being a leader, wife," Kolton rumbled in my ear, pulling me back against his warm chest. "Thinking is part of the job requirement."

I huffed a laugh, realizing I'd been thinking a little too hard. "But how do you know when to *act*?"

"You don't always know. Listening to your gut is a good first step. Taking the advice of those closest to you. Learning to trust your instincts."

I groaned. "I have a *lot* to learn."

Chuckling, he tightened his arms around me and said, "I'll be right beside you every step of the way, sweetness. I promise. You'll never have to do it alone."

I snuggled against him and shut my eyes, allowing his promise to lull me into a dreamless sleep.

Days went by.

Days and days without a single peep from Arrow or the coven. No more boxes arrived. No more messages, not even in my dreams.

We'd canceled the meeting with Arrow's pack, too focused on the coven's impending attack. My parents had been safely secured, and Hendrix's head had been returned to his pack. I still hadn't grieved his death. Maybe never would. But his fate still troubled me. Still filled me with fear.

I hadn't turned myself in. Hadn't given in to Keisha's demands. She could retaliate at any moment. Could pick her next target. She may be blind, but that didn't seem to stop her. We'd prepared as best we could, keeping watch at night. Keeping to ourselves so the rest of the pack wouldn't get involved. They couldn't shift at will like we could, and Kolton still didn't want our abilities to become public knowledge. Plus, the more they stayed out of it, the safer they were from the coven.

If only Brielle felt the same way. She *refused* to leave, despite my best efforts to scare her off. Each day that passed was harder than the last. I spent most of my waking hours training, which allowed me to keep a better eye out for witches, but my worry grew and grew.

It was like waiting for a bomb to drop.

On the evening of the fifth day, after another grueling afternoon of training, I headed upstairs for a quick shower. It had become my routine. Mornings were for meetings. Afternoons for training. Before a hearty dinner, I went upstairs to wash the sweat from my body. That way, I was smelling fresh for my evening alone-time with Kolton.

Not that he cared either way what I smelled like. He just wanted *me*. We'd been mated for a little over a week now and things hadn't cooled between us. If anything, the threat of danger and long days of training only heightened our need for each other. We'd spent more than one night passionately making love until the wee hours of the morning.

I marveled at how much stronger our bond felt after each encounter. Even my own body felt stronger, which was another perk of our union. Kolton's strength was now mine, and mine was his. The closer we became, the more we could feed off each other. The more we could *give*. Not just physically, but mentally and emotionally.

Our bond was like a channel, flowing freely between us. The more we fueled it, the stronger it flowed. Discovering all our bond had to offer was worth every hour of lost sleep.

It was like an addiction. One that I unapologetically gave myself to.

He'd taken me from behind again last night, knotting me more than once. The thought of a repeat performance tonight filled my body with an all-too-familiar heat. Groaning, I switched the shower to cold. How long was this mating frenzy going to last? Not that I was complaining. Sex with Kolton was the highlight of my day. Each time was new, exciting, and filled me with more and more love for him. I couldn't be happier to be his soulmate.

Still . . . the constant need to bone was a tad bit distracting. Not just for me but for the entire household. Knowing they could hear us and were probably losing sleep almost made me feel guilty. Except that I was too ridiculously happy to stop.

When my stomach rumbled with hunger, I turned off the shower and toweled myself dry. Just knowing that *Kolton* was preparing dinner made me hurry to finish up. We'd missed having the staff around this past week, but I would always love Kolton's cooking best.

Donning a tank top and shorts, I released my hair from its messy bun and shook out the curls. Ever since Kolton had saved me from a bad haircut, I'd paid more attention to its maintenance. I even oiled it on a regular basis. Coconut was my current favorite.

Softly humming, I finished up with my hair and headed into the bedroom. I was almost to the door when something in the corner caught my eye. I paused, remembering the cartful of blankets I'd purchased this past weekend. After everything that had happened, I'd almost forgotten about them. They were still inside shopping bags, sitting neglected on the floor. Normally meticulous, Kolton hadn't even seemed to notice them.

A powerful urge suddenly shivered through my limbs. An *itch*, one that I couldn't help but scratch. Completely ignoring my growling stomach, I beelined for the blankets. One by one, I removed their tags and placed them on the bed. Each blanket I'd chosen was super soft. Not a single one chafed against my skin.

I hummed my approval and started to arrange them in an overlapping pattern, like the petals on a rose. Each blanket represented a petal, an important part of the whole. When I reached the center, I paused to inspect my creation, then decided to leave it empty.

Stepping back, I stared at the bundle of soft blankets . . . and smiled.

Perfect. It was *perfect*.

The door suddenly opened. I turned to find Kolton entering, and my smile stretched a mile wide. When he immediately returned the smile, I stepped aside to let him see my creation. His gaze landed on the blankets, and he froze. The smile started to slip. Shock sparked through our bond, followed by disbelief.

His chest heaved, like he was struggling to pull in air.

"Nora," he said, his voice rough with emotion.

A violent tremor shook him as he continued to stare at the blankets.

"Nora," he repeated, finally lifting his eyes to mine.

I gasped at what I found.
Fear. His eyes were filled with *fear*.

CHAPTER 33

NORA

Alarmed, I stepped toward him. "Kolton, what is it?"

He opened his mouth, only to be interrupted by Jagger's sudden arrival.

"Brielle's missing."

At the slight panic in his voice, all the blood drained from my face. "What do you mean *missing?* Did she leave?"

"Her car's still in the garage. I just checked. We've started a more thorough search of the house and grounds. Still no sign of her."

At that, Kolton snapped out of it. The fear vanished as he turned to Jagger and said, "Tell me everything. When and where you saw her last, who she was with. No detail is too small."

When they started to exit the room, I quickly followed.

Kolton stopped me at the door. "Stay here, Nora. We don't know what we're dealing with yet."

"But—"

"It could be the witches. You're safest here."

"Yes, but—"

He stepped into me and cupped my face. "*Stay,*" he fiercely said, yet his eyes pleaded with me to obey him. "Please stay, Nora."

Before I could respond, he captured my lips in an almost desperate kiss, then turned and strode from the room. I gaped after him, my mind reeling. Jagger's voice carried down the stairs and across the foyer, fading as they exited the front door. I stood still for a long moment, listening to the urgent calls and footsteps inside the house as everyone searched for Brielle.

For my *best friend*. The human girl I'd allowed into this dangerous world. Into *my* world, when I'd been told again and again not to. But I'd done it anyway, because I'd been *selfish*.

Guilt punched me in the gut, robbing me of air. If anything happened to her, I'd never forgive myself.

My mind made up, I finally moved. Hurrying past my blanket creation, I grabbed my new phone from the nightstand, then left the room behind. More guilt hit me, guilt for ignoring Kolton's order, but I couldn't wait this time. Every instinct I possessed told me to *go, go, go*. Brielle needed me. I could feel it in my bones.

Slipping down the stairs, I headed in the opposite direction that Kolton and Jagger had gone. Ever since I'd told Brielle to leave five days ago, our relationship had been strained. And when Brielle was upset, she tended to eat her feelings. So I beelined for the kitchen. Maybe she'd decided to sneak some ice cream before dinner. She could have been waiting until Kolton left, then hid inside the pantry with her spoils.

I'd done it myself when I'd first come here. Vi had found me, but only after I'd managed to eat half the jar of peanut butter.

As I opened the kitchen door, I held onto hope that I'd find my best friend there. "Brielle?" I called, immediately bombarded by the smells of Kolton's dinner. The food was neatly laid out on the island, kept warm inside covered serving dishes. Ignoring the loud growl of my stomach, I crossed the room and peered inside the pantry.

Empty.

Trying not to panic, I searched the kitchen for any sign of her. *There!* A single spoon and pint of ice cream on the counter. She'd been here then, not too long ago. But where was she now? I scanned the space for more signs, but nothing stood out to me.

Until I glanced at the door. The door that led outside. The one I'd used a long time ago to make my escape. It was cracked open. Less than an inch, but enough to make the hairs on my body stand on end.

No one in this house would so carelessly leave an outside door open, not even Melanie. Unless they'd been leaving in a hurry.

Approaching the door, I focused my heightened senses on detecting Brielle's scent. When I caught a strong whiff of it on the doorknob, my alarm grew. I whipped open the door and stepped outside, dialing her number at the same time. When it started to ring, I paused, straining my ears for any sound.

At first, all I heard was the chirp of crickets and the wind rustling through the trees. And then I heard it.

Her *ringtone*. The one she'd selected simply because she knew it annoyed the hell out of me.

It was faint. Barely a whisper. But as the song drifted through the air, I began to run. Straight into the woods.

This late in the day, the woods were nearly pitch black. That didn't stop me. As I raced barefoot into the darkness, my night vision kicked in. Still clutching my phone, I followed the sound of that annoying ringtone, praying it wouldn't—

The sound stopped.

Yeah. That.

Didn't matter. I'd already picked up hints of Brielle's scent, just enough to track her. As I went, another scent tickled my senses. One that caused dread to slither down my spine. I almost stopped. Almost did the *smart* thing and sought out Kolton through our bond. But, at the last moment, I set my jaw and forged ahead.

This confrontation was *long* overdue. It was time I took care of this problem once and for all.

The farther into the woods I traveled, the stronger both of their scents became, until I finally slowed to scan my surroundings. Except for the typical nighttime activity, I couldn't see or hear anything abnormal. Still, their scents were too strong. Too *fresh*. They had to be close.

"Show yourself, Arrow," I called into the night. The frantic rustling of bat wings greeted my words. As they faded away, silence descended once again. Then . . .

"I knew you would figure it out."

Arrow materialized from behind a tree, but he wasn't alone. He had my best friend clutched against him, one hand circling her throat. At the sight of me, she began to struggle.

"Shh, shh, shh," he crooned in Brielle's ear, tightening his hold on her neck. When she flinched, I zeroed in on his fingers.

Claws. He had his *claws* out.

"Are you out of your mind?" I hissed, stepping toward them. "You're going to *scratch* her."

He tightened his hold even more, and I stopped dead.

"Don't. Please don't hurt her, Arrow. Don't . . . don't cut her."

"I won't, Nora. You have my word, so long as everyone cooperates. I'll forgive the ringing phone, but no more outbursts." He eyed me hard. "That includes any communication with your *mate*. If I find out you contacted him, Brielle pays the price."

I slipped my phone into my pocket and held up my hands. "I didn't contact him. No one knows I'm out here. But they know Brielle is missing. It won't be long before they pick up her scent trail too."

He shrugged. "We'll be long gone before that happens."

"We?"

"You and me, of course. I came to rescue you from this place."

I barked an incredulous laugh. "You're insane, Arrow. I should

312

have known from the beginning not to make that deal with you. After what you went through with the witches, I tried to be sympathetic, but there's no reasoning with you. Why can't you see that I'm perfectly *happy* here?"

His eyes flashed dangerously bright. "Happy? With *them*? How could you still be so stupidly naive after everything I told you, Nora?"

I dropped my hands to my sides, squeezing them into fists. "You're the one who stabbed me in the back by contacting the Blackstone Coven. Do you know what Keisha *did*? She killed Hendrix. Probably as punishment for giving us his phone. And if I don't turn myself in soon, she's going to kill again."

He shook his head. "I didn't stab you in the back, Nora. I stabbed *them* in the back, the demons masquerading as a happy little family. It was my plan all along. Once I heard about the Blackstone Coven, I gave myself up for testing. I needed to see if they were legit. And they are. They can't exorcise angelic spirits, but they can cast out *demons*. It's the taint they can remove. The *filth*. When I realized that, I started to plan my escape, and that's when you showed up.

"I knew almost immediately that your celestial wasn't demonic. The witches' magic didn't work on you, not even a little. You were *untouchable*. And when I managed to grab your hand that one time through the bars, I sensed who your celestial was. The bond she still shares with Zuriel stirred awake, filling me with *hope* for the first time in years. It renewed my strength. My purpose. Divine fate sent you there to *help* me.

"Everything started falling into place after that. You revealed your connection to the Midnight Pack, which allowed me to get close to the demons like I hadn't in years. With you there, it was all too easy to set my plans into motion. All I needed was that phone to light a fire under the witches, and it worked. They figured out I wasn't

Hendrix, but assumed the texts were from you. I let them think so, only because I knew that would eventually lead them here. I never wanted to kill them. I've only ever wanted to rid the world of the demon spawn you've been living with. And now I have the proper leverage to do so."

All the blood drained from my face. "Oh, Arrow, what have you done?" I whispered, staring at him in disbelief. In *horror*. But he didn't seem to notice. He was too busy trying to *convince* me.

"When you failed to turn yourself in, the coven sent me one last message a few hours ago," he went on, his voice growing more and more animated. "They're coming. They're coming for you all. Maybe even today. It's why I came here, Nora. For *you*. I don't care that you're mated, not anymore. I know our bond is strong enough to wash away the taint. You will be pure again, once you're mated to me.

"And when the demons are cast from this earth, I'm prepared to strike a bargain with the Blackstone Coven. In exchange for sparing us, we hand over any werewolves with demonic spirits to them. With the resources I'll be gaining once I'm crowned the new alpha of Midnight Pack, it shouldn't be hard to track down more of them. We could even find more like us and create our very own legion again. We'll be a *family*."

The wide-eyed look Brielle was giving me no doubt mirrored my own expression. I could barely understand what Arrow was saying. It was insane. All of it. Certifiably *insane*. He wanted to *mate* me?

"So you're telling me," I began, barely able to contain my fury, "that your pack *didn't* betray you? That you *let* the coven capture and torture you, all so you could prove their ability to cast out spirits?"

"I know it sounds crazy, Nora, but it's my calling. I can't protect the world from demons like I used to, so finding someone who can was the next best option."

What the hell?

"You? Like *you* used to? Do you hear yourself, Arrow? You're not *Zuriel.*" At my sharp tone, his eyes narrowed in warning. But I wasn't done. Not even close. "And there's no way the witches will agree to that bargain. They don't care what kind of spirits werewolves possess. They don't want *any* of us to possess them, be they angels or demons or Fallen. All you'll be doing is fueling their exorcism crusade. And really? You think I'm going to *let* you become the alpha of Midnight Pack? You think I'm going to *let* you destroy my family? Think again. I will stop you. I will fight you myself if I have to."

Brielle gasped as Arrow dug his claws into her vulnerable throat, impossibly close to breaking the skin.

"Defy me and your friend loses her humanity," he bit out, his voice more guttural than moments before.

At the sound, heat surged through me. So overpowering that I had no choice but to snarl back, "Harm her and you will be no better than the demons you so desperately hate."

A smile slowly curled Arrow's lips. "Seraphina," he said, in that same guttural tone. "It's about time you showed up. Have you come to challenge me then? Or will you run away like last time? Either way, I will have your submission. I will have your *loyalty.*"

At his roar, my claws shot out. "You will have *neither,*" I roared back. Or rather, *Storm* did. "I am done, Zuriel. Done serving you. Done obeying your narcissistic orders. Bond or no bond, I *reject* you."

Arrow reared his head back as if I'd struck him, yet managed to keep his firm grip on Brielle. "Reject me? I *made* you, Seraphina. You would be *nothing* without me. The only reason why we are here right now, stuck in these miserable mortal bodies, is because of you. You owe me your allegiance. You owe me *everything.*"

Holy hell, this was escalating fast.

Storm and Zuriel were totally in charge now. If I didn't gain back control, a fight was certainly going to break out. And Brielle was still stuck in the middle.

Kolton, I need you! I desperately cried out through our bond, struggling as Storm gained more and more control over my body. *Arrow has Brielle. Storm is about to fight him.*

Sure enough, fur erupted over my arms and legs. Arrow saw and, with a growl, started shifting too. Brielle whimpered, her eyes filled with stark fear.

Where are you? Kolton's voice came through loud and clear. Just the sound of it made me want to cry tears of relief.

In the woods. Not far from the path I took that time I tried escaping.

I'm on my way. Whatever you do, don't engage Arrow.

I'm trying not to, but Storm is forcing the shift.

STORM!

At the violent force of the word, I froze. *Storm* froze.

You will not fight Arrow, Storm, Kolton commanded, his authority absolute. *You will stand down right this instant.*

I felt my lips pull back in a defiant snarl.

If you allow harm to come to my mate, I will never forgive you.

Surprise pricked my chest. Then shame.

A soft whine left my throat. Storm's whine.

She's my whole world, Storm. Whatever happens to her happens to me.

The whine intensified, and then I felt it. Her retreat. Her submission. The fur on my skin began to recede.

Confusion flickered in Arrow's gaze. "What's happening? Why is Seraphina retreating?"

Finally able to speak again, I said, "Because she chose to submit. Just not to you."

Frowning, he opened his mouth. But before he could say anything, a terrifying howl shuddered through the trees. Followed by loud crashing as something *huge* tore through the woods.

I shivered, but not with fear. My days of being afraid of Kolton— of *Shadow*—were long gone.

Arrow, on the other hand, noticeably flinched. Brielle released a startled hiss and reached for her throat.

When her fingers came away red with blood, my heart stopped.

"Brielle," I whimpered, staring in horror at the growing stain on her neck.

When she saw the blood, a strangled laugh left her. "Crap. Does this mean I'm infected? Am I going to sprout fur and a tail now?"

Instead of answering, I shot Arrow the darkest glare I could muster and roared, "How could you? *How could you?!*"

He quickly released her like he'd been burned and backed away, the fire in his eyes dimming. "It was an accident. I *swear*, Nora. I would never . . ."

Another howl ripped through the air, terrifying in its intensity.

More fur sprouted over Arrow. His bones began to crack as he allowed the shift to overtake him. His canines elongated, yet he still managed to say, "Come with me, Nora. I can't protect you from the witches if you stay. We weren't meant to be enemies. We can fix this. Fix *us*."

I watched him shift, forcing myself to remain where I was. "That's where you're wrong, Arrow. We were enemies far before we met. There's no undoing that now."

His lips pulled back in a grimace as the rest of his body transformed into a silver wolf. Kolton was seconds away now. The urge to stop Arrow from leaving—to pin him down so I could watch my mate tear him to pieces—was a temptation I could barely resist.

But I didn't move an inch. As Arrow shook off the change and cast me one last glance—almost *pleading* with me to follow him—I looked away. I *dismissed* him. As he rightly deserved.

A moment later, he took off like a shot, racing through the woods as if the devil himself was on his tail. And he *was*. So close that I could feel the ground tremble beneath my feet.

He was suddenly there. A wall of shadow and blood-red eyes. Bloodlust and violent fury burned in his gaze, nearly driving me to my knees.

Brielle made a choking sound but was too shocked to move. "Please don't let him eat me. Please, please, please."

"He's not going to eat you, Brie," I said. But he *was* going to eat Arrow if I didn't stop him. I only had a split second. *One* second to take action before he charged on by like a freight train.

Bracing for a collision, I stepped into his path.

He immediately slammed on the brakes. Dirt and rocks pelted my legs as he skidded across the ground, stopping just in the nick of time.

Holy hell, that was close. *Too* close.

As he towered above me, I craned my neck back, marveling at how massive he was. Yup. He was still the stuff of nightmares in his demon form. If I didn't know him better now, I'd be peeing myself.

"I must go. I must *kill*," Shadow growled, his powerful chest heaving. "Can't let him get away."

Despite his monstrous appearance and searing red gaze, I didn't back away. Didn't even flinch. More surprisingly, neither did Storm. For the first time ever, she didn't react to Shadow's presence.

Tell him to settle, Kolton said through our bond.

Me? I incredulously asked, certain I'd heard him wrong.

Yes, sweetness. He respects you. He'll listen.

Oh, wow. This terrifying beast respected *me?* That pleased me more than I thought it would. So much so that any remaining fear I might have had melted away.

Stepping even closer to him, I reached up and placed my hand on his chest, directly over his thundering heart. "Settle, big guy," I quietly, yet firmly, said. "We can't fight Arrow right now. He's not the threat we need to be worried about. The witches are coming."

Alarm flared through our bond.

When? Kolton said. *What did Arrow tell you?*

Only that they could arrive at any moment and plan to take us all out. To kill or capture, I don't know.

Shadow growled again, so forcefully that my whole arm shook. "I will kill them all this time. I will rip them to pieces with my teeth and claws. I will bathe the ground in their blood and entrails."

A swallow got stuck in my throat. "Wow, you really *are* violent."

Told you. I could have sworn Kolton chuckled.

"Hey, guys?" Brielle interrupted, keeping a safe distance from Shadow. "I know how the whole werewolf and moon thing works, but I think my eyesight is already changing. Everything's brighter and a little orange. Is that normal?"

Shadow stiffened. Lifting his head, he sniffed at the air. His ears immediately flattened against his skull. "Fire. *Magic* fire."

The blood in my veins turned to ice.

The witches.

They were here.

CHAPTER 34

Shadow.

One word from Kolton was all it took.

Shadow immediately dropped to all fours and barked, "Get on."

I didn't have time to panic. Didn't have time to hesitate. I hurried over to Brielle and dragged her forward.

"No way," she yelled, struggling to break loose. "There's no way I'm getting on that thing!"

"It's not a thing, it's *Shadow*," I shot back, using my supernatural strength to overpower her. "He won't hurt you, trust me."

As I forced her to Shadow's side, he crouched down.

She shook her head. "No—"

"Get *on*, Brielle," I snapped, tossing her onto Shadow's sloped back.

Cursing, she grabbed his fur and straddled him like a horse. "You and I are going to have *words*, Nora!"

I jumped on behind her, holding on tight as Shadow surged upward. "Looking forward to it, *bestie*."

Shadow lunged forward and Brielle screamed, clutching his fur for dear life.

"I'm going to need *therapy* after this," she wailed as we crashed through the woods at breakneck speed. "Therapy and tubs of ice cream!"

Despite her hysterics, we made it through the woods in one

piece. As soon as Shadow loped onto the lawn, it became perfectly clear where the orange glow was coming from.

"Kolton, the house!" I cried, staring in horror at the roof. It was on fire and quickly spreading, driven wild by a sudden wind. A *magic* wind.

Shadow picked up speed. I grabbed Brielle to keep her from tumbling off.

Yards away from the house, voices drifted on the wind. An eerie chant. A *spell*.

Shadow abruptly veered to the left, shooting straight toward the gap between the house and garage.

The voices grew louder and louder.

Shadow, NO, Kolton's voice thundered through my mind. *Find the others first. PROTECT.*

Shadow growled and shook his head, but changed course again. I breathed easier, tightly gripping his sides as he raced toward the kitchen door. Only when we were feet away did he skid to a halt and crouch to let us scramble off.

The moment we did, he began to shift. Faster than I thought possible, he morphed into Kolton. His muscles rippled as he stood, a sheen of sweat covering his naked form.

"*Jagger*," he hollered, ushering us both inside the house ahead of him. "*Vi. Griff. Mellie.*"

"Kol!" a frightened little voice immediately called back.

"*Mellie*," he shouted again, practically picking me and Brielle up in his haste to find the others.

"Over here!" another voice yelled, Vi this time.

Kolton surged ahead, racing through the kitchen and dining room. As we did, the air thickened with smoke and obscured our vision. Brielle began to loudly cough.

We were suddenly surrounded by familiar faces. I glanced around, nearly crying out with relief when each one was accounted for. Even Miss Gabby was here, looking more than a little frightened. She held Melanie, tightening her hold when the girl squirmed to be let down.

"You all know the plan," Kolton said, his voice rising above the crackling flames that were quickly eating the house from the top down. "Mellie, Miss Gabby, Brielle, it's time to leave. Head through the tunnel and don't look back. There's a car already waiting for you at the end. We'll meet you at the location we agreed upon."

Miss Gabby obediently nodded and turned toward the den. She knew what to do. Knew where to find the hidden button that opened up a secret staircase leading down to a tunnel below the house. The tunnel went deep into the woods, ending at a crude path barely wide enough for a car.

"Princess!" Melanie screamed, struggling in her nanny's arms. "I forgot Princess!"

The smoke swallowed them from view.

Fighting back tears, I pulled Brielle into a fierce hug. "Go. Miss Gabby will help you adjust if we don't—"

"Don't you dare say it," she snapped, pulling away to glare at me. "You're not dying, and I'm *not* leaving. I can *fight*. I'm one of you now."

"You know that's not how it works, Brie," I argued back. "You're basically still human. Still *weak*. One little cut isn't going to magically make you *Superwoman*."

"Cut? She got *cut?*" Vi said, reaching for Brielle.

Jagger beat her to it, tipping up Brielle's chin to expose the scratch on her throat. Even through the smoke, I could see his eyes flash yellow. "How did this happen?"

"Arrow," was all I said.

"We can talk about this later," Kolton firmly spoke. "She's leaving. Jagger, see that it's done."

Brielle jerked her face away and narrowed her gaze on Jagger. He stared back, his expression unreadable. "Don't. You. Dare," she quietly spat.

In one swift move, he had her over his shoulder.

"Put me down," she yelled, uselessly beating at his back. "Mark my words. When I wolf out, I'm going to rip you a new one. Jagger. *Jagger!*"

They vanished into the smoke.

Sighing, I turned to Kolton. "Okay, what now? Do we just walk out the front door and confront the witches?"

"Yes," he replied. Then quietly added, "But not you."

I blinked up at him, clearly having heard wrong. "What?"

His lips thinned. "You can't stay, Nora. You need to leave."

He might as well have suckerpunched me.

"Since when?" I demanded, not hiding my hurt. "That was never the plan, Kolton."

He stared at me, then looked away. "Griff, see that Nora is—"

"NO," I shouted, swiping my hand through the air when Griff stepped toward me. "I am the alpha female, and I say that I'm staying. You can't order me to leave, Kolton. I'm your wife. Your *mate*. I belong by your side, no matter what. I won't let anything tear us apart, remember? Even you."

At the desperation in my voice, he turned to look at me. When I found that same *fear* in his eyes, my breath caught. "Nora," he croaked, reaching up to touch my cheek. "I can't let you stay. You're—"

A deafening *crack* drowned out his voice.

"Look out!" Griff roared. He dove to the side, tackling Vi to the floor just as the ceiling caved.

I was suddenly airborne, wrapped tightly in arms made of steel. The world was fire and ash, but all I could feel was him, protecting me from it all. We hit the floor and rolled, barely dodging a wooden beam as it splintered the tiles. We were up a second later, scrambling to avoid being buried alive.

Griff and Vi joined us, racing for the foyer. As we neared the stairs, the giant crystal chandelier high above snapped free. It fell, fell, fell, slamming to the ground inches from our feet. We didn't stop. Didn't look back. Didn't slow. Not even when we reached the front door. Kolton simply lowered his shoulder and plowed through it. The frame snapped, and the door exploded outward.

We surged onto the porch in a billow of smoke, coughing and gasping for breath. When the house groaned menacingly above our heads, we moved for the steps.

"Jagger's still in there," I panted, wildly looking about. Tears from the smoke blurred my vision, but I could tell there were only four of us. "We need to go back."

When I turned, Kolton lifted me and leapt down the porch steps. Just in time too. A roar filled my ears as the entire house came down. Trembling. Screaming. A great ball of flame hurtling toward the ground.

When it struck, a powerful blast of glass and shrapnel flew through the air. Kolton covered my head, protecting me from the debris with his own body. Heat seared my skin. Smoke filled my lungs. I buried my face in his chest, a scream building in my throat. A scream that became a ragged cough as I choked on ash.

"Vi! Griff!" Kolton bellowed moments later, halting in the roundabout.

"Here," Vi called out from not far away, followed by a fit of coughing.

"You guys okay?" Griff this time.

"Yeah. You see Jag?"

"Here."

At the sound of the new voice, Kolton's relief surged through our bond. Still holding me, he made for the voice and dragged his second into a tight embrace.

"The others?" he said, pulling back to check Jagger over. Through the haze, I could just make out his features. He had a large gash on his cheek and was covered in soot, but otherwise looked unharmed.

"Safe. All three of them," Jagger replied, his voice gruff from the smoke.

More relief flooded our bond.

Kolton clapped him on the shoulder. "Thank you."

He nodded, then jerked his chin at something behind us. "Looks like the fight has just begun."

We turned, and that's when we saw them.

Standing in a single line on the front lawn like a row of soldiers was the Blackstone Coven. They were all dressed the same in long black robes, eerily blending into the night. If not for the violent blaze behind us, they would be hard to see. I recognized each one, easily picking out Raelyn and Fritz.

And standing at their center was Keisha, their new leader. I immediately noticed the black cloth around her eyes, hiding her blindness. Her *weakness*.

A violent shudder ripped through Kolton, as if he too had just spotted her. But he didn't move. Didn't do anything but stare her down.

Keisha, on the other hand, was smiling. As if she could *feel* our eyes on her.

Hello, little wolf, she crooned. *Long time no see.*

Everything in me went cold.

Her lips hadn't moved. She'd spoken inside my *head.*

Careful, Nora, Storm warned. *The forced blood bond has made our mind vulnerable to her mental attacks. She could trap us without lifting a finger.*

Push her out, Nora, Kolton spoke next. *Block her with a mental shield before she can sink her hooks into your mind.*

Remembering my brief training about mental shields, I focused on erecting an invisible wall. Kolton and I could do the same thing with our bond. It was the only surefire way to keep our thoughts private. I hadn't really practiced before now though. Hadn't *needed* to. Still, I got to work on blocking Keisha, not wanting her to take me out of the fight before it even began.

Kolton suddenly released me and stepped forward. He stood tall and strong. An intimidating figure, even without a stitch of clothing on. Maybe even *more* so because of it. Every muscle, every sinewy line, stood out in stark relief. He was power made flesh. A literal *beast* prowled just beneath his skin.

As I continued to protect my mind from Keisha, Kolton said loud enough for the witches to hear, "You shouldn't have come here. There will be no escape for you this time. Blackstone Coven will cease to exist after this day."

Keisha's smile slowly widened. "Oh, we have no intention of running, *alpha.* You're the one who's cornered. Soon, you will all be in cages. I'm looking forward to getting my hands on you and your *spirit.* Demon, is it? But I'm even more excited to get my hands on your little wife again. I almost broke her last time. This time, I'll tear her apart until she willingly *gives* me the spirit I seek."

Just like that, dark fur exploded over Kolton's body. In seconds,

Shadow was shaking off the shift, standing a solid nine feet tall.

Several of the witches flinched, but Keisha only smiled more. "Witches at the ready!" she yelled, raising her arms in the air.

"*Wolves*," Shadow roared, ordering us to shift. The sound of crackling flames was soon replaced by the vicious cracking of bones. I shifted in record time, but not as quickly as the others. They had all taken on their demon forms, leaving me the only one on all fours. They stood on their hind legs, nearly as tall as Kolton.

Storm tensed as they surrounded her, but I didn't sense an ounce of fear. She was determined. *Focused*. She wanted a piece of those witches as much as they did.

"Show no mercy," Shadow growled, and the others growled their approval. To my surprise, so did Storm. "Fight hard. Fight *fast*. Fight together."

When he threw his head back and released a guttural howl, we all raised our heads as one and joined him.

Stay close to me at all times, Nora, Kolton said through our bond, right before the witches unleashed their magic.

As it streaked toward us, Shadow lunged forward. Storm tore after him, sticking close behind as he led the charge. Magic blasted him left and right, but he didn't slow. Didn't flinch as he gained on the witches with terrifying speed. Storm managed to keep up, a streak of white trailing his dark form. He headed straight down the middle, Keisha clearly his target. His claws tore up the grass as he bore down on her, completely ignoring the others.

He was feet away. *Feet* away from reaching her.

At the last second, Keisha vanished behind the line. Shadow didn't slow. He crashed into the line and witches went flying. Jagger, Griff, and Vi hit the line a second later.

Screams lit up the night as Kolton caught a warlock midair and practically tore him in half. Blood sprayed, striking Storm's muzzle. With a snarl, she pounced on one of the fallen witches, going for the jugular. Unable to look away, I watched in horror as Storm bit down and shook her like a rabbit, silencing her screams.

Only when the witch was dead did Storm whirl and lunge for another. Before she could bite down, pain seared her side from a magic attack. She yelped and looked up to see Fritz about to blast her again. Unable to avoid the attack, she braced for more pain. Shadow was suddenly there, picking Fritz up as if he weighed nothing. Fritz froze, his eyes rounded in terror. When he opened his mouth to scream, Shadow roared in his face.

Then struck.

Fritz's head went one way, his body another as Shadow swiftly decapitated him. He wasn't the only one Shadow had decapitated, I quickly noticed. It seemed that he wanted to give Keisha a taste of her own medicine.

Except that, when I looked around, I couldn't spot her.

The coven was falling left and right, unable to defend against the swift and savage attack. Griff, Jagger, and Vi were equally ferocious, protecting each other's backs whenever a witch got too close. They powered through the magic attacks, taking turns delivering the killing blows.

Griff suddenly choked, as if struggling to breathe. When he coughed and blood spilled from his mouth, dread filled me. I wildly looked about, searching for the culprit. I found her feet away, gaze locked on Griff as she used her magic to drown him in his own blood. Before I could move toward her, Vi appeared out of nowhere and clawed through Raelyn's neck with one vicious swipe. She crumpled to the ground in a pool of her own blood.

Within minutes, there were only a few witches left. They tried to portal away, but Kolton mercilessly cut off their escape. One by one, they fell prey to his teeth and claws. Their screams were terrified, yet short-lived, as he quickly dispatched them.

We all slowed to watch, reveling in our victory. Griff threw back his massive head to release an excited howl.

We'd done it. We'd defeated the coven.

I made a grave mistake then. I dropped my mental shields. Only a little, but it was enough.

Keisha struck like an adder, whispering inside my mind, *Come to me, little wolf, come swift and silent. Your will is mine, no need for violence. Come to me, little wolf. Come . . .*

The words wrapped around me and squeezed, stealing my control. I struggled to break free, but her hold was too tight. Too *powerful.*

I was suddenly moving. Moving *away.* Away from safety. Away from my *pack.*

Storm's body quivered as she too fought to free us, but Keisha had ensnared us both. I could hear Storm trying to reach me, to break through the fog in my brain, but her words were faint. Dull.

Only one voice was loud and clear, demanding all my attention. *Come to me, little wolf. Come, come, come.*

I obeyed, slipping away before anyone could stop me. I followed the voice's pull, heading toward a copse of trees. Toward *her.* I could see her now, her dark form illuminated by a sparkling cerulean portal at her back.

She was smiling. Beckoning to me with open arms.

Come to me, little wolf. Come . . .

So close. I was so close to reaching her. Only a few more feet to go.

A roar suddenly cleaved the air. So powerful that it shook the ground beneath Storm's paws.

Keisha's head snapped up, and I stumbled, suddenly confused.

NORA!

The word blasted through my mind, snatching me from the haze. Storm shook her head, trying to reorient herself.

Baring her teeth, Keisha focused on me again. *Come to me, little wolf—*

Another roar cut her off, the sound so devastating and filled with *pain* that I whined. A whine that left Storm's mouth as we shared in Kolton's misery.

"Nora, no!" he bellowed, clearly in human form now. I could hear him racing toward us. Could hear his keen desperation. But I was unable to turn around.

I was *trapped*. Stuck in a cage. This time, my very own body.

Realizing that I wasn't going to budge another inch, Keisha sealed up her portal and ran toward me. It took her seconds to reach me. Seconds to form another portal.

I internally screamed at my body to *move*, frantic to get away. Storm thrashed and howled alongside me, but there was no outward evidence of our struggle.

Keisha's fingers were inches away from touching us. From pulling us inside the portal.

A *crack* suddenly rent the air. Like a sharp whip.

Keisha yanked her hand back with a startled cry. I watched in amazement as blood gushed from a deep cut on that same hand.

"You will not touch her again, *witch*," Kolton seethed, still too far away to reach me.

"Impossible," Keisha whispered, touching the cut. She gasped and raised her head, looking toward Kolton as if she could *see* him. "This magic doesn't belong to you. It's utter *blasphemy*."

"Oh, you have no idea how *blasphemous* I can be," Kolton quietly growled. "How about you stick around and find out?"

Hissing, Keisha reached for me again.

Another *crack.*

She screamed this time, yanking her hand away once more to clutch her face. Blood trickled through her fingers and dripped to the ground below.

Another *crack.* Followed by another. And another.

Keisha wailed and staggered back. "You will pay," she cried, still clutching her face. "You will pay *dearly* for this day. I will curse you. I will rain *hellfire* on your heads. My coven will be avenged. I will gather witches from every corner of the earth and—"

Another *crack* and she stumbled back. Just like that, she fell into her portal and vanished.

The moment she did, the spell she'd placed on us broke. Storm collapsed, but Kolton caught her. Lowering himself to the ground, he buried his face in her fur and groaned, "I need my mate, Storm. I need to hold her."

At the pure anguish in his voice, another whine left us.

Storm immediately allowed the shift, pulling back to give me control. I struggled to the surface, responding to my mate's distress. His anguish continued to flood our bond. Even when I'd fully shifted into human form, he rocked me in his arms, quietly groaning every few seconds.

When I reached up and touched his face, trying to reassure him, a shudder rocked his frame.

"I almost lost you," he said against my neck, holding me impossibly tight. "I almost lost you."

Again and again he said it, each time more heartbreaking than the last.

I tried offering words of comfort, but he didn't seem to hear me. I whispered them through our bond, pushing what little calm I had toward him.

No response.

He continued to rock me, uttering the same phrase again and again.

The others joined us then, also back in their human forms. I threw them all helpless looks, but they seemed at a loss as well.

Their fearless leader, their powerful alpha, had completely shut down.

Defeat curved his body inward, when he should be howling his victory at the moon. He'd saved me. He'd saved us *all*. And yet . . .

Something was dreadfully wrong.

My mate. My beautifully strong mate.

Felt broken.

CHAPTER 35

KOLTON

She's okay, she's okay, she's okay.

I chanted the words in my mind, but they held no meaning.

All I could see was that witch reaching for her. One second. *One second* more and my life would have been over.

It didn't matter that I could feel her in my arms. Didn't matter that I'd saved her in the nick of time.

The pain of nearly losing her had ripped me wide open. I thought I could handle it. Thought I was strong enough. But I couldn't have been more wrong.

History was repeating itself.

We might have survived today, but our enemies wouldn't stop coming. Wouldn't stop trying to tear us apart.

We couldn't keep going like this. Not anymore.

She's okay, she's okay, she's okay.

No, she wasn't. And neither was I.

My world had just been turned upside down.

I was slipping. Slipping into insanity.

History was repeating itself, my parents' fate becoming ours.

There was no escaping it. No denying what I'd seen in our bedroom earlier.

My mate. My perfect mate.

Was pregnant.

ALSO BY BECKY MOYNIHAN

WOLVES OF MIDNIGHT
Midnight Vow
Midnight Claim
Midnight Queen

A TOUCH OF VAMPIRE
Shadow Touched
Curse Touched
Fate Touched
Sun Touched (spin-off standalone)

THE ELITE TRIALS
Reactive
Adaptive
Immersive

GENESIS CRYSTAL SAGA
Dawn till Dusk
Fall of Night
Stars till Sun

ACKNOWLEDGMENTS

Aaaah, the family dynamics of this story is giving me all the feels!! It's one of my favorite things about werewolves. Pack is family, and family is everything. Even better when it's found family. I'm so excited to write the conclusion of Nora and Kolton's love story, especially with the new addition. Their story will have a guaranteed HEA, promise!!

A huge thank you goes to Kate, Morgan, Melissa, and Allie for being rockstar beta readers. Your dedication and feedback mean the world to me!

To my amazing ARC team: thank you, thank you, thank you for your continued loyalty and for loving on my books!! I value you and your reviews so much!

Lastly, thank you to my lovely readers for giving my books a chance! You keep my dreams alive!

BECKY MOYNIHAN is a bestselling, award-winning author of paranormal romance and urban fantasy. Her books include the A Touch of Vampire series, Wolves of Midnight series, The Elite Trials series, and the co-written Genesis Crystal Saga.

When she's not writing, you can find Becky curled up on the couch in her North Carolina home, binge-watching shows and sipping Mountain Dew.

To stay up to date on new releases, sign up for her monthly newsletter: www.beckymoynihan.com/newsletter